PRAISE FOR CAITLIN ROTHER

Praise for *Staged*, the second in the Katrina & Goode thriller series

"Densely developed characters and an addictive plotline led to a sleepless night as I whisked through *Staged* at record speed. I couldn't put it down. Rother's years writing true crime have given her fiction a rare authenticity. Highly recommended. Such a good read!"

—Kathryn Casey, author of *Bone Cold*

"In *Staged*, the latest thriller by Caitlin Rother, investigative team Goode and Stone are put to the challenge with a complex case involving the judiciary, familial conflict, corporate greed, and, of course, murder. And not just one murder. Not by a long shot. Clues abound, but are they real . . . or staged? Rother takes us on an exciting, edge-of-your seat ride to find out. She is masterful at portraying the setting of San Diego, both celebrating and undercutting its idyllic image. With Katrina, the novel's investigative reporter, Rother also gives us a behind-the-scenes look at how crime gets represented, something she is well poised to depict. Her experience as a journalist and true crime writer is particularly evident in the meticulous details, making the story both compelling and believable. A great read!"

—Ona Russell, author of the award-winning
Sarah Kaufman historical mysteries

"*Staged* is the thrilling second book in Caitlin Rother's scintillating series. The chemistry between Katrina and Ken is electric. The alluring coastal setting and unexpected twists make this book a must read."

—Alana Albertson, *USA Today* bestselling author of *My Fair Señor*

Praise for *Hooked*, the first in the Katrina & Goode thriller series

"Rother delivers a gripping, expertly woven crime thriller from the first page. *Hooked* is a tense, multifaceted plot filled with murder, secrets, and a brilliantly plotted cover-up that keeps the pages flying."
—Audrey J. Cole, *USA Today* bestselling author of *Missing in Flight*

"Smart, gritty, and intricately plotted, this addictive police procedural features unforgettable characters and a plot that cuts as deep as it twists. The chemistry between investigative reporter Katrina Chopin and homicide detective Ken Goode is electric . . . and the plot multilayered, delving into corruption and the many masks it hides behind. I was hooked from the start!"
—Christina McDonald, *USA Today* bestselling author of *What Lies in Darkness*

"Caitlin Rother sets the hook early and reels you in chapter by chapter in this fascinating murder mystery. Rother's attention to detail and crime scene knowledge, which have made her the best true crime writer of our time, give the novel a gritty sense of verisimilitude. Goode and Katrina are layered and complex characters who come together to make a formidable investigative team. I can't wait to read about their next case!"
—Matt Coyle, author of the bestselling Rick Cahill crime novels

"*Hooked* had me hooked from the first chapter. Rother's true crime fans will devour her new thriller. Sharp dialogue and fast paced, *Hooked* is an excellent start to a new series. Can't wait for the next one!"
—Alana Albertson, #3 Amazon bestselling author of *Badass*

Praise for *Naked Addiction*, the prequel to *Hooked*

"With a journalist's eye for the telling details of life, Caitlin Rother is a keen architect of the most important part of storytelling: character. The people in her prose grip you tightly with their truth."
—Michael Connelly, #1 *New York Times* bestselling crime novelist

"*Naked Addiction* is a strong debut from a perceptive and unflinching writer. Detailed and tightly focused, the story unfolds on the sun-drenched but dangerous streets of San Diego."
—T. Jefferson Parker, *New York Times* bestselling crime novelist

"Caitlin Rother walked the walk as an award-winning journalist, and now she talks the talk in her debut novel, *Naked Addiction*. Rother's honed reportorial eye gives us the five *W*'s of murder set out on turf she knows so well. With a deft hand, Rother puts a bloody fingerprint on the picture-postcard setting of San Diego. The sun and surf are a gorgeous backdrop, but in Rother's *Naked Addiction*, trouble in paradise abounds."
—Alan Russell, author of *Political Suicide*

"*Naked Addiction* . . . is one of the most well-constructed murder mysteries that I have ever read in forty years of reading that genre. Rother's years as an investigative reporter put her on the front line of crime, and she has used that experience to construct real and authentic characters and scenarios that are so factual that you feel you could be reading a newspaper account of a crime. The plot . . . is so complex and elaborate that you never suspect who the murderer is until Rother decides to let you know—at the end of the book. Rother's debut into the fiction genre is impressive and has a long life ahead of it."
—Book Hunters

Praise for *Down to the Bone*

"Rother presents the riveting story of a botched investigation, multiple suspects, and a web of lies. Was justice ever served? The question will remain with you long after you finish reading."

—Diane Fanning, author of *Written in Blood*

"If you love true crime books where the author goes far beyond what is already known, and raises questions that need to be asked, this is a book for you."

—Justin Brooks, founding director, California Innocence Project

Praise for *Death on Ocean Boulevard*

"The Rebecca Zahau case is one of the great crime mysteries of modern times. It took an author of Caitlin Rother's caliber to bring it into sharp focus. A riveting read."

—Gregg Olsen, #1 *New York Times* bestselling author

"Gripping. Propulsive. A tour de force of true crime storytelling. Rother is a rare talent, and *Death on Ocean Boulevard* an instant classic of the genre."

—Kevin Deutsch, author and host of *A Dark Turn* podcast

"Caitlin Rother skillfully chronicles one of the most fascinating and controversial cases of the past decade. Big money, sex, and a questionable death makes for an addictive read."

—Kathryn Casey, author of *In Plain Sight*

Praise for *Poisoned Love*

"A true crime thriller that will keep you on the edge of your seat. This first-time author has done a brilliant job of captivating the inner workings of a female killer . . . someone who uses her cunning ways to commit murder."

—Aphrodite Jones, *New York Times* bestselling author of *Cruel Sacrifice*

"Caitlin Rother, a seasoned reporter with integrity, class, and skill, weaves this complex story seamlessly, offering it up in the page-turning fashion of a suspenseful novel . . . An exciting debut from a tirelessly hardworking reporter."

—M. William Phelps, *New York Times* bestselling author of *Obsessed*

Praise for *Twisted Triangle*

"A harrowing tale of one woman's struggle to maintain a balance between being a mother, an FBI agent, and dealing with a corrupt husband, also an FBI agent. A must read."

—Joseph D. Pistone, a.k.a. Donnie Brasco, author of *The Way of the Wiseguy*

"Hitchcock wishes he'd dreamed it up. Capote wishes he'd written it. Rother's mesmerizing narrative chronicles a wife's heroic struggle against great odds to survive her psychopath husband's elaborate scheme to make her murder the perfect crime. This spellbinding tale offers an added treat—it's true."

—Marcus Stern, Pulitzer Prize–winning journalist and coauthor of *The Wrong Stuff*

Praise for *Body Parts*

"This kind of frightening and fascinating glimpse into a killer's mind is rare, and an extremely intuitive Rother makes the most of it."
—Ron Franscell, *New York Times* bestselling author

"Caitlin Rother is the model for serious crime journalism today. She's bold, meticulous, and exhaustive, returning to cases with loose ends to update us on the latest innovations and developments."
—Katherine Ramsland, Anthony Award–winning author of *The Serial Killer's Apprentice*

"The updated material in this new edition of *Body Parts* not only brings the story full circle by giving a name, face, and tragic backstory to the mystery that set the nightmare in motion, it adds another layer of depth. Caitlin Rother never lets the horrific nature of the crimes overshadow the humanity of the victims."
—Simon Read, author of *Scotland Yard*

Praise for *Dead Reckoning*

"Well researched and a quick, engrossing read, this should be popular with true crime readers, especially the Ann Rule crowd."
—Starred review in *Library Journal*

"We've finally found the next Ann Rule! Caitlin Rother writes with heart and suspense. *Dead Reckoning* is a chilling read by a writer at the top of her game."
—Author Gregg Olsen

"*Dead Reckoning* by Caitlin Rother is one of the best true crime books I have read in years. First, it's one of those 'too wild and crazy to have made up' stories about the horrific murder of Tom and Jackie Hawks on their yacht *Well Deserved* off Catalina Island by Skylar Deleon, a con man, killer, and hermaphrodite, along with his wife Jennifer and three other accomplices. However, it took Rother's investigative journalist's tenacity and eye for detail and her knack for telling a good detective story that reads like a novel to set this book above most in the genre."
—Steve Jackson, *New York Times* bestselling author

Praise for *Lost Girls*

"*Lost Girls*, by veteran journalist and true crime writer Caitlin Rother, is a deeply reported, dispassionately written attempt to determine what created that monster and predator. It is a cautionary tale and a horror story, done superbly by a writer who knows how to burrow into a complex case without becoming captive to her sources."
—*Los Angeles Times*

"[Caitlin Rother] is one of the best storytellers going in the true crime genre today. Written with the verve, pacing, and characterizations of a detective novel, combined with her reporter's eye for detail, *Lost Girls* should be on every true crime fan's bookshelf."
—Author Steve Jackson

Praise for *I'll Take Care of You*

"Rother has written another 'ripped from the headlines' page-turner. Journalistic and thorough, this title is sure to be popular. Purchase for public libraries with large true crime collections."
—*Library Journal*

"Riveting . . . a story that will haunt you . . . Rother presents a fascinating study of one woman's evil and greed—that ultimately leads to the murder of a kind-hearted millionaire. The compassion the author shows for the victim and [his] . . . family makes this book an emotional, gripping tale."

—Author Aphrodite Jones

Praise for *Then No One Can Have Her*

"I honestly could not stop reading Caitlin Rother's *Then No One Can Have Her*. It's riveting, revealing, and insightful . . . Her closing chapters, written in first person, made my eyes water. What a fabulous, fabulous book!"

—Suzy Spencer, *New York Times* bestselling author

"Prepare to be hooked by Rother's absorbing narrative of greed, desperation, and twisty relationships . . . Between lies, financial shenanigans, shady legal maneuverings, and divided families, this tale sounds like fiction, but it's all true. And very dark."

—Author Katherine Ramsland

STAGED

ALSO BY CAITLIN ROTHER

Poisoned Love (updated)

Twisted Triangle (by Caitlin Rother with John Hess)

Where Hope Begins/Deadly Devotion (by Alysia Sofios with

Caitlin Rother)

My Life, Deleted (by Scott and Joan Bolzan and Caitlin Rother)

Lost Girls

I'll Take Care of You

Then No One Can Have Her

Hunting Charles Manson (by Lis Wiehl with Caitlin Rother)

Naked Addiction

Love Gone Wrong

Secrets, Lies, and Shoelaces

Dead Reckoning (updated)

Death on Ocean Boulevard

Body Parts (updated)

Down to the Bone

Hooked

STAGED

A THRILLER

CAITLIN ROTHER

THOMAS & MERCER

Published by Thomas & Mercer, Seattle

www.apub.com

Amazon, the Amazon logo, and Thomas & Mercer are trademarks of Amazon.com, Inc., or its affiliates.

EU product safety contact:
Amazon Media EU S. à r.l.
38, avenue John F. Kennedy, L-1855 Luxembourg
amazonpublishing-gpsr@amazon.com

ISBN-13: 9781662532368 (paperback)
ISBN-13: 9781662532375 (digital)

Cover design by Shasti O'Leary Soudant
Cover image: © Wirestock, Inc. / Alamy; © Tom Grubbe / Getty

Printed in the United States of America

Staged, the second in the Katrina & Goode thriller series, is set in late 2015, as newspapers were transitioning from print to online editions, but long before newsrooms were decimated by the resulting industry implosion and many were closed entirely due to COVID shutdowns. This was before "fake news" evolved into the misinformation and disinformation campaigns of today—when communities relied on the media to print the truth and to keep politicians honest, and on the police to keep us safe. When journalists were held to higher ethical standards and when people still believed in science and technology.

PROLOGUE
PETER CHOPIN

June 3, 2010

Judge Peter Chopin eased his black Mercedes sedan toward the curb to pick up his wife in front of the federal courthouse that cool Thursday evening in June. Even after thirty-one years of marriage, Peter still gazed at her longingly as the breeze blew her dark shoulder-length hair into her face, her sticky pink lipstick capturing several strands.

Judge Aphrodite Chopin, or Aphy, as she liked to be called outside the courtroom, always waited for Peter under the overhead walkway on Front Street. Because that area acted like a wind tunnel, he often wondered why she always glossed up her full, pouty lips when she knew the couple was heading straight home. He wanted to think she did it to look pretty for him, but he knew deep down that she still felt like she was onstage. Partly due to the public nature of being a federal judge, but mostly because she'd been a Tony-winning actress before she became a lawyer. To this day, drama still flowed through her veins like hemoglobin in everyone else.

Aphy had blown into his life like a storm. Ever since they met in law school, she'd kept the energy buzzing through his body. The sound of her throaty laugh, even fuller after a glass of red wine, warmed his skin. The way she emphasized certain words when she spoke made him hang on all the rest. He thought he knew everything about her, or at least tried to. But he knew he could never possess her. She was a force unto herself, unlike any other.

Peter was the calm to her storm. Steady, loyal, and attentive, he was a dependable creature of habit who gave little thought to changing his routine, oblivious to safety concerns. He saw no need for caution in provincial San Diego, once known as a navy town and still in training to be a big city. The command he held over his courtroom gave him a sense of control in his orderly, mundane personal life, fostering an inattention to detail and a false, even naïve, feeling of security.

That's why Peter didn't notice the beat-up blue Toyota Corolla that pulled up behind him, then followed at a distance. Or that the driver was wearing a black ski mask—quite the odd accessory for driving in broad daylight.

"Hello, beautiful," Peter said as Aphy got into the car. After freeing the hair from her lips, he kissed her. "You smell good. And you taste sweet too."

"That's because I'm sucking on a mint," she said, sticking out her tongue, which was encircled by a round white candy. "I felt like doing that during trial today, but I had to keep decorum since no one else was. It was a circus in there. None of the attorneys knew who or what was on first, and I had to hold two of their clients in contempt for unruly behavior. I'm so relieved that we're dark tomorrow."

"My day wasn't nearly that exciting," Peter replied, smiling thankfully. "But I'm looking forward to ending the week with some wine on the back deck. My hearing tomorrow was canceled, so I don't need to go in either."

"Good, we can lie around and lollygag," she said, using one of her favorite crossword puzzle words. "I can't wait to get out of these damned heels. They're brand new, and I've got blisters on my blisters."

Peter still felt like a lucky man for capturing Aphy's attention all those years ago, though he'd never really understood how he managed to steal her away from her then-boyfriend Vincey, a cocksure and handsome man from a wealthy family, wealthier than hers, and the Rockefellers compared to his. When Peter asked why she chose him over Vincey, Aphy said she wanted stability. She preferred his constancy, and his dry wit amused her. She never said she loved him more. She simply refused to discuss the matter further.

Her walled-off emotions often confused him. Especially lately, when she'd seemed more distracted and distant than usual, pulling away from his reaffirming touches. But when he asked her what was wrong, she said, "Nothing. Don't worry, we're fine. We're a family, and we always will be." This struck him as a non sequitur, but he tried to take her word for it. He needed to, for the sake of his own sanity.

A month after they'd started dating, Peter was thrilled—and yet terrified—when Aphy announced that she was pregnant, with not just one child, but fraternal twins, a boy and a girl. Peter had been a fraternal twin himself, but his brother died in the womb before they were born. He'd always felt like a part of him was missing, which only made him feel more confident that this coupling was meant to be.

It had all happened so fast, but he was too infatuated to question the timing. All he knew was that he loved her more than he thought he could love anyone. They were married in Founders Chapel on the University of San Diego campus a month before the babies were due.

At twenty-five, Peter was several years younger than Aphy. He was in awe of her talent and accomplishments, and her stack of *Playbills* to prove it. She didn't like to discuss why she'd given up the theater to become a lawyer. She later tried to persuade their daughter, Katrina, to follow in their footsteps, but Katrina politely declined, saying she wanted to tell stories, not sit in judgment of others.

When Aphy and Peter got married, they both had one more year of law school before they could take the bar, a year Peter spent fraught with fear. Every day, he questioned whether he was up to the task of starting a family and keeping his new wife happy while they were both launching busy law careers. He hadn't dated many other women, and he couldn't help but notice men staring a little too appreciatively at his beautiful, inspiring wife.

Having grown up as an only child, he also knew nothing about raising more than one child at a time. But somehow, they managed to get through it, thanks in large part to Peter's mother, an empty nester who was happy to babysit while her engineer husband worked late at General Dynamics.

After graduation, Aphy and Peter landed jobs as prosecutors at the local US Attorney's Office, which allowed them to keep semiregular hours—at the office, anyway—as they raised Katrina and Francis.

Katrina was born first; Franny came seven minutes later. Peter was relieved that all their parts were intact and that they grew up without lighting themselves on fire or blowing up the car with fireworks like their neighbor's boy. The twins were intelligent and ambitious, like their parents, though Peter thought Franny was too emotional and Katrina lived in her head too much.

Sometimes he wondered how they could have such vastly different dispositions from his. Katrina was a storm like her mother, long before there was a hurricane by that name, and she focused that force on getting things accomplished.

Franny was named after the Polish composer Frédéric François Chopin, a distant relative on Peter's side, but he earned his nickname early on from his T-ball teammates, several of whom had lisps and couldn't pronounce his real name. Creative and brilliant like his sister, Franny was much more moody. Although he inherited his mother's flair for drama, he lost out on the rest of her judicious temperament.

As parents, all Peter and Aphy could do was be supportive. When Franny landed himself in jail and was ordered by the court to enroll in the McDonald Center's substance abuse treatment program in La Jolla, they agreed to join the family support group. There, Peter was forced to meet Aphy's ex-boyfriend, Vincent "Vincey" Battrelle, whose older son, Alex, was in the program. Although Peter, Aphy, and Vincent had attended the same law school, Peter never had any classes with Vincent and had successfully avoided interacting with him.

But after engaging with Vincent during group meetings, Peter was proud of how he'd managed to swallow his past insecurities, going so far as to enter into a business deal with Vincent and his investment partner, Dr. Simon Fontaine, whose daughter, Victoria, was in the program as well. Dr. Fontaine was not only the go-to cosmetic surgeon in the wealthy coastal enclave of La Jolla but a pharmaceutical entrepreneur to boot.

Simon had been developing a promising sex drug at Vitaleron, a new biotech company for which he and Vincent were trying to raise capital. He said the groundbreaking drug would combine physical effects that heightened sexual pleasure with psychological effects that boosted the brain's dopamine receptors. The lucrative end result was a vehicle to perpetuate the infatuation and sexual attraction between romantic partners to keep them coming back for more. Simon planned to market the drug as a panacea to ennui in marriages and long-term relationships, targeting those preaching monogamy in the evangelical Christian community in particular.

After several years of sharing their innermost thoughts about the challenges of their children's relapses and recovery, Simon, Vincent, and Peter had formed a bond. Peter was also excited enough by the venture's potential that he became a cofounder by investing a good-sized nut. Aphy was all in too.

But Peter's insecurities were triggered when he saw her laughing and joking with Vincent at a couple of mixers at the University Club. Vincent had done well for himself since law school, investing his family's money in hotel and housing projects all over Southern California. He'd also acquired the region's biggest newspaper, the *San Diego Sun-Dispatch*, which gave him more power and prestige than Peter could even dream of.

When Peter saw Vincent touching his wife's lower back and gazing knowingly into her eyes, it was a painful reminder that she kept her eyes shut when Peter made love to her. She claimed she was focusing on the sensations, but he couldn't help but imagine that she was fantasizing about Vincent.

Driving himself crazy, Peter felt he had no choice but to step away from Vitaleron. Peter had already made the mistake of letting his self-doubts lead him into an intimate coupling with his longtime clerk in his chambers one night. He immediately had her transferred to another judge, because he couldn't chance Aphy finding out. Not after all they'd built and suffered through together.

That suffering culminated a few years later, when their life under the cloud of their son's demons finally burst. Just before the twins' thirtieth birthday, Franny was found dead in his bayfront home. On the coffee table next to his body, a bottle of lemon-infused vodka sat next to an assortment of pills, some crushed into powder. The medical examiner ruled that Franny, who had been sober for more than a year, had overdosed on this narcotic cocktail.

Although Katrina was not typically a conspiracy theorist, her job as an investigative reporter made her naturally suspicious. She was convinced that her brother had been murdered.

"He doesn't even like lemons," she kept saying.

While Peter generally accepted Franny's death as a suicide, Aphy said she wasn't sure what to think.

As sad as the loss of their son was for both of them, the couple's lives settled down dramatically after the funeral. Over the next six months, Franny's emotional wreckage slowly dissipated, and opportunities began to arise, such as the Mediterranean cruise the district court's presiding judge and his wife had invited them to join.

As Peter turned down their street in the upscale community of Point Loma that Thursday evening in June, he could practically taste the bottle of Pinot Noir he was going to open on the back deck. Also focused on making love to his wife later in the evening, he didn't notice that the beat-up blue Toyota was still trailing them.

"I'll pour the wine and meet you outside," he said as they pulled into the driveway.

"Thanks, hon. I'll be down as soon as I put on my comfy clothes," she said.

Peter climbed out of the car and leaned into the back seat to grab his briefcase and gym bag. He was rounding the rear bumper to help Aphy carry in her things when the first shots rang out.

Struck multiple times in the head and upper torso, Peter went down face first onto the cement driveway. While ducking and dodging around a bush, Aphy dropped her purse. She then tripped while running toward the house and fell to the ground. The killer continued shooting, firing seventeen bullets—a full magazine—into Peter's and Aphy's bodies by the time he was done.

Two neighbors, who were in their front yards at the time, told police they couldn't identify the driver because of the ski mask. One of them saw the Toyota's license plate number but could remember only the first few digits. However, both neighbors recalled that the Toyota had a loose muffler, which made a horrible grating sound and set off sparks on the asphalt as it sped off. They also remembered that the Beatles song "Let It Be" was blaring out of the passenger side window.

The media dubbed this the "Double-Judge Murder" case. But after an initial spate of articles, the coverage dribbled off because the police refused to comment any further on their "ongoing" investigation.

FIVE AND A HALF YEARS LATER . . .

CHAPTER 1
KEN GOODE

December 2015

Detective Ken Goode was blocked. He sat at his desk, staring at the thick stack of investigative reports about the murder of Dr. Simon Fontaine and his daughter, Victoria, which he had to review one last time before forwarding them to his sergeant. But he couldn't get his brain to focus. It was useless. His mind was elsewhere.

The pressure of this case was brain bending. Calling it *high profile* was a massive understatement. With such wealthy, influential victims and suspects, every detail had to be double- and triple-checked.

"I need more coffee," Goode muttered.

He'd started the morning with a mug of strong home brew, then downed a double latte that afternoon. But he'd learned the hard way that too much caffeine only made his brain short-circuit, so he tried to limit his daily intake—unless, of course, he was working a breaking homicide case, in which case all bets were off. Still, deep down, he knew caffeine wasn't the answer.

What he really needed to break through the fog was a quick escape to the beach. Glancing at his watch, he noted that it was four fifteen. If he hurried, he could make it just in time to catch Sunset, the glorious daily ritual at Windansea, his second home in La Jolla.

His cubicle was lined with photos of Windansea, with its iconic palm-frond shack and craggy shore. The pictures helped get him through the day, but to actually recharge his soul he needed to get out from under the fluorescent lights to feel the sand under his feet and the foam lapping over his toes as he watched the sun sink into the ocean.

Knowing he often couldn't break away in the late afternoon, he tried to hit the water at dawn to catch a few sets before work. Even on a day when the surf barely hit his knees, he paddled out and meditated on his board, his legs dangling in the water as the sunlight danced on the ripples around him.

But under the circumstances, Goode knew better than to ask to leave early today. Not when the stakes were this high and everyone was watching.

"Report procrastination is really a thing with you, isn't it?" his sergeant, Rusty Stone, said only half jokingly from his desk, kitty-corner to Goode's. "Does your inner child need nurturing, or are you just lazy? Because the brass is crawling up my ass for those reports. The mayor's office wants us to sew this baby up ASAP so we can start healing as a city, blah blah blah."

"Give me a break. There's a lot of detail in these pages," Goode said, holding up the stack of reports. "I don't think they want the case thrown out because of shoddy police work. Or maybe they do. The mayor should've stayed under the radar if he wanted to keep his name out of the paper. How stupid can you be to get mixed up with high rollers like the Fontaines, McMurphys, and Battrelles and still expect to keep it quiet? For a sex enhancement drug, no less. Anyway, they should be happy that we've got Darren McMurphy behind bars awaiting trial for murder and that we're picking up his dad in the morning for conspiracy to commit murder."

Although Stone was technically Goode's boss, they were more like partners. They were also best friends. After growing up on the same street a few blocks from the beach, Rusty Stone had stepped in as Kenny

Goode's big brother from another mother after Kenny lost his mom when he was only six. Kenny's dad died a few years later, leaving him and his younger sister, Maureen, orphaned.

Kenny's mom had announced that she was going out for a drive one weekend afternoon and reluctantly agreed to bring him along. Only later did he realize that her reluctance stemmed from plans that shouldn't have included him and a deep depression that her little pink pills couldn't lift.

So, after stopping to get them both some ice cream, she pulled over to the far-right lane of the Coronado Bridge, a bustling but narrow throughway where there was no shoulder. With the engine still running, she gave him a droopy smile as she dropped her red pumps through the driver's side window onto her seat, then walked behind the car, where she dropped herself over the railing and plunged two hundred feet to the water below.

Still hoping she would come back, Kenny was anxiously gripping his seat belt when the flashing red light of a police cruiser caught his eye in the rearview mirror. Moments later, a young police officer poked his head through the same window.

"Where are your parents, son?" he asked.

Faced with a mute, traumatized boy and the red heels on the driver's seat, the officer pieced together what had happened and took Kenny home, driving the rest of the way across the bridge that connected downtown San Diego to Coronado Island, then doing a U-turn to return to the freeway that took them back to La Jolla.

Goode attributed that experience to his decision years later to join the police force himself. Probably gave rise to his savior complex too.

After that, Rusty Stone, who was five years older than Kenny Goode, taught his new little brother to surf. Both sons of working families—Kenny's parents taught at the high school, while Rusty's bartended and waited tables at Chuck's Steak House—they were raised among the wealthy elites, only to discover that they were equal, if not superior, out on the water, where money didn't matter.

Now that Goode reported to Stone in the Homicide unit, the sergeant enjoyed flexing his supervisory muscles even though he knew Goode would diss him right back. They were still bantering when Stone's phone rang.

The sergeant was quiet for a moment after answering. "Oh, shit. Really?" he asked rhetorically, sighing loudly. "Okay, we're on our way. I'm sure I don't need to tell you not to let your people touch him or anything in the cell, do I?"

Stone paused. "Wait, what? You already cut him down? Did you take photos first?" He paused again. "Aw, geez, I wish you guys had left his body where it was, so we could've documented that." Another pause. "Yeah, I know it's your jurisdiction, but it's clearly related to the Fontaine case. You *have* been following the news lately, haven't you? Kinda hard to miss."

After he hung up, Stone shook his head. "That was a lieutenant at the jail downtown. Darren McMurphy was just found dead, hanging by a bedsheet in his cell," he said through gritted teeth. "But as you heard, some idiot deputy cut him down without taking any pictures first. Effing idiots. Anyway, McMurphy left a suicide note. *Allegedly.*"

"He seemed more indignant than suicidal to me," Goode said, recalling his first exchange with McMurphy at the hospital about a month earlier. Despite being under arrest and handcuffed to the bed, the suspect practically spat on him with disdain. McMurphy flatly denied killing the Fontaines with the paralytic drug succinylcholine, which was especially ludicrous because he'd just been captured at the Hotel del Coronado after injecting Katrina Chopin, a *Sun-Dispatch* reporter, with the very same drug.

Katrina managed to survive the harrowing episode only because Goode responded to her call for help in time to give her CPR until the paramedics could arrive with oxygen.

Later, Darren McMurphy only agreed to cooperate with police after learning that his father, Patrick, had turned his back on him. Patrick denied the claim that his son was doing his bidding, insisting that Darren had acted on his own when he murdered the Fontaines and attempted to kill Katrina Chopin. But Darren refused to take the fall alone, insisting that he was only following orders.

Darren revealed that his father was the leader of a cabal of rich power brokers who ran the city behind closed doors and had ordered him to "take care of this mess," referring to some thorny issues at Vitaleron, where Darren and his father were on the board. "Or we, and a lot of other important people, will be out a lot of cash," he quoted Patrick as saying, noting that Patrick had invested the McMurphy family's entire nest egg in the biotech company, as had many of his cohorts.

Goode had hoped that putting both McMurphys in jail would make it easier to squeeze the weakest links in the conspiracy scheme—which also involved a congressman and his fiancée—and bring down the whole shebang. However, Darren had now died before Goode could pin him down about how this cabal worked and get him to generate a membership list.

"The way this case has gone, nothing is what it appears to be," said Goode, who had anticipated more unexpected curveballs in this case, and Darren's alleged suicide proved him right. "But I'll withhold judgment until we know who had access to Darren in that cell. He was in a single cell, in protective custody, wasn't he?"

"Yep. That's why I said he *allegedly* wrote a suicide note," Stone said. "Daddy was mad at Darren for implicating him, but was he mad enough to put a hit out on his own son? Or did Daddy just cut off the family money and leave Sonny Boy hanging, as it were, to pay for his own defense? Either way, that's some cold shit right there."

"Darren's fiancée did say there was someone on the inside helping them at the PD, but she didn't name names," Goode said. "And since the jail is the sheriff's turf, maybe this 'inside' mole has dug a tunnel across law enforcement jurisdictions."

Stone nodded approvingly. "I wouldn't be surprised. It feels like we're peeling back the layers of a very sick old house lately. Why don't you call and have a forensic tech meet us there to take photos? I have a feeling the lieutenant didn't do that either."

"I'll give a heads-up to Artie Hayes at the ME's office too," Goode said, referring to his investigator buddy. "I'm sure the sheriff's department wants to keep this on the down-low because of all the suspicious deaths at the jail lately. How many does this make this year?"

"I have no idea," Stone said. "There've been so many drug overdoses, medical mishaps, and random suicides, I've lost count."

"Only this one doesn't seem so random."

"No, it doesn't. I've got to take a whiz. Meet you at the car in five."

After working so hard to put the Fontaine case together, Goode wasn't thrilled about this turn of events. He also wasn't feeling very talkative because his funk went beyond the obvious challenge of having their primary murder defendant—and the linchpin of their case—die on them. But he knew he couldn't hide his feelings from his oldest friend for long.

Goode had only been pretending to abide by Stone's order to keep his distance from Katrina Chopin, at least until the case got closer to trial. The truth was, he was falling in love with her. He couldn't stop thinking about her knowing hyacinth blue eyes, her long legs and inviting mouth, and the round, firm breasts he'd unveiled all too briefly a month ago during a perfect storm of events that caused him to break protocol.

Katrina had only just started working at the *Sun-Dispatch* a week before Dr. Simon Fontaine, the founder and CEO of Vitaleron, was found dead on a Friday, Halloween night, on the back patio of his La Jolla Farms mansion. The body of a thirty-five-year-old woman, who turned out to be his daughter and CFO, Victoria, was discovered upstairs on her bedroom floor.

Earlier that same night, Katrina and Goode had met by chance at Piatti, his favorite Italian restaurant in La Jolla. They'd barely started chatting at the bar when Stone called him away to investigate two deaths in

La Jolla Farms. By the next morning, Katrina had been assigned to cover the Fontaines' deaths, which by then had been categorized as "suspicious." Long story short, Victoria and Simon Fontaine were murdered, but their deaths were staged to look like suicides, which took a while to shake out.

Doing their damnedest to stay on their respective sides of the ethical wall separating a homicide detective and the reporter covering his case, he and Katrina ended up competing, and yet also helped each other by building off the other's investigative discoveries. But, unable to deny the chemistry between them, they lost their heads one night a week into the case. Or at least he did. He could blame it on the wine they drank on her balcony, but, really, he was simply unable to resist her.

They were rolling around on the sleeping bag in her unfurnished apartment, on their way to being naked, when they were interrupted by the sound of tires crunching on the driveway below her balcony. It was a black Infiniti whose driver was built like a linebacker, who crept up the stairs leading to Katrina's apartment and tried to enter her front door. Thankfully, Goode had already turned the deadbolt.

"Linebacker Dude," as they called him, had not come back since. But because they were unsure what he'd been trying to accomplish that night, they both feared, and even expected, that he would.

I swear I was only there to protect her, which, by the way, proved to be a prescient move. What happens if I'm not there the next time?

Still, as much as Goode wanted to share another bottle of Cabernet on that balcony and pick up where they'd left off, there were other, more practical complications.

"It was great that you happened to be there that night, but you and Stone are key sources in pretty much every one of my stories, so we can't let that happen again, at least not right now," Katrina said to him recently. "I don't want either one of us to get fired."

He couldn't disagree with that logic, so the two of them had been playing it cool, talking almost every day, but primarily by phone. On the slim chance they could both break away from work, they met at Windansea at sunset for some eye contact and a dose of positive ions.

Meanwhile, Goode and his team worked with the feds to build a strong case against the McMurphys, with the goal of exposing and breaking up this powerful cabal of elites. The narrative was complicated and messy, but much of the heavy lifting had already been done. This was all described in the arrest warrant for Patrick McMurphy, which they were going to serve at his house in the morning.

Even though Patrick didn't kill the Fontaines with his own hands, the warrant contended that he had orchestrated the conspiracy to do so and ordered his son to do his dirty work. Just like in the bloody slayings carried out by the Manson Family, the law was clear: Conspiracy to commit murder carried the same punishment as murder. But now the obvious question was, did Patrick have something to do with his son's death as well?

"I know this McMurphy development sucks, but what is up with you? You seem to be in perpetual sulk mode lately," Stone said, turning to look at Goode while they were stopped at a red light. "Is it that reporter? Dude, I told you to wait. Did you do something you shouldn't have—again?"

"No, not exactly," Goode said, willing the light to change.

"What does that mean?"

"We haven't had sex, if that's what you're asking. She's taken the same position as you. We can't go out on a real date until she's done covering this case."

"Smart woman."

"Yeah, well, my job is getting in the way of my life. She's the first woman I've met in a long time who isn't bad for my mental health."

Preparing to hand the case over to the district attorney's office had distracted Goode, at least temporarily, from his carnal urges. He'd almost given up on finding a good woman after a long bout of self-imposed celibacy. Katrina was the most promising prospect since he'd been dumb enough to agree to remarry his ex-wife Miranda, years after they'd divorced, and soon after he'd joined the San Diego Police Department (SDPD).

Although it was humiliating in the moment, he realized he'd dodged a bullet when Miranda left him at the altar to run off to the Caribbean with her boss. The experience also drove the point home that he shouldn't trust women who made promises they couldn't keep.

But Katrina seemed like the real deal. Unlike the damaged women he too frequently attracted, she seemed unusually healthy, confident, and fearless. Once he got to know her better, he sensed that she pushed down her emotions like he did, but her scars and experiences seemed to make her even stronger. Like a superhero whose bloody gash cleaves together within moments, leaving only a faint memory of the injury.

"I don't think she's going anywhere," Stone said. "Just chill."

"Not my favorite thing, unless I'm surfing or drinking a dirty martini, neither of which I can do on the clock," Goode retorted.

"I know, buddy, but you can hang in a little bit longer. Think of how long you've waited already."

"That's what makes it even harder," Goode said. Patience wasn't one of his strongest traits.

"Think of it this way. Katrina is like the Baked Alaska at a five-star restaurant. You have to wait for it to finish cooking while you savor the first few courses. Not that I'm encouraging you to savor anything. As your supervisor, I'm still saying 'keepa-you-hands-off.'"

It wasn't like Goode was sitting on his hands, pining for this woman. But it had been a few long weeks since their make-out session had been spontaneously aborted, so the Baked Alaska was getting a little toasty for his liking. That said, he had to respect her and her strong ethics. They were so hard to find these days.

CHAPTER 2
GOODE

Thursday

When Goode and Stone arrived at the Central Jail, they were escorted to the cell where Darren McMurphy's body lay on the cement floor with a twisted bedsheet still partially wrapped around his neck. The sheet had been sheared with a knife or sharp object, leaving remnants still attached to the light fixture on the ceiling.

Back at La Jolla High School, McMurphy had been one of Goode's teammates on the varsity baseball team. A quintessential pretty boy with long eyelashes and heart-shaped lips, McMurphy was also an arrogant little shit. Twenty years later, he'd proved he was still the latter, but his once-handsome face looked more like a giant blueberry.

Tony Allegro, the lieutenant who had called Stone, reached around his protruding belly to unlock the cell and let them inside. He pointed toward a note, scribbled in pencil on a piece of notebook paper, that was sitting on Darren's thin mattress:

> I was only following your orders, Dad. But by denying
> me that truth, and cutting me off from the family trust,
> you've failed me as a father and killed my will to live.

You leave me no choice but to do this. So, now you
have my death on your head as well.

Dwight Pepper, the same roly-poly forensic tech who had worked the Fontaine case, arrived moments after they did to take photos of the body, the note, the cut bedsheet, and the threads still clinging to the light fixture, as well as a few overall shots of the cell.

"Do you see a pencil anywhere?" Stone whispered.

"Nope," Goode whispered back. "Who else was in here before us, Lieutenant?"

"Just the deputy who cut him down and checked to see if he was breathing."

"Even though his face had turned blue," Goode whispered to Stone.

"He locked up and notified me immediately," Allegro said, pulling his pants up over his beach ball stomach and sniffing authoritatively. "Even though this is our jurisdiction, I *have* been watching the news, so I called you as a professional courtesy."

"I appreciate that," Stone said. "I'll need the deputy's name and a copy of your staff roster for this shift."

Apparently, that demand caught Allegro by surprise. "Really? Why?" he asked, frowning. "It's a pretty obvious suicide, and it's our case, not yours. So, I'll need that *request* in writing, Sergeant."

"Considering there's no pencil in the cell, and he couldn't have written his own suicide note without one, we have a bit of a quandary, don't you think?" Goode said.

"No, not necessarily," Allegro said, shrugging. "It probably got kicked out of the way when the deputy came in or when you all piled in here. Or maybe it's in or on McMurphy's person somewhere."

"Okaaaay. I hope you're not saying what I think you're saying," Stone said. "I don't see a guy about to kill himself sticking his pencil where you're suggesting. Let's see what they find at the autopsy before we say what's what."

"He wasn't on suicide watch, right?" Goode asked.

"Nope," Allegro said. "We had no indication that he wanted to harm himself, though he was pretty uncooperative with everyone he came in contact with. Seemed like a real angry guy. Probably holding a lot of fury inside. It's written up in multiple shift logs."

"Yeah, I'm not surprised. He's always had a bad case of entitlement syndrome. Plus, he was in withdrawal from the sex drug, which was stolen from the lab at Vitaleron, and who knows what else he was taking. I hear you can get all kinds of good narcotics in here," Goode said, unable to restrain his sarcasm. "When was the last time someone checked on him?"

"Whenever the last rounds were. I'd have to look," Allegro said, ignoring Goode's attempt to provoke him.

"You have cameras monitoring each cellblock, right?"

"Yes, but not literally into each cell, so there's no footage of this particular area."

"Well, that's convenient," Goode muttered.

"What was that, Detective?" asked Allegro, whose tone conveyed that he'd had enough of the detective's lip.

"Nothing."

They waited outside the cell until Artie Hayes, Goode's lanky, nerdy investigator friend, showed up from the medical examiner's office. As a marathon runner, Artie stayed extremely fit, inspired by all the evil nasties he'd witnessed in people's bodies during autopsies over the years.

While Goode was a homicide relief detective, working his way out of Vice, Artie had been a helpful, generous mentor, and his contributions to the Fontaine case so far had been crucial. Looking around the cell, Artie took a few notes and snapped a couple of photos with his phone. With the help of a second investigator he was mentoring, Artie zipped McMurphy into a body bag and wheeled him out to the ME's white van.

On the short drive back to police headquarters, Stone called the chief's office to brief him.

"I know you're not on the best terms with Sheriff Helmsley, but I strongly suggest you request that we handle this death investigation, since it's obviously related to the Fontaine case," Stone said. "I asked for the shift log and the name of the deputy who cut him down, but the lieutenant gave me a shit ton of attitude and demanded the request in writing. I think it would be mighty bad PR for the sheriff's already-tainted public image if McMurphy was murdered in his jail cell by someone who was enabled to stage it as a suicide."

"I'll see what I can do," Chief Baxter said. "We're all under the microscope with this case, and we need to make sure things are done right. But that man's never liked the concept of transparency. Though I'll deny having said that, Stone."

"Yes, sir. Duly noted."

As the Homicide unit's media spokesman, Stone asked if he should call a news conference to discuss how McMurphy's death would affect the Fontaine case, because he knew the media would be hounding him for answers. But the chief told him to wait until he heard from Helmsley first.

When Baxter called back a while later, Goode could hear him yelling expletives at Stone. The sheriff's answer was, essentially, "sorry, not sorry, no," Stone's team couldn't handle the death investigation. Baxter said Helmsley had also dodged the request for the shift log, so he was going to send it in writing himself.

"Maybe that will shame him into sharing it, but he's probably thinking you're going to try to make him look like he's part of this alleged cabal you guys keep talking about," the chief said. "I'll make sure he understands that the feds have their own Fontaine investigation going, and it would be better for us to determine if there *is* an inside mole rather than have the feds turn us upside down trying to find one. For all we know, Darren McMurphy's fiancée may have raised that specter as a straw man or to deflect blame from herself."

"Good point, Chief," Stone said.

Helmsley was obviously holding on to the case to save face, but Goode figured the sheriff also wanted to have some sway with how the ME categorized the manner and cause of yet another jailhouse death. Although the two county departments publicly claimed to work independently, it was well known to insiders that the ME generally agreed with whatever "facts" the sheriff put forward so their findings would be consistent. It was only in rare cases that they weren't, and even then, fingers were never pointed to malign any police agency.

San Diego County had its own law enforcement triumvirate of power, comprising the San Diego police chief, the county sheriff, and the district attorney. The triad was protected by a culture of silence that maintained the status quo, which Vincent Battrelle and his staff of newspaper editors had historically preserved and protected.

That is, until Katrina Chopin showed up. She'd already warned Goode that she was planning to break that power structure wide open.

CHAPTER 3
GOODE

It was 8:00 p.m. by the time Goode said good night to Stone in the parking lot behind the police station.

From there, Goode was headed to his neighborhood deli to grab a roast beef and Swiss cheese sandwich with Russian dressing. But before eating it at his kitchen table, he would fix himself a vodka tonic and call Katrina. He wanted to give her a heads-up about the day's political shenanigans by the sheriff's department and a little encouragement—not that she needed any—to start making calls. If anyone could shake things up, it was her.

He also wanted to ask whether she'd checked to see if Sheriff Marcus Helmsley, like Police Chief Tom Baxter, was on the donors' list for the reportedly independent political action committee that funneled money to Congressman Brandon Winchester's reelection campaign. It had surprised them all a few weeks earlier when she'd found the chief and the mayor on the list, especially when Baxter denied making any such payment. They later learned that Darren McMurphy had made a slew of campaign payments in the name of numerous Vitaleron investors—without their knowledge or authorization, which violated any number of laws. McMurphy had also bribed Winchester and an FDA official in exchange for a promise to try to expedite approval of the sex drug, which was in the second of three required phases of human trials.

A lot of good that will do us now that Darren McMurphy's dead. But it would help to know if the sheriff is part of the cabal, the Vitaleron campaign scheme, or both.

Goode hadn't been able to prove it yet, but if the chief, the mayor, *and* the sheriff were silent investors in the biotech firm, that would answer a lot of questions, not to mention pose a serious conflict of interest with the Fontaine investigation.

But Stone called before Goode was even halfway to La Jolla, where he lived in a one-bedroom rental cottage near the high school, in the same neighborhood where he grew up.

"You miss me already?" Goode quipped.

"You're not going to believe this, but Patrick McMurphy's wife just called 911 to report finding him dead in his home office. They live on Hillside Drive, on the north side of Mount Soledad. I'm heading over there now. I'll text you the address."

"Any sign of foul play?"

"Nothing obvious."

"I love it when our entire case collapses in just four hours," Goode said, writing off his sudden wave of nausea to getting irritated on an empty stomach.

"Not necessarily. Depends on what we find over there. Maybe Patrick found a conscience and offed himself out of guilt over his son's alleged hanging death," Stone said. "I just hope it's not another shit show like the Fontaine scene."

Stone was referring to the ambiguous state of the plastic surgeon's three-story mansion, which had caused confusion that wasn't even the killer's intention.

Darren McMurphy had asked his nurse fiancée to sedate Victoria Fontaine by putting Xanax in her chicken soup, then showed up wearing lipstick and a police uniform, claiming it was a Halloween costume. He ordered the nurse to inject Victoria with succinylcholine, knowing it would go undetected in a routine toxicology screen. When she refused, he did it himself, poking Victoria's arm with the needle multiple times to make it look like she, as a recovering addict, had injected herself with an illicit drug. McMurphy also stuffed several oxycodone pills down Victoria's throat and left open vials of Xanax and oxy—prescriptions filled fraudulently in her name that morning—on her bedside table.

After Dr. Fontaine came home unexpectedly, McMurphy injected him with the paralytic drug as well, hoping it would appear that the doctor had suffered a heart attack from the shock of discovering his daughter's fatal overdose, which sent him tumbling down the carpeted stairs.

McMurphy's goal in all this was to prevent Victoria from carrying out her threat to expose his illegal efforts to speed the Vitaleron sex drug's approval by falsifying the results of the human drug trials and bribing Winchester, who was on a key committee involved in monitoring the FDA. Although Dr. Fontaine had not originally been a murder target, he instantly became collateral damage.

The confusion for police came into play when Vincent Battrelle and his son Michael showed up independently at the mansion hours later. Michael had come to check on Victoria, who had shocked him by breaking up with him that morning, and immediately thought his older addict brother Alex was somehow to blame for the two deaths. To protect the family name and Vitaleron's future, Michael and Vincent Battrelle decided to stage a double-suicide scene, unaware that they were disrupting McMurphy's earlier staging effort. So, they moved the doctor's body, first to an upstairs balcony, where Vincent shot the corpse in the head, then down to the back patio, where they placed a gun next to Dr. Fontaine as if he'd shot himself there.

Goode recognized right away that the physical evidence at the mansion didn't make sense. But it took several rounds of toxicology screens at a private lab before he and Artie Hayes from the ME's office could determine that it was succinylcholine, not the sex drug or the meds on Victoria's bedside table, that had killed her and her father.

"After all the scene tampering at the Fontaines', I'm not taking anything at face value," Stone said. "So, let's try to chill until we get there, buddy."

"You're right," Goode said. "I'm taking deep breaths as we speak."

Turning left off Torrey Pines Road, Goode was amazed at how much the upscale neighborhood had changed since he'd last driven through it. As he drove up the twisty Hillside Drive, he passed a vast assortment of homes, ranging from ginormous multilevel villas, set back behind tall iron-gated fences, to comparatively modest, yet still ungodly priced, single-story bungalows.

When Goode was growing up, his mother told him stories about the cluster of short, stout older homes with low ceilings on that street, known as the "Munchkin houses," where actual cast members of *The Wizard of Oz* purportedly lived. Built in the 1930s, they overlooked the long slope that was now covered with multimillion-dollar homes all the way down to La Jolla Shores. Although the "Munchkin" stories never proved true, the La Jolla legend carried on.

Pulling up to the address, Goode was shocked to see that the McMurphys lived in what was probably the last remaining "Munchkin" bungalow, the only one that had yet to be torn down and replaced with a huge mansion. It didn't fit with the home he'd envisioned for the leader of a group of wealthy elites, but he knew appearances could be deceiving. It did jibe with the claim that Patrick had invested the family's entire nest egg in Vitaleron, which apparently had left no money for remodeling.

As Goode approached the yellow stucco house with blue trim, he was surprised to see Katrina leaning against her Land Rover, talking to a patrol officer and scribbling in her notebook. With her slender runner's body standing at five foot six, she was only a few inches shorter than the officer, and her confident posture conveyed that she wasn't intimidated by him one bit. When her dark-brown hair fell into her eyes, she ran her hands through the wavy curls underneath. As Goode remembered grabbing hold of them that night on her balcony, the prurient memory flash sent a spike of arousal through his body like an electric current.

Not now, I'm working. How did she hear about this so soon? I'm happy to see her, but I've got work to do, and I always seem to let her distract me. I'm doomed.

CHAPTER 4
KATRINA CHOPIN

Earlier that afternoon, several hours before Katrina heard about the two McMurphy domino deaths, she was discussing next steps in her editor Joanne Wagner's glass-walled office in the *Sun-Dispatch* newsroom.

"After your great series on the Fontaine murders this past month, which I'm sure will win countless awards, I'm ready to shift the story over to the courts team. You good with that?" Joanne asked, more out of politeness than anything else. Court reporters typically stepped in after the initial arrest and follow-up stories were done anyway.

"Sure," Katrina said. "I'm ready to move on."

Although she hoped to get back into the mix closer to trial, Katrina was more than ready. She was *thrilled* to hear this development. In fact, she'd already been plotting how to facilitate her escape from the frustrating ethical constraints that had kept her and Goode apart for weeks. Antsy to go out on a proper date with the sexy surfing detective, she'd come up with a story idea that would steer clear of law enforcement sources almost entirely.

"It's perfect timing, actually, because I was about to pitch an investigative feature," she told Joanne.

"Pitch away."

The story, Katrina explained, would chronicle her personal journey as she explored her family's ethnic history by submitting her DNA to Ancestry and 23andMe, two popular commercial genetic genealogy websites. By taking a first-person approach to a trend story with a consumer-review angle, she could share her emotional discoveries in real time.

"I could use a break," she said. "I did almost die by lethal injection a few weeks ago, and we still don't know who smashed my car window with a rock and left that threatening note."

"You don't need to keep selling it to me. I think it's a wonderful idea," Joanne said. "Very creative. And I agree. Enough of this cops-and-murder stuff for a while."

Linda Kelley, Joanne's hard-assed boss, was equally excited about the story. Katrina suspected this was partly because it meant she would be in safer reporting territory all around. Linda didn't want reporters taking unnecessary risks that could turn into liabilities for the paper, which is exactly why, after Darren McMurphy had tried to take Katrina's life at the Hotel Del, they jumped at the chance to take her out of the line of fire.

The only downside was that it could take up to two months to get all the DNA results. Processing time for 23andMe was only three to four weeks, but Ancestry took twice as long, which seemed like an eternity. Still, after signing up with both services that afternoon, Katrina just had to wait for the DNA kits to come in the mail, spit into both vials, and send them back.

What she didn't tell her editors was that freeing herself from her ethical constraints wasn't her only ulterior motive. By drawing the public's focus to her family, she hoped to light a fire under the SDPD's complacent ass to reignite its investigation into her parents' murder—a case that was still technically open, but had long gone cold—and to take a deeper look at her brother's suspicious suicide as an adjacent and possibly related crime. She hoped the genealogy story might generate new tips and leads that she and

Goode could use to investigate the Double-Judge killings in their off-hours as they'd secretly planned.

But her immediate incentive was the freedom to frolic with the handsome detective, because her attraction to him had been hard to ignore these past few weeks. It wasn't just his sarcastic wit. He also was nice to look at. In addition to his sinewy six-foot-tall athletic frame, broad shoulders, muscular arms, and pecs, his mirthful green eyes triggered her sexometer with a funky bass guitar riff. She'd heard that same riff in her head the night they first kissed on her balcony.

The two of them proceeded to cross a number of lines that night, but circumstances forced them to stop before they did something she would regret. She didn't rue the make-out session—rather, she'd gotten swept up by it. But she was determined not to let their powerful and relentless chemistry disarm her journalistic ethics again until they were clear of this story.

They suspected Linebacker Dude was involved in the Fontaine case somehow, but Katrina couldn't tell her editors about his attempted break-in, let alone report it to police, because she would have been taken off the story. If either her or Goode's bosses had learned that he'd been there, shirtless with his pants half off, they both would have been fired. So, she was trying to tough it out, pushing the fear from her mind that the dude would reoffend by making sure that her front and sliding glass doors were locked at all times. She'd also started carrying a can of pepper spray in her purse.

Her efforts to keep Goode at a distance were motivated by another factor as well: Having sex with unavailable men had been an unhealthy coping mechanism for too long. It had sent her into therapy, in fact, where she vowed to remain celibate until she could safely withstand the persistent urges that had driven her behavior. Although she still hadn't broken that vow, Goode wasn't making things any easier with their long phone calls after work, which were growing increasingly salty and spicy.

"Our time will come, and delayed gratification is always better," she told him. "That's what my therapist said, anyway."

"That's what you keep saying," he said. "But now that I've seen your perfect breasts, I can't stop thinking about how the rest of you would look in the moonlight."

"How did they look?" she said.

"Like two ripe peaches."

"Really."

"Yes."

"Does that make you want to eat peaches?"

"As a matter of fact, yes. So, that's what I visualize at night when I'm trying to fall asleep."

"Eating peaches?"

"No, eating *your* peaches. I also picture what would have happened next if that dude hadn't pulled up outside and sent me into an adrenaline-fueled frenzy to make sure he didn't get into your apartment."

All that aside, it was also a relief that the other source of drama in Katrina's life—the paper's publisher, Vincent Battrelle—had let up. Not long after she was hired, Vincent tried to hire her off the books to search for his missing son Alex and wouldn't accept her polite refusal, even after she explained that the side job posed a major conflict of interest with her coverage of the Fontaine case.

With Simon Fontaine dead, Vincent was now Vitaleron's biggest investor. He was also on its board of directors along with his son Michael, who, after Victoria Fontaine's death, had stepped in to replace her as chief financial officer, all of which seemed suspiciously convenient in hindsight. Not to mention that she'd learned they'd both tampered with evidence at the crime scene.

At the time, when Katrina cited these factors as her rationale for turning down the side job, Vincent and the paper's then–executive editor, John Palmer, tried to push her off the story, blaming it on pressure from the SDPD and mayor's office. She resisted, and, supported by her advocates Joanne and Linda, they all forced Vincent and his lapdog to withdraw, warning that such a move could taint the entire staff's reputation.

The situation got worse before it got better, but in the past few weeks, all these wrongs had been righted. Katrina's investigative reporting exposed Palmer for contributing to Congressman Winchester's reelection campaign. Because such a donation was strictly against newsroom rules—and Winchester was arrested as one of Darren McMurphy's coconspirators—Palmer was forced to resign. The editor slunk off to a resort in the Bahamas, where he was reportedly poolside, applying madly for PR jobs while drunk on dark 'n' stormies, a ginger-beer-and-rum drink befitting his circumstances.

Unless John Palmer has a trust fund we don't know about, I have to wonder how he's able to afford that kind of hideout. Was he getting payoffs from the cabal all along?

Linda, the Metro editor who had recruited Katrina the day she won a national investigative reporting award at a newspaper back east, had since moved into Palmer's job and his corner fishbowl office. Joanne, in turn, was promoted to take Linda's place. Although Linda was still rough around the edges, she seemed less agitated and more comfortable in her new role, because she no longer had to worry about pleasing Palmer.

"I never respected that man," she told Katrina and Joanne the day he was escorted out by security. "I feel like I can breathe again. I don't know why Vincent hired him in the first place."

After her successful genealogy story pitch to Joanne, Katrina was leisurely browsing the internet at her desk, surrounded by the sound of her coworkers conducting phone interviews. Working in a newsroom, she'd learned to block out most of her coworkers' phone calls. But some of the more bizarre one-way conversations were hard to ignore, and it was considered bad form to admit that you'd been listening.

"Let me ask you this: Are you on medication right now?" one of her pod-mates asked. "Yeah, I thought so."

Looking forward to her first weekend off since she'd started working at the *Sun-Dispatch*, Katrina was finally going to get her broken car window fixed and move some furniture into her new apartment from the storage units containing her family's belongings. It wasn't just a matter of free time that had kept her from doing this before. She'd also been waiting until she felt emotionally capable of doing so.

I think I'm finally ready to paw through those boxes now, even though I know it will trigger all kinds of memories.

Her aunt Athena hadn't been much help with packing up the Chopin family house in Point Loma. She was too broken up by the cumulative loss of her sister, brother-in-law, and nephew in just six months. So, Katrina spent two weeks alternating between comforting her aunt, culling out items she could sell at an estate sale on the front lawn, and resolving the financial detritus that came with losing both parents simultaneously. By the time she'd emptied the house to rent it out, she'd filled three adjacent storage lockers with furniture and boxes.

Thankfully, her parents had been organized and efficient in their estate planning. After Franny died, they'd updated their wills to leave everything to each other, or, if they were both dead, to Katrina. They'd also set up a trust with investments and a trustee, to ensure that Katrina would be well cared for, and if she lost a job, or wanted to spend six months vagabonding in Europe, she could. With an aggressive investment portfolio, Katrina could even live, sparingly, off the inheritance.

But none of these options was remotely interesting to her. Money wasn't all that important to Katrina, because she didn't work to live, she lived to work. Other than playing her guitars and writing the occasional song, being a journalist had been the main plank of her identity since she'd felt the high of her first big news story back in college. After that, she fit the more routine parts of her life into nights and weekends between deadlines.

Once her parents' estate was settled, she left for a job at the *Northampton Record*, a little paper in western Massachusetts. From there, she worked with a rental manager to lease her parents' house for two years to a family of four, which had renewed the lease year to year ever since.

Now that she was back in town, she'd notified the tenants that she would be moving into the house when the renewal expired in five months. So, there was no point to filling her new apartment with furniture that she would just have to move again.

That said, the sleeping-bag-on-the-living-room-floor arrangement was getting old. She was excited by the prospect of putting sheets and blankets on her old familiar mattress in the master bedroom. She also planned to dig out a couple of bedside tables, a chest of drawers, a dining table and chairs, and a desk to make a home office out of the second bedroom.

But not wanting to tempt fate, she didn't ask Goode to help her move, knowing they might slip given the chance to cavort in a dark private space on a Saturday afternoon. That, however, left her without a set of strong arms to do the heavy lifting.

Working nights and weekends had paid plenty of overtime over the past month but left her with no time or motivation to make new friends. So, it was a combination of impulse and random events that prompted her to ask Norman Klein, the cops reporter, to help her.

While Katrina had been in Joanne's office earlier, Norman had quietly sent in a news brief about a thirty-eight-year-old inmate who had been found dead in his jail cell. Norman didn't give anyone a heads-up, because the sheriff's news release didn't disclose that it was Darren McMurphy.

The only reason Katrina even had a clue came via a voicemail that was waiting for her when she returned from the restroom, but even then, the male caller disguised his voice with an electronic device:

"The inmate who died in the downtown jail today was Darren McMurphy. He hung himself in his cell."

As adrenaline flushed through her body, Katrina ran back to Joanne's office with the news: "You're not going to believe this!" she said, repeating the message. "I guess it's not over till it's over."

"Call your detective friend for confirmation and ask what it means for the Fontaine case moving forward," Joanne said eagerly. "In the meantime, write up a quick history of the case. We'll only run the name if you can confirm it. Worst case, we'll go with Klein's brief, which few people will probably even see. You know my preference. Get to work."

Katrina tried calling Goode, but he didn't answer. She figured she'd try him again in a bit rather than leave him a message he might not get in time.

She was busy writing up the Fontaine/McMurphy case background when an editorial assistant rushed over to recount what she'd just heard on the scanner:

"The San Diego PD dispatcher was trying to reach Sergeant Stone and Detective Goode in the field because Patrick McMurphy's wife called 911 to report that her husband died suddenly at home. The wife said, 'I don't want any more trouble after what happened to my son today, so I thought I'd better call this in right away.'"

"Oh, wow, thanks," Katrina said. For a few moments she was happy to get near confirmation about Darren McMurphy. That is, until the ramifications hit her between the eyes.

Goode and I were so close to freedom, and now we get this double whammy. That said, it's a great story, and it's still my *story. I'm not about to give it up now.*

Back in Joanne's office, Katrina gave her the latest: "I think we can say that first tip is correct, which means we'll need to write up a different top to the story. I'm going to head over to Patrick McMurphy's house and try to catch Goode in person and confirm."

"Sounds like a plan. Just write up the A-matter first," Joanne said, referring to the background and context portion of the story.

While Katrina was typing away, Norman showed up in the newsroom. He was hovering outside Joanne's office, waiting for her to get off the phone to ask why the new investigative reporter had been allowed to usurp another story on his beat and, worse yet, why no one even had the courtesy to tell him. Everyone sitting near Joanne's office could hear how upset he was.

"I had to read it on the daily story budget, where you replaced my jail-inmate brief with a story under Katrina's byline," he told Joanne heatedly.

Katrina had met Norman only once before, because he worked out of a cubbyhole at the police station. But she felt like she knew him after reading his first-person account of how Goode had saved his life a year earlier on the cliffs of Black's Beach, where a mentally ill woman with a gun threatened to jump and take him with her. Because Goode had saved Katrina's life, too, she felt like that gave her and Norman an unspoken bond. She hoped he'd think so as well.

Other reporters described Norman with a mix of sympathy and admiration. He always looked like he'd rolled out of bed and put on whatever clothes were lying on the floor. He also failed to wipe newsprint smudges from his face, which earned him a not-so-secret nickname, "Inky."

But despite his iffy social and personal grooming skills, Norman was determined. After getting a late start as an editorial assistant in his mid-twenties, he was soon promoted to night cops reporter. From there, he moved up to the daytime beat due to his coverage of the Tania Marcus case, which culminated in an account of his near-death experience at Black's Beach. Although he was now in his late twenties, he was still considered a cub reporter because he had so much to learn.

Knowing she'd taken his story, Katrina tried to soften the blow with a personal greeting on her way out.

"Hi, Norman," she said in her perkiest voice, extending her hand to shake his. "Katrina Chopin."

"Yes, I know. We've met," he said dourly.

He's definitely pissed.

Katrina plowed ahead. "I wanted to ask you, are you busy this Saturday?"

She could see by his tight lips and contorted brow that he was unsure how to take the question, but it seemed to break his sulk. "Um, maybe," he said in a noticeable New Jersey accent. "What's up?"

"I thought it would be good to get to know each other better so you don't think I'm purposely trying to snake your stories all the time," she said.

She'd heard through the grapevine that Norman was intimidated and not just a little upset that she'd been assigned to the Fontaine story her first week at the paper, because he'd been the first to inform the Metro desk after hearing about the 911 call on the scanner in his car. But Katrina knew the night editor had written a brief under Norman's name after doing the brunt of the work himself—consulting the crisscross directory to determine that the house in La Jolla Farms was owned by Dr. Simon Fontaine. So, when Katrina was assigned an investigative breakout piece the next morning, she didn't feel bad for a second. That said, she figured Norman's ego needed some massaging.

Norman nodded, so she proceeded. "I need help moving some stuff out of storage on Saturday, and I wondered if you were available," she said. "We can hang out, and maybe I can give you some investigative tips while we're at it."

Given the impetus for his visit to the newsroom, Norman blushed, revealing his embarrassment that she was capable not only of stealing his stories and doing a better job than he ever could, but of reading his mind as well.

"Sure. I guess I can do that," he said, smiling awkwardly. He seemed flattered by the invitation. "Where do you want to meet?"

"How 'bout that coffee bean place down the street?" she suggested. "We can take one car to the truck-rental place. We might need another set of hands to help carry the heavier stuff, but I don't know anyone else to ask. Do you? My only request is that it isn't Jerry."

Norman let out a snort. "Why's that?" he asked.

"I don't know if you guys are friends," she said, referring to the arrogant City Hall reporter as she leaned in to whisper the rest, "but he's kind of a dick. He's been spying on me since I got here, leaving half-eaten pieces of cake on my desk and going through my emails."

This time, Norman laughed out loud. "He *is* kind of a dick. I agree, no Jerry."

"Well, I've got to run to La Jolla and see if I can grab Detective Goode or Sergeant Stone for a quote," she said, leaving Norman with his mouth agape that she'd just done it again.

CHAPTER 5
KATRINA

Thursday

Goode walked toward Katrina in front of the McMurphy house, where the patrol officer was giving her the runaround. As Goode approached, Katrina switched her focus to the detective, whose eyebrows were raised with the silent question she knew he was thinking.

"Heard it on the scanner," she said.

The officer seemed confused until he realized she was talking to Goode. "Detective, this is Katrina Chopin from the *Sun-Dispatch*. I was telling her that we have no comment because we're still investigating the scene."

"Yes, we've met, and that is correct," Goode said. "I'll take it from here, Officer."

"Sergeant Stone is inside. He's handling media, no?" the officer asked, confused.

"Yes, he is. Thank you," Goode said, clearly annoyed with the officer's passive-aggressive reminder that it wasn't his job to talk to the press. "Why don't you string up some yellow tape to keep the lookie-loos at bay?"

Once the officer was out of earshot, Goode rolled his eyes and gave Katrina his telltale smirk. A lock of sun-bleached brown hair fell over his forehead as he gazed down at her in the moonlight. If she were in a Jane Austen novel, she would have swooned. But instead, she tried to keep her cool.

"I didn't expect to see you here, but I guess I should've known better," he said. His tone sounded professional, but his laughing eyes sparked with an unnerving flirtation that only she could see on the dark street.

"Thought I'd surprise you for a change."

"For a change? You're always surprising me."

"Yeah, well, this case is one big, long surprise. You said you had it all tied up and were about to send it over to the DA's office, so I was hoping to finally have time to finish moving into my apartment and do the other stuff we talked about," she said, lowering her voice, "like investigate my parents' murder. But this changes everything. So, Darren McMurphy hung himself in his cell this afternoon? And now his dad is dead too? I never expected that to happen."

"How did you—never mind," he said.

"So, is that a confirmation?"

"Is what a confirmation?"

"Of the suicide. Do you think his dad killed himself too?"

Goode shook his head and took a breath before he answered. "Off the record," he said carefully, "we don't know if Darren's death was a suicide or a murder. I just got here, and so far, my understanding is that there's no obvious sign of foul play in Patrick's death. But knowing this case, who knows. So, it's too early to announce anything publicly."

"Well, thanks for the nonclarification. To answer your question, I didn't know for sure if the dead inmate was Darren or not. The sheriff's news release didn't say. But since it was, maybe Patrick did the same thing out of guilt. That would make sense."

"Wait, what *did* the sheriff's department release say?"

"That a thirty-eight-year-old male inmate was found dead in his cell, name pending, autopsy tomorrow."

Goode shook his head again and frowned with apparent frustration. "So, how did you know it was Darren, and who gave you the hanging information?"

"Anonymous tip to my voicemail. The guy disguised his voice with one of those *Star Wars* doohickeys."

"So, you tricked me. Thanks for the heads-up."

"Sorry, just doing my job."

She enjoyed their banter, especially when it gave her the information she needed. Until he threw her a curveball.

"Back to where we were," he said. "Off the record, it might make sense, but I can guarantee you it's not going to be that simple. This family didn't feel feelings like regular people. I didn't see any empathy or compassion, let alone guilt, in their DNA."

"You know, this off-the-record thing feels like a whole lot of déjà vu," she said, referring to the start of the Fontaine case. He'd given her the same nondenial denials and no solid information on the record for days, still reeling from the shock that the beautiful woman he'd chatted up at Piatti was now reporting on his case. "But what happens to your case now that your two primary defendants are dead? Could be another Vitaleron power grab."

"I'm not exactly sure. I guess it'll save taxpayers a lot of money on trials that won't go forward, and we won't get to the whole truth. Although I doubt we would have gotten to it even if this hadn't happened."

Goode was right about that. Darren McMurphy may have implicated his father as a leader in a cabal of wealthy men who secretly ran the city. But he didn't seem like the kind of guy to hang himself, even after being forced to go cold turkey, with no sex drug, cocaine, or God knows what else he'd been taking.

He could've been in the tailspin of withdrawal, feeling mentally unstable in a quagmire of hopelessness: He was facing a possible death sentence after being abandoned by his father, whose instructions to "take care of this mess" had put him behind bars in the first place. That would be a lot to deal with for anyone. But then what or who killed Patrick?

"Can you guys give me anything I can run with tonight?" she asked.

"Give us an hour, and one of us will let you know. Seems like you've kicked Norman Klein off his beat."

"Over my dead body. I'm an investigative reporter, not a cops reporter. That would be a demotion."

"Sorry, didn't mean to hit a nerve," he said, smirking again. He reached out and squeezed the side of her waist, glancing around to make sure that no one had seen. "Gotta go."

"You make me insane. I'm starving, and I'm on a deadline," she said, playfully angry.

"Go home. Eat. Stone or I will try to let you know what we can in a bit."

"What do you mean, try? I can't go home now. They need some kind of confirmation or quote for my story. We're going to write about these two deaths either way."

"I know, but that's all I've got right now. I'd love to chat more, but I need to get inside. I was on my way home to call you about the internal political shenanigans that went down earlier today when I got called over here."

"I'll be back," Katrina called out as Goode turned and started heading back inside.

She got into her car and drove down the hill into the Village, as the locals called downtown La Jolla, to find something to eat. If she didn't hear from him by the time she finished eating, she would come back. Maybe by then she could get a cell phone shot of the ME loading Patrick's body into the van, the go-to photo for this kind of story.

She hadn't known Goode and his buddy Stone for that long, but they were notorious for not calling back or answering their phones when they were busy, which was basically all the time. She was still working on getting them trained.

CHAPTER 6
GOODE

Thursday

Goode shook his head. He should have known this salacious news would leak out quickly; he just didn't think it would be *this* quickly. But who would call Katrina with that tip? It had to be someone who knew what had really happened but wanted everyone to think Darren McMurphy had killed himself, when none of them knew anything for sure yet.

Walking through the McMurphys' kitchen, he smiled and nodded respectfully to an older woman with stark-white, perfectly coiffed hair, whom he assumed was Patrick's widow. She was cloistered in the breakfast nook, staring blankly into a full glass of white wine cradled in both hands. He headed past her, down the hallway, to find Stone.

Once again, Katrina somehow knows as much or more than we do about our own damn case. This doesn't bode well.

He found Stone standing next to a dark-stained oak desk in Patrick's home office, where the deceased was sitting upright in his chair, with a shiny new laptop and a bottle of lemon-infused vodka in front of him. He must have just purchased the laptop, because the Regional

Computer Forensic Laboratory (RCFL) still had his desktop computer, which they'd seized during the previous search.

On the laptop screen was an unfinished game of solitaire. Dressed in powder blue shorts and a lavender golf shirt, Patrick looked as if he'd been playing the game while sipping a glass of vodka and smoking a cigar whose nasty stink still hung in the air.

At seventy, he had a full head of white hair, and his slender frame seemed to be in pretty good shape, at least from the outside. There were no pills, rope, blood, visible injuries, weapon, or any other obvious sign of what could have caused his death.

"What do you think, heart attack?" Goode asked.

"Could be."

"From the stress of ordering a hit on his son today?"

"With this family? Anything's possible."

"I'm not taking any chances, or making any assumptions, but based on what happened at the jail this afternoon, and Patrick's imminent arrest, we should treat this death as suspicious," Goode said.

"Agreed," Stone said.

"We should have Artie's lab test the contents of this glass and the vodka bottle, too, in case he was poisoned."

"Yes, absolutely. Good call. His cigar too," Stone said, pointing to the nub in the ashtray, most of which had burned into a caterpillar-like curl of ash.

"But before we do that, we should get Dwight Pepper over here to dust the glass and bottle for prints and swab them for DNA. He should swab Patrick's keyboard, too, in case there's any weird powder on it. What's that stuff they put on mail to try to kill politicians?"

"Anthrax."

"Yeah, that stuff. Wait a minute, I have a hunch," Goode said, slipping on a pair of latex gloves. He toggled the keyboard to a split screen and clicked on one of the open windows, where he found the start of what looked like a will in a Word document:

To whom it may concern, I, Patrick McMurphy, hereby leave all my possessions to my wife, Doreen, and my younger son Matthew, to be split 50-50. Since my older son Darren has disgraced the family and will be spending the rest of his life in prison, he is in no need of the family trust and shall have no access to family money for his defense. I leave my

The unfinished sentence was the end of the text. Not all computers were set to save text automatically, so Goode couldn't tell if Patrick had saved the document yet. But he knew better than to mess with the file before the RCFL had a chance to duplicate the hard drive.

"So, he was writing his will when he stopped to play a game of solitaire, then suddenly keeled over?" Stone asked, reading over Goode's shoulder.

"Yeah, something's fishy. He had to know he was about to be arrested. We pretty much told him as much in the last couple of interrogations, not to mention the searches of this house and his office downtown. But someone else could have typed this up after he was already dead."

"Good point."

"The DNA swab on the keyboard will show if there was another contributor," Goode said. "The fact that this document was left unfinished could have been on purpose, so it would look like his heart stopped while he was writing it. Have you talked to the widow yet?"

"No, I was waiting for you," Stone said. "Even though she called to notify us, it seems like she wants to be left alone. It's got to be tough, two losses like this in one day. Then we descend on the house, giving her no privacy or opportunity to grieve."

"You never know. She could be relieved that this is all over. Who knows what went on or was said in this house before today. I'm going to ask if she's able or willing to talk. Last I checked, she was drowning herself in a bottle of Chardonnay."

Making his way back to the kitchen, he found Doreen humming as she made herself a ham, cheese, and sweet pickle sandwich.

"You want one, Detective?" she asked, giving him a wooden half smile, as if she were greeting an acquaintance at the beach club. "I was getting ready to make one for Patty when I found him. But I guess he won't be needing one now."

Um, okay, is she not upset, or does she always use dark humor to handle tough situations?

"Sure, that's nice of you. I'd love one. I was heading to the deli for a sandwich when I got called over here," he said. "I'm so sorry for your loss, Mrs. McMurphy. You must be having a very difficult day."

"Yes, you could say that," she said, taking a deep breath and letting out a long sigh. "But that's all I'm going to say unless and until I have a lawyer present, Detective. I know how this must look."

"How what must look?"

Doreen held his gaze as she sliced cleanly through the first sandwich with a carving knife—without looking down—then did the same with the second one. "That's all I'm going to say."

Neat trick. She's certainly good with knives. Is she suggesting that he didn't die of natural causes while, faced with an impending arrest in the morning, he was writing up a new will? I know everyone handles grief differently, but this family seems like a school of cold fish.

She took a couple of plates out of the cupboard, put a sandwich on each one, and slid one toward him. After slamming the cork into the wine bottle, she tucked it under her arm.

"There's soda and water in the fridge. Help yourself. I'll be in my bedroom," she said flatly, heading down the hallway with her glass of wine and sandwich plate. "I've got nothing to hide, so feel free to look around, take whatever you want, and let yourself out. I need to call my son Matthew. He lives in Hong Kong, and he's got no idea what's been going on here."

Well, that was a weird exchange.

Sandwich plate in hand, Goode was on his way to tell Stone about the surprising carte blanche Doreen had given them to search the house without a warrant when he stopped at a bathroom to wash his hands. If there really was some poisonous powder on the laptop that had seeped through his gloves, he didn't want to ingest it.

It was a half bathroom, with a small sink and a toilet. Peeking in the medicine cabinet behind the mirror, he saw nothing out of the ordinary—no pills, syringes, or drug paraphernalia of any kind that could have been used to poison Patrick. The deaths of father and son within just four hours definitely pointed to foul play.

Once his hands were clean, he went back to eating the sandwich, which was tasty with those sweet pickle chips and just the right amount of mayonnaise. He was hungry, but he stopped chewing for a moment when he realized he could hear Doreen's muffled voice through the wall to her bedroom.

Cocking his head, he tried but couldn't make out what she was saying. So, he grabbed the empty glass on the sink and put it up to the wall, like he was playing telephone as a kid.

"Yes, as soon as I found him dead, I called the police just like you said, Vincey. Then I made the detective a sandwich and came straight in here to call you. I told him I couldn't say anything more without an attorney present. I can meet with Milton tomorrow if you want, and go over my statement, before they force me to make one. But right now, I've got to call Matty. I'm not really looking forward to that conversation, but I just keep telling myself what you said, 'It'll all be over soon, and hopefully we can go back to the way things were.' I can't wait for that damn sex drug to be approved so I can start the next chapter of my life."

The way things were? When was that? And Vincey, was that Vincent Battrelle? Were they having an affair? Was this why she was feeling guilty and paranoid? That was as good a motive as any for Vincent—or both of them—wanting Patrick McMurphy dead. Or was it a power play and money grab on the Vitaleron board like Katrina suggested? She was a smart cookie, possibly even smarter than him, he hated to admit. Did Vincent and Doreen plot this out together? But then how did her son Darren end up dead too? Or was Patrick's death an act of retribution for killing her son?

Some answers to these questions would be helpful, because so far, Goode hadn't been able to pin anything on Vincent other than obstruction and evidence tampering at the Fontaine crime scene. And thanks to Vincent's high-powered attorney, those felony charges had been negotiated down to misdemeanors for both him and his son Michael.

Nonetheless, Vincent's behavior had been that of a guilty man all along—overreacting to accusations, calling Katrina and asking if Goode was at her apartment, as if he knew the detective was standing right next to her. That behavior almost had him convinced that Vincent had someone watching her place and that he could've been responsible for the threatening note she'd received, crafted out of letters sliced out of a magazine and attached to a rock that broke her car window. Whether Vincent did all of that himself, or had one of his lackeys do it, was immaterial. These behind-the-scenes dealings between him and Doreen made them both look complicit in Patrick's death.

Heading back to Patrick's office, Goode outlined for Stone the conversation he'd just overheard.

"Hmmm, that's interesting," Stone said, clearly distracted.

Stone said it was nice that Doreen gave them permission to search her house, but he had their teammate, Detective Ted Byron, applying for a warrant anyway.

"Better to do this by the book," Stone said. "Besides, grief does strange things to people. She could change her mind in a flash, and we'd lose crucial hours."

Stone didn't seem impressed with the new Vincent development, probably because he didn't know the whole history of events and the theory that Goode and Katrina had been discussing, that the people behind the Fontaine murders could also be involved with her parents' murder and brother's alleged suicide. Why else would the threatening note she'd received be worded that way?

> Hey, Miss Rock Star Reporter, we see you're back in town, digging where you shouldn't be. Watch your back or it won't be your car window that gets whacked next time. Could even look like another suicide.

At the time, Goode and Katrina weren't sure if the words *suicide* and *whacked* were references to her brother Franny's death, which she'd always suspected was a murder staged as a suicide, or if they were references to the staged suicides at the Fontaine mansion. If it was the former, they'd come up with a possible motive: Vincent was angry at Franny for losing his money on the resort deal that failed right before Franny was found dead.

But what are the chances that the lemon-infused vodka is a coincidental element of both Franny's and Patrick's death scenes? Even though there are no visible pills lying around here, like there were in Franny's house, my gut says they're related.

"This could prove to be the missing link we've been looking for," Goode told Stone excitedly. "I always felt like Vincent was more involved in Patrick's cabal than he let on, and therefore more complicit in the hit on the Fontaines."

"Yeah, I don't know," said Stone, still sounding distracted. "I'm sure he, like the McMurphys, was frustrated with the time it's taking for the FDA to approve the sex drug and how long his big investment is taking to pay off. But why would he want Patrick out of the way now? Unless it has more to do with Vitaleron or his real estate developments, where the cabal might have more influence in the city planning process."

How about because Patrick knew too much, so the cabal wanted to shut him up before he squealed like his son did?

Goode hesitated to delve into the details of Katrina's family's backstory, because he could tell that Stone wouldn't be able to process them right now. Stone often got overwhelmed at the start of a new case, even though the two McMurphy deaths were really more of an outgrowth of the Fontaine case. But Goode knew his private investigation with Katrina would generate theories that he couldn't explain in a vacuum, and that once they started pulling more threads, he'd have to fully brief Stone. So, seeing an opening to what he really wanted, he took it.

"Maybe the Fontaine case isn't as screwed as we thought now, even without the McMurphys," he said. "Katrina and I were talking before and—"

"Hold on," Stone said. "Why are you sharing information with her when I've specifically told you not to? When did Katrina become part of our team?"

Which is why I didn't want to bring this up right now. But this is the moment to push through.

"She's not, but you know she's really good at her job. I should also preface this by saying that Marty Watts, our new special buddy at the FBI, raised this possibility as well."

"Okay, then, that's a little better. But you know how I feel about outside opinions influencing our investigations."

"I think there's more to this case that may go back in time and connect to the Double-Judge murders. Just listen," Goode said, attempting to connect the dots for him. "So, I'd like to dig into the judges' case file for leads that could help us in this new chapter of the investigation. Vincent could've gotten lucky because he's got such a well-connected lawyer, but we know Katrina was in danger before, and even with the McMurphys gone, she's still in danger as long as someone is still killing people connected to Vitaleron. Did I ever tell you that Katrina's father was one of the original cofounders and investors in the company but pulled out because he was jealous of Vincent hitting on his wife?"

Stone frowned. "No, I don't think you did," he said. After thinking a moment, he said, "In that case, I guess it can't hurt to ask. But I'm going to proceed carefully, and so should you. Don't do anything until I run this up the chain. You know detectives don't like their colleagues Monday-morning quarterbacking their cases."

"And you know that the Double-Judge case never went anywhere. I don't know why, but if I did, we wouldn't be having this conversation."

"True. But for now, let's focus on processing this scene before Queen Doreen changes her mind."

"Got it. I just got a text from Pepper that he's on his way. Artie should be here soon too. I left the RCFL a message that we're bringing the laptop over in the morning."

CHAPTER 7
KATRINA

Thursday

Katrina was thankful to find a sandwich shop on Girard that was still open, where she devoured a tuna melt with a bag of whole-grain chips. She passed on the meal deal that came with a giant cup of diet soda because she had a rule against drinking caffeine in the evening. She didn't want to be up all night, and she'd also been working to eliminate brain-rotting aspartame from her life. Despite that cloying artificial-sweetener taste, she'd come to rely on a quick pick-me-up soda when a story broke late in the afternoon and she needed to sharpen her wits. That made it not just physically addictive, but emotionally, too, because she felt like she couldn't be smart without it.

And I don't want to be addicted to anything.

She tried texting Goode, but he didn't answer. So, she hopped into her Land Rover and drove back up the hill to collect that quote—and any other tidbits he and Stone might throw her way.

The same patrol officer was blocking the opening in the white stucco wall, even though the slate pathway leading to the McMurphys' front door was now cordoned off with yellow tape.

"Hey, Katrina. Back so soon?" he said. "I still don't think we have any information for you."

"Yeah, I figured, but I told those guys I'd check back for a quote. Could you ask Detective Goode or Sergeant Stone if they could come out for a minute?"

"I can try," he said, heading inside.

"One of them will be out shortly," he said when he reemerged, walking far enough down the sidewalk that they didn't have to interact.

Fine with me.

Five minutes later, Goode came outside, appearing a little frayed around the edges. "What's up? I thought you were going home," he said.

Katrina shook her head. "I told you I'd be back. I need a quote for my story, remember?"

"Oh, yeah, you did say that. Sorry, there's a lot going on here."

"These deaths have really screwed up your case, right? You seem kind of frazzled."

When Goode's expression turned to frustration, Katrina was confused. Seemed like that should have been not only a natural question, but an anticipated one.

I must have hit a nerve.

"You know I can't give you a quote on the record," he said.

Oh, maybe that's the source of his frustration. He has something to say but knows he shouldn't.

"Well, then, can Sergeant Stone come out and play? You know I'm on a deadline."

"You're always on a deadline. Listen, here's what I can tell you, off the record—" he said, leading her farther away from the police officer.

"How 'bout on the record, not for attribution?" she asked.

"I think I've got this from last time—that means you use what I say but don't quote me by name?"

"Right."

"Okay, here, you can use this, but please don't make it come back on me: Darren McMurphy's 'suicide' note was written with a pencil that was not found in the cell. We don't see how he could write a note without one, and conveniently, there were no working cameras monitoring his cell. So, I wouldn't call it a suicide. It seems more like it was staged to look like one. Technically, Darren's death is under the jurisdiction of the sheriff, who is under the gun right now because of all these jail deaths. Clearly, your anonymous tipster has an agenda. He could be a sheriff's deputy, or even the watch commander, trying to protect the boss and the department's reputation. Hopefully we'll know more tomorrow after the autopsy."

"How about the basics—like the time and place where Patrick McMurphy was found?"

Goode pulled out a scrap of paper where he'd scribbled some notes. "Stone said you can quote him on this: 'Patrick McMurphy was found dead in his home office at 7:27 p.m. Although there were no visible signs of foul play, the San Diego PD's Homicide unit has categorized his death as suspicious because it came so soon after his son's violent death at the Central Jail this afternoon, so we think the two may be related. We'll be looking to the ME's office for a cause of death, but it will be a while before we get the toxicology results."

"That'll work," she said. "Although I could have just written that for you guys."

"Hey, I got you something, didn't I?"

"Yeah, but where's the juice you wanted to tell me earlier?"

"We'll have to talk about that later. The sheriff's department can try to make Darren's death seem like a nothingburger, but the fact that the two deaths occurred only a few hours apart is clearly some kind of burger. Please don't mention this in the story, but Patrick's wife, Doreen, was also acting kinda strange tonight."

"How so?"

"She was ice cold when I first walked in. Then later, she offered to make me a sandwich, like it was an ordinary day. And then she says, 'I'm not going to say anything else until or unless I have an attorney, because I know how this must look.'"

"What does that mean?"

"That's what I said. But wait, there's more."

He told her about overhearing Doreen's call to "Vincey," when she said she called the police right after she found Patrick, "just like you told me to."

"It was like she and Vincent knew Patrick was going to die. So, I saw that as a major lead. It also gave me an opening to ask Stone for access to your parents' murder case file. Vincent Battrelle has been way too involved in your life, trying to buy you off the Vitaleron story and distract you with the search for Alex Battrelle, who turned out to be in the Caymans making illegal transactions for Congressman Winchester, both of whom were subsequently arrested by the feds. Seems like Vincent's business associates are being charged with crimes, or worse, murdered or dying suspiciously, yet nothing comes back on him."

The feds had charged Congressman Winchester for his role in the overall conspiracy, which involved soliciting a bribe from Darren McMurphy, then later luring Katrina to the Hotel del Coronado to meet Winchester and his fiancée, Darla Johansen, who worked at Vitaleron, allegedly to discuss the congressman's campaign finances. But the real motivation was to get Katrina into a hotel room, where McMurphy could inject her with succinylcholine.

When Katrina told Goode she was going to meet Winchester and Darla in a bar at the hotel, he said he would sit nearby to make sure she was safe. What he didn't tell her was that McMurphy and his fiancée were suspects in the Fontaine murders and that they were hiding out at the hotel. He also didn't tell her that he and Stone had set up a sting operation with the FBI, hoping to implicate Winchester in a recorded conversation with Katrina while also catching the Fontaines' killer, all by using Katrina as bait. Winchester and Darla did manage to lure a reluctant Katrina up to their room, but their bizarre exchange prompted her to leave before McMurphy could arrive with his deadly syringe.

Once Goode thought he had the situation under control, he told Katrina to go home and let him do his job. But she stubbornly insisted on staying, only to be lured upstairs to another room by McMurphy's fiancée, Esperanza Cepeda, who had been Simon Fontaine's surgical nurse. After Esperanza described to Katrina how McMurphy had forced her to watch him inject Simon and Victoria Fontaine with a paralytic drug, McMurphy burst in, injected Katrina with the same drug, and left her to die.

Meanwhile, McMurphy tried to make a run for it with Esperanza, whom he'd repeatedly threatened to kill if she didn't cooperate. But once they were in the crowded lobby, she took her chance to escape by reaching into his pocket, grabbing the syringe he'd used to try to kill Katrina, and injecting him with the succinylcholine that remained in the chamber, which was enough to take him out. She then fled to the restroom where she'd tracked down Katrina earlier, so Goode knew where to find her. Esperanza subsequently agreed to be the prosecution's star witness.

At the same time, Winchester's fiancée, Darla Johansen, tried to wrangle an immunity deal from the feds. But because she'd acted as a lookout for McMurphy while he'd injected Katrina at the hotel, the feds weren't sure whether to trust her claim of coerced involvement. And neither was Goode. Darla also refused to talk to them about her fiancé Winchester's involvement in the scheme.

After spending the night in the hospital and then writing up the whole account in the newspaper over the next couple of weeks, Katrina had been enjoying the resulting reprieve from the pressure that her publisher, Vincent Battrelle, had been inflicting on her to protect his family and business associates.

"Vincent did admit to evidence tampering at the Fontaine mansion, but he doesn't seem to be involved in the rest of all this, right?" she told Goode outside the McMurphys' house. "He's also been leaving me alone lately, which is a nice change."

"But what if he's been having an affair with Patrick McMurphy's wife? That would put Patrick's sudden death into a whole new light, wouldn't it? Did I tell you that we were planning to arrest Patrick in the morning for conspiracy to commit murder in the Fontaine case?"

"No, that's some important context that you neglected to mention. Can I put that in the story?"

"Yeah, I guess that's okay since it's not going to happen now."

"So, you're not giving me much to work with here, but what if someone else has been involved in these murders all along, and if that person knew you were about to arrest Patrick, he killed both McMurphys to keep them from spilling more incriminating information about the cabal? Like the names of its other leaders?"

"Right. Like Vincent Battrelle?"

"Maybe. Or whoever else."

"You might have something there, but honestly, we really didn't see any obvious forensic signs of foul play here tonight. No pills or gun, nothing like the plethora of clues we found at the Fontaines', even if they did turn out to be staged."

"I'm just saying, anything is possible."

"Yes, you're right. It could also be a natural death, or even a suicide by some means we haven't found yet. But while we're waiting for the toxicology results, this puts Vincent back into the game. And even though the guy who gave you a lethal injection is dead, as long as people related to Vitaleron and the Fontaine case are still dying, you're still in danger, whether it's from this potential killer, from Vincent, Linebacker Dude, whoever broke your car window, or whoever killed your family."

Just when she'd finally felt like the heat was off enough to sleep through the night, Katrina was caught off guard by Goode's predictive pronouncement of impending doom.

"Well, that's not very reassuring," she said, staring at him for a minute, trying to get her bearings. "Speaking of which, are you still looking for Linebacker Dude and his black Infiniti?"

"It's kind of hard to openly investigate an event that neither of us wants anyone to know about," he said, referring to their interrupted half-naked interlude. "But I'm definitely keeping my eyes and ears open for any leads that might intersect."

"What about the bodyguard outside of Winchester's hotel room at the Del?" she asked. "Didn't you say he had the same build as the Dude?"

"Yes, Walter Hall. Didn't I tell you? When I tried to pick him up for questioning a week ago, Winchester's staff said he took a leave of absence right after his boss was arrested, and they're not sure where he is. Possibly the Bahamas."

"No, you didn't tell me that either. Do you know who else is in the Bahamas?"

"No, who?"

"John Palmer, the former executive editor who tried to kick me off the Vitaleron story at Vincent's request. The one whose name was on the donor list to the Christian PAC that funneled money to Winchester's campaign."

"That's a good lead, actually. I guess I should check airline manifests for the Bahamas." He paused for a minute. "Listen, sorry, but I've really got to get back inside."

"Okay," she said. "I'll call in these few factoids about the McMurphys, then go home and try to process all of this."

Goode nodded. "Sorry, I didn't mean to scare and then abandon you. Let's talk tomorrow after the autopsies," he said. "Maybe I'll know more by then."

He puckered his lips into a silent kiss and gave her an empathetic smile before heading into the house.

Katrina was getting used to the professional blow-off from Goode. If they didn't know each other as well as they did, she probably wouldn't mind as much, but she knew that he'd spent the day gathering other leads that he hadn't shared with her.

After everything that had happened since they'd met a month ago, she wished he would quit keeping things from her. It had almost gotten her killed at the Hotel Del, although he probably wouldn't see it that way. When she put on her rational hat, she told herself that he was just doing his job. Just like her.

CHAPTER 8
KATRINA

Thursday

Katrina called Joanne from the car to dictate the juicy new tidbits she'd gotten so her editor could weave them into the story on deadline.

"Nice work," Joanne said. "Now go home and get some rest so you can write a follow-up on the autopsies tomorrow. Just when you thought you could rest on your laurels—"

"That's never going to happen. You're only as good as your last story."

"Right. Not until you and I are in a nursing home. Me first," Joanne said, laughing. "Have a good night."

When Katrina got back to her apartment, she poured herself a splash of buttery, oaky Chardonnay in an oversize glass, a favorite possession that she'd found in a thrift store back in Northampton. The wine tasted better and stayed cold longer if she kept pouring splashes rather than filling a smaller glass to the top. At least that's what she told herself.

After giving away most of her belongings to friends, she'd shipped the glass and a few other necessary items from the East Coast. Those of more immediate need—like her corkscrew—made the cross-country trip in her Land Rover. She also hand carried her and Franny's guitars, because she didn't want them thrown around by careless airport workers and postal carriers.

That was nice of Goode to remind me that even with the McMurphys out of the picture, the person who killed my parents, and possibly my brother, is still out there, waiting to get me.

"I can't seem to find safety no matter where I go or what I do," she said to herself.

She thought about playing her guitar for a while, but she wasn't in the mood. So, she poured herself another splash and checked to make sure that her story had been posted, and without any errors. Then she checked the local TV news websites to see if they'd managed to catch up. It always gave her immense satisfaction when, on a night like that, none of them had.

CHAPTER 9
GOODE

Thursday/Friday

Goode and Stone chatted outside in the street where Patrick's wife, Doreen, couldn't hear them while they waited for the forensic tech and ME investigator to show up.

They'd already searched the house a few weeks ago after Darren made his claims about his father being a cabal leader and had gathered enough incriminating emails and documentation from both of their computers to write up Patrick's arrest warrant.

Now that Patrick was dead, they reexamined his home office and did a quick run-through of the rest of the house. But other than the half-written will on the laptop and the lemon-infused vodka, they found nothing noteworthy or suspicious.

"If Doreen won't talk, there's nothing more we can do tonight," Goode said.

Once Dwight Pepper and Artie Hayes arrived, Goode had Pepper swab Patrick's glass, the vodka bottle, and the laptop for DNA and noxious powder. Pepper also dusted the glass and bottle for prints before Artie poured the glass's contents into a vial for toxicology testing.

Before heading out, Goode tapped on Doreen's bedroom door, where she'd locked herself inside. She didn't want to open it, so he told her through the door that they needed her to come down to police headquarters to give a formal statement the next morning at ten o'clock.

"With or without an attorney, it's up to you," he said.

"Okay, thank you, Detective," she said, slurring her words.

"Also, just wanted to let you know we're taking Patrick's laptop," he added. "We'll copy the hard drive and return it to you in a few days."

"That's fine," she said. "Good night, Detective."

"Good night, Mrs. McMurphy."

The next morning, Doreen McMurphy showed up at the station with her attorney, Milton Biggs. Over the past month, Goode and Stone had already met several times with Biggs, whose firm represented the Battrelle family and its various business enterprises, including Vitaleron. He was a big man, but he'd gained even more weight in the past few weeks.

His neck looks jowly. Like Jabba the Hutt's. Stress eating?

Stone and Goode sat facing Doreen and Biggs across the table in the interrogation room and turned on the video recorder. Dressed in a navy blue skirt suit and pearls, Doreen seemed anxious, but at the same time, she also looked like she was going to nod off. He still couldn't tell what was going on behind her blank expression.

Seems like she didn't sleep well last night, which isn't surprising given the day's events. Especially after drinking all that wine. Maybe I can crack that stiff exterior.

Biggs kept shifting around in the old wooden chair, which squeaked with his every move. Goode attributed it to the extra weight.

"Again, we're very sorry for your loss, Mrs. McMurphy," Goode said. "Can we get you some coffee or water?"

"No, thank you," she said through pursed lips. "We won't be here long."

"Oh, really?" Stone asked. "How's that?"

"Go ahead and ask your questions," she said. "I've got to be somewhere."

That comment rubbed Goode the wrong way. He had half a mind to get up and leave for a while without disclosing why, just to annoy her.

You'll leave when we say you can leave, lady.

He had to remind himself that she was grieving, even if it was for two such unsavory characters. But she came off as an unsympathetic character herself, no matter how hard he tried to find a chink in her armor. Maybe she just didn't like or trust men.

"Did your husband seem under the weather or show any signs of medical distress yesterday?" he asked.

"No, he seemed fine," she said.

"Did he have a heart condition?"

"Not that I know of. His doctor told him to stop with the cigars, which I asked him not to smoke in the house, but that's another story."

"When was the last time you talked to him?"

"We had a late lunch, then he went into his office. Said he had some things to take care of."

"Okay, how did you find your husband in his office? Was he unconscious, face down on the desk? Or was he dead, sitting up in his chair like we found him?"

"He was dead, but face down on the desk," she said flatly. Her eyes were as lifeless as her husband's body.

"So, you sat him up?"

"Yes. I wanted to get a better look to see if I could revive him. But he wasn't breathing."

"What made you go in there? Did you hear a noise?"

"No, like I told you, I went in to ask if he wanted a sandwich, because I was about to make myself one. That was around seven o'clock."

"Okay. What time was lunch?"

"About two o'clock. I made us some nice poached salmon with baby potatoes and green beans."

"So, he was in his office for five hours before you found him?"

"Yes. But that's not unusual."

"Did he see or talk to anyone after lunch?"

Doreen looked at Biggs, who nodded at her.

"At the advice of my attorney, I'm invoking the Fifth Amendment."

Stone and Goode frowned at each other and shook their heads almost imperceptibly, so as not to draw notice. "Okay, that doesn't seem like a tough question if he died of natural causes," Goode said.

"Ask your next question, Detective," Biggs said as Doreen maintained the blank expression, blinking several times, like a lizard.

"Okay. Was it Vincent Battrelle?"

"Same answer."

"We know that you spoke with Vincent Battrelle last night, because I overheard you talking to him on the phone," Goode said.

Doreen stared down at the table and put her hands in her lap.

"I heard you tell him that you called us just like he told you to. What did you mean by that? Did you know in advance that your husband was going to die?"

Still looking down, Doreen blinked a few more times. "Same answer."

"When you and I were in the kitchen, you said, 'I know how this must look.' Should we suspect you had something to do with his death?"

"Same answer."

"Did Vincent Battrelle threaten you or your husband, Mrs. McMurphy?"

Doreen glanced up at that question, defensive and protective. "I've known Vincey since I was in college, Detective. He was just trying to help me."

"Okay, that doesn't really answer my question. Did Vincent Battrelle threaten you?"

"No."

"Did he threaten your husband?"

"Not exactly."

"Did he or someone else come to the house after lunch, or did Patrick speak to someone else on the phone yesterday in the hours before he died?"

Doreen turned toward Biggs, who nodded at her again. "I'm invoking the Fifth Amendment," she said.

Goode was growing exasperated by this game she was playing. What was she hiding? Did someone help her or Vincent kill Patrick?

"Do you know who it was? If you don't answer, we can easily subpoena your phone records, Mrs. McMurphy."

"At the advice of my attorney, I'm invoking the Fifth Amendment," she said.

"Okay. So, he talked to someone you don't want to name. Is that because you're scared of this person?"

"Same answer."

"Did this same person come to the house after he or she called?"

"Same answer."

Goode ran his fingers through his hair, which seemed to help him think better. Got the blood flowing, anyway.

"Did your husband have a recent will, Mrs. McMurphy? As in locked up and kept somewhere, signed and notarized?"

"I'm not sure how recent it was, but I think so."

Goode shifted his gaze to the attorney. "Do you know, Mr. Biggs?"

"I'll have to check, but I believe so. It would have been drafted before the Fontaine incidents, though."

Interesting that he used a neutral word like incidents *instead of* murders.

"So, why do you think he would start typing one up on his laptop yesterday afternoon?"

"Who are you directing that question to, Detective?" Biggs asked.

"To you."

"I don't really know. But since it wasn't printed out, signed, or notarized, I highly doubt it would hold up in court, especially since the narrative stopped mid-sentence."

Unless the purpose of it wasn't the distribution of assets, but something else.

"Did he have advance warning that we were going to arrest him this morning?"

"He could have. You know he had an office at City Hall and many friends in high places. You also haven't hidden your intentions these past few weeks."

"Yes, but plans for an imminent arrest aren't something we spread around town, Mr. Biggs, unless we arrange for the suspect to turn himself in, which we didn't in this case. Can you please research the will issue and get back to us?"

"Certainly," Biggs said.

"Mrs. McMurphy, do you think your son killed himself?"

Doreen squeezed her eyes tight and shook her head.

"I need you to answer out loud for the recording, please."

"No," she said softly.

Goode tried to keep any accusatory tone out of his voice for his next question. "Did your husband ask someone to put an end to Darren's life in jail?"

"I don't know. I can't believe that my husband would do that to his own child, but he was pretty angry," Doreen replied. "I told him to leave it alone."

"Do you know whom he might have talked to about that?"

"I'm invoking the Fifth Amendment."

"Was it the same person who called or came over yesterday?"

"Same answer."

After running into the same brick wall, Goode was frustrated and out of questions, so he looked to Stone for any others. Stone raised his eyebrows and shrugged.

"Okay, then, I guess that's all we've got. Thank you, Mrs. McMurphy. If you change your mind and would like to tell us who called or came over, please do. We can protect you if that's the issue and help you the best we can. Otherwise, we'll just subpoena those phone records. It'll take longer, but we'll get them."

Sounds like we need to get Vincent Battrelle down here and ask him the same questions.

Scraping his chair on the linoleum as he stood up, Biggs led Doreen out into the hallway, where they were whispering when Goode closed the door to debrief with Stone. A few minutes later, Biggs came barging back in, with panic in his eyes and beads of sweat on his upper lip.

"Call an ambulance! Doreen fainted while I was in the men's room. I just left her for a couple minutes, and now she's not breathing."

Goode ran into the hallway to see for himself. Biggs was right. Doreen wasn't breathing. Three members of the same family collapsing or dying in different locations within twenty-four hours was the definition of suspicious, especially after what Doreen had to say—and wouldn't say.

What could the common denominator be? Goode already suspected poisoning for Patrick, but that seemed unlikely in Doreen's case because she'd been with them and then was alone in the hallway when she collapsed.

It was possible that she felt hopeless and sad and decided to end it all, but why do it at the police station? Goode didn't have time to ponder the possibilities. During his years in Vice as an undercover narcotics detective, he'd dealt with a lot of street-drug users in Ocean Beach. He had a hunch.

It's worth a try. It's not going to hurt her if her heart gave out. And if we wait for the paramedics, it'll be too late.

Goode ran back into the interrogation room, where he opened the first aid wall cabinet and grabbed a container of naloxone spray, which reverses the effects of an opioid overdose. Kneeling next to her body, he shoved the spray nozzle into her nose and hit the plunger.

Within a few seconds, Doreen started moving and opened her eyes. *Bingo.*

"What happened?" she asked weakly.

"Yes, what did you just do?" Biggs asked.

"We keep naloxone around for this very reason," he said, explaining its purpose. "It looks like she either took a pill laced with fentanyl without knowing, or she took it on purpose. The number of fentanyl deaths is booming nationally, because it's getting into black market prescription drugs that people are getting or buying from friends or acquaintances, not knowing they contain fentanyl, which is one hundred times stronger than morphine. Even a tiny amount can be fatal."

They sat Doreen up against the wall and brought her some water.

"Did you take something before you passed out?" Goode asked.

"I took a Xanax because I'm overtired, and I was having heart palpitations from all of this. I just wanted to calm down," she said.

"Where did you get it?"

"From—" she said, pausing to look at Biggs. "From a friend. I was all out."

"Was this the same friend who came over to the house before Patrick died?"

She looked at Biggs again, who answered for her.

"This is not an opportunity for a backdoor interrogation, Detective. She never said anyone came over, and she's not comfortable answering that question right now," he said. "Her previous answer stands."

"I'm only trying to help her. If someone is trying to kill her entire family, they've almost succeeded, and they will likely try again. We can provide her some measure of witness protection if she cooperates, but we can't do anything if she won't tell us what's going on."

"It's complicated, Detective," Biggs said. "We'll be in touch if she changes her mind. In the meantime, I'm going to arrange for private security to keep watch over her and her house."

"Good idea. Mrs. McMurphy, why don't you give me the rest of the Xanax pills that this person gave you. We can have them tested."

Doreen acquiesced and handed over a plastic baggie containing several small white oblong pills.

It's your funeral if you don't let us help you, Doreen. Whoever gave you these will likely have no trouble overcoming a damned rent-a-cop. But this turn of events certainly made Doreen seem more like a victim than a perpetrator.

CHAPTER 10
GOODE

Friday

By the time they'd finished interrogating Doreen, both autopsies had been completed. Deputy Chief Medical Examiner Clarence Thompson didn't invite Goode to observe, so Artie Hayes called afterward to report the findings as a professional courtesy. He also delivered his personal frustrations with the internal politics of the case.

"I told them you wanted to be there, but that sheriff's lieutenant, Tony Allegro, was adamant that he didn't want to wait for anyone else to show up. He didn't say it explicitly, but I could tell from his tone that he specifically didn't want you there. They did them back-to-back. There was nothing I could do. Sorry."

"Figures. This already smells like yesterday's diapers, and I haven't even heard the findings yet," Goode said. "What were they, anyway?"

Artie said there were no broken bones in Darren McMurphy's neck, only fractured cartilage. They also didn't find any pencil in his clothing or on his person. These types of neck injuries are generally more consistent with manual strangulation than a self-inflicted hanging, he said, so he was baffled when Thompson ruled the death a suicide.

"Frankly, I was speechless," Artie said.

Recounting what Thompson stated for the official autopsy report, Artie said, "McMurphy was in a single cell, so these injuries must be self-inflicted. Lieutenant Allegro said the pencil used to write the suicide note must have gotten kicked out of the way during the chaos of having outside parties in the cell investigating."

"Oh, so, this is our fault now?"

"I know, right? It's like an echo chamber, but no one is making any sense," Artie said. "Thompson totally ignored me in there. He never does that. It was like he'd been abducted, but his body was still there, going through the motions."

"This sounds like the Rebecca Zahau case," Goode said, referring to a local case with similar injuries, which the ME's office also ruled a suicide by hanging. The ME stubbornly refused to change the determination despite subsequent findings by renowned pathologist Cyril Wecht, who was hired by the victim's family and contended she'd been hit over the head with a blunt object, strangled, then dropped over a balcony railing in a staged hanging. "There seem to be some parallels here between the cabal of power brokers and the Zahau family's allegations that the sheriff's department gave special treatment to Rebecca's multimillionaire boyfriend. Once again, it seems that wealthy white men are being protected, but by whom?"

"Good question. So, with Patrick McMurphy dead, who's calling the shots in this cabal?"

"Another good question. Do you think Thompson has been compromised?" Goode asked. "You know him better than I do."

"I hate to say it, but I think so. He's always seemed like a good guy to me, but something's definitely off about this. He wouldn't look me in the eye all morning. Then, after the second autopsy, he muttered something about his mother being sick and ran off, saying he wasn't coming back for at least two weeks."

"Really? That's odd. What were the findings in Patrick's autopsy?"

"Nothing unusual there either. Due to the lack of obvious signs of foul play, Thompson called it a natural death by cardiac arrest, but he didn't even order a full tox screen, just a blood analysis for alcohol."

"Huh. Why's that?"

"Yeah, weird, I know. We almost always run a full tox screen. When I asked why, he said it was because he didn't suspect drug use."

"So, what did the blood analysis show?"

"That he was drunk, with a 0.23 percent blood alcohol level."

"Lucky he wasn't driving. But, as you know, I *do* suspect drugs, so can you do a full tox screen for me on the down-low? And can we also send out the blood, the contents of Patrick's glass, and the vodka bottle to a private lab? When you test it in-house, don't mention the outside lab to anyone until we can compare the results. Might be a good rat trap, or should I say *mole* trap," Goode said.

"We're on the same page," Artie said. "I already did all that as soon as Thompson left. We should have comparative results from the outside lab within a couple of days."

"Awesome. You're always one step ahead of me," Goode said. "I'm going to take your advice and try to figure out who the shot caller is over at cabal headquarters."

Goode requested that Artie also send Doreen's Xanax pills to the outside lab for testing. "Maybe we can trace them back to a local source," he said. "She kept taking the Fifth during the interrogation. She's clearly trying to protect someone, or to protect herself from someone she fears."

"Will do," Artie said. "Drop them off when you get a chance."

That afternoon, the sheriff's department and ME's office issued a joint news release stating the results of the autopsies: that Darren McMurphy died by suicide, by hanging himself in his cell, and his father, Patrick, died of natural causes, by cardiac arrest.

Katrina texted Goode as soon as she read it. **Did you see the joint release from ME/SDSD? WTF?**

Goode felt his blood pressure rising as soon as he called it up on his screen. The release mentioned that Patrick had died at home, playing solitaire on his computer, but made no mention of his blood alcohol level or the partially written will. Not surprisingly, it also didn't mention that the pencil allegedly used to write Darren's suicide note was missing from his jail cell or that the findings were pending toxicology results.

"Take a look at this," Goode said, motioning for Stone to read over his shoulder. "This is total collusion bullshit. They never issue joint releases. And why are they including Patrick's death in this? That's *our* investigation."

When Katrina called Stone for a comment a few seconds later, the sergeant put the call on speaker and motioned for Goode to scribble notes if he had something to add.

"Hey, Sergeant Stone," she said. "I assume you saw the joint release that just came out?"

"Yes, ma'am. Goode and I were just discussing it."

"What do you think?"

"Well, off the record—"

"I need you to talk to me on the record today, Sergeant. I can't write a story without quotes."

"There's a lot going on behind the scenes, so there's not much I can say for attribution," he said, pausing. "But the Darren McMurphy death case is not in our jurisdiction. The Patrick McMurphy autopsy findings, as stated, are technically accurate, but we need toxicology results before anyone knows what happened at the McMurphy house last night."

"What possible scenarios are you looking at?"

"Patrick may have been drinking heavily because he was upset about his son's death that afternoon. He also may have found out that we were going to arrest him this morning, and I'm sure he felt apprehensive about that. Either one could have caused a heart attack. His blood alcohol level was at 0.23 percent, almost triple the legal limit. Thankfully he wasn't driving, or he could've taken someone else with him."

"What charges were you going to arrest him on?"

"Conspiracy to commit murder, among others, including conspiracy to steal proprietary intellectual property. The feds had some charges in the works as well."

"So, is it possible that he conspired to put a hit out on his own son to keep him from cooperating with authorities?"

"Anything is possible, Katrina, but we have no definitive proof of that at this point. We're still investigating."

"How will the two McMurphy deaths affect your investigation and the prosecution of the Fontaine murder case?"

Goode scribbled "following up on loose ends" on a piece of paper and shoved it at Stone.

"The McMurphys' deaths necessitate that we close the cases against both men. However, we're regrouping to see what loose ends we still need to pursue, with regard to these deaths and to the Fontaine murders."

"Such as?"

"That's all I can say right now."

"What about other possible parties to the conspiracy, such as this cabal of wealthy men I keep hearing about? Like Darla Johansen, who acted as a lookout while Darren injected me with succinylcholine?"

"We're still interviewing witnesses and investigating suspects, including her."

"What about Vincent Battrelle? What is his current status? Is he a witness, person of interest, or suspect?"

Stone made an *ugh* face and looked to Goode for assistance, who scribbled another note. "I can't comment on specifics of pending arrests, because it's an ongoing investigation, but we're compiling a list of Vitaleron investors to determine who else may have been involved. We're still trying to get a handle on the cabal that Darren McMurphy told us about."

"Okay, but I'm going to keep asking," Katrina said. "You know that, right?"

"Yes, Katrina, I do know that."

"I heard you had Doreen McMurphy in for questioning this morning," she said. "Is she a suspect or person of interest in her husband's death?"

Stone gestured with an open-palm *how did she know that?* to Goode. "No comment," he said. "Listen, I've got to run, Katrina. Lots to do today."

Stone hung up and made another face, indicating he'd just been put through the wringer. "Dang, she's persistent. The Klein kid must have seen Doreen come in through the lobby. When do we get him back on the beat?"

Goode laughed. "Probably once the smoke clears on all of this. I told you Katrina's good. Let's see where she goes with that. I wish we could tell her more. Maybe she could loosen some of the bricks in Doreen's wall."

"Well, as usual, use your best judgment, but if you're going to tell her anything, keep it off the record, and make sure you keep your name—and mine—out of the paper," Stone said.

Goode took that as a go-ahead to use her help to determine whoever had killed Darren in his cell. He was pleased to have saved Doreen's life, because she likely could answer that question—if she ever agreed to talk. Because if she hadn't helped kill her husband, she was in danger of being killed herself, as they'd just witnessed.

"By the way, don't forget about my request for the Double-Judge case file," Goode said.

"Thanks for reminding me. I'll email the lieutenant right now."

CHAPTER 11
KATRINA

Friday

After finishing the Stone interview, Katrina went up to the roof patio because she wanted to feel the early-afternoon sun on her face. The air-conditioning had caused goose bumps to erupt all over her legs, and her toes felt like ice cubes. Back in Northampton, she'd kept a space heater under her desk, but she'd left it with a pod-mate, mistakenly assuming she wouldn't need it in sunny California.

The sun was bright and high in the clear blue sky, but the air was cool and a bit windy. The forecast said it might rain, and some low clouds were forming to the north that seemed to be blowing her way.

Even so, she was still happy to be home. Spending the holidays in San Diego was far more enjoyable than in Chicago or Northampton, Massachusetts, her last two locales, where, instead of a skirt and heels, she would be wearing a long, heavy jacket with pants, snow boots, a scarf, a beanie cap, and gloves in December.

I don't miss running the car engine for ten minutes while I scrape the ice off the windows every morning, that's for damn sure.

The interview with Stone had gone well. He didn't shut down her questions as fast as he used to, and he seemed to be sharing more.

Running through the key points in her head, she crafted a lede and headed back down to write up her weekender. She was happy to learn that Joanne and Linda planned to make it the A-1 lead on Sunday.

While the story was being edited, Katrina started reporting on her genetic genealogy project. She learned that once the two services had developed her DNA profiles, the information would be entered into their respective websites. Each one would send her a report with names and contact information for close and distant relatives who had also joined the site, as well as an ethnic breakdown for her family, its origins, and common traits. One site offered access to external databases for researching ties to her matched relatives. It also offered the added bonus of listing genetic risks of developing various medical conditions such as diabetes or celiac disease.

Katrina wasn't expecting any big surprises. She knew her mom's family was Greek and that her father's family was a Euro mix of mostly English and Irish, with a bit of Polish. Still, she couldn't help but feel excited about the possibility of surprise.

She was already aware of the health risks on her father's side, which carried the gene for Huntington's disease. Her father had chosen to be proactively tested and was thrilled to learn that he'd managed to avoid that fate. She, on the other hand, had decided not to take that specialized genetic test. She didn't want to risk discovering that her lifetime carried an unknown expiration date, waking each day with dread and wondering when the neurodegenerative symptoms would begin as her brain started to disintegrate, eventually rendering her unable to walk, talk, or take care of herself. She would just live her life, hoping that she was born lucky like her dad. But unlike him, she'd always steered clear of committed relationships that could produce children. She wasn't willing to risk the potential of burdening a husband or their offspring with any of that.

Neither genealogy website warned that its consumer-grade DNA test would give her specific medical information, or she wouldn't have pitched the story. In fact, she'd chosen 23andMe because it listed Huntington's as a disease that was specifically excluded.

Around three o'clock, Joanne called Katrina into her office. "You've been working so hard, you can leave early today. Take the night off!" she joked.

Katrina didn't hesitate to pick up her things and skedaddle, pleased that she could get a run in before heading out to explore Mission Hills and try a new restaurant or bar. But with a big day of hauling furniture and potentially traumatic memories awaiting her, she planned to make it an early night.

CHAPTER 12
KATRINA

Saturday

Norman was fifteen minutes late when he arrived at the coffee place the next morning. His hair was more tousled than usual, his T-shirt was covered with pizza stains, and his jeans needed a good wash, but he was smiling as he approached her table outside.

Seeing him eye her egg bites and cappuccino, she handed him a ten-dollar bill. "It's on me. Get whatever you want," she said.

"Oh, nice. Thanks," he said, grinning.

He came back with a jumbo chocolate chip cookie and a large coffee, white with cream. "I'm not much of a breakfast eater," he said.

Or a healthy one either.

"I don't mean to sound like your mother, but with all that sugar, we'd better get you some protein, or you could crash trying to lift heavy furniture," she said.

He shrugged, apparently trying to pretend he didn't care that a beautiful, talented woman saw him as more of a son or little brother than a potential dating prospect. "We can always take a pizza break, right?"

"I was thinking of something more nutritious, but pizza is good," she said, chuckling as she pulled a ziplock bag of nuts out of her purse.

"I brought these for a protein snack. Did you come up with another guy to help us?"

"No, sorry. I work a lot, so I don't have that many friends. I tried a couple guys, but they're busy today."

Katrina felt bad for him. She could tell he was fibbing because he wouldn't meet her gaze. "No worries," she said. "I can always hire someone if we can't load it all today."

Norman's narrow, hunched shoulders visibly relaxed as he sat back, sipped his coffee, and munched on the cookie. Soon, the front of his shirt was covered with chocolaty crumbs that would leave stains as soon as they melted.

After breakfast, they climbed into his old clunker and drove to the U-Haul place down the street. The gossip was accurate—his back seat was, in fact, crammed with old newspapers and soiled fast-food containers.

She'd planned on renting a truck, but the only vehicle available was a van. Katrina had made a mental list of the main pieces she wanted to take home, but with this bigger vehicle, she could transport any additional items that caught her fancy.

"The storage units are off Rosecrans in Point Loma," she told Norman. "Just follow me."

After locating the three adjacent lockers, Norman helped Katrina lift the accordion-folding doors. She then stood back to survey the contents of each one, trying to remember which held stuff from which parts of the house. At this point, it seemed like a guessing game.

Five years earlier, her mind had been in a haze of emotional paralysis. She hadn't considered that she might want to pull out a couple pieces at a time. She did recall, however, that as the movers unloaded their van into the units, she'd asked them to put furniture into just one of them. Otherwise, she was staring at a mess of boxes, only some of which were labeled. But she had to forgive herself. It was such a traumatic shock to lose her entire family within six months. She'd been in no state to make lasting organizational decisions.

"What's the matter?" she asked Norman, noticing his troubled expression. She wondered if he was embarrassed to admit he was out of shape and clueless how the two of them were going to accomplish this on their own. When she'd accidentally bumped into him as they were jostling around to get the doors open, he was soft and squishy like the Pillsbury Doughboy.

Norman squinted, scrunching up his nose and mouth. "I didn't realize all your stuff would be stacked up in boxes like this," he said. "Do you even know what's in them?"

"No, not really, but it's okay. We'll start with the furniture, and take it slow."

She'd been prepared for memories to surface as she went through her dead family's things, but she wasn't ready for the grief-packed punch that hit her once she stopped worrying about Norman's feelings.

It started with the king-and-queen set of red antique leather armchairs in which her parents used to watch TV in the family room. She felt a pinch in her nose and her eyes started misting at the sight of the chairs, which were passed down from her mother's family. The bigger one was for the man of the house, and the smaller one was for his wife, and each had its own ottoman. They were too much for her apartment, but she pictured sitting in them with Goode, watching movies, after she moved back into the house.

Don't get ahead of yourself. You were the one who told him to back off. Now you're fantasizing about sitting in the king-and-queen chairs together?

Moving the queen's chair to the side a bit, she was hit with another unexpected wave of memories at the sight of the rocking horse on springs in the corner, which she and Franny rode when they were in preschool. As soon as she touched one of the horse's ears, flashes of them taking turns on it came back to her, and her eyes welled up with tears. Feeling her fingertips tingle, she gasped.

Is that you, Franny? Are you here? God, I miss you.

She wasn't sure if she felt another round of tingles or if it was pins and needles from the first round.

I'll never be able to part with this horse now. Maybe I can give it to a close friend, so I can watch their child enjoy it since I won't be having kids.

Her breathing was coming harder and faster now. Unable to temper the surge of emotion, her body began to shake. The tears turned to full-on sobs, sending her scurrying toward the parking lot. She couldn't break down in front of Norman.

She hadn't done this the whole time they had been loading in five years ago. Why now, in front of a coworker?

"Because you were too busy consoling your aunt," her therapist's voice echoed in her head. *"If you have no one to console you, you'll have to do it yourself. Or let someone else get close enough to do it."*

"Are you okay?" Norman asked, following several steps behind to give her space.

"Yeah, just give me a few minutes," she said over her shoulder.

She kept walking away from him until she turned the corner. After taking a few deep breaths, she wiped her eyes with her T-shirt sleeve and headed back. Embarrassed at losing control, she tried to be all business.

"Sorry," she said. "Let's keep going."

Norman nodded, smiled, and patted her awkwardly on the shoulder. "Okay, but let me know if you want to talk about it."

She nodded and smiled back, taking a few more deep breaths.

He's actually kind of sweet. Okay, first things first.

The last items she recalled moving into the lockers were boxes from her parents' courthouse offices, which had been delivered to the house. After confirming they were in the front of one unit, she labeled them with a black marker and directed Norman to load them into the van. She hoped they contained some juicy leads, like personal letters that had been hidden in desk drawers.

"There, that was easy!" she said. She figured the best approach to shifting the focus away from her meltdown was to get Norman talking about his job, for which he clearly had a passion.

"I was reading your first-person piece about Detective Goode saving your life last year," she said, pulling out her ace-in-the-hole bonding move, which elicited a grin.

See? It's working already.

"What was that like? Did you hold back or feel like you couldn't say anything in the article?"

"I didn't want to gush or sound like I had some bromance with the guy," he said, "but I'd be dead if he hadn't been there to call for help and to keep Clover Ziegler talking so she didn't pull me over that cliff with her."

"I felt the same way when I wrote my first-person account about him saving me at the Del."

"Yours was really well written," he said. "I felt like I was there with you every step of the way."

"Thanks, Norman. That's nice of you to say."

"I can't believe that guy shot you up and left you to die. And now that he's dead, he won't have to go to trial and face you or his other victims' families. What a coward."

"Yeah, I've never been so scared in my life. I was on my hands and knees, trying to buck him off me, but he was bigger and stronger. He basically sat on me, put all his weight on my back, and pushed me to the ground. Then he injected me in the butt. After he left, I slowly lost control of my body. It was horrible." She shuddered at the memory. "I don't like thinking about it. It was like being buried alive. I couldn't breathe. I thought I was going to die."

"Wow. How scary," he said. "If it's any consolation, you're the best writer at the paper now. You came out of nowhere and started taking my stories away, which kind of pissed me off. But then I thought, I should try to get to know her. Maybe she'll teach me a few things. So, when you asked me to help you today, I figured that was a good sign."

"You can call and ask for help anytime," she said, slapping him lightly on the shoulder.

"That would be awesome," he said with a grin.

She got him talking about growing up in New Jersey and working his way up at the paper. Then she walked him back to the day he followed Clover Ziegler, who talked to voices only she could hear, to the cliffs of Black's Beach.

"I was so scared. I was thinking about all the things I still wanted to do," he said. "She had a gun to my neck and kept dragging me down these ledges till we got to the edge of the cliff. It was terrifying. Goode was standing back, like she demanded, but he still tried to talk some sense into her. He told her to let me go and to back away from the cliffs. But he'd also called for a helicopter, and by the time it came—with a guy talking to her on a loudspeaker—she was off in her own world. The people on the beach looked so free, she said. 'I want to be free.' Then she let go of me, dropped the gun, and stepped off the cliff. When Goode ran over to see if I was okay, I told him she said she hadn't killed anyone. Goode took off in his VW, and within a few hours, he and Stone had captured the real killer. I never got a chance to thank him, but I think he knows. He's not a super expressive guy, but he seems to have a good heart."

"Yes, I think so too."

"Clover's mother was mad, though. She complained to me later that Goode should have done more to save her daughter, and said he took a female witness home to his house. Like something funny was going on."

Whaaat? That doesn't sound like him. He told me he'd been celibate for years and that if we ever got there, I would be the first in a long time.

"When was that?"

"About a year ago, during the Tania Marcus case, but after Clover was dead."

"Huh."

"Yeah, that's what I said. Clover's mother said she was going to report him, but I never heard anything more, so I figured she was as unstable as her daughter."

"I'm sure there's some explanation," she said.

There'd better be.

She and Norman moved more of the furniture out of the way to get to the pieces she wanted, then loaded them into the van. The chest of drawers, the desk, and the couch proved to be too heavy, so she resigned herself to having to ask Goode for help. They'd have to bring a metal dolly next time.

But at least now she had a bed, a dining room table and chairs, and a few other odds and ends, like dishes, glasses, cutlery, towels, and bed linens.

"Ready for a pizza break?" she asked.

"I thought you'd never ask," he said. "Although I'm so hungry I could eat a cheeseburger and fries."

"You got it."

CHAPTER 13
KATRINA

Saturday/Sunday

By the time Katrina said goodbye to Norman that afternoon, she had just enough time to run to the auto repair shop to get her broken passenger side window replaced. For the past month, she'd been driving around with duct tape holding the cracked pieces together, which gave her PTSD every time she looked at it. Although she'd reported the incident to the police, she never heard another word about it.

I wonder if they even tried looking for the culprit. Probably not, since no detective ever contacted me.

She'd felt safer once the McMurphys were out of the picture. But that ignorant bliss ended as soon as Goode outlined all the remaining potential sources of danger.

On the way home from the repair shop, she didn't feel like cooking dinner after such a strenuous day. But she pictured eating a nice meal at her family's dining table in her apartment, overlooking the lush green canyon that sloped down to the freeway below.

She found the solution at the upscale organic grocery in Mission Hills, where she picked up a nice bottle of Cabernet Sauvignon, a preroasted chicken, a premade Caesar salad, a sourdough baguette, and some butter.

After six weeks of eating takeout on paper plates with plastic utensils, she was excited to have a tasty, civilized meal with ceramic plates, place mats, and stainless steel cutlery.

The antique wooden table and chairs were too big for the corner next to the kitchen, which she remedied by removing one of the chairs and pushing the table against the window next to the sliding glass doors.

After dinner, she poured herself another glass of wine and sipped it as she paced from room to room. Even though the apartment was still sparsely furnished, it finally felt like she *lived* there. Now that the queen-size bed was made up in the master bedroom, she happily rolled up her sleeping bag from the living room floor and shoved it into the hallway closet.

That made room on the carpet for her to go through the six boxes from her parents' offices, which the homicide detectives had never asked to search. The first four mostly contained law reference books, boxes of business cards, and a stack of framed family photos, which she was grateful to have but weren't helpful for investigative purposes.

She perked up when she opened the last two boxes and discovered that each parent had kept a hardcover datebook. Starting with her mother's, she flipped through the pages to find a curious series of lunch dates at "the Grant" with "Vincey" that started right after Franny died.

Maybe Daddy wasn't there for her because he was preoccupied with his own grief. She'd heard of couples breaking up after a child was killed or died by suicide, but not when the child was about to turn thirty. *Still, maybe Mom needed a shoulder to cry on? Vincent did mention that Daddy thought he and Mom were having an affair, but he didn't say when that was. And he didn't deny it either.*

She put down her mother's datebook to flip through her father's and compare what he was doing during that same period. On Friday afternoons, when court was typically dark, he listed regular golf tee times and a few entries for Dr. Laurel, whoever that was.

Dr. Laurel? Was he seeing a therapist, or was he sick?

She pulled out her father's box of business cards and thumbed through them until she found one for Dr. Laurel Castaneda, who had a doctorate in psychology and was also a licensed family therapist.

I wonder if he was jealous that Mom was having lunch with an old lover. Why does Vincent keep popping up in my life no matter how hard I try to put him away?

Setting the two datebooks aside, Katrina pulled out file folders until one of them caught her eye. Inside was a stack of handwritten cards and letters from Julia Frangello, her father's longtime clerk. Katrina remembered her name because she used to answer the phone when Katrina called from Chicago to talk to her father. At the time, it didn't register that Julia had stopped answering, but she did recall now that a couple of other women had taken over.

Julia's cards and letters started a few years before Katrina's parents were killed and ended with a sympathy card for Franny's death. As she read through the handwritten messages, she was shocked by Julia's intimate tone, realizing there was more to her relationship with Katrina's father than she'd known.

All this time I thought my parents had such a happy, healthy marriage, and yet all these shenanigans were going on behind closed doors while I was away at school?

> Dear Peter, I understand why you felt you had to have me transferred, but I really wish you hadn't. I think we could've continued to work together even after what happened between us. It was only once, and I believed you when you said it would never happen again. I've really grown to love you after working together for so many years. I hate clerking for someone else. Judge Martinelli is so cold and distant, he might as well be the king of Iceland. Anyway, I hope

you have a lovely holiday with your family and that
Franny can keep his drinking under control.
Fondly yours, always, Julia.

Wow. Okay, so he slipped one night, but then did the right thing. Maybe he was trying to get his head straight with the therapist. So, he was not a bad guy, just an insecure one who made a mistake. How did I not know any of this? He always seemed so, well, judge-like, and so did Mom. But then, she had all those lunches with "Vincey."

The other letters were more of the same, with Julia pouring out her feelings about how much she missed him and wished he'd let her come back. She promised she could be professional.

I just want to get back to how things used to be before I ruined everything. I'm sorry, she wrote, only to switch tone and say, I don't regret us making love that one glorious night one bit. I think about it a lot.

The note in the final card, which read "Deepest Sympathies" in white frosted letters across the front, was short and sweet:

Dearest Peter,

I'm so, so sorry that you've lost your son. I know you guys had your issues, but I also know you loved him very much. My heart is hurting right along with yours. I wish you'd let me help. But since you've asked me to stop writing, this will be my last note. I know you're trying to make things right with your wife, and that's one of the reasons why I've always loved and respected you so much. I hope you have a happy life. I got a new job at the state courthouse, so we don't have to run into each other in the hallways and cafeteria anymore.

My love and best, always,

Julia

Katrina would have to dig deeper to determine what her mother had been up to, and whether her parents' dalliances could have led to their murders somehow. The only scenario that came to mind was revenge.

Julia seemed emotional, yet rational, but Katrina could only judge by what she wrote in the cards. Could she have become unstable enough to kill both of Katrina's parents? Or could Vincent have put someone up to shooting her dad, not knowing that her mother would become collateral damage, just like Simon Fontaine did when Darren set out to kill Simon's daughter, Victoria? Either way, these items were a major find.

I can't wait to show them to Goode.

On Sunday morning, Katrina got up early to go for a run, intending to pick up a cappuccino and muffin toward the end of her route. After that, she planned to head over to IKEA to buy a few contemporary items, like shelves for the photos, to balance out the antiques. If she found a chest of drawers she liked, she could assemble it herself and not have to ask Goode for help.

But she didn't make it past her carport. When she reached the top of the stairs, the air went out of her lungs.

"Nooooo," she moaned. "Not again!"

The same passenger side window she'd just fixed was smashed again, obviously by the same person, because the scene was re-created to a T: A rock sat on the hood with a note attached, crafted out of glossy magazine letters cut with an X-ACTO knife. The only difference was the heightened threatening nature of the note:

> We told you to stop digging where you have no business or there would be repercussions. Darren McMurphy hung himself and his father died of a heart attack. Leave it alone and move on or you will end up like them and the rest of your family: Dead.

This time, Katrina wasn't going to waste time calling for a patrol officer to take a report. This was directly related to the cases Goode was investigating, and this note was far more specific—and direct—than the last. But her fingers were shaking so much she could barely hit the number in her contacts to call him.

"Ms. Chopin," he said, sounding even more caffeinated than usual. "I was just reading your illuminating story. So, to what do I owe the honor on this beautiful Sunday? The surf was awesome this morning. The waves were—"

"Can you come over?" she interrupted, unable to keep the fear out of her voice. "I finally got my car window fixed yesterday, and when I came out just now, it was smashed again, just like last time, but with a way more threatening note. I can't even—" She was unable to finish her thought because her throat constricted, closing off her airway.

Goode jumped right in. "Stay right there. I'm in Bird Rock, and I'm leaving now. I'll be there in a few minutes," he said. "Call 911 if you see anything or anyone that makes you feel like you're in imminent danger."

Katrina fought to take a deep breath and gasped for air, repeating the exercise until she could breathe normally again. Shifting into crisis mode, she snapped photos with her phone of the window, the rock, and the note.

"Can I just have one day off to relax?" she said out loud. "This feels like Northampton all over again."

Five years ago, she'd left San Diego on the advice of the police detectives working her parents' murder. She moved to Northampton, a small town in Massachusetts where she'd been offered a newspaper job. Not good at staying under the radar, however, she uncovered a scheme involving a corrupt school district that contracted with a waste company tied to the Polish mafia. The woman who gave her the incriminating documents ended up dead—strangled with a thin metal wire, her eyes gouged out and displayed next to her body as a warning to Katrina and anyone else who might want to feed her information.

But Katrina, determined to be a badass, would not be deterred. While she wrote the series that won her an investigative award and ultimately resulted in her being recruited by Linda Kelley, the then–Metro editor of the *Sun-Dispatch*, she had to live under constant intimidation and threats. Whispered phone calls to her private cell number, and a black Town Car that sat outside her apartment with the barrel of a gun pointing at her bedroom window. The police had a patrol car do regular checks on her place at night, and her editors were sympathetic, but she slept fitfully due to recurrent nightmares that lasted until the perpetrators were put behind bars. The case still hadn't gone to trial yet, so for all she knew, the stalker smashing her car window now could be part of the Polish mafia. Apparently, geographical relocation had done nothing to stop trouble from following her home to San Diego.

But it wasn't just the notes, the vandalism, or the attempted break-in that was the most disturbing. It was the realization that she'd never really been out of danger since her parents, and quite possibly her brother, had been murdered, the notion that *all* these events could be related. Also, as Goode had telegraphed, this new note confirmed that she was no safer after the apprehension—and deaths—of the McMurphys, because whoever was behind all of this was bigger than them.

Is this the work of the cabal Goode keeps talking about? I still don't really know who's involved or how it works, or why they're so threatened by me.

But whoever it was had been watching her and her apartment closely enough to know that her window had only just been repaired. They didn't even wait twenty-four hours to break it again.

Message received. Loud and clear.

"And screw you, whoever you are," she muttered.

If this *was* the cabal's work, then the La Jolla rich man's mafia was no different from the Polish gangsters who'd come after her in Northampton.

Always under the cover of darkness, it seems. So, what am I supposed to do now? Today's story didn't even reveal much, if anything, new. It only raised questions about where the Fontaine murder investigation would go from here.

But now that the initial shock had worn off, Katrina was feeling more angry than scared.

Do they really think I'm going to back off? Because this only makes me want to go deeper and ram more stories down their throats. Apparently, these people would like to see my investigation go no further, but that's too effing bad, because that's not how I roll.

Katrina had told Joanne about the first threatening note, but she hadn't let her tell Linda or HR for fear they would take her off the Fontaine story. This time, she was going to go "balls to the wall," as one salty old editor of hers used to say, and propose that they run photos of both notes and detail their contents. Rather than cower and hide, she would illustrate how hard certain parties, including her stalkers—plural based on the *we* in the note—were fighting to promote the narrative that the McMurphys' deaths were a suicide and a natural death. That this violent threat only served to convince her that they were both homicides.

As examples, she would reveal the anonymous phone tip she'd received from the man who disguised his voice and compare the language in her threatening note to the joint release by the sheriff's department and ME's office. That would show her stalkers—and her readers—that she would not bend the truth in the face of threats and manipulation.

But playing devil's advocate, she had to ask herself: Were her stalkers truly involved in these murders, or were they simply capitalizing on the fear that went with them?

Bottom line, Katrina hoped that shining a light on these ploys would flush out the cowards and show "investigators," specifically the sheriff's and ME's offices, that they couldn't get away with doing a half-assed job. That would be her argument to Joanne, anyway. And if

Joanne or Linda tried to take her off the story—for her own safety, or any other reason—she would respectfully decline. She was done being scared. Maybe it was even time to buy a gun and go John Wick on these asshats.

Katrina was pacing around the carport when Goode pulled up in his personal vehicle, a sky blue vintage Volkswagen van with a bleating engine. He tried to give her a comforting hug, but she pulled away after giving him a quick, loose embrace. She was too pissed to be comforted.

"You sounded so upset and scared on the phone, I thought you'd be in pieces when I got here," he said. "I was all ready to sweep you away to breakfast, but you seem too worked up for that."

"You're right. I'm ready to show these asshats that they can't intimidate me."

Her body flooded with adrenaline as she detailed her plan in rapid-fire spurts. Goode seemed okay with everything but the gun.

"I'm all for the Second Amendment. If you really feel like you need a weapon for personal protection, I'll support you and help you find the right one. But I'm concerned that you don't have the training to use one, and if this stalker, or Linebacker Dude, comes back to break into your apartment and tries to wrestle the gun away from you, it's not like you're a bodybuilder with the strength to stop him. Look what happened with Darren McMurphy. He sat on you, and that was it. One of these guys could easily overpower you and shoot you dead. So, let's talk this through."

Katrina knew he was right. She conceded that she needed to approach this calmly and rationally, but that would involve blowing off some steam first.

"You want to go for a run with me?" she asked.

"Um, sure, but I'm not really dressed for it," he said, pointing at his flip-flops. "We could head over to the Shores and I could jog there without shoes if you want. I'll take you to Harry's for brunch afterward."

"That's fine. First things first, though. I purposely called you, rather than 911, because I wanted to report this incident and death threat to the detective investigating the Fontaine–McMurphy case, since this latest note specifically refers to it. Also, don't try to talk me out of this, but I'm going to pitch this to my editors as a follow-up story to Darren's attempt to murder me at the Del."

Cautioning that Katrina could be throwing fuel on the fire, Goode said he didn't like the sound of that, but he could see that she'd made up her mind.

"That's your right, Katrina, but then you should be prepared for this to escalate. I can only protect you to a certain point without actually moving into your apartment," he said, half serious and half smirking.

"I do finally have a bed," she said, smiling to indicate that her anger was wearing off. "But you're still going to have to wait for that."

"I know, Stone keeps telling me the same thing."

"And what did you say?"

"I told him this case is bad for my mental health."

Katrina grabbed a light athletic jacket from her apartment, and they headed for the Shores in Goode's noisy van. He promised to duct tape her cracked window again when they got back, by which time he had talked her out of buying a gun and relying on her pepper spray instead. She also satisfied him that he didn't need to camp out in her apartment overnight as long as she promised to wait until Monday to pitch the story to her editors. After that, they agreed to reassess the situation on a daily basis.

"Maybe I can get the paper to hire an armed guard to park below my balcony from sunset to sunrise and stop anyone who tries to climb up and break into my place," she said.

CHAPTER 14
GOODE

Monday

Mug of coffee in hand, Stone was going through his emails on Monday morning when Goode walked in after a much-needed dawn surf. As Goode filled him in about Katrina's death threat the day before, he could see Stone frowning with helpless frustration that Goode was back to intimate-protection mode with this reporter, as if no time had passed since they were in the same situation a month earlier.

"Remember what I said about her being in danger? Well, this death threat not only proves that out, it also supports the theory that both McMurphys were murdered and that these events are all related. So, the jeopardy dial has been cranked up to ninety-five," Goode said.

"Well, that seems like an exaggeration, but I agree, it's not good," Stone said. "Just when you think it's over, they drag you back in."

"I'll type up a report about the threat and her smashed window, put it in the case file, and attach it to a copy of the first incident report that patrol took a month ago. She's right to be upset, because no detective in the Double-Judge case ever followed up on it, even though it clearly seems related to her parents' murder. Another example of that case team falling down on the job. Speaking of which, what's up with my request to get access to that murder book?"

Stone had submitted the request on Friday to the lieutenant, who kicked it upstairs to the chief, who had already responded himself that morning, before Goode had come in with a belly full of fire.

"I hate to mess with your chi, but I've got more bad news for you," Stone said. "Check your inbox."

As Goode read the email Stone had forwarded, the chief basically said no dice. But what struck Goode was the speed of the response. Such a quick turnaround on a seemingly routine request was unprecedented, and the fact that the chief felt he needed to respond personally was odd on its face. That case is still open and under active investigation by a team of capable detectives that has worked hard on it for the past five years, Chief Baxter wrote. Detective Goode has no evidence, only a half-baked suspicion, that the murders of the Chopin judges are in any way connected to any pending danger to their daughter, Katrina.

But it was the next section that really triggered Goode's hinky meter:

> I talked this over with the mayor and we agreed that it would be a dangerous precedent to open up this case to other detectives, specifically Detective Goode, who has been seen canoodling with Katrina, the same investigative reporter who was almost killed by a suspect who was actively under investigation by Goode. If this conspiracy theory or related concerns are coming from her, she's welcome to meet with the lead detective on the "Double-Judge" case and convey her thoughts as she did at the start. But that team has found no conspiracy in their investigation thus far, despite the *San Diego Advocate*'s attempts to invent one over five years ago.

"What the hell is he doing discussing internal SDPD business with the mayor?" Goode asked rhetorically. "It's none of the mayor's goddamned business. We should leak this email to Katrina and blow this whole thing wide open."

"I don't know about that," Stone said, "but I do agree that it's none of the mayor's business."

"Well, this little stalker incident from yesterday will turn that whole bullshit excuse on its head, won't it? The threatening note she got pretty much proves that these murders are all related, or at least the stalker wants Katrina to think so. Either way, she's not imagining the danger to her safety, and neither are we."

On the surface, the chief's email seemed straightforward. But as Goode scrolled down into the thread below, he saw that the chief had made a major error by neglecting to delete earlier responses from other people—besides the mayor—whom he'd decided, bizarrely and inappropriately, to consult *over the weekend.*

More importantly, it was actually the mayor's chief of staff, Lawrence Rayburn, who had come up with the language that the chief wrote to Stone. That indicated this case was now a political football, because it involved the recent deaths of Patrick McMurphy and his son, who had been the mayor's unofficial adviser and campaign manager, respectively.

"That is a whole lot of political bullshit right there," Goode said. "This isn't even the chief talking, it's this dude, Lawrence Rayburn. Look down in the thread. Why is he involved in responding to a direct request to your lieutenant?"

"Good question," Stone said. "He was the PD's legal counsel and liaison with the mayor's office until he moved over to City Hall about five years ago. And now he's the mayor's chief of staff."

"Five years ago, as in before or after the judges were murdered?"

"After, if I recall. Never thought of that, but that's an interesting observation. Could be a coincidence. Who knows. All I can tell you is that I never liked him. He's one of those rich La Jolla punks who thinks he knows everything. Insists on being called Lawrence, not Larry, and he always wears a bow tie. He's my age and went to Bishop's while you and I were at Muirlands and La Jolla High, so maybe that's why you don't know him. His dad, Elmore Rayburn, is one of the original partners of SBOD, the defense contractor in La Jolla that grew into a multibillion-dollar corporation after developing all kinds of spy technology."

"That's fitting, then, isn't it? You're right, I've never met him, but I already know I don't like him. What else can you tell me about him?"

"Remember last month, when we decided to get an injunction to force Vitaleron to produce a sample of its sex drug to see if it could have killed the Fontaines because nothing was coming up in the toxicology tests, and they wouldn't produce the sample voluntarily? Then we got word from up the chain to stand down, and we both said, 'That is some Tammany Hall bullshit'?"

"Yeah, like it was yesterday. Why?"

"Because I found out that the stand-down order actually came from Lawrence Rayburn, who is no longer the PD's legal counsel but inserted himself into this case," Stone said. "That's some context for you."

"Yeah, and when we found out that the chief and the mayor had donated to the PAC that funneled money to Congressman Winchester's campaign, and the chief denied it, we wondered if it had been done without his authorization or knowledge, as he claimed it was."

"Right. So maybe this Bow Tie Rayburn guy was the one funneling names to Darren McMurphy and Darla Johansen at Vitaleron, who worked with investors and tracked their campaign donations. Speaking of which, where are we with putting that list of cabal members together? I thought Darla promised to do that on day one as part of her immunity deal with the feds," Stone said.

After Winchester and his fiancée, Darla Johansen, and Darren McMurphy and his fiancée, Esperanza Cepeda, were arrested at the Hotel Del, Darla ran off to a friend's house, where she immediately called the FBI and tried to make an immunity deal in exchange for information on the cabal behind the Fontaine murders. The authorities didn't give her much credibility at first, but Goode started listening more closely once he heard that her claims echoed Darren's. The problem was that both of them were withholding crucial details, hoping to make a deal.

"My FBI friend, Marty Watts, tells me that negotiations on that deal fell apart because Darla refused to provide any dirt on her fiancé, so no such list was ever compiled," Goode said. "We can take a run at her now that the federal deal is no longer in play."

"Definitely. We don't need her to testify against Winchester for our side of the case. Acting as Darren McMurphy's lookout while he injected Katrina makes Darla good for conspiracy to commit murder, just like Patrick McMurphy. We can even use the same arrest warrant language. She's also good for the theft of intellectual property since we have her on camera stealing doses of the sex drug to share with Winchester, Darren McMurphy, and his fiancée. You still have Darla's number, right?"

"Yep, I'll give her a call."

While Stone went back to reading his emails, Goode pondered next steps.

"Damn. Sorry to pile on," Stone said, "but I just got another negatory from the chief on our request for the name of the sheriff's deputy who cut Darren McMurphy down and also for that day's shift log. Can you believe this? Do they not know how bad this smells?"

"Once again, after Katrina's death threat, we can argue that they're trying to hide something. What's the reason for the denial?"

"Same as before—it's not our case and there's no need for us to investigate a jail death that's under the sheriff's jurisdiction, plus the ME says it's a suicide, blah blah blah. Get this, he also said that we are free to file a complaint with the Citizens Law Enforcement Review Board. Unbelievable. Do we look like citizens? I'm an effing police sergeant, for Christ's sake."

"Can you forward the email to me? I want to see if the chief was careless enough to leave the thread below like last time."

Sure enough, the chief repeated his mistake.

"There he is—Bow Tie Rayburn weighed in on this one too," Goode said. "The sheriff used the same language to the chief that Rayburn suggested in his response down below. These people are idiots. So, it appears that this isn't just a mole in the attic of a sick house, but rather a whole mole family, and the rot is trickling down into every room. How do we even tackle that?"

His brow furrowed, Stone shook his head. "I honestly don't know," he said. "But if you send me both reports on Katrina's smashed windows and the death threat, I can craft a double-barreled response and fire it back at the chief. I'll be sure to mention that she's planning to write a story about both threatening notes and the PD's lack of response thus far. That should get his attention."

In the meantime, Goode racked his brain to find another way to get the name of the deputy who cut Darren down. The shift log would be tougher, but someone in the sheriff's department who was on the right side of justice could get both items to them.

"I'm going to call Artie and see if he might have a deputy friend who could get that to us on the QT," he said. Worst case, he would do undercover recon at one of the bars where the jail deputies hung out after work. Low-level cops loved to gripe and gossip, especially after a few too many beers.

"That's a great idea. Just make sure to tell Artie this is a sensitive situation, so sensitive I don't even feel comfortable alerting Internal Affairs," Stone said. "In fact, it might be time for you to have a chat with your FBI buddy. This has 'Public Corruption Unit' written all over it."

"Let me try Artie first. I want to keep this between close allies for as long as we can, especially now that it affects Katrina's safety too."

"Be careful what you share with her, okay? She's free to expose her personal challenges to the masses, but we'll need to proceed with caution to ensure she doesn't end up dead."

That warning triggered yet another stealth ploy, which Goode didn't share, to give Stone plausible deniability if anyone came at them.

If he couldn't get official access to the Double-Judge file, he would sneak in the back door by signing into the Case Agent Investigative Review, or CAIR, system on his laptop. All he needed was the case number. He wasn't sure if this would leave a digital fingerprint, but what could the other detective team say? He had no authorization to do anything with the information. Yet.

CHAPTER 15
GOODE

Monday

After a day of setbacks, the sound of the waves crashing on the shore of Windansea at dusk was as soothing to Goode as the warm body of a woman wrapping her arms and legs around him on a chilly night. At least what he remembered of that feeling.

But from his perch at the top of the wooden stairs leading down to the beach, he couldn't even conjure up a visceral memory. It had been too long. Even his fallback, the mental picture of Katrina's breasts in the moonlight, was getting worn out from overuse.

Sure, Goode appreciated the lithe bikini-clad *chiquitas* who paraded up and down the beach, trying to win the attention of the surfers who hung out at the shack. But after the years of trouble with damaged damsels and manipulative she-devils like his ex-wife, he found that the ocean—his muse, his therapist, and his friend—could fill that niche better, and with no emotional hassle.

He and the sea had had a symbiotic relationship dating back to when his dad first brought him down to Windansea. They would watch the waves crash as his father told his tales, like the one about the night he'd met Goode's mom at a beach bonfire. Her long brown hair blew in the wind as she scooped up her long diaphanous blue dress in her arms and danced like she was sailing in the wind. Goode's subconscious must have linked those images to this particular stretch of beach, because he'd felt a powerful spiritual connection to it ever since.

After Goode's mother jumped off the Coronado Bridge, his dad went back to live on his family's farm in Montana. Kenny and his sister, Maureen, moved in with their dad's sister, Katherine, and visited their father for a few summers until he died. The doctors said it was a heart attack, but Katherine said their mom's death literally broke his heart. They stayed with their aunt until they both graduated high school, after which she moved to Maui.

Long before then, Rusty Stone had taken over the role of Kenny Goode's storyteller and mentor, until the student outgrew the teacher. But Rusty was a cool big brother that way. He was never one to compete, only to support. Goode may have been the better surfer and ultimately a better detective, but they were best friends, so Stone always seemed to take it in stride.

"If you look good, I look good, so it don't matter to me none," Stone would say in his country-western voice.

The orange-yellow sky was turning red as the sun slipped down toward the horizon when Goode's cell phone rang. It was Artie Hayes.

"Give me some good news," Goode said. "I could really use some."

"Are you sitting down?"

"Yes. Tell me."

"We got the results back for Patrick's laptop. It's negative for anthrax and any other poisonous substance. No hits on the cigar either. But listen to this—the vodka bottle came back positive for narcotics, and so did the contents of his glass."

"No shit. Like what narcotics?"

"Like, enough that there's no way he would put them into his own drink, because it would ruin the taste. If he wanted to kill himself with pills, why not chase a few of each drug with something that tastes good? But it looks like someone crushed the pills into that bottle of lemon-infused vodka to hide the bitter taste, then gave it to him as a gift, and he was so bent on getting trashed that he didn't notice or care."

"So, what specifically did they find?"

"OxyContin, Xanax, Ambien, and Adderall," Artie said.

Something about that particular combination sounded familiar. "Can you repeat those, slowly?"

As Artie ran through them again, Goode closed his eyes and tried to recall where he'd heard them before. Then it hit him.

"I'm catching the sunset at Windansea. Are you at your computer?" he asked.

"Yep."

"Google 'Franny Chopin' and 'suicide' and '*San Diego Advocate*,'" he said.

Goode heard the click of keys on Artie's keyboard, then a pause while the search results were loading. "You have got to be effing kidding me," Artie said.

"Is it there?"

"That cannot be a coincidence."

"Yeah, I know. Katrina said her brother hated lemons and would never drink that stuff. She's always thought that someone aware of his history of drug and alcohol addiction set him up or forced him to swallow that narcotic cocktail so it would look like a suicide."

"Wow. No kidding. So, what's next?"

"I'll tell Stone, but I think we keep this between us for right now. Don't enter the results into your system, and make sure to hide the lab paperwork somewhere safe at home or in your car. We'll wait to see what results your in-house lab comes back with after analyzing Patrick's blood, urine, and stomach contents. If someone tries to hide or change those results, which I'm betting they will, we can pull these out and expose the culprit. How long will that take?"

"Should be sometime this week."

"Okay, so we'll look to see whose digital fingerprints are in the computer for any modified results and go from there."

"After the way he handled those autopsies, my money's on Thompson. He'll be back right about the same time."

"Stone and I are seeing some bad shit on our side too. He's already thinking we should take this to my new friend at the FBI, but I wanted to keep this under local control for as long as possible. Because if we make too much noise, one of us could be targeted next. That includes my friend Katrina Chopin at the *Sun-Dispatch*."

"Sounds like a plan," Artie said. "I'm in."

Now that the sun had set, the air was growing cooler and the wind picked up. Goode debated whether to tell Katrina about these latest findings. Of course she would want to know, because even her own parents never bought her murder theory. But he kept coming back to Stone's warning, that she was still reporting on this story, and they couldn't afford to have information going public with so much at stake. Especially when Vincent Battrelle, the owner of her newspaper, could be involved. She had her rules and boundaries, and so did he.

Still, he had to be realistic. He knew he wouldn't be able to keep the recent developments from her for too long, especially if he headed over to her apartment to protect her, which, after this news from Artie, seemed like the right thing to do. Things were going to keep growing messier, so Stone would have to cut him some slack about restrictions on preserving the "integrity" of their investigation.

But he kept coming back to the same question: The killers were clearly a part of something bigger than just the McMurphys. It could be the cabal, but he kept coming back to what seemed like the most obvious common thread between all the deaths: Vincent Battrelle. Goode started drafting a list of connecting dots that he could show Stone and share with the feds to prove his theory, if necessary:

- Vincent lost a bundle in Franny's resort hotel deal that went bad right before he died. Franny overdosed on the same vodka-narcotic cocktail that killed Patrick McMurphy, and both deaths were staged not to look like homicides.

• Vincent was so startled by Goode's question about his ties to Peter Chopin that he dropped a crystal tumbler of whiskey, cut a bloody gash in his finger, and admitted that Peter suspected he was having an affair with Katrina's mother, then divested from the Vitaleron start-up. The Chopins were subsequently mowed down in their driveway.

• Simon Fontaine pushed Vincent's son Alex off the Vitaleron board due to addiction issues. Simon and his daughter, Victoria, were later killed, their deaths staged to look like suicides. Vincent admitted to shooting Simon in the head after he was dead, though he claimed it was to protect his investment in Vitaleron.

• Darren McMurphy took over the Vitaleron board after bullying Vincent's other son, Michael. Darren later claimed that he murdered the Fontaines on his father's orders. They were about to arrest Patrick McMurphy when Darren was found dead in his cell with injuries that Artie Hayes said were more consistent with manual strangulation than hanging. Hours later, Doreen called police and then Vincent, as instructed, as if they knew Patrick was going to die after drinking the spiked vodka.

What if Patrick had ordered the hit on the Fontaines, not to protect his family's money, as Darren claimed, but on behalf of the cabal, or a larger group of investors that wanted to wrest control of Vitaleron away from Simon Fontaine and Vincent Battrelle? If so, did Vincent bring that bottle over as a "gift" to Patrick to preemptively stop a coup? Or did Vincent, or members of the cabal, have prior knowledge that Patrick was about to be arrested and kill him (after also having Darren killed) before either of them could reveal names and other incriminating details about the cabal to police? As a corruption scheme, this latter scenario made a whole lot of sense.

I need to listen to my gut. Thank God I was prescient enough to take Vincent's bloody paper towel from his house and send it to the crime lab to see if his DNA matches any of the items from Patrick's desk. It's time to activate that sleeping evidence into a possible arrest.

Because it was after hours, Goode was going to leave Dwight Pepper a message at the crime lab. He didn't have the proper supervisor's authorization, but he was worried Stone would deem this request premature or unsubstantiated, or worse, try to run it up the damn chain, only to have Bow Tie Rayburn inject himself again and put the kibosh on it.

Not this time.

Goode was surprised when Pepper answered.

"What's up, Detective?" he said, apparently seeing Goode's name on the caller ID.

"Oh, you're there. Do you remember that paper towel I sent over with Vincent Battrelle's blood on it about a month ago?"

"Sure do."

"Did you happen to submit it for a DNA profile?"

"No, I can't do that without authorization, and I assume you didn't give that to me at the time because you didn't have probable cause. Has that changed?"

"Yes. I was just hoping I'd asked you at the time. It was more of a stretch then, but it's not now, so go ahead and do that. Once you get it back, I'd like you to compare it to the DNA swabs you took of the glass and bottle you collected from Patrick McMurphy's home office the other night, and the swab of his keyboard."

"You know I need that request in writing and signed by your division head, Detective."

"Yeah, I'm aware that's the usual protocol, but I'm wondering if we can do it verbally this time, because this has to stay hush hush. If not, then I'll bring you a piece of paper, but either way, I need you to take extreme security measures with this request and call me, rather than email, with the results. We have a leak somewhere, and I want to keep this off the grid, if possible. Is that clear?"

"Yes, but I still need that piece of paper."

Goode sighed. *He's not going to play ball.*

"I'll bring it to you in the morning," he said. "If we put a rush on it, how long will that take?"

"We can get it done in a few days if we can make a good case that a murderer is on the loose."

"I'd say the chances are pretty good. I'm just waiting for a second set of toxicology results to confirm the first, and if you find a match, that would give me the identity of a suspect who could be the perpetrator in as many as five murders."

"Wow. Okay. I'll see what I can do."

Within a minute of his hanging up, Katrina called.

"What are you up to?" she asked.

"I'm at Windansea. Just watched the sunset. It was awesome. Lots going on today, so I'm just trying to process it all."

"You want some company?"

"I don't know how much longer I'll be here, but if you're close, sure."

Seconds later, he felt the toe of a pointy shoe in his lower back. He turned around and there she was, wearing jeans and a white cashmere sweater that fit snugly in the chest.

"Were you here the whole time? Why didn't you just come over and talk to me?"

"Because you were on the phone and you looked intense," she said. "Didn't want to disturb."

"Yeah, I was. Sit down with me."

Katrina lowered herself onto the stairs next to him but left a good six inches of space between them since they were in public. They both stared out at the ocean, a safe neutral space, as the daylight waned.

"What's going on?" she asked, turning to look at him.

"You mean what part can I tell you off the record?"

"Yeah, or more than that would be nice."

Thoughts flew through his brain like bees around a hive as he debated what he could and couldn't tell her.

I can start with the Vincent stuff. That's safe.

"I've been compiling a mental list of all the reasons why Vincent Battrelle is a common and connecting factor in this whole case, starting with your brother's death," he said. "Tell me if you agree."

Katrina listened patiently, nodding silently, as he ran through his points, omitting certain details that he couldn't share with her, such as the matching contents of Patrick's and her brother's last drinks. He didn't realize until afterward that he'd spilled more than intended about Doreen's call with Vincent, but he went with it, as if it were no big deal. Unsure if Stone would be convinced by his list, Goode was eager to hear Katrina's take on it.

"Makes sense to me. But I didn't know that about Doreen McMurphy," she said. "If you or Stone can't tell me that on the record, I'll call and ask her about Vincent myself, since he used to date my mom. When are you questioning him again?"

"I overstepped by telling you that, actually, so do me a favor and let me talk to Stone about Doreen before you call her, okay? He might agree that it could help us if you try to soften her up a bit. You're good at that. Maybe she'll slip and tell you something she wouldn't tell us, which would help all of us. As for Vincent, I'm waiting for some test results to come back before I take another run at him. Hopefully I'll have some proof to back up these speculative connections in a few days."

"What test results?"

"I'll see if I can share them if they're positive, but until then, they've got to stay in here," he said, pointing to his forehead. "Hey, I wanted to ask you, did you pitch Joanne the tell-all column about your smashed car windows and threatening notes?"

"Yeah, I did. She got all motherly with me, hugged me, and said she didn't want me to get hurt."

"Uh-huh," Goode said, waiting to hear whether he was staying overnight at her apartment.

"I told her that this was too important, and that it had to do with my brother and my parents. That I was tired of living like a scared victim, waiting for someone to come get me. That it was time to go on the offensive. I also told her this would grease the wheels for the genetic genealogy story, since it'll be a few weeks before my DNA profile comes back. Then we talked to Linda, who said she had to think about it.

"A couple of hours later, Linda handed me a liability waiver and said I had to sign it if I wanted to stay on the story. So, I made a pitch for a private armed security guard to park under my balcony every night, and that's when shit got real. I said, 'It'll only be until the cops get to the bottom of what happened with the McMurphys and this whole cabal thing. If that doesn't come to a head within two weeks, we can reassess.'

"So, then Linda said, 'Well, that's going to cost a pretty penny,' so I said, 'Think of the readership. It's like a soap opera. People will eat this up!' That's when her eyes got big and round. It was kind of funny. She was like putty in my hands. Anyway, bottom line is it's on. My bodyguard does his first shift tonight, and I write up the story tomorrow. I'll be calling you guys for a quote since I've reported these threats to you twice now, with little or no follow-up."

"Hey, that's not fair," he said. "I came right over when you called."

"That's true. Sorry, I really meant the first one wasn't followed up on, and now it's happened twice. Don't worry, I'll say it right in the story."

"Okay, good."

A little disappointed that he wouldn't be staying overnight, Goode also knew that this hired-guard plan, for all practical matters, was the wiser one all around. Still, he felt like he'd just spent five minutes on a roller coaster, only to get whiplash when the ride ended.

His expression must have betrayed his feelings, because Katrina put her arm around his shoulder and squeezed. "It's better this way, trust me," she said. "I don't want some killer breaking into my apartment when you have your pants half off again. The headlines would be so embarrassing for you. And so would your suspension."

"I know, I know. 'It'll be so much better if we wait to take off our clothes until this is all over.' Or so you guys keep saying."

"You want to grab a drink before I head home?" Katrina asked. "My night watchman is coming over as soon as I tell him I'm on my way."

"Sure, why not. I'll drink my sorrows away."

CHAPTER 16
KATRINA

Monday

Katrina eyed the handsome detective next to her at Piatti with a feeling of déjà vu, and in spite of the circumstances, smiled at her own good fortune.

"Little did we know when we met here five weeks ago what was about to happen," she said, poking Goode's bicep playfully. "What a whirlwind of romance, murder, and mayhem."

"I'll say," he said, "and then some."

Goode sipped his dirty martini almost wistfully, as if he had the weight of several planets on his head.

"What's going on in that noggin of yours?" she asked. "Something happened today that you can't talk about, but you want to, right?"

He shook his head and laughed through his nose. "How do you do that?" he asked.

"Do what?"

"See into my brain like that? It's really unnerving."

"Well, I kinda know you by now."

"How could you? I barely even know me."

"So, tell me what it is you want to tell me but don't think you should."

Goode met her eyes for about twenty seconds, apparently mulling whether to share whatever it was.

"I knew this was going to happen," he said, looking away. "That's why I almost said no when you suggested a drink."

"Okay, spill. I don't have all night."

"Actually, for this, you do. But listen, this is huge, and you cannot, I repeat, cannot print this in any form or tell anyone at the paper about this right now. Promise me, or I won't tell you."

Now I almost don't want to agree to that, because it's got to be really big. But it's clearly weighing on him, so I can't say no. I'll just have to figure out a way to get it into the paper.

"I promise," she said.

He took a deep breath and took her hand in his. "We had the contents of both the liquor bottle and glass from Patrick McMurphy's desk tested by a private toxicology lab," he said. "They contained the same cocktail of narcotics that killed your brother, and both were delivered in the same liquid carrier: lemon-infused vodka."

Katrina felt numb for a minute before she realized that he was squeezing her hand, so she squeezed him back. He was looking at her, waiting for a response. She felt sad and yet redeemed, relieved and yet all fired up. The warm, empathetic look in his eyes made hers fill with tears that soon flowed down her face.

"I knew it," she said quietly. "I effing knew it, and no one believed me."

"I know you did," he said. Putting his arm around her, he held her tight, then let her cry against his shoulder. His shirt was soaked within moments. They sat like that for a couple of minutes before she pulled back, wiped her eyes with a cocktail napkin, and blew her nose.

"Is there more?"

"Yes, but I can't tell you much of it. All I can say now is that you and I were right, and that your family's deaths—your brother's, anyway—are definitely connected to the McMurphys' deaths, which means they're probably also linked to the Fontaine murders. It also confirms what my gut said all along, that all of these deaths, staged to look natural or like suicides, are murders. It fits the pattern."

"Then I guess it's damn lucky that I've got a retired cop to watch over me while I sleep and make sure I'm not next. Because I'm really not up for that," she said.

"Absolutely. I'll share one more piece of information, which, again, is for your ears only. I'm also having the glass and the bottle tested for DNA to see if the profile matches the bloody paper towel I took from Vincent's house the night I asked him about the original Vitaleron partnership deal with your father. He was so startled, he dropped his tumbler of whiskey and cut a gash in his finger. If his DNA matches, we'll have him for murder."

"You suspect Vincent because you overheard Doreen McMurphy telling him she called the police as soon as she found Patrick dead, like he told her to?"

"Yes, among the other points I listed earlier."

"What if his DNA isn't on the bottle?"

"Then Doreen needs to tell us who gave it to Patrick or whether she put those drugs into it herself as part of a plan with Vincent or someone else."

"It doesn't necessarily mean that Vincent killed Patrick or my brother, though. Vincent and Franny were friends."

"So, now you've developed a soft spot for him? Since when?"

"It's just been nice not having to worry about him being mad at me, or expecting something from me, or calling to harass me like he was doing a month ago. But Patrick drinking the same lethal cocktail of narcotics as my brother can't be a coincidence," she said, finishing her last sip of wine.

"That's what my buddy Artie Hayes, from the ME's office, said."

"Can I have a Glenlivet with one big rock?" she asked the bartender. "I definitely need something stronger."

"Make that two," Goode chimed in. "I'll join you. What the hell."

"So that's why you didn't want me to talk to Doreen yet?"

"That's one of the reasons. She kept pleading the Fifth during our interrogation, but she did say that she and Vincent were old friends. What little she said made it sound like she was scared of someone who came over that afternoon before she found Patrick dead. But she wouldn't say that it wasn't Vincent, so that might have been a cover story for the two of them. Even if his DNA isn't on the bottle, my gut still says he's involved in this."

"Are you going to open a murder case on my brother?"

"I will at some point, but we've got to keep these private lab results quiet for the moment. Artie is the only one besides you who knows about them, and I told him to hide the paperwork. I haven't even told Stone yet. There's some really bad internal political shit going on. The sheriff has closed the door to us on Darren McMurphy's death case, which is clearly suspicious, and the ME's office kept us out of both Darren's and his father's autopsies even though Patrick's death is our case. It all seems to track back to the mayor's office. But your question reminds me, I should check to see which pathologist did your brother's autopsy."

"I was just going to suggest that. I think I have that report somewhere. If it's not in my parents' stuff in storage, they have to give that to me as a family member, right?"

"Yeah. But we think the deputy chief ME has been compromised, so he could try to block the request if you don't have the report already. He's the same guy who did the Fontaine autopsies. They seemed to be on the up-and-up, but the McMurphys' did not."

"Have you had any luck getting access to my parents' case file yet?"

"No, I was blocked by the chief, because of this dude in the mayor's office, who is blocking us on other fronts too. But I'm not giving up."

"Good. Why is the mayor's office involved in this, especially if Darren's death is under the county sheriff's jurisdiction? It has to be something bigger."

"That's what I kept saying throughout the Fontaine case, remember? Why did the mayor call a news conference at police headquarters, where all those hair-gelled Vitaleron jackals talked about changes to the board?"

"Yes, I remember, and I agreed that was completely inappropriate. But other than the fact that the mayor, the police chief, and most of these victims are Vitaleron investors, what other connection is there?"

"I've been banging my head against the wall trying to figure that out, and all I come up with is Vincent Battrelle."

"Two heads are better than one, but I think I'll refrain from banging mine and just drink my scotch."

"Good idea," he said, clinking her glass with his. "Cheers."

Katrina had planned to share her news about the love letters from her father's clerk and ask Goode about the witness from the Tania Marcus case who reportedly went into his house. But she'd lost track of all that amid the spiked-vodka news.

We're going to get justice for you yet, Franny.

CHAPTER 17
KATRINA

Tuesday

After getting a good night's sleep, thanks to the presence of retired SDPD sergeant Teddy Kincaid, Katrina went to work early to write her column. She crafted it as a first-person account of two incidents of car vandalism and death threats, reminding the readers of her near-death experience at the Hotel Del, which she'd written about previously.

"It wasn't enough for Darren McMurphy to try to kill me with a lethal injection of succinylcholine, a paralytic drug, in the butt cheek at the Del," she wrote. "Now I have to deal with a stalker who is threatening to finish the job. All I know for sure is that the stalker isn't Darren or his father, Patrick, because they're both dead."

The photos she took of the rocks, notes, and smashed windows would accompany the column, with a pull quote from the second note as a graphic element.

"Clearly, all the perpetrators in this conspiracy to murder the Fontaines have not been caught. Whoever smashed my car window and left threatening notes has done so on two separate occasions over the past month. I didn't feel the need to write about the first incident, which occurred before I was attacked at the Del. But I can't stay silent now that this stalker has returned for a repeat performance less than twenty-four hours after I had my broken window repaired.

"What's curious is that the note specifically referred to my story about the McMurphys' deaths. The sheriff and medical examiner claim they were a suicide and a natural death, and that they are neither suspicious nor related. But my sources say otherwise," she wrote, elaborating on the false narrative.

"'Ms. Chopin reported her death threat to the SDPD Homicide unit on Sunday because the note specifically referred to the Fontaine case, which we are still actively investigating,'" she quoted Sergeant Rusty Stone as saying. "'We are taking the threat very seriously, because we believe the recent McMurphy deaths are, in fact, related *and* suspicious, so this case is still very much active.'"

Katrina also revealed that this wasn't the first time she'd been stalked and threatened while reporting on a dangerous murder case. Tempting fate, she briefly described her experience with the Polish mafia in Northampton and her recurring nightmare, in which she was abducted, thrown into a black Lincoln Town Car, and taken to a recycling plant, noting that she always woke up before getting sucked into the giant plastic-bottle crusher.

What she didn't mention was that these nightmares had started up again a month ago, when Vincent Battrelle was pressuring her to search for his son Alex as a side job, which created a conflict of interest with her investigation into who, including him and his sons, might have killed the Fontaines. Stressed out, she'd woken up sweating and gasping for air at 4:30 a.m. and grabbed her inhaler. A few hours later, her anxiety went into hyperdrive when she found her car window smashed for the first time.

At the time, her fears were tempered only by the fact that Goode was not-so-secretly camping out in his VW van overnight in her carport, watching for intruders or Fontaine murder suspects who might try to harm her. In between the alerts of his bleating engine coming and going, she was able to get some sleep.

The nightmares stopped once she thought she was in the clear, after Darren McMurphy was behind bars and Brandon Winchester had been arrested. Linebacker Dude, whom she and Goode now believed was Winchester's bodyguard, Walter Hall, also hadn't reappeared, so she'd figured the worst was over.

But as soon as Goode made her aware that she was still very much in danger, her fears, the 4:00 a.m. tachycardia, and the anxiety dreams had returned. She hoped she could counter, and even combat, all of this by standing up in print to whoever was persecuting her, because some bullies were known to back down when confronted.

"I refuse to live in fear like a victim while I do my job to expose the truth, no matter what these or any other stalkers threaten to do," Katrina wrote with bravado. "We not only have the SDPD investigating this situation, we also now have my residence under armed surveillance. So, a warning to whoever did this: If you come back and try to harm me in any way, you will be met with lethal force."

Although she didn't specifically mention Walter Hall, this was a warning to him as well.

By the time she'd turned in the column, Katrina felt empowered, especially when Joanne said she could fix her rebroken window during work hours—and expense it. Doing so, she had the mechanic snap a couple shots of her making a thumbs-up gesture next to the glass as it was being replaced again. She posted them on social media with the hashtag *#livingfearlessly*.

After picking up Thai takeout on her way home, she stopped by her bodyguard's car, parked in the driveway below her balcony, before she headed up to her apartment. With his shaved head and big ears, Teddy Kincaid reminded her of the character Mike Ehrmantraut on *Breaking Bad*, the strong-arm hit man who took no BS from thugs and competing drug traffickers and loved to play with his granddaughter.

"My column is running tonight, announcing that you're here watching over me," Katrina announced proudly.

"You think that's a good idea?" Teddy asked, wincing. "It might be better to let me catch these bastards unawares. Now they'll know there's only one of me. I hope a gang of them doesn't show up."

"I'm sure it'll be fine," she said. "I didn't specifically state there was only one armed guard. Plus, I trust you can take care of who- or whatever comes at you."

But as she trudged up the stairs, she realized that he might be right. She'd gotten so caught up in her *I won't be a victim* mind-set, she didn't ponder whether she might have made things more difficult for herself—and Teddy—by exposing so much personal information.

Naaah, he can handle it. And so can I. We're both professionals.

She pushed the momentary trepidation and fear from her mind as she sat down to enjoy her meal, safe and secure at her table with the canyon view.

Posted online at eight o'clock, her column drew hits immediately and went on to rack up more than any other article that night. Several readers commented that, perhaps, she and her editors didn't think this through, because the piece almost seemed to dare the culprit to strike again.

"Because you are the last surviving member of the Chopin family," one woman wrote, "the column makes me feel like I'm waiting to watch a fight to the death at the Roman Colosseum."

Katrina, who had hoped for a carefree night under Teddy's watch, took note of the comments stacking up, then snapped her laptop closed, as if ignoring them would make them disappear. All she really wanted was some peace.

She took a long hot shower before getting into bed with a suspense novel she'd purchased a year earlier but still hadn't read. Within an hour, her eyelids felt heavy enough that she could turn out the light.

With her head resting comfortably on the pillow, she was able to turn off the worry switches in her brain for the first time in months. That, in turn, set off a chain reaction of releasing the cramped and tight muscles all over her body, like a generator powering down to the off position.

When she opened her eyes again, she was amazed that she'd packed in a solid eight hours of uninterrupted, nightmare-free sleep.

Maybe it's denial, maybe it's real. All I know is I'm tired of being scared all the time. Something had to give. I've got work to do.

CHAPTER 18
GOODE

Wednesday

Goode was pleasantly surprised when Stone accepted his invitation to go dawn surfing on Wednesday morning for the first time in years. Given how stressful work had been lately, Stone decided he was willing to brave the fifty-seven-degree water, only to learn that his wetsuit was a tighter fit over his paunch than he'd been expecting.

They got changed in the dark and damp morning air as they leaned against Goode's van, which was parked facing Pumphouse, just before the sun came up. The waves were cranking, but Goode refrained from commenting for fear that Stone might chicken out.

"Man, I've got to lose some weight," Stone said, wriggling around until he could pull the strained front flaps of his wetsuit together to zip it up. "It's got to be the nightly bowl of ice cream. Or maybe it's the two chocolate-covered macaroons I crumble on top. Lucky I quit drinking, or it would be even worse."

"You just need to do this more often, that's all," Goode said. "Isn't it beautiful? This never gets old. I'll probably still be doing this in my eighties."

After Goode slid his van door shut, they walked single file down the dirt path toward the shack, boards under their arms, rekindling memories of the old days, when Stone used to call them Tuber and Mini Tuber.

"So, I told Katrina about overhearing Doreen McMurphy calling Vincent Battrelle while we were at their house the other night, and she wants to interview her," Goode said. "I told her I would ask if that was okay with you, since what I told her was off the record."

Stone stopped walking, turned around, and gave him an annoyed look. "What did you do that for?"

"I was going over that list I read you of all the common factors connecting Vincent to all these people who've died, including her family members, and it kind of slipped out. But I thought you would support the idea since she managed to pull personal details out of Michael Battrelle about the Fontaine case that he wouldn't tell us. You have to admit, she's good at it."

"Yeah, yeah, I know," Stone said, pausing before walking forward again. "I guess it's okay since Doreen was so uncooperative. Maybe she'll say more in an unofficial setting with another woman now that she's had a few days to settle down. We did talk to her the morning after her son was found hanging in a jail cell and she found her husband dead at his desk. I think she's scared to death she's next."

"I think so too. Just wanted to make sure you were on board before I give her the go-ahead."

Not that she needs our permission, but it's better if Stone feels he's got some say in it.

"Glad to hear it," Stone said. "We don't need you going Lone Wolf again and making your own decisions on this one. It's too sensitive."

Cutting ahead of Stone, who was plodding along the path, Goode let the comment go, but not without rolling his eyes.

You don't know the half of it, buddy.

When they reached the shack, which had been rebuilt numerous times after being destroyed by storms since the original structure went up in 1946, they stopped to watch the waves rise and fall to get a feel for the rhythm, the time between each swell and between sets.

"You go on in first," Stone said. "I'll just sit here and observe for a minute."

Goode could tell Stone was feeling old and out of shape and needed some coaxing.

"It's not even that big today. You'll be fine," he fibbed. "I'll be right there with you the whole time."

"Yeah, okay," Stone said reluctantly. "But I'm no Big Wave Dave like you."

They didn't get much of a chance to chat except during lulls between sets.

"You seem a little disappointed that some retired cop was hired to watch Katrina's place. I know you really wanted that job," Stone joked.

There was some truth to that. "Actually, I'm a little relieved because it removes the temptation for at least a couple of weeks," Goode called over his shoulder, paddling into position to catch the next swell.

Goode caught a sweet ride, but it was nothing like the high of mastering a twenty-five-footer at Jaws on Maui, where he'd hung out for a week right before the Fontaines were murdered. Stone held his own on one gnarly wave, but he wiped out more often than not.

By the time they toweled off and headed back to Goode's van, the morning sun felt bright with hope. Goode felt zen and relaxed while Stone laughed and joked, probably more out of embarrassment than anything else. Still, it was the perfect way to start the day.

After showering at Stone's place, the two of them strolled into the Homicide unit on a natural high. But Stone didn't even get a chance to sit down before they both saw the handwritten note, dashed off in angry capital letters, sitting on his desk:

GET YOUR ASS DOWN TO MY OFFICE NOW! Baxter

Chief Baxter had never left a note like that before. He usually called or had his assistant call. Maybe he'd already left a couple of voicemails and was frustrated that Stone hadn't answered, but Baxter had quite a temper, and many of the sworn officers, especially Stone, as the unit's media spokesman, had felt the brunt of it at one time or another.

"What's his beef?" Goode asked.

"Probably Katrina's story. I read it as soon as it was posted online last night, but maybe he just saw it in the paper this morning while I was out reliving my youth with you. I'm guessing he didn't like what he read with his Cheerios."

CHAPTER 19
RUSTY STONE

Wednesday

Stone's skull felt like it was caught in a vise, squeezing both temples, as he stepped into the elevator.

Great timing. I think I'm getting a migraine.

Just thirty minutes earlier, he'd felt so light and carefree, whistling and picturing the cheeseburger he was going to eat as a treat for working out so hard that morning.

I really need to do that more often. As much as I love having breakfast with Kelly and our three little weasels, it felt good to be out in the water at sunrise with the Mini Tuber, just like old times. Made me feel young again. Well, younger.

When he reached the chief's office, his secretary, Maria Martinez, gave Stone a sympathetic look.

"Hope you had a strong cup of coffee and are on top of your game, because he's on fire in there. I haven't seen him like this in, well, never."

"Oh, geez," Stone said, feeling the acid rising in his throat. "What's the deal?"

Maria gave him a half smile and said, "I think you already know it was that quote this morning, where you said you thought both of the McMurphy deaths were suspicious *and* related. He didn't authorize that, and it directly conflicted with what the sheriff already put out, so Helmsley took his head off this morning, and now the chief wants to kick the dog. You're the dog."

She picked up the phone to buzz the chief. "Sergeant Stone is here," she said.

"Go on in," she told Stone. "Duck and cover, and good luck."

Stone opened the door to a big office with a massive desk at one end and a conference table with comfy vinyl chairs at the other. Usually, Baxter would be sitting at the table with his coffee and wave Stone over collegially to join him.

But this time, Baxter was hunkered down behind the desk, silently glaring at one of the empty stiff-backed chairs opposite him. That meant he expected Stone to sit there and take his drubbing like a child.

The sergeant sat down cautiously, glancing around, anywhere but the chief's face.

"What the hell were you thinking?" Baxter asked in a low growl.

"Excuse me, Chief? I'm not sure what you mean."

"Where do you get off commenting on a death case that isn't even ours and calling it suspicious when you know this whole Fontaine case is as sensitive as just about any you've handled your entire time with this department?"

Stone was confused. He knew the case was sensitive, but he didn't see it as radioactive.

I guess I should've listened more closely to Goode.

He tended to think of his buddy as a smart but ornery upstart with little regard for protocol, but maybe he shouldn't have dismissed Goode's theory about Doreen McMurphy and Vincent Battrelle. Stone could see now that it wasn't a conspiracy theory, it was right on point. Now he'd gone and dropped the political football, which had come at him so fast he hadn't even seen it coming.

The chief was known for having a temper, but he seemed to be reacting even more strongly than usual, which was a red flag for Stone.

"I'm sorry, sir, I didn't think I needed to check that quote with you, but I see now that was an oversight on my part," he said. "But if I may—"

"No, you may not. You're aware that the sheriff and I don't get along. I reminded you of that a couple of days ago, and now you've made a bad situation worse. He ripped me a new one this morning, and when I didn't kiss his ass hard enough, I heard that he immediately called the mayor and told him that I needed to step down in a month unless this situation was rectified."

The sheriff, who was elected by the voters, had no direct authority over Baxter. But as the longtime head of the county's law enforcement agency who had a close political alliance with the mayor *and* the district attorney, the sheriff had enough clout and political influence that he could make Baxter's life difficult.

However, before Stone had a chance to respond, the chief emptied his throbbing forehead vein of anger in one stream of consciousness. It was like watching dominos falling, where the first one set off the sequential toppling of an entire structure built from many rows of small black blocks, until they all collapsed into one big heap.

Where is all this bile coming from?

"I learned through a friend at the shooting range yesterday afternoon that the deputy who cut Darren McMurphy down in his cell was Walter Hall, Brandon Winchester's bodyguard, who has since taken off for the Bahamas. Winchester, meanwhile, is out on bail, roaming around like a ghost dragging chains, due to charges you guys helped the FBI put together. I've been getting calls about his arrest, the arrest of Alex Battrelle, who was everyone's favorite investment broker, and now about the deaths of both McMurphys. These recent events have made a lot of influential people in this town very nervous that their investments in Vitaleron, and the precious sex drug under development, are going to tank. Many of them put their retirement savings into that company, and they need their investments to pay off.

"Part and parcel with that, they were strongly encouraged to give sizable donations to Winchester's reelection campaign, which is now obviously a useless cause. They're also worried they'll be named as part of that cabal your team keeps talking to the media about. Many of these callers are Alex Battrelle's clients, so they're also concerned that their secret dealings in the Caymans will come out in divorce court, causing them to lose those funds as well.

"As if that wasn't enough, you guys asked me, in writing, for that incident report about Darren McMurphy's death, not to mention the sheriff's shift log. Then you had to write me again, challenging my decision, which I told you was made in light of the conference call I had with the sheriff and the mayor, where all of this was laid out to me. So, now it looks like I can't control my own men, because they don't respect my authority.

"All of this puts the sheriff's reelection campaign in a precarious position with the Lincoln Club, which, as you know, funds the Republican candidates in this town. Helmsley doesn't want to lose the next election because of you and your boy, stirring up all this trouble. Goode, by the way, was seen canoodling with that reporter at Piatti the other night, without a care in the world that everyone knows they're sleeping together. Were you aware of this? You and I just talked about him and that complaint regarding the female witness in the Tania Marcus case, and you promised me that he would not step over that line again or there would be repercussions. Look, I know he's smart and does good police work, but he has got to be reprimanded. Dammit, Stone, I can't take another morning like this."

Stone's mouth had fallen open, and stayed open, at the mention of Walter Hall, the bodyguard that had tried to stop him from getting Katrina out of Congressman Winchester's room at the Del, where they had planned for Darren McMurphy to give her a fatal shot of succinylcholine.

If Hall was working for Winchester, then how was he also working as a jail deputy? And how did he coincidentally happen to be near Darren

McMurphy's cell at just the right time to cut him down? Probably because McMurphy wasn't hanging in the first place. None of that is coincidence.

Stone felt his chest tightening further with each of the chief's complaints. After a few unsuccessful attempts to pull air into his lungs, he simply. Stopped. Breathing.

"Stone, are you all right?" the chief asked. "You don't look so good."

But the sergeant couldn't hear anything except a buzzing sound, like a fly in his ear. The vise had tightened to the point where his skull felt like it would implode from the pressure. His ears had started ringing when he first sat in the chair, and now that sound was alternating with the buzzing.

Ring, buzz, ring, buzz.

Too dizzy to sit up straight, Stone lost control of his body and slumped forward in his chair. The last thing he remembered was hitting his forehead, hard, on the sharp edge of the chief's desk.

Thwack.

Then everything went black.

When Stone came to, his vision was fuzzy, his head was throbbing, and he felt a warm liquid dribbling down his face and into his mouth. It tasted like metal.

Is that my blood?

Baxter's voice still sounded like a fly buzzing as he came around the desk and lowered Stone from the chair onto the floor. Stone couldn't make out what the chief was saying as he pushed on Stone's chest, then pinched his nose and breathed into his mouth.

It was all a blur of sensations until he felt the plastic mask over his nose and mouth and the cool stream of oxygen flowing into his sinuses and down his throat. Gasping loudly, Stone sputtered and realized that he was able, once again, to breathe on his own. But he still felt dizzy, even though he was lying down.

He could almost focus on the paramedic who was kneeling next to him, dabbing at his forehead and down his face with a gauze square. It smelled like rubbing alcohol and came away with blood on it. The medic taped a bandage over the cut on Stone's forehead.

"You've got quite a gash there, Sergeant," the paramedic said. "How does your head feel?"

"It hurts."

"Just the cut or your whole head?"

"My whole head."

"Okay, we're going to take you to the ER to get you checked out to see if you had a heart attack or stroke. Have you ever had either one, or do they run in your family?"

"No."

"Panic attacks?"

"No. But I did feel like I was getting a migraine earlier. I get them sometimes when I'm under a lot of stress."

"Gotcha. Good to know," the medic said as they wheeled the gurney toward the door. "Anyone you want us to call for you?"

"Yes, can you call Detective Goode and ask him to meet me at the hospital? I need to talk to him. It's important."

"What about your wife? Or other family members?"

"Yes, my wife, Kelly. But Goode is my brother. He can handle that. We go way back."

"I'll give him a call," the chief offered. "I should probably tell him what I told you, so it doesn't get lost in translation."

Feeling protective of his buddy but also a little scared of what Goode might say, unbridled, in a room with the chief, Stone didn't know how to respond.

"That's your choice, Chief, but please tell him to meet me at the ER. I'd like to talk to my detective."

"You just worry about your health, Sergeant. I'll take things from here," Baxter said.

As if he hadn't had a rough enough morning, Stone felt a pang of apprehension as they wheeled him toward the elevator. Not a slight pang, more like a massive feeling of dread. People were dying, their jobs were being threatened, and he and Goode still didn't know who was behind it all.

Goode thought Vincent Battrelle was the common thread, but Stone still thought this was too big to be the work of one man. He remembered dismissing Goode's warnings as paranoia that one of them could be the next target for going after these guys. But even with the fuzzy memory of the chief's rant, he knew this situation was serious enough to have brought on this attack. And now they were taking him out of action to the ER.

"My phone. I don't have my phone. Can you guys go back and grab it?" Stone said to the younger paramedic. "I think I dropped it in the chief's office."

The medic must have recognized the urgency in Stone's eyes, because he ran back to retrieve the phone while his partner held the elevator door open.

"Here you go, sir," he said, placing the device in Stone's hand and squeezing his shoulder. "It'll be okay, don't worry. We got you."

Not trusting the chief to follow through, Stone thought he'd better call Goode himself. But the detective didn't pick up, so Stone left him a message: "Just left the chief's office in an ambulance. We're headed to the ER at Scripps Mercy in Hillcrest. Meet me there."

CHAPTER 20
GOODE

Wednesday

Maria, the chief's secretary, called Goode at his desk about twenty minutes after Stone left the Homicide unit.

"Chief wants to see you right away," she said.

While Goode was on the office phone with her, Stone called his cell. Not wanting to interrupt his call with Maria, he put her off, then listened to Stone's cryptic message about leaving the chief's office in an ambulance.

What the hell happened down there? I know Baxter has a nasty temper, but the ER? Stone sounds bad. Shaky and weak. So, now what do I do? It sounds like he's trying to warn me about the chief. Maybe I can beg off and ask to reschedule. No, I'll tell Maria I'm rescheduling because Stone is my family and he asked me to meet him at the ER. What's she going to say, no?

Goode called Maria back from his car on the way to the hospital. But he didn't have to worry. She said she'd handle Baxter for him.

"Go take care of your family," she said. "I know you guys are brothers. But get your ass down here as soon as you get back. The chief is super pissed. Hopefully he'll have calmed down by then, or you might end up in the ER too."

Parking was always a bitch around the hospital in Hillcrest, so Goode pulled into a parking garage without even checking the price. From there, he ran over to the ambulance bay, where he saw one of them pulling away, then burst through the hospital doors used by the paramedics.

"I'm looking for the police sergeant who was just brought in," he said, flashing his badge at a nurse, who pointed him toward a gurney down the hallway.

Stone didn't look any better than he'd sounded in his message. His face was so pale it almost matched the white bandage taped across his forehead. When Goode grabbed his hand, it felt clammy. None of these indicated a positive outcome.

"What happened? Did the chief do this to you?" Goode asked, only half joking.

"Yes and no," Stone said weakly. "He didn't hit me, but he launched into a tirade. Then I passed out and bonked my head on the edge of his desk."

"Passed out? Ouch. Why do they have you in the hallway? Don't they know who you are?"

"They do, but the ER is full of sick homeless people and addicts who OD'd and were brought back with naloxone. I'm on the short list for a bed, though. They think I might've had a stroke or heart attack. Or both."

"Jesus, dude. Did I work you too hard this morning? I thought you were up to it."

"Yeah, no, I don't think that had anything to do with it," Stone said. "I felt a migraine coming on in the elevator down to see the chief. I expected him to be angry, but I wasn't prepared for the endless rant."

"What did he say?"

"First, he makes me sit in the punishment chair, and then he starts frothing at the mouth with this litany of corrupt bullshit. I think I got overwhelmed, because it sounds like he's up to his eyeballs in it, and

I didn't know what to say. That's why I wanted to warn you before he puts you through the same thing."

"Yeah, at first, Maria told me to come down, but then she said she'd hold him off until I could take care of you, brah. What kind of corrupt bullshit?"

Goode pulled up a chair to be at Stone's eye level and have a more private conversation since they were smack in the middle of a public hospital hallway with ears everywhere. But as soon as he sat down and leaned in, he noticed a glaze come over Stone's eyes. It was as if he'd gone inside himself.

"Stone! Are you okay?" he asked, grabbing him by the shoulder. No response.

Stone's upper body started to shake, a little at first, before turning into a full-on seizure.

"A little help!" Goode yelled. "We need help over here! He's seizing!"

Goode jumped up and grabbed Stone by both shoulders, not because he knew what to do, but because he didn't.

A male nurse and a female doctor came running from opposite directions. "Step back," the nurse ordered as he and the doctor turned Stone on his side and put a pillow under his neck and head for support.

"It's okay, Sergeant, you're okay," the doctor said in a calm, soothing voice.

The seizure didn't last much longer before it stopped, by which time Stone's face was covered with sweat, soaking the bandage until it was pink with blood seeping through. Finally lying still, he opened his eyes.

Goode hated to see his buddy looking lost and fearful like this. Other than his sister, Maureen, whom he rarely saw these days, Stone was the only family he had. But he was relieved that this hadn't happened earlier at the beach, where he wouldn't have had the slightest clue what to do.

"What the hell was that?" Stone asked the doctor pleadingly. "It was like an earthquake shooting through my system. That's never happened before."

"Try to stay calm. We're going to get you something to lower your blood pressure. It's really high, and that could be the cause not only of the seizure, but of your other symptoms today as well," the doctor said, a no-nonsense brunette with dark-rimmed glasses whose name tag read NANCY COSTELLO.

"They gave me aspirin in the ambulance," he said.

"Yes, I see that," Dr. Costello said. "That was in case you'd had a heart attack before they picked you up. You're next in line to be admitted, but we're going to take some blood now to find out what's going on. Based on your symptoms and now this seizure, we're going to do a CT scan of your head, an EEG, and an ECG to look at the activity in your brain and your heart."

"That's a lot of tests. Is all that really necessary?"

"Absolutely. That's standard protocol. Have you been under a lot of stress lately?" she asked.

"Yes, but I didn't think it was enough to cause all of this."

Goode didn't want to miss anything, but he stepped down the hall to check his phone after it buzzed with a text from Maria:

Everything OK down there? The chief is getting anxious with how Stone is doing. He still thinks you're coming back to talk to him.

Is she serious? This is one of the busiest ERs in the city, for Christ's sake. It's the definition of "everything is wrong and takes forever."

Stone just had seizure, so no, not OK, he texted back. I'm here 4 rest of day. He's getting tests for possible heart attack/stroke. Pls tell chief I'll call or stop by in a.m.

Maria texted back: Sounds serious! I'll let him know. Give Stone our best and tell him we hope he's OK. Chief feels bad. Wonders if he did this by yelling at Stone.

Good! Goode replied. He should be sorry. I'm sure he didn't help matters.

That's what I told him, Maria wrote. I keep telling him he needs anger management. Stay safe, Detective.

By the time Goode was back at Stone's bedside, they had connected him to an IV and were giving him intravenous meds to prevent a repeat of what had just occurred, without interfering with the tests they were conducting.

"I bought us, well, me, some time with Maria," Goode said. "I said I would be here all day, so the chief will have to wait till tomorrow to take my head off."

Stone had sweated so much during the seizure that the nurse had to change his bandage. He'd regained some of his color, but he still had fear in his eyes.

"You know, when I stopped drinking in my twenties, I thought my health would be pretty good going forward," Stone said. "This doesn't seem fair."

"I'm not a doctor, but I'm going to venture that it might be all the cheeseburgers, pizza, and ice cream you eat," Goode said. "Fat, sugar, and hammock riding are *no bueno*. You're always talking about how you need to get more exercise, but I rarely see you do it. You should surf with me more often. It would do you a world of good."

"I don't know. Seems like it had the opposite effect today."

"That was just a coincidence. Let's wait and see what your tests show before we start diagnosing you. Just try to relax, buddy. Whatever is going on, this is a good hospital, and they're going to take care of you."

Stone closed his eyes, took a deep breath, and nodded. Then his eyes popped open. "Did anyone call Kelly?" he asked, panicked. "The paramedics asked if they should call anyone, and I think I asked them to call her, but I was so dizzy. Maybe I said *you* would call her. I don't remember much from the ambulance ride over."

"No worries. I'll call her right now," Goode said, heading off down the hall.

Stone was right—in all the chaos, no one had called his wife, Kelly, so she was not happy. Stone was only forty-two. A little more stocky than overweight, and not in great shape. But this day had come as a shock for all of them.

"I'll be there as soon as I can," she said. "I just need to make sure my mom can pick the kids up at school. It's a half day today."

"Okay, we'll see you when we see you. Right now, we're in the hallway, but we should have a room by the time you get here."

Trying to exude calm, Goode put on his *all good* face. "She's on her way," he told Stone. "Now that you're sedated, do you feel well enough to give me a few highlights from the chief's rant, or do you want to wait till later?"

"I feel like I should tell you now before anything else happens," Stone said. "In case I don't get another chance."

Stone spent the next ten minutes running through what he could recall, which, as Goode had anticipated, was enough to give anyone a stress attack. Goode was perfectly healthy, and even he felt his blood pressure rising at the remark about him and Katrina at Piatti.

"Jesus! We were not *canoodling*, and we're not sleeping together either," he said. "She got some news while we were having a drink, and she was so upset she was literally crying on my shoulder. The reason we were having a drink was because you told me not to do anything to step over that line, so we were out in public on purpose. Who is the spy spreading this misinformation, anyway?"

"I don't know, but you need to be careful. People see what they want to see, and anyone who isn't blind can tell that you two want to be in bed, even if you haven't gotten there yet."

Goode shrugged. "That's fair, I suppose, but we're doing our best. She's still on this story, the investigation is proceeding, and someone did just threaten her life—again. It was concerning enough to convince the paper to hire her an overnight armed guard for a couple of weeks. She did that to keep you and her editors happy. Geez, I mean, if everyone is going to accuse us anyway, maybe I should just go ahead and stay the night."

Shaking his head, Stone had to chuckle. "If you stay on the right side of the line, I can defend you. But this whole female-witness-in-your-house thing keeps cropping back up. I don't know why Clover

Ziegler's mother is still complaining about you a year later. What did you do to that woman?"

"I told you at the time, she flirted her ass off with me that afternoon before Clover jumped off the cliffs at Black's, and I politely declined her advances. She's acting like a woman scorned, and let me remind you, her daughter was mentally ill. Could be genetic."

"That's a good point I'll make to the chief the next time it comes up. But you were right about this whole case being politically charged. I thought you were being paranoid, but I've never had the chief tell me to stand down and leave a case alone like this, especially when the evidence is so egregious."

"Exactly. What I don't get is how he thinks we're going to bury a corruption scheme that's spreading like a virus through the mayor's office and the county's two largest law enforcement agencies. He's basically saying we should just accept orders from politicians and Vitaleron investors who have no business horning into our investigations."

"Worse than that, he basically dismissed the whole cabal idea. Like it doesn't exist."

"That's probably because he's scared shitless of losing his job. Unless he's more involved than we know."

"Yeah, I forgot to tell you, the sheriff told the mayor to fire the chief within a month unless—how did he put it?—'this situation is rectified.'"

"What does that mean?"

"Like I said, back off and stand down. Stop trying to put this whole case together, and now that the McMurphys are dead, accept that there is no larger conspiracy, because too many rich white men are worried their wives will take them to divorce court for the money that Alex Battrelle hid in the Caymans and, worse, that they'll lose their precious Vitaleron investments, not to mention the magical pill that promises erections until they die."

"Well, that's not going to happen. I don't know about you, but I'm not standing down. If I have to work under the radar, I'll do that to protect your health, but I'm not going to leave this alone. I already saw this coming, though, so I haven't even told you everything I'm doing so you'd have plausible deniability."

Stone looked stricken again, and this time he wasn't joking. "Don't even tell me that, or I'll have another seizure," he said. "Do what you need to do, but please make sure neither one of us gets in trouble for it."

"So, I have your unofficial approval to do whatever it takes?"

"Yes. They won't be able to say anything when the house of cards comes crashing down and you prove, unequivocally, that we were right. Some of them may even end up in jail, including the mayor. Maybe the sheriff, too, if we can prove Darren McMurphy was murdered under his watch. Wait, I forgot to tell you something. Walter Hall, Winchester's bodyguard, also works as a jail deputy. He's the one who cut Darren down in his cell."

"Holy shit, you're kidding me!" Goode said. Then something else hit him. The pieces were starting to come together.

"Wait, now that you mention it, I forgot to tell you something too," Goode said. "I was keeping this on the back burner, because I thought maybe McMurphy was just throwing mud at the wall to see what would stick, but now I'm seeing that it's pure gold. Remember the dirt he gave us on the mayor?"

"Yes, but remind me. I just had a seizure."

Goode explained that Darren McMurphy had said that one of his father's shell corporations bought a mansion as a bribe for the mayor to create a new district so Patrick McMurphy could build a big hotel on Mission Bay—on the same site as Katrina's brother Franny's failed project.

"I also just learned that Franny died from the same cocktail of narcotics that was in the bottle of lemon-infused vodka from

Patrick's desk. So, Franny didn't kill himself—he was murdered, just like Patrick."

Stone's eyes almost rolled back into his head. "Whaaat?"

"Yes, so now we can open up two new homicide cases, one for Katrina's brother and one for Patrick McMurphy," he said, explaining that Artie had sent the vodka bottle to a private toxicology lab to keep the ME's office out of the loop, because they suspected Dr. Thompson had been compromised. "Anyway, *that* juicy tidbit about the lethal vodka cocktail is what I was telling Katrina when she started crying on my shoulder at Piatti. She's always thought that her brother was murdered, but no one believed her. And *that* was the extent of our 'canoodling.'"

"I wish you'd told me this sooner," Stone said. "Does anyone else know that Darren told us about the bribe for the Mission Bay hotel district? If not, it's the perfect motive to keep him and his father quiet—permanently. There was so much going down after the sting operation at the Del, I lost track of that tidbit, and I don't remember seeing it in the reports."

"That's because I held it back as leverage. I figured, with all this shit swirling around, we should have a major chit at our disposal."

"Good man," Stone said, ready once again with the puns, his eyes twinkling.

"You're back, I see."

"Yes, I think so. I'm starting to feel better."

"I love you, brother," Goode said, hugging Stone. "You're the best."

"No, you're the best," Stone said. "I love you too, buddy."

That's when Kelly came running in, looking stricken. But her face relaxed as soon as she saw the smiles and hugging going on.

"I'm going to step out and give you two some privacy," Goode said, giving her a quick hug before heading outside to call Katrina.

It was tricky when the reporter on your mondo homicide-corruption case was also the first person you wanted to spill all your big personal news to. He held a lot back, but he did share that he had

Stone's implicit permission to do what had to be done to get these bastards now that he had linked her brother's and Patrick's deaths to the lethal spiked vodka.

"And you're just the reporter to help me bring them down," he said.

"I'd be happy to," she said.

"Starting with Vincent Battrelle," he said. "I'm going to pay him a visit as soon as I make sure Stone is okay."

CHAPTER 21
GOODE

Wednesday

After Stone finished all his tests, Dr. Costello consulted a few other specialists, then came by that evening to deliver her diagnosis: Stone had high blood pressure and high cholesterol, an unhealthy foundation that probably contributed to the episode. But it was more likely triggered by a stress-related migraine, coupled with a panic attack, that caused him to get dizzy, hit his head, and pass out. The seizure at the hospital was also caused by stress, which is rare, she said, but can happen even when the patient has no history of epilepsy.

"We're going to keep you overnight to monitor your vitals and make sure you don't fall and hurt yourself if you have another seizure or dizzy spell," Costello said. "I've already added a sedative and blood pressure medication to your IV meds. Once you're discharged, you should see a nutritionist about your diet, talk to a psychiatrist about starting antianxiety meds, and see a therapist to help you deal with stress. The body and mind are intricately connected, and we want you to send more positive messages to your brain so your body doesn't give out like this."

"Yeah, I've been feeling pretty anxious lately. Lying awake for hours at night too," Stone said. "Can't turn my brain off."

"So, you have insomnia as well? Your body can't heal and regenerate itself if you don't get enough sleep," she said. "That will also make you more tired and anxious, which can set you up for an episode like this. Based on your cholesterol numbers, I'm guessing you don't eat well, especially if you're running from homicide to homicide and not sleeping much for days at a time."

"That's my life in a nutshell," Stone said. "Plus, this particular case we're working is the doozy of all doozies."

"Well, I recommend that you take a medical leave for two weeks to give your body a chance to recover and get back into balance. Seizures take a toll on your brain. You'll need to just do nothing for a little bit, okay?"

Stone looked at Goode and shook his head as if to say the doctor has no idea what she's suggesting.

"I'm not sure I can take two weeks off right now," Stone said. "Like I just said, we're in the middle of a highly sensitive investigation."

"That may be so, but if you don't, you'll be back here in short order, and every seizure will do more damage. So, let's nip this in the bud before you fall down some stairs or seriously hurt yourself. If you like, I can call your chief to deliver my recommendation personally. I'll tell him that your body sent you a message that we all need to listen to."

"Honey, please listen to the doctor," Kelly said. "You need to rest. Let Goode take over the case while you're gone. He's fully capable, aren't you, Uncle Goode?"

Kelly smiled wryly at the detective, who was so much a part of the family that he'd earned the title of uncle. Goode nodded affirmatively.

She knows the drill. Listen to her, buddy.

"They're both right, and you know it," Goode told Stone. "We need to get you back into fighting shape. I had no idea you were this bad off, or I never would have taken you surfing this morning."

Costello looked at Goode and said, "He was out in those big waves today? Did he go deep underwater?"

"No, I don't think so," he said. "He wiped out a few hundred times, but it's not like we were scuba diving."

"Did you hit your head with your surfboard, Sergeant?" the doctor asked.

"Yeah, actually, I did, a couple of times. Didn't think it would make much difference. I've got a hard head," he said, chuckling to make light of his lack of surfing prowess.

"Well, concussions don't show up on the CT scan, but that may be part of the picture here as well. You gave your head a good bump when you hit the edge of the desk, so if that's in addition to multiple thumps with the surfboard, we'll need to follow that protocol as well, which means I'm keeping you for a couple of nights, not just one."

"I'd really like to go home, plunk myself down on the couch, and watch TV," Stone said.

"Sorry, but we've got too many variables at play here to do that. Let's make sure you're out of the danger zone first."

Kelly nodded. "This case will still be there when you get better. Or maybe Goode will solve the whole thing while you're gone, and we can get back to our normal level of crazy."

A spontaneous burst of laughter came out of Goode before he could stop it. "Sorry," he said, covering his mouth. "You have no idea how complicated and messy this case is, but thanks for the compliment, Kelly."

Turning to Stone, he said, "The chief is going to love it when he hears this news."

He'll think we have no choice but to stand down. It's the perfect cover for me to work on the down-low.

But that was not exactly the case. The chief felt guilty that his rant had put Stone in the hospital, so he consulted with his pastor, who helped bring his emotions down to where he was prepared to ask Stone for forgiveness when he returned to work. At least that's what Maria told Goode when she called to check in, noting that Dr. Costello had already talked to the chief on Stone's behalf.

"So, I'm calling to say that you don't need to come in to see him after all," Maria said. "The chief doesn't want to see anyone else hurt, and he figures that Stone can pass on the gist of what they discussed when he's feeling better. He does remember it, right?"

"Yes, he does, and he's already done that. That's actually what triggered the seizure in the ER," he said, milking it.

"Oh, no."

"Yeah, the doctor said it was stress related, like the rest of this episode. They also think he may have gotten a concussion when he hit his head on the desk."

"Geez. I hope he's okay."

"We hope so too. But you can let the chief know that I've been briefed and will proceed accordingly."

"Okay, sounds good. Please tell Stone that the chief approved his two-week medical leave, no problem. I'll handle the paperwork, so he doesn't have to do anything else."

CHAPTER 22
KATRINA

Wednesday

As Katrina formulated her questions for her father's former clerk, she remembered having lunch with him in chambers during the summer when she came home from college, snarfing down tuna fish subs with hot peppers from the Italian deli. She wasn't much for hot or spicy foods, but she loved those pepperoncini peppers. Julia was always so welcoming on these visits, cooing over Katrina.

"Look at you, all pretty and grown up," Julia would say.

Thinking back with twenty-twenty hindsight, Katrina wondered if Julia fantasized about being her stepmother and going shopping together someday.

At the time, Katrina appreciated Julia for taking care of her dad, who could get so deeply focused on his cases that he would forget to change out of his sneakers after taking a walk during the lunch break.

In contrast, her mother was always über-efficient at home and at work. Aphy had her creative and analytical sides, which was what made her so intriguing. It also didn't hurt that, as a former homecoming queen who'd made her way to the Broadway stage, she had always been beautiful.

As these memories flooded back, Katrina felt a hole in her heart. She tried not to dwell on the past or the fact that she'd never see her parents or twin brother again, because it did her no good. But she was sad they would never have another family dinner at Piatti, even if Franny sometimes threw a tantrum, smashing a wine bottle on the patio and storming out. It was better to focus on the happier times. Like when they gathered for Christmas or went sailing on their boat around Coronado.

Thinking back to the months after Franny died, Katrina remembered that her mom seemed down and more distracted than usual. But with Katrina away at school in Chicago, they didn't talk much because they were both so busy, so Katrina had no idea about her mom's lunches with "Vincey," a name that made her cringe.

When she said "lunch at the Grant," did she mean the Grant Grill, or was "lunch" a code word for sex at the US Grant Hotel?

The thought of such a rendezvous between her mother and Vincent Battrelle was beyond her comprehension. His well-preserved appearance only bolstered her suspicion that he'd made a deal with the devil or Dorian Gray, but he was too Machiavellian to be described as attractive.

She wanted to press him about those lunchtime rendezvous, but thought she'd explore them with Doreen first. If their friendship did go way back, Doreen might be able to give Katrina some intel on her mom's relationship with Vincent. But what if he'd been having affairs with both of them?

Katrina was tired of waiting for Goode's go-ahead to give Doreen a call. She'd tried to be patient out of respect for her professional and personal relationship with the detective, but the last couple of times they'd talked, he was in his own world.

Since when do I have to wait for police permission to do an interview anyway? Since never. Screw waiting. I'm done.

Because she already knew where Doreen lived, she decided it might be better to show up unannounced. Maybe Doreen would invite her in for a chat.

It was hot in the sun but chilly in the shade in Mission Valley when Katrina got into her car. She headed north on the freeway, then headed west on La Jolla Parkway, where the sun disappeared behind the marine layer of clouds that hugged the coast. Oftentimes, it didn't burn off until the afternoon, and sometimes, it didn't burn off at all. Still, it was almost always sunny at the beach on Christmas. *With no family left, who am I going to spend the holidays with?*

Once again, she pushed those thoughts out of her mind. She had more important things to think about.

As she cruised up the twisty Hillside Drive, she admired the historic architecture of the few remaining older homes. She wished people could be satisfied with celebrating the original architectural styles by preserving, not destroying, their natural charm.

Parking down the street from the McMurphys' house, she realized that her nighttime visit had not allowed her to appreciate the full scale of the property, which flowed down the hill behind the house. Thus, the street name, Hillside Drive.

As luck would have it, a woman with a straight white bob under her visor was tending to flowers in the front garden, cloistered behind the stucco wall.

Perfect. Now I don't even have to knock.

"Mrs. McMurphy?" Katrina asked brightly.

Holding a few blooms in her free hand, the woman smiled as she glanced up from her task of clipping dead rosebuds.

"Yes," she said. "And who might you be? Are you the new family in the Robertson house?"

"No, actually, I'm with the *Sun-Dispatch*. I was in the neighborhood, so I thought I'd stop by and see if you were free."

"Thanks, but I already take the paper," Doreen said, turning her back to Katrina.

"I'm actually not selling the paper. I'm a reporter, and I'm writing a story about your husband and his legacy. Can we chat for a few minutes?"

That got Doreen's attention, and as Katrina hoped, lowered her defenses. As Doreen slowly turned back around, Katrina could see the corners of Doreen's mouth go from a suspicious and apprehensive downturn to a more relaxed and open upturn, though her eyes still reflected a blankness that Katrina couldn't pinpoint.

Katrina purposely didn't introduce herself by name in case Doreen had read her first-person columns about Darren's attempt to kill her. She would own up to it eventually, but opening with that detail could potentially end the interview before it started.

Besides, Katrina's introduction wasn't entirely a fib. She could always use more background as she continued to write about this case. Although Goode said he thought the deaths of Darren and Patrick McMurphy were suspicious, he hadn't provided her with any proof that she could publish, so she would proceed with her own investigation into the official narrative of suicide and natural death.

"Sure. I was just gathering up a bouquet for my dining room table," Doreen said. "They help cheer up the house at a time like this."

"Of course," Katrina said, smiling empathetically. "I was here, outside, talking to the police the other night after you called 911. I'm so sorry for your loss. Both of your losses."

Now, she saw some emotion as Doreen teared up.

So, she's in there somewhere. Maybe she's relieved that the chaos is over and she doesn't have to live with her family's evil deeds any longer. Unless she was in on the whole scheme.

Katrina had been pondering this possibility quite a bit. What kind of mother could produce a son who could kill two people and attempt to kill a third, with no remorse? And for what? Did the family live by greed, doing whatever it took to get what they wanted? Did Patrick's wealth destroy any goodness they may have once had, or did he choose Doreen as a mate because she was just as greedy and callous as him and the wicked *Rosemary's Baby* son they'd produced?

"Thank you, dear," Doreen said. "Follow me. We can take some iced tea to the veranda. The view is lovely."

Speaking of Rosemary's Baby, *let's hope she doesn't put something into my drink.*

"Your garden is beautiful," Katrina said as they meandered along the front path through the rainbow panoply of flowers, from roses to pansies, daisies to hydrangeas, and cyclamen to lavender.

Hearing a vehicle pull up, Katrina turned to see a car marked with the logo of a security company park in front of the house. Doreen turned as well and waved to the male driver, a uniformed guard who called out his greeting from the sidewalk.

"Hi, Mrs. McMurphy. I'm here to start my shift," he said.

"Very good!" she replied. Then, speaking in a low voice to Katrina, she said, "Milty Biggs, my attorney, hired some security to watch over me because of what happened."

The front door was painted a welcoming periwinkle, leading into a low-ceilinged foyer and down several stairs to a long room with a cathedral window at the end, which offered a glorious view of the hillside and ocean beyond.

The furniture seemed a bit drab and worn in comparison, as if Doreen had lost the desire to keep up with the latest fabrics or trendy styles. Maybe she suffered from depression. Or maybe the McMurphys weren't as rich as she'd thought.

Doreen led her into the kitchen, which had a more modern and yet still retro feel, with a center island, breakfast nook, and dining room. Beyond that was a wide, open family room with a curved sitting area centered on a massive flat-screen TV.

"My boys liked to watch a lot of sports here every Sunday," she said.

"Your boys?"

"Yes, my husband, Patrick, and our sons Darren and Matty, when he was in town, and all their friends from the beach club. It could get pretty loud in here, especially if they had money on the game," she said, retrieving a pitcher of iced tea from the fridge.

"Matty is your other son?"

"Yes, my younger son, Matthew. He lives in Hong Kong. He said he'd fly in as soon as he could, but that was a week ago now. He's pretty busy, I guess."

There were those dark, blank eyes again. Was she holding in her emotions so she didn't have to feel them? Or was she in so much pain it made her eyes go dark from the anger building up inside? Katrina couldn't tell.

"It must be really hard going through all of this alone," Katrina said.

That did it. The dam burst and Doreen started crying, which turned to sobbing within seconds.

"I'm sorry," Doreen said, running out of the room and down a hallway, where Katrina heard a door close.

During Doreen's absence, which lasted a good ten minutes, Katrina felt free to wander around and snoop, her ear cocked for her host's return. She found a collection of family photos of Patrick and his sons fishing, and a few featuring just the boys. From their body language, the brothers didn't seem to like each other much. Maybe they were too different, or they were forced to compete for their father's approval and affection. That was never an issue for Katrina and Franny, because Franny's addictions took him out of the running.

Based on what she'd previously learned about Victoria Fontaine and Vincent's son Alex, growing up with money in La Jolla did not ensure happiness. Rather, it seemed to breed self-destructive behavior and unhappiness. More interested in pursuing their own livelihoods, these egocentric parents left their kids to essentially raise themselves. Instead, they threw money at their children, or in Darren's case, purposely withheld it, as his "suicide" note so blatantly stated. Money was not love, but that was the language they learned to speak.

I have so many questions, but I'm sure Doreen would kick me out if I asked most of them. So, I'm going to approach this with no overt assumptions, and let her talk. I won't ask anything that might shut her down.

When Doreen emerged, her eyes were swollen and damp, and her nose looked as if she'd blown it a few times, but she seemed noticeably calmer.

"Excuse me," she said. "Everything is just too much lately."

"No need to explain," Katrina said. "That's perfectly understandable."

Doreen poured two glasses of iced tea, handed one to Katrina, and headed for the veranda. The clouds were starting to burn off, but the moisture in the air actually made it seem brighter, as if the sun's rays reflected off each minuscule water droplet. Doreen led her over to a round glass table with an umbrella, facing the ocean, and sat in a green polyester director's chair, gesturing toward the one next to her.

"So, what do you want to know?" Doreen asked.

Starting with a few softball questions, Katrina asked how she and Patrick met, what big hotels he'd built, and what she did for a living while he was off developing resorts. She was careful not to load her questions with opinions, and not to mention anything that might trigger Doreen's memory about Katrina or her family. Not yet, anyway.

Doreen said she'd met Patrick while they were both attending the University of San Diego. They got married right after graduation.

"Is that where you first met Vincent Battrelle?" Katrina asked, kicking herself for playing that card too soon.

Doreen frowned again but shook it off, probably remembering that she'd already mentioned Vincent.

"Yes, Vincey and I actually dated for a while—I was an undergrad and he was a law student—until he met another woman and fell in love. She married someone else, and eventually so did he, but we've stayed friends ever since. Why are you asking me about Vincey?"

She calls him that too? Odd.

Katrina made a quick recovery. "Well, he's my boss, and I know you all know each other because your husband and son were officers on the Vitaleron board with him."

The tense moment quickly passed, and Doreen settled back down.

"Oh, right. But Patrick wasn't an officer. That was Darren."

"Right, yes. I was lumping them together for conversational purposes."

"Just make sure you get those details right when you write the obituary, dear."

"Yes, of course."

Still trying to build trust, Katrina held her tongue for the moment and let Doreen think she was writing a standard obit.

Doreen said she and Patrick were both from local families who had been in San Diego for at least two generations, although their parents didn't grow up with money. They worked hard and saved their pennies while their kids did well enough in school to earn scholarships to USD.

"Patrick's fortune was self-made as well," she said. "He went on to earn an MBA from San Diego State, which he put to good use with the connections he'd made at both schools."

Doreen said that as if the money he'd made while she raised their two kids had nothing to do with her. That was a red flag for Katrina, a sign that Patrick had drilled that message into her head to control her and make her feel small and powerless.

"I dabbled in real estate before the boys were born, but I quit to be home for them while Patrick did his deals," she said. "He was rarely here, but we joined the beach club when the boys were young, so I had plenty of company when he was working late. In fact, I served as our agent when we bought this house all those years ago. After Darren was born, Patrick wanted to move to a more modern place with lots of marble and granite, but I've always enjoyed this house just the way it is. So, I refused to sell or do a major remodel, and we stayed put. Patrick spent his money on cars and, well, other things."

Katrina wasn't sure if she meant women or something more illicit, but the "his money" comment fell in line with her earlier thoughts. She decided not to press it, but to let the truth come out organically.

"This other woman that Vincent Battrelle met when you were dating, do you remember her name?"

Doreen's expression turned quizzical. "Now what in God's name does that have to do with Patrick's obituary?" she asked.

That was the end of the softball questions. Katrina had no choice now but to come clean. Sort of.

"I didn't actually say I was writing an obituary, Mrs. McMurphy. I am writing a story about Patrick, so I need to know about his past accomplishments, but it's not just about that."

"So what does Vincey have to do with this, and this woman he was dating?"

"Because I think that woman was my mother," Katrina said, hoping that detail would elicit sympathy, and was enough off topic from the Fontaine murders, her family's deaths, and Vitaleron that she could work her way back after this short detour.

"What did you say your name was again?"

"Katrina Chopin."

"You're Peter and Aphy Chopin's daughter?"

"Yes, I am."

"Now that you mention it, I do see the resemblance," Doreen said, pulling back to gaze at Katrina as if she were a sculpture. "I guess I should offer my condolences as well. You've lost everyone, just like me. I still have Matty, but he's so far away it still feels like I've lost everyone too. I'm so sorry."

"Thank you. So, was it my mom?"

"Yes, dear, it was."

"I need to ask you kind of a delicate question. It's not for the story. It's for me."

"Okay," Doreen said, leaning in closer, her curiosity visibly piqued. Katrina had her now. Doreen would tell Katrina whatever she wanted to know, and she wouldn't be so defensive when the questions came back around. "What did you want to know?"

"You say you're still friends with Vincent. Do you know if they were, possibly, um . . . Did they rekindle their friendship or possibly a romantic affair in the months before she was murdered? I just found her datebook a week ago and saw some strange entries. I'm trying to figure out what they mean."

Doreen raised her eyebrows and sniffed, twisting her lips to one side. "Well, I'm not really sure, but I do know they met for lunch. Quite often."

"Right. That's what the datebook said. Do you think it was really just lunch? Or something more?"

"Hmmm, how do I say this? I know that Vincey hadn't been happy in his marriage for quite some time. Ruth is a dear, but she can be kind of, well, cold. And your mother was lovely. So charming, smart, and, of course, beautiful. I think he was still in love with her, but she chose your father over him, and that was that."

"Or maybe it wasn't, if they were having lunch so often. She wrote 'lunch at the Grant' in her datebook. But the Grant is also a hotel, so I'm not really sure what to make of that."

Doreen laughed, shaking her head. "Me either, but most people who go for lunch would say, 'I'll meet you *at the Grill*,' not '*at the Grant*.' That Vincey. He's always up to something."

"How close are you two, you and Vincent, if you don't mind my asking?"

"We're very close. He's one of my best friends, actually. Patrick wasn't around much, and he didn't pay me all that much attention anyway, which over the years was fine by me. Please don't put this in the story, but I was lonely in my marriage, and, well, Vincey filled a hole in my life that needed to be filled."

Was that a sexual reference? She's not crass. Surely she wouldn't be so vulgar to come out and say it like that.

"So, you trust him?"

"Oh, yes, completely."

But I need to ask her directly, because it goes to Goode's theory about a possible motive to kill her husband.

"Are you two having an affair?"

Doreen frowned, like that was a crazy idea. "No, of course not. Like I said, Vincey is just a good friend. And so, for that matter, is his wife, Ruth."

Katrina figured that was as far as she could go without breaking Goode's trust or Doreen shutting down the interview.

"Back to your family. What was the relationship like between your son and his father? The suicide note he left made it sound like things got pretty bad," she said, casting out the bait.

"Well," Doreen said, pausing, as if she wasn't sure how much to say.

"Go on."

"I don't think my son killed himself," Doreen blurted out. "I know the sheriff said he did, but I know my son, and I had only just talked to him that morning. I know he and his dad were mad at each other, but I just . . . I don't think he would hang himself like that."

Yes! That's what I was hoping for.

"Have you thought about hiring an expert to do a second autopsy and reexamine the ME's ruling?"

"I can do that?"

"Yes, absolutely."

"Hmm. Maybe I should. Patrick isn't here to stop me now. He was so angry at the boy for being so reckless and bringing shame to our family, not to mention jeopardizing our entire nest egg, which is tied up in Vitaleron. I'm just scared that Patrick did something he shouldn't have. I almost don't want to know."

"Like what?"

"I probably should stop there."

"What if I don't attribute it to you? Why don't you tell me, and then we can discuss how I can investigate further. I should have mentioned this earlier, but I'm an investigative reporter."

"Okay. Well, Patrick had contacts who work inside the government, and I'm worried—angry, actually—that he may have done something to get Darren killed."

"Why do you think that?"

"Because Patrick had a string of visitors the day he died, one after the other. They started coming in the morning and continued in the afternoon. After we got the call that Darren was dead, there were even a couple after that. I was beside myself, but he didn't seem very upset. Anyway, one of them brought him that fake-lemon vodka. Awful stuff. I've never known him to drink anything like that. I went into his office a while later to ask if he wanted a sandwich, and there he was, collapsed on his desk."

It was difficult for Katrina not to tell Doreen about the toxicology tests and the drugs used to spike that vodka, but she'd promised Goode to keep that a secret. For now.

"So, what are you saying? I'm confused. It's possible that someone put something in that vodka, Doreen. Have you thought of that?"

"Yes, I have, because he didn't have any heart problems. Neither did anyone in his family. That's what scares me. I called Vincey as soon as I found out that Darren had died, and he said he had a feeling that something was iffy. And since Patrick was having all of those visitors, Vincey had said earlier that if something happened to Patrick, I should call 911 and report it immediately, before anything happened to me."

The way Goode described it, it was more like call the police as soon as he's dead. *I wonder if Goode heard it wrong or if he didn't describe it to me properly.*

"Wow, you must have been scared," Katrina said. "And you've been holding on to this this whole time? You poor thing."

"Yes, it's been a lot."

"Have you told the police any of this?"

"No, Vincey told me not to."

Katrina was hesitant to ask this next question, but she had to know. "Was Vincent one of the visitors that day?"

"Yes, why?"

"Do you know if he was the one who brought the vodka?"

"I asked him that, and he said it wasn't his, which didn't really answer the question. So, I don't actually know where it came from, and Vincey was pretty vague. I assumed he was trying to protect me, so I didn't press him. But I thought the timing between Patrick's and Darren's deaths was too close to be a coincidence, don't you think?"

"Yes, I would have to agree," Katrina said. She paused and took a deep breath, knowing she was about to ask Doreen to take a risk that might give her some protection but could also backfire and put her in danger. "So, let's figure out how I can get this into the paper without making you feel unsafe. Since you've got a security guard watching over you and your house, it could actually help if you were to tell me this on the record, because it could serve as a public warning to whoever brought the vodka that day that you—and the people who read my story—are onto them. Shining light on the truth could set you free."

"I don't know."

"What if I say, 'Patrick had a number of visitors in the morning and afternoon that day. One of them brought him a bottle of vodka, and he collapsed after drinking some of it.' That way you're not outing anyone by name, because you don't know who it was anyway."

"That might work, but let me think about it. I'll talk to Vincey and see what he says. It is his newspaper, after all."

"That's fine, but since he was one of the visitors, just keep in mind that he may have other motives that have nothing to do with your safety, Doreen. I know he's your friend, but he usually thinks about business first and people second."

"All right," Doreen said, standing up abruptly. "I've said more than I should have."

Shit, now I've gone too far. But I've got to take one last shot.

"There's one more thing. You'll want to sit down for this, and then I promise I'll go."

Glancing around furtively, Doreen sat down again, but she was perched on the edge of the chair, ready to jump up at any provocation.

"Vincent will probably tell you this anyway, but I wanted you to hear it from me first."

"Okay."

"I'm the one your son tried to kill at the Hotel Del. I had to be resuscitated by Detective Goode and paramedics. I almost died. You may have read my first-person story in the paper. I didn't want you to think I was hiding anything from you or had ulterior motives for coming here. I have more questions, and I'd like to talk some more, but I agree, I think we've covered enough for today."

A strange expression crept onto Doreen's face. That dark, blank look was back in her eyes, and her mouth was pursed into a tight line. Then the dam burst again. She reached out, grabbed Katrina, and hugged her.

"I'm so, so sorry," she said, tearing up again. "I did not raise him to be like that. He turned into a monster after being abused by his father. When he was younger, Patrick would take Darren into his room and close the door, and I heard horrible noises, like Patrick was throwing him and the furniture around. I was too scared to say anything. I tried questioning my husband once, and he threatened to do the same thing to me."

Katrina nodded. "I'm so sorry for what you went through all these years too. That's awful."

"To tell you the truth, I'm glad he's dead. I didn't know him or my son anymore. I just want to live in peace and take care of my garden."

"Maybe it's time to let the world know that," Katrina said, touching Doreen's forearm. "He can't hurt you anymore."

Doreen shrugged. "You might be right. But let me think about it. I'm really glad you came by today. I can see now that I needed to let all of this out."

"Me too. I'm going to write up this story this afternoon, so I can call you in a little while to see what you've decided, and we can work out language you're comfortable with. But remember what I said about Vincent. It might be better to talk this over with someone more neutral, someone who doesn't have anything to do with Vitaleron. This isn't about money or protecting the future of that damned sex drug that has obsessed so many rich men in La Jolla. This is about the truth, your safety, and your freedom."

Doreen nodded. With that, they both stood up and headed back to the front door, where they hugged goodbye.

"Thanks again, Doreen," Katrina said.

"I'm so sorry about what my son did to you, and to the Fontaines," Doreen said. "It's just unfathomable to me."

CHAPTER 23
KATRINA

Wednesday

The air felt electric as Katrina walked to her car, like she was vibrating. She felt good, on a natural high, but she also felt torn in different directions. It would take some time to process what Doreen had said. But she was sure of one thing: This story was going to break new ground in the case.

I've got some intel on my mom and Vincent now, too, so it's been a good day, and it's not over yet.

Back in the newsroom, Katrina was typing up the story when she saw Vincent's name on her caller ID. She wasn't surprised.

"Vincent. It's been a while," she said nonchalantly.

"I know, and I was enjoying the break, but Doreen tells me that you're trying to put her life in danger."

"Now, come on, she didn't say that."

"No, you're right. *I'm* saying that. You can't print that story."

Is Vincent just trying to use Doreen for his own ends, to protect himself by preventing me from printing what she told me? Or is he really trying to protect both of them? Either way, I have to get him to tell me the truth. The truth matters.

"What are you talking about? It's on the budget and it's going online in a few hours. You aren't going to make me pull the conflict of interest card again, are you?"

"Katrina, I called to talk some common sense into you. Not everything has to be an argument between us."

"Good. But Doreen is a grown woman, and she talked to me on the record. She said she wanted to talk to you about how to phrase the part about who brought over the vodka bottle that day, but that's the only thing we left hanging."

"That's the crucial part that has to be left out."

"But she didn't tell me about the vodka bottle, Vincent. I already knew about it, so that's not the part that's up in the air, only who brought it over. Do you know who that was?"

"Yes, I do."

"Okay, who was it? She said you told her that it wasn't yours, whatever that means. Are you saying it *was* yours?"

"No, I'm not. But I just finished telling you that you can't write about this."

"Well, I'm sorry, but I'm writing this story. It's newsworthy and it's important. That's what we do here."

"Don't get smart with me, young lady, or I'll have you fired."

"You tried that once and it didn't work, but we can run the gamut again if you insist. I'll go tell Linda that you're trying to protect one of your friends and that you put me into another conflict of interest by threatening my job. You know what she'll say."

"You're being selfish and insensitive. Doreen just lost her son and her husband. Are you trying to get her killed too?"

Was that a Freudian slip?

"Did you just say they were both killed? That's not what the sheriff says."

"I didn't mean to say 'too.' Are you trying to get her killed, is what I meant to say."

"No, I'm not. All I want to say in the story is that one of the people who came over to visit Patrick brought a bottle of vodka over that afternoon. Was it you? Is that what this is about? Because it's a fact, Vincent. He drank it, then he keeled over and died, so that raises some serious questions, doesn't it? Especially when you told Doreen to call the police as soon as he died. It was like you knew he was going to keel over."

"Is that what she told you? Because that's not true."

"Pretty much."

"I said to call the police right away if anything happened to Patrick that night. I didn't want her to be next."

"Aha. Thanks for the clarification. Did you want to tell me where you bought the bottle of vodka?"

"I *didn't* buy it, and I just finished telling you that you can't say I'm the one who brought it, because that's not true either. Someone handed it to me on my way in and said they forgot to leave it, so they asked if I would carry it inside, because it was actually a group gift."

Finally, the truth! At least part of it.

"But you can't use that either," he added.

"Vincent, you need to say something is off the record before you tell me. That was all on the record. And it's important. I'm using it. So, are you going to tell me who this 'someone' is?"

"No, I can't, and I won't. You're impossible. I'm calling Linda."

Click.

The last thing Katrina wanted was to get Doreen killed, but Vincent had let some of the truth slip out during their argument. What did he mean by a "group gift"? Was he admitting that Darren and Patrick McMurphy had reported to the cabal, a group that had them both killed? And was this a confirmation that Vincent was part of that group?

Goode had already told her his gut feeling that Vincent was involved in this somehow, and that there were other things he knew but couldn't tell her. He'd also described the McMurphys' deaths as suspicious, which would indicate that other people didn't want them talking to the authorities. But now she was confused about whether Darren had said it was his father or the whole cabal that had, essentially, ordered the hit on the Fontaines.

Either way, these deaths were all connected to people invested in Vitaleron, and the same killer or group of killers could have ordered a hit on her father, since he was one of the original cofounders, a little-known secret that Goode had discovered in the corporate formation paperwork and that she still hadn't disclosed to her editors for fear they'd take her off the story.

She and Goode had planned to investigate her parents' death together, but he'd gotten caught up in the McMurphy domino-death debacle and then Stone's hospitalization, so she'd proceeded on her own. She wished that Vincent hadn't hung up on her before she had a chance to ask him about those lunches with her mother, but that would probably be best saved for another conversation anyway.

Katrina was typing up the highlights of their conversation when her desk phone rang. It was Linda's executive assistant, Patricia. Since Linda had been promoted, she'd stopped paying visits to Katrina's desk, frothing at the mouth over a story, and telling Katrina to follow her to her office like a dog.

"Ms. Kelley would like to see you, Katrina," Patricia said.

"Okay, thanks. Be right there."

Ever since Linda had taken over for John Palmer, orders or feedback usually came through Katrina's direct supervisor, Joanne. The management hierarchy at the *Sun-Dispatch* felt like the military sometimes. But this session was different.

Katrina stood at the door of Linda's glass office until the editor motioned for her to come inside and sit down.

"Vincent just called, as I'm sure you expected," Linda said.

"Yes, and he's doing it again."

"What's that?"

"Creating a conflict of interest by trying to get between me and a source who wants to tell her story, and to fill in a missing part of the most important case in the city right now."

"Well, I don't know that it's *the* most important case in the city."

Is Linda really trying to put me in my place right now? Or is she scared that what Vincent is saying is right, that Doreen could get hurt? Or, as the paper's executive editor now, is she trying to protect Vincent, her job, and the paper's reputation? If it's the latter, I know he's her boss, and he will decide if she ultimately keeps her job, but I thought we were past all that after the last time he tried—and failed—to compromise me.

"I do. Doreen McMurphy told me some crucial details that she wouldn't even tell the police, and it's not our job, or Vincent's, to protect her if she wants to give us her perspective. He's an old friend of hers, and it sounds to me like he's trying to manipulate her for his own agenda, which I'm not really clear about at this point. But it sounds like he's in the middle of something pretty shady, so that's *his* personal business, not the paper's."

"We don't want to get anyone killed, Katrina."

"No, but it was her decision, and she willingly told me these things on the record today. I think he's trying to talk her out of it to protect himself, and that's not right."

"You can't say that he was the one who brought the bottle of vodka over or that it was from a group of friends."

"Why not?"

"Because that would implicate him in a possible murder and open up a whole can of liabilities."

"It's getting conflated now anyway, but he didn't say that was off the record until he'd already said it."

"I just explained why we're going to let him have that one. You know, he's not very good at watching what he says to you. It's almost like he thinks of you as one of his children. You two have a history now, and you seem to get under his skin very easily. He did try to hire you to work as his own private investigator, so I know he respects you, but just remember that he pays our salaries."

This isn't a good situation, but at least it's not as bad as my last paper.

The *Record* was also family owned, and stories were quietly killed if reporters unknowingly wrote a negative article about someone on the publisher's secret list of friends and sacred cows. Readers, however, had no way of knowing this, or that internal political pressures at a newspaper—to protect or criticize certain people—could often be more difficult to deal with than those that arose in the coverage of elected officials.

"Okay, I'm not supposed to tell anyone this, because I was told in strict confidence, but I know for a fact that that bottle of lemon-infused vodka was spiked with narcotics. It was the same lethal cocktail that killed my brother, Franny, who allegedly overdosed, so I'm positive that this was no ordinary heart attack. I always said Franny was murdered, and now I know I was right. I didn't tell Vincent that, and you can't, either, or I'll lose my source at the PD. I don't think anyone else in the department even knows this yet."

Linda's face was one long, open mouth as she stared at Katrina. "Wait, whaaat?" she asked. Then, after a lengthy pause, added, "Shit, that's not good."

"Now you know why it's important to say that someone brought over that bottle of vodka and that Patrick keeled over and died sometime after drinking it. I guess he didn't tell you that I already knew about the vodka from another source, so Vincent can't keep that out of the story, because Doreen isn't the one who told me about it in the first place."

"Oh. I see what you're saying. Who told you about the vodka?"

"Doreen confirmed it, but originally it was Detective Goode. He told me off the record, and more as a personal favor because he knows I didn't believe my brother killed himself. Franny hated lemons, so lemon-infused vodka was not something he'd choose to drink. Ironically, Doreen said the same thing about Patrick."

"So, we can say there was a bottle of vodka that someone brought over that afternoon, and we know he drank some before he died."

"Yes, that's all I was trying to write in the first place. Although we're losing the 'group gift' part of it."

"Right. You can use all but that detail—just don't attribute it to anyone, and see if you can get your detective to either go on the record or let you print the part about what drugs were in the bottle as soon as you can. That's huge."

"I know. That was my plan. There's a lot going on behind the scenes right now that I can't talk about, mostly because I don't know enough, but I'm not going to get it for this story tonight."

"Still, incredible reporting, Katrina. Well done. I'll keep that to myself for now, and I won't mention it to Vincent. You're right, we don't know what he's gotten himself mixed up with, but it doesn't sound good," she said, letting out a long sigh. "This new job isn't any easier than my old one, you know."

"I'll bet. Thanks, Linda. We need to watch Vincent moving forward. The police want to talk to him again. You know he's still facing obstruction and evidence-tampering charges, right?"

"Yes, although I heard his lawyer got them down to misdemeanors. I'm not surprised to hear about this vodka, actually, and it makes me concerned about the future of our newspaper. I should probably talk to our lawyers."

"No, please don't, because then we'll have to explain all of this, which we can't. Not yet."

"Okay, Katrina. I'll stand by and wait for the word. I can already see that this is going to get very messy."

Other than that blip of internal politics, Joanne and Linda loved the story. They barely touched what Katrina wrote, which was nice. They were starting to trust her.

Katrina tried calling Goode to give him a heads-up about the story and her call with Vincent, but he didn't answer. She figured he must still be at the hospital with Stone.

I hope he's not mad at me when he reads this, but this story will help his investigation. As long as he can get past the ego bruising that I was able to pull this juicy stuff out of Doreen and he wasn't. He should thank me.

The story went online at eight o'clock, and within ninety minutes it racked up more clicks than her first-person column about her death threats and smashed car window. Her strategy to grow a following with her personal-narrative touch was not only working, it was earning her points with management. The question was, how would her rock-wielding stalkers feel about it?

CHAPTER 24
GOODE

When Katrina called Goode that evening, he didn't pick up because he and Kelly were at Stone's bedside. It was pretty late once he got home and listened to her message, by which time her story was already online.

He read it in bed, propped up on a couple of pillows, hoping that a nightcap of warmed Courvoisier would take the edge off so he could fall asleep. It had been a long day of worrying about his buddy.

But even after what was supposed to be a comforting drink, it gnawed at him that Katrina had proved once again that she could pull the very facts out of a witness/suspect that he'd tried and failed to get himself. This hurt mostly because Doreen would've died if he hadn't given her a snort of naloxone, and yet she still wouldn't tell him what he needed to know, even though the details could save her life. How did Katrina win her trust and extract such intimate personal details? Was it easier for a distraught woman to open up to another woman, or was it Katrina and her wily ways?

Like I told Stone, Katrina is damn good. She's helping us do our job, so does it really matter how we get there? I'd like to think it doesn't, if I could just get out of my own way. The good thing is that this will put pressure on the chief to let me do my job and expose those crap autopsy findings for what they are.

Goode was aware that Katrina didn't have to wait for his permission to interview Doreen, yet part of him was still hurt, and a little annoyed, that she'd gone ahead when he'd asked her not to.

This is a pure technicality, because Stone gave the go-ahead, even if she didn't know that. If you want to be with her, you'd better get used to this. She is her own woman, which means that she's not clingy or needy, and you actually like *that, remember?*

Rolling over, he turned out the light, but tossed and turned for a while before he finally fell asleep.

Goode returned to the station the next morning, but he was still too distracted by Stone's health problems to focus on the job. The whole episode made him realize how much he cared for his buddy and that he needed to show that love while Stone was still around to appreciate it.

It also made Goode realize that no matter how indifferent his sister, Maureen, seemed to his repeated breakfast invitations, he had to keep trying. Even if she said she was busy hanging with her loser coworkers from the steak house, he knew she cared about him. But family was family and shouldn't be taken for granted.

He tried calling her again as he stared at the photo of the two of them with their surfboards that hung in his cubicle. Still no answer. So, he left her another message.

"Hey, Maureen, it's me. Just checking in again. Is everything okay? You know I worry when you don't call me back. Stone is in the hospital, and I really want to talk to you. I feel like I need my family more than ever right now."

When Maureen finally called back, it was after her shift at 12:30 a.m. and he was asleep. She said she was on the freeway, heading to Malibu for some night surfing. Alone. No wonder he worried. But his phone was in airplane mode, so he didn't get her message until the next morning:

"Hey, bro. I'm fine, everything is good," she said. "Sorry to hear about Stone. That sucks. But we can meet for breakfast any time after eleven. I'm usually at that outdoor café on Cass Street. Miss you too. Ciao."

As he listened to her voicemail, he wondered about her grasp on reality. Didn't she stop to think that he had a real job and that eleven o'clock was in the middle of his workday? She was smart, but sometimes she acted like a surfer chick with water on the brain.

Taking a break for lunch, Goode arrived at the hospital just in time for the celebratory news that Stone was ready to be released—two days after his collapse. With plenty of rest, a new diet, more regular exercise, and a few drugs to get him through the transition period, Dr. Costello said he should be able to return to work after his two-week leave.

"But you really need to keep that stress level down," she told Stone. "You can't change events, but you can change the way you react to events." Seeing his bemused expression, she added, "I know that's easier said than done, but you're going to have to try. No offense, but I don't want to see you back here."

"None taken," Stone said, laughing. "The feeling's mutual. I'm happy to be going home."

Stone was still wobbly on his feet as Goode and Kelly each took one arm and made sure he didn't slip on his way into the Stone family's SUV, into their house, and onto the couch, where he planned to spend his vacay watching sports and movies on the new flat-screen TV that Kelly had bought as a surprise welcome-home-get-well-soon gift.

Goode really wanted to discuss Katrina's story about Doreen, but he didn't mention it because he and Kelly were trying to keep Stone's mind off work. He would only do so if Stone brought it up or if he got to the point where he couldn't hold his tongue another minute.

Once Stone was safely ensconced with a pharmacy of meds on the coffee table next to him, Goode felt like he could finally get his mind back on the job. The past few days had seemed like he was driving through a long, hazy tunnel.

Back at his desk with a latte, Goode pulled out his latest to-do list to reorient himself as he flipped through the same case file of investigative reports that Stone had sent to the chief right before his hospitalization. Goode believed this file was the trigger for the chief's outburst, because Baxter had derisively referred to the "so-called cabal" that had been mentioned throughout the reports. Goode wondered if he didn't like the reference because he didn't know what it meant, if it seemed offensive or stupid to him, or if he was simply trying to convince Stone that the group didn't exist to protect his own ass.

The chief could be involved with the cabal, as a member or a mercenary. In fact, he *could be the mole inside the PD.*

With that epiphany in mind, Goode jotted down a few new tasks, in no particular order, that had been flitting around his brain.

First, to catch up with Artie Hayes to see if the in-house toxicology results were in for Patrick McMurphy, and if they differed from the private lab's, which could confirm whether Thompson was a mole as well.

Second, to track down Darla Johansen, the congressman's fiancée, and get her to compile the list of cabal leaders as promised.

Third was a higher priority, and that was to ask Vincent about the links Goode had identified between him and his dead friends and associates, to see if he could offer an explanation that pointed toward innocence. Goode was skeptical.

But before he had a chance to do anything, Artie called.

"I was just about to call you," Goode said.

"I got a notification that Patrick McMurphy's tox results are in," Artie said. "But when I checked the computer, they were 'pending review.' I tried to get access to them, but I was locked out, which is unusual. Seems like someone doesn't want me to see what he's doing."

"Is Thompson back from his two-week leave?"

"Yeah, this morning, as a matter of fact, so I assume he's the one behind this. I'll find out as soon as I can get back in there."

"Okay, keep me posted. What do we do if the results don't match the outside lab's?"

"I'm already assuming they won't. I'll go chat with my friend in the tox lab. There's a reason I bring her pan dulce every Friday. These situations don't happen often, but when they do, she gets me the info I need."

"Awesome."

"One other curious thing."

"Yeah, what's that?"

"Doreen McMurphy called to say that she's commissioning outside autopsies for both her son and husband, and she'll call us with the name of the pathologist as soon as she hires one. I didn't see that coming."

"No, me either. That will definitely force this charade out into the light."

Who advised her to do that? That would counter the theory that she had something to do with Patrick's death, and if Vincent was the one who delivered the spiked vodka, then it wouldn't be coming from him. It's definitely time to pay him a visit.

CHAPTER 25
GOODE

Friday

Catching Vincent Battrelle by surprise had worked well the last time, when Goode showed up at his palatial home on Whale Watch Way. But because he'd waited until 7:00 p.m., Vincent was already pretty sloshed, so, Goode decided to try to catch him during the day this time.

It was straight up noon, and Vincent answered his cell on the third ring. Hearing a man yell "Fore!" in the background, Goode figured he was on the green at Torrey Pines, where he claimed to have spent the afternoon that the Fontaines were murdered.

"Detective Goode," Vincent said. "What can I do for you?"

"We need to talk, Mr. Battrelle. How soon can we meet?"

"I'm only on the ninth hole right now. Can't this wait until Monday?"

"No, I'm sorry, it can't. I can meet you at the Lodge at Torrey Pines in a couple of hours since it sounds like you're already there."

"I am, but I've got a lot of money riding on this round, Detective. Golf might not seem important to you, but that's because you don't play, and you live on a public wage," Vincent said, chuckling. "What's this about, anyway? I thought you'd wrapped up the Fontaine case."

"No, not at all. We'll talk about it at the Lodge. I'll see you at two o'clock."

Goode was sipping his Arnold Palmer for a good twenty-five minutes before Vincent strolled into the bar, passive-aggressively late for their meeting. He didn't apologize, because he'd already made it clear that this was supremely inconvenient. But his face was pale, and he looked stressed, even after a relaxing sunny day on the golf course, which made Goode feel better.

"Mr. Battrelle," he said. "Fair warning: Next time you keep me waiting, I'll call your attorney instead and have him bring you down to the station."

"I thought you wanted to talk, Detective, not provoke me," Vincent said, flashing him a disingenuous smile as he slid onto the adjacent stool. "Besides, I told you I had money on this round, and I had to cut out early as it was. Very unsportsmanlike. What more is there to discuss?"

"Our investigation is still open and active, and you are still very much in our sights, because your name keeps popping up in all the wrong places."

Vincent looked at Goode with a mockingly bewildered expression. "I don't know what you're talking about. I already told you what happened that night at Simon's house," he said, as if he didn't give a damn about his dead friend and fellow investor. Goode also took it as a poke at him and his authority.

You'd better start taking me seriously, old man, or we're going to have a problem. And, if you don't stop turning my crank, I'm going to pop you one.

Vincent nodded at the bartender, who poured him a whiskey on the rocks and set it down on a coaster in front of him. "Thanks, Freddy. Put that on my tab, would you?

"So, let's get to it, then," he said, turning toward Goode. "What's so important that couldn't wait?"

"I understand you came to see Patrick McMurphy shortly before he died," Goode said, staring Vincent right in the eye.

"Yes, I did. So what? You're going to accuse me of giving him a heart attack now?"

"Well, that depends. Did you bring him a bottle of lemon-infused vodka?"

If a veiled expression was a sign of guilt, then Vincent was guilty. He stared back at Goode with a piercing glare through hooded eyes. "I don't drink that nonsense, and he didn't like it either," he said.

"That's not what I asked. Did you bring him a bottle of it that afternoon?" He could see that Vincent didn't want to answer, but knew that Goode wasn't going to let up. "Well, did you?"

"Yes and no. I carried it in for someone who said they'd forgotten to leave it. It was supposed to be a group gift to lighten the mood."

"Kind of odd timing, considering his son had allegedly just killed himself. And who was that someone?"

"I'd rather not say."

"Why's that?"

"Because since you're asking, there must be an issue with it, and I don't want to get mixed up in anything."

"Too late. If you don't tell me who it was, I'll have to take you downtown and ask you in a more formal setting."

"I'm not going to tell you even if you drag me downtown."

"Okay, so then what group was this gift from?"

"Some of Patrick's friends and business associates."

Sounds like the cabal to me.

"I'm going to need you to name names."

"And I'm going to have to take the Fifth, Detective. I'm not going to answer anything more about the bottle."

"But you're admitting that you were the bagman?"

"I wouldn't call it that, but yes, I was the one who delivered it, as a favor to a friend. That's all I'm going to say."

"So why would you tell Doreen to call the police as soon as Patrick died? It was like you both knew he was going to die after he drank it."

Goode could see the sweat beading on Vincent's upper lip as he downed his whiskey and set his gaze on the TV above them. "I didn't say that. I said that she should call the police if anything happened to Patrick, because I was concerned for her well-being. Neither one of us knew he was going to die."

"I was in the bathroom, and I overheard her talking to you on the phone, Vincent. Time to fess up. This is serious."

"I've already told you what I know. If that's all you've got, then I'm going to get back to what's left of my game," Vincent said, getting up to leave.

"Not so fast. I'm not done," Goode said, grabbing his forearm. "I've got more questions."

"Don't you touch me. Ever," Vincent growled, jerking his arm free. "I'm not going to answer anything more without an attorney present. You've harassed me enough."

Going in for the coup de grâce, Goode leaned over and asked quietly, "So, you were aware that the bottle was spiked, right?"

But this time he didn't get the reaction he was hoping for. Vincent kept his mouth tight and his expression blank as he cracked his neck from side to side like a thug. Then he turned and headed for the door that led back to the course.

"Call my lawyer," he said over his shoulder. "And make an appointment next time."

Stonewalled. I can't push any harder or the chief will know that I'm not standing down as ordered.

Mulling Vincent's nonanswers and defensive responses, Goode came up with more follow-up questions that he hadn't gotten to ask. Once Patrick was arrested, he couldn't have bailed out, because judges didn't release suspects charged with murder or conspiracy to commit murder. So, did he know he was on his way to jail and drink the vodka, knowing it was spiked? Like a Russian spy who takes a cyanide pill after he's been captured so he can't be tortured or give his captors any information? Or was he just pissed off and decided to get drunk? Maybe everyone *but* him knew the bottle was spiked.

Either way, Goode needed the names of these "friends and business associates." But even if Vincent had named names, Goode probably wouldn't have known who they were anyway. He needed Darla Johansen to provide context.

No time like the present.

Opening the Notes folder on his phone, he punched in her number and arranged to meet her at Jose's Courtroom on Prospect Street in the Village, which was about fifteen minutes away.

CHAPTER 26
GOODE

Friday

Jose's was packed and loud as usual on a Friday evening, when pitchers of cheap margaritas were flowing, sports events were playing on TVs hung around the bar, and tables were stacked with oversize hot plates of traditional Mexican entrées and bottomless baskets of salty chips and salsa.

Still reeling from his frustrating meeting with Vincent, Goode couldn't help but call Stone to vent about it. Of course, that only made Stone want to join him at Jose's, or at least have Goode bring him some leftovers. But Goode had to draw the line.

"You know what the doctor said: no chips, no cheese, no sour cream. No refried beans either," he said, sitting in a booth in the back, where he was waiting for Darla. "You also know you can't leave the couch, brother. No beef tacos and no work talk-o's."

"Oh, ha ha. You sound like Mrs. Robertson from La Jolla Elementary. You're not going to let me do anything fun, are you?"

"Not right now, I'm not. Dr. Costello told me to keep an eye on you, so that's what I'm doing. For you, Kelly, and your three little weasels."

"Okay, call me when you're done with Darla. Unless you do something I don't want to know about. If you won't tell me, I'll know you did something you shouldn't have. Geez," Stone said, pausing. "I don't see how I get information no matter how this goes."

"Probably for the best."

"Yeah, well, call me anyway. You can pretend I'm Katrina and only give me the fat around the meat."

"Let's see how it goes."

"You're enjoying all this power, aren't you?"

"Yes, and it's going to my head. Gotta go. She just walked in."

Goode stood up and motioned to Darla, who was looking around for him. A tall and pretty blonde, Darla may have resembled a Barbie doll, but she was no dummy. Although she'd been filling in for the receptionist at Vitaleron when he met her, he later learned that she had a chemistry degree, helped with the company's IT, and managed the investors' financial contributions and campaign donations. She also administered doses of the sex drug to human trial participants as part of the company's application for FDA approval. But she'd been fired after getting caught on security cameras—which were secretly installed in the lab after the Fontaines' deaths—stealing doses of the drug.

Wearing a wraparound sundress, Darla was showing plenty of cleavage. Maybe she thought that would distract him, not knowing that he was all business and certainly not about to fall prey to another manipulative woman, no matter how attractive she was. That's what his ex-wife had taught him.

Goode had planned to do a formal sit-down with Darla, but that was before the chief's recent stand-down order. So, he had no choice but to take a more casual approach to see what she would offer willingly.

Since her attempts at making an immunity deal with the FBI had fallen apart, she was now a free agent. At least until the SDPD and the FBI could decide which of them was going to file charges and arrest her.

Gesturing for her to sit across from him, Goode settled back into the booth, but she seemed nervous, shifting around on the seat.

"What are you drinking?" she asked, eyeing his iced tea and lemonade.

"Arnold Palmer," he said.

"I'm going to have a margarita. You aren't going to arrest me tonight, are you?" she said, laughing a little too loud.

She's a little jumpy.

"I don't have a warrant in hand, if that's what you're asking," he said, giving her his slow Joe Cool smile, as Stone liked to call it.

"Okay, awesome."

Leaning back with her chest out, she pulled her hair up and into a bun to expose her long neck. Either Darla was out of practice with her seductress act, or she wrongly assumed that he liked whatever Brandon Winchester liked.

He noticed she was still waving around her ginormous yellow diamond ring, which he now knew Winchester had given her to mark their engagement.

"So, you two are still together?" he asked. "You know he's going away for a long time, right?"

"He's out on bail until he goes to trial and while he appeals any conviction, so he doesn't seem too worried. We've done some research, and political corruption convictions are pretty rare. Even Senator John Edwards from North Carolina got off."

"I wouldn't be so sure. Remember Randy Duke Cunningham, our local favorite who went to prison? And this is not just a simple corruption case. The bribery charge is tied up with a conspiracy to commit two murders and to attempt a third."

"You guys will never make that stick, though," she said. "Not without my help. Like I told you before, I'm not going to give you dirt on him. That's part of the deal, or there is no deal."

"Well, the way I hear it, that already killed your deal, so I assure you that charges will be coming your way. It's just a matter of time."

Darla shrugged. "Whatever. That just means I can make one with you right now. I couldn't talk to you before because I was negotiating with the feds." She cocked her head to one side, trying a different sex kitten tactic. "So, what did you want to ask me?"

"Isn't he still married?" Goode asked.

"Really? That's your opening question?" Darla shook her head and rolled her eyes. "Yes, technically, but his wife is much more amenable to divorce now. She thought he'd get tired of me, but after everything came out in the newspaper, she filed her own papers, so it's all good. Except for Brandon, of course, because she has more leverage for all the property now. And also the money he had hidden in the Caymans with Alex Battrelle. He'll have to split that with her since Alex was arrested too. So much for our luxury honeymoon in Greece."

"You have to get married first."

"That's the plan. That way no one can force me to testify against him either."

The waitress brought over a basket of chips and took Darla's drink order. "Margarita, rocks, with salt," she said. "And can I get a Cuervo Gold shot on the side?"

"I'll have another one of these," Goode said, pointing to his glass.

"You're going to make me drink alone?"

"Unlike you, I still have a job," he said. "And I'm working right now."

"You're no fun. Are you sure? Not even one?"

"I don't need to drink to have fun. Trust me."

Darla made a sad, pouty face. Maybe she thought she could get him to compromise himself if he had a couple of drinks. That seemed to be the go-to ploy in her wheelhouse based on Katrina's description of their meeting at the Del. Darla didn't seem to realize this was her last chance to offer him some information, and if she didn't start taking it seriously, she would be in handcuffs the next time they met.

"Did you bring me a list of the cabal members, or at least the leaders, like I asked? That would be a good place to start," he said.

"I thought we should talk first."

"No, Miss Johansen, you need to bring something to the table first. That's what you offered for us to even have this meeting."

Don't think I'm buying you drinks for nothing, missy.

"I'll give you information if you give me a deal."

"And I can't give you a deal unless you give me information. Are you a slow learner, Miss Johansen?"

"Oh, all right. I'll give you some of the names I know, but I'm not handing you a list in my handwriting."

"You could have typed one up."

Darla raised her eyebrows and shrugged again. "Same difference."

"So, shoot. I'll make a list on my phone."

The waitress brought the drinks, which gave Darla an excuse to try another seductress trick—provocatively licking the salt from her glass. She downed the shot, sucked the lime, then licked a chip and ate it.

Jesus, woman. Enough with the licking and sucking already.

"I'm waiting."

She giggled as she chewed her chip.

"You think this is funny?" he asked. "I can go back to the station right now and draft an arrest warrant for conspiracy to commit murder, theft of intellectual property, conspiracy to commit fraud, and whatever other charges we've got lying around."

"Fine," she said, and rattled off a dozen names as he scrambled to type them into his phone with his index finger. A few of them sounded vaguely familiar, because he'd seen or heard them in the news—until she got to Lawrence Rayburn.

"Wait, back up," he said. "Lawrence Rayburn?"

"Yeah, do you know him?"

"That's the mayor's chief of staff. I thought these were all rich guys who were on the outside, working the elected officials with their power, money, and influence."

"He's one of their inside guys," she said.

"One of them?"

"Yeah, I'm not going to give you everyone right off the bat. I need my deal in writing first."

"I need some clarification here. Is he a rich guy or an inside guy?"

"Both. He's kind of a double agent."

"If he's rich, what's he doing working at City Hall? He was legal counsel at the PD before moving over there."

"What's your point? Don't you know who his father is?"

"No, who?"

"I mentioned him already. Elmore Rayburn."

"Why does that name sound familiar?"

"After Elmore Rayburn got tired of working for SBOD, the defense contractor, he kept his shares but branched out to serve his other interests. He joined the San Diego Padres as president, left to form a real estate development company with the club owner, then broke away again to form his own. It's a whole Rayburn family enterprise now. They've been building luxury hotel resorts and developing top-secret spy technology ever since. The family is smart, powerful, and loaded. All his kids work for him but Lawrence, who's always been a bit 'different' and went the public service route. But in the end, those rich boys are all the same. Always fighting with their siblings for Daddy's attention and approval."

"I've heard that story before."

"Right, so have I, like the Trumps and the Murdochs."

"I was going to say the Battrelles and the McMurphys. They're part of the cabal, right?"

"I don't think Vincent is an official member. Patrick McMurphy was. Darren was not. I think Vincent is more of an honorary member, like an FOTC, Friend of the Cabal. He probably could be if he wanted, but he didn't take the blood oath. From what I understand, Vincent is aware of what they're doing, but because he never joined, he has no voting power, which gives him plausible deniability. His son Alex hasn't joined either. He just handles cabal members' funny money in the Caymans, and his other son Michael doesn't have the stomach for it. Besides, the Battrelles have enough power from running Vitaleron and owning the newspaper that they don't need to get their hands dirty, if you know what I mean."

"When you shoot your dead business partner in the head like Vincent did, I'd say you were still getting your hands dirty."

"Yeah, well, I'm sure that was done in a panic. Michael was not in on the murders, and Vincent is not a stupid man. Nor is he incapable of letting others do the scut work so he doesn't have to."

But now that Darren and Patrick McMurphy were gone, she said, they were no longer battling the Battrelles for control of Vitaleron. Vincent was now the board chairman, and his younger son, Michael, had taken over the company's day-to-day operations. That meant Vitaleron was now completely under the Battrelle family's control, all of which were key developments in terms of motive for killing the McMurphys, or at least supporting the idea of putting out a hit on them.

"So, you wouldn't consider Vincent a leader of the cabal, even unofficially?" he asked.

"That's not how it works."

"Okay, so how does it work?"

"There's a group of five leaders who are the shot callers, known as the Circle of Five. The next tier is the caucus. Below them are the soldiers, although they all see themselves as kings in their own right. But it's hierarchical, largely according to time as a member, age, wealth, and stature in the community. Most of them are corporate businessmen—landowners, developers, investment executives—but some are lawyers and surgeons. They do super secret man-club activities like going to sex parties with hot young girls. They also have to take a blood oath to join, so it's basically like *Fight Club*. Whatever the cabal does stays within the cabal. Or there are serious repercussions."

"How do you know all of this?"

"I can't say."

"Can't or won't?"

"Both."

"So, we can find all these people on your fiancé's campaign donation statements?"

"I told you I'm not going to talk about Brandon."

"We're talking about public documents."

"Then put it in another context."

"Okay, where else can I find a list of the full cabal membership?"

"I believe they're all Vitaleron investors. You seized the company's computers, right?"

"Yes."

"I managed the investor list for the board so we could keep track of who had given how much and when, which is an SEC reporting requirement. I was constantly updating it as investors jostled for position, trying to get a board seat. Mostly, they wanted to get their hands on that drug without waiting for it to go to market. I know that Dr. Fontaine and the board were planning to market it as a way to maintain long-term relationships, and to Christian conservatives in particular, but some of the older men I know are already fantasizing about landing younger girlfriends or prettier wives. I'd be rich now if I'd sold the stuff I used personally—for research purposes, of course. You can ask Dallas Fairchild, our senior biochemist. Now that Dr. Fontaine is gone, the board has put him in charge of getting this drug to market as quickly as possible."

"But legally, I hope. And I already have talked to Dallas. He's the one who had those cameras installed that caught your ass stealing the drug without permission."

"Well, that was his perspective. Since I managed the human trials, I added myself as a participant. He's not going to be able to prove otherwise."

"I'm sure that's not cool under FDA testing protocols."

"But you don't really know that, do you?"

"So, are all the Vitaleron investors members of this cabal?"

"No."

"Then the two groups are not mutually exclusive. I need a real list. A short list of cabal members."

"I can't give you that."

"Why not?"

"Why do you think?" Darla asked.

"I don't know."

"I thought you were a detective," Darla said, leaning over and lowering her voice. "Do you think I have a death wish? I went for a deal with the FBI because I thought they would protect me. But it seems that they're more interested in putting Brandon in prison. When I refused to budge on that, they left me hanging out to dry."

Darla ordered a second margarita even though she was already tipsy, but Goode quickly paid the bill and stood up to leave before things got any more awkward, snagging a few chips for the road.

"I've got to go," he said. "Thanks for these names. I'll be in touch once I find that list of Vitaleron investors. Maybe you can help me whittle it down."

Prospect Street was festive at night during the holidays, with snockered revelers straggling from one bar to the next under the brightly colored lights. There were no parking spots near Jose's, so Goode had had to park his Explorer in one of the bank building lots on Ivanhoe, a few blocks away.

Artie Hayes called on the hike back. "Hey, buddy, you have news for me?" Goode asked.

"I finally got into Patrick McMurphy's file, and it's just like we thought. The tox results state that his blood was normal, no sign of narcotics, which makes no sense, because he definitely made a dent in that bottle, so there's no way he didn't die from the drugs that the private lab found."

"Right," Goode said. "Could you tell who last signed off on the file?"

"Yeah, it was Thompson. He has nothing to do with the toxicology lab and has no reason to mess with the file, but he's one of the few people in the office with administrative powers to edit these forms. So, I'll see if I can find a paper report of the original that proves he changed the results."

"What about your girl in the lab?"

"That's why I'm calling. I'm taking her out for a drink. She's the one who ran the tox screen and can tell us whether the drugs showed up in his system. You want to come? If I tell her she can trust you, maybe she'll agree to go on the record."

"Sounds good. Where?"

"I'm purposely taking her to a dive where no one will see us. I'll meet you at the Alibi in Hillcrest. Thirty minutes?"

"Perfect."

Parking in Hillcrest was even worse than in the Village, forcing Goode to cruise up and down the residential streets south of University Avenue to find a spot big enough for his Explorer.

By the time he walked into the dark little bar, Artie was sitting in a back-corner booth with a young Latina, drinking tequila shots. The place was crowded with college students, older single men, and groups of gay men of various ages, which was typical for a Friday night in Hillcrest.

"Goode!" Artie called out. "Over here."

"*Buenas noches*," Goode said, sliding into the booth next to his buddy so they were both facing the young woman.

"*Buenas noches*," Artie replied. "This is Rosa Valdez, my colleague who works in the toxicology lab. Rosa, this is Ken Goode. He's a homicide detective I work with on a lot of cases. Great guy. Funny as hell."

Artie slid a tequila shot over to Goode, who took one look at it, shrugged, and said, "Okay, just one. But then I'm switching to beer. It's been a long week, and I've still got work to do this weekend."

They made small talk to make Rosa feel comfortable with Goode before Artie opened the door.

"So, Rosa and I were talking about the Patrick McMurphy case," Artie said.

"Uh-huh."

"Rosa is concerned because she said she ran the tox screen on his blood and found Xanax, OxyContin, Ambien, Adderall, and a high alcohol content. But I was telling her that I just looked at the investigative report and it only mentioned the alcohol, stating that his blood was otherwise normal. So, she's not really sure how that happened, because that's not what she entered into the computer yesterday."

"Rosa, did you make a copy or take notes on your results before entering them into the system?" Goode asked.

"Of course. I always write in my notebook as I'm going along, and I use my notes to type the narrative into the system. Then afterward, I print out a copy for my files, because this has happened before."

"What's happened before?"

"Sometimes there are weird changes that don't match my work. I usually don't say anything if they're minor. But this time it's such a high-profile case, and this was a big change. I was going to tell someone even before Artie asked me about it this afternoon."

"Well, now you don't have to. If it's all right with you, we'll make copies of your notes and your paper file copy, and most importantly, don't tell anyone," Goode said. "This is part of a bigger case we're working on. If you give me your notebook, I can make you a copy, but that way I'll have your original notations as evidence that no one can question."

Goode could see in Rosa's eyes that she was on board. She was only in her mid-twenties, but she was already a pro. Her whole demeanor said she was the best kind of nerdy good girl he could hope for, the type who'd studied hard in her college chemistry classes to land an internship at the ME's office as a stepping stone to the dream job she now had, as a county toxicologist. She believed in fighting crime, getting the bad guys, and doing the right thing. And although she was a little scared, she was excited to get involved in something bigger.

"I'm not going to get fired, am I?" she asked.

"Not if I have anything to say about it," Artie said. "And you can trust Goode. He's the best."

Rosa nodded and smiled. "Okay," she said. "Let's go."

Goode and Artie looked at each other and laughed.

"Okay!" Goode said. "No time like the present. You never know who might be going through your desk as we speak. I'll meet you guys at the morgue."

"Back door it," Artie said. "No security cameras."

"Gotcha."

CHAPTER 27
GOODE

Friday

An hour later, Goode left the ME's office with a manila envelope containing Rosa's notebook and printed copies of the toxicology report as it was originally entered, as well as a printout of the fraudulent altered aversion with Clarence Thompson's initials on the bottom.

Artie also told him that Doreen McMurphy's gifted Xanax pills had tested positive for fentanyl, but they had no distinctive markings that would allow their origins to be traced.

She's lucky she took one while I was nearby, or she'd be dead right now.

"Thanks. I'm hoping I can turn that into an attempted murder charge down the road, so can you email those results to me?"

"Sure thing."

On the drive home, Goode's stomach churned. He felt like he needed to get some food into his stomach to soak up the alcohol, which he told himself he'd consumed as part of his job. His and Artie's plan to recruit the young woman's help had been successful, after all, so that was a call to celebrate as well.

I deserved those drinks as a way to cap my productive, albeit somewhat frustrating, day. The cabal corruption ring is finally taking shape, and the best part is that the chief and that flunky in the mayor's office are none the wiser.

He'd planned to sign into the CAIR system on his laptop and dig into the Double-Judge case file that night, but his brain was already on overload, the tequila shot and beer notwithstanding. So, he made himself a ham and cheese sandwich and called Katrina instead.

"Hey, Surfer Man, I was about to call you," she said. "We must be having a mind meld."

"That or something else," he said, picturing something more physical.

"You and your oversexed brain."

"Just didn't want you to think I'd forgotten."

"No worries there. So, what's up? What are you going to tell me off the record tonight that I can't use?"

"Let's just say what I could tell you would make a week's worth of stories, but I'm only going to give you highlights, and even then, you can't print any of it."

"As usual."

"First, good story about Doreen. It was helpful when I talked to Vincent today. He's definitely in this deeper than we know, but he's one treacherously elusive Teflon dude. I can't ever get him to implicate himself in a way that I can grab on to."

"I know, same here. But I can tell that he's very nervous about that vodka bottle. After telling me that I couldn't write about its existence, he let it slip that he carried it in for a friend as a group gift. Then he called Linda Kelley, our top editor, and tried to convince her not to let me mention it in my story. Luckily, I fought back and won, at least in part."

"He pretty much told me the same thing today, but in a more cagey way. He denied knowing Patrick would die after he drank it, though."

"Are you sure of what he said in the first place? You did only hear one side of the conversation. He said he told Doreen to call the police 'if anything happened' to Patrick, which is not nearly as incriminating."

"True. That's the line he gave me too. So, I don't know, maybe I conflated or jumped to conclusions, because based on what Doreen told you, it doesn't sound like *she* knew Patrick was going to die. She also told the ME's office that she's going to have a second autopsy done on both Darren and Patrick, which tells me she's not complicit. Did she seem genuine to you? She seemed scared to me, but she also seemed like she was hiding something."

"Her tears seemed real. She ran off crying before I'd even asked her anything, and then she said some other stuff I didn't print, so, yes, I believe her."

"Well, you printed that she suspected Patrick did something to Darren, but she didn't really want to know, and that she was relieved that Patrick was dead, which was great stuff, by the way. It'll help me moving forward now that Stone and I were basically told to leave their deaths alone. That was before your story, of course, but I've found out some good shit since."

"Like what?"

Goode told her about Clarence Thompson altering Patrick's toxicology report. "So, now we know he's been compromised and is most likely taking orders from someone outside the department, maybe for money. Although if the cabal works like the Mexican drug cartels, it could be threatening to kill family members if their moles don't do what they're told."

"So, how are you going to prove that?"

"I have a couple of people in the ME's office who gave me some documentation tonight. Got it right here in my hand, in fact."

"That's huge. Can you leak me a copy?"

"Not now, but maybe later. I also met with Darla tonight. She wouldn't give me a list of the cabal members, because she's worried that could get her killed, but she indicated that most of them are investors at Vitaleron. Also, this got lost in the shuffle earlier, so we don't know how many investors there are, because that's proprietary information. But Darren McMurphy gave me some prime dirt to use as leverage against the mayor and his dad."

"What's that?"

Goode explained the bribery scheme to give the mayor a mansion to help grease the way for a new special district where Patrick could build a new resort on the same parcel where her brother, Franny, had planned to put his.

"I can't believe you never told me this!" Katrina said.

"Yeah, as you probably know, it's a protected area of rare creature and plant species, so no resort could go there without specific zoning changes. And since your brother wasn't involved in Vitaleron, it's clear that this cabal has other active tentacles that reach into big land use and development deals. Darla gave me a short list of names tonight, but I've been trying to think of other ways to compile a full list of leaders and members. What about the Winchester reelection campaign records you wrote about?"

"You can download those records to cross-check against the other lists, but it'll be like looking for a needle in a barrel of needles," Katrina said. "I think the Vitaleron investor list will be more helpful. But wait a minute. If Vincent loses a bundle on Franny's resort project, and then Patrick snakes a deal for the same property without cutting Vincent in, doesn't that give Vincent motive to kill Patrick or have him killed?"

"Yes, but according to Darla, Vincent is only an honorary Friend of the Cabal, an FOTC, as she called it. So, it doesn't sound like he would have access to the cabal's resources for a hit like that, and especially not when the target is a cabal leader, which is how Darren described his father. But someone—or a group of someones—obviously saw both of them as liabilities. They were probably worried the McMurphys would expose that mayoral bribe, not knowing that Darren had already told us. I purposely left it out of the investigative reports for that reason."

"What makes Darla the expert? What if she's wrong? Vincent could be working behind the scenes with the cabal to smash my car window and send me death threats so I'll back off the story."

"He could be, and I'm still looking at him—hard—but until we know who these other dudes are, I'm not going to do anything but talk to him like I did this afternoon. He's already accused me of harassing him, so I'm screwed if our meeting today gets back to the chief. I'm trying to do this quietly, especially while Stone is still out."

"When does he come back?"

"Week and a half."

"I'm going back to the storage units tomorrow to pull out my parents' computers and search for any relevant emails. I'm also looking for journals, paper cards, or letters they might have kept. You want to come and help me? I still need to get a few pieces of heavy furniture that I couldn't get on the last trip. Like a couch, a desk, and a chest of drawers."

"Sure, but I don't think they'll fit into my VW van."

"Do you know someone with a truck you could borrow? We'll need one of those heavy-duty dollies too."

"Yeah, Byron, a detective on my team, has both, and he owes me one. In the meantime, I'll do a quick check in the CAIR system to see if we seized a list of Vitaleron investors along the way."

Before hanging up, they arranged to meet at the storage facility at ten o'clock.

CHAPTER 28
KATRINA

Saturday

Katrina arrived an hour before the rendezvous time to get a head start on trying to locate the items she wanted. But more importantly, she came early so she didn't break down sobbing like she had with Norman Klein. If that was going to happen again, she wanted to get it out of the way before Goode showed up.

Her family's two-story house had plenty of space for both parents to have their own home office. Each of them had a personal and a work laptop, the latter of which they'd brought home in briefcases the day they were shot. Katrina specifically remembered her aunt Athena handing them to her as soon as she arrived from Chicago, as if she were responsible for safeguarding the family jewels. She recalled packing the work laptops separately from their home office computers, papers, and books, and never understood why the cops never got a warrant to seize any of these materials.

In hindsight, she realized that the police investigation was even more flawed and incomplete than she'd remembered. Goode said he was going to look for holes in the investigative reports, but she already had a gut feeling that the cops knew nothing about her mom's relationship with Vincent or her father's fling with his clerk.

Opening the doors to the first two lockers, she stared helplessly at the floor-to-ceiling stacks of boxes. On the last trip, it was easy to grab the ones from her parents' courthouse offices and to maneuver the furniture enough to pull out a few pieces. But because she knew that the items she wanted this time were deeper in each locker, the task loomed larger. She felt a headache coming on.

What was I thinking? Pull yourself together before he gets here. Hopefully he'll come up with a good plan of attack.

By the time Goode arrived in a white pickup truck, Katrina had managed to compose herself. Just seeing him get out of the truck in his jeans and black T-shirt, which was form fitted to his broad shoulders and pecs, was enough to distract her from feeling overwhelmed. He soon allayed her remaining concerns about the task at hand.

"I suggest we keep taking stuff out and stack it on the driveway here until we find what you need," he said. "Then we can put it back in a more organized way—sorted by category or room—so you can find it more easily next time," he said.

See? I knew he'd be good at this.

"Sounds good to me. Let's go for it."

Goode got to work on the furniture, pulling out the smaller items, such as the coffee and end tables she'd chosen, and making his way to the bigger items. She felt much better once the pieces she'd picked were stacked into the truck.

He suggested they take the same approach with the boxes: Take them out and reorganize them by room, looking inside if necessary, and label them with the black markers she'd brought. Luckily, those from her parents' offices were already marked.

"I still can't believe the detectives didn't get a warrant for their work laptops and files," she said.

Goode was uncharacteristically silent about this revelation as he stopped to lift his T-shirt and wipe his sweaty face, exposing his six-pack abs. She tried not to stare, but he was watching her to see if she was watching him, and she couldn't help but blush, smile, and glance away.

"I know," he said finally. "It's embarrassing. It's almost like they didn't want to catch your parents' killer. But that fits the pattern of the more recent deaths—the 'investigators' aren't really investigating. They don't have to question anyone, let alone file any charges. Thank God Stone assigned the Fontaine murders to me when I wasn't even back from vacation yet, or they might have been written off as suicides, just like the McMurphys and Battrelles wanted."

Katrina felt sick to her stomach that the corruption went so deep and so wide that her family had been swept up in it. What had they done or gotten mixed up in to be a part of this?

Goode must have gauged her thoughts by her expression, because he came over to give her a hug, taking her by the shoulders and seeking consent before doing so. She hadn't planned on allowing this to happen, but it was almost a reflex as she buried her face in his neck and let him comfort her. Then the tears came, despite her prep work to prevent them.

They stayed like that for a good minute until she let go, gave him a quick smile, and then averted her eyes. She felt uncomfortable that, despite her best intentions, she'd let her guard down and allowed herself to be so vulnerable in front of him.

Back to business.

By opening various boxes, she found the towels, linens, kitchen pots, pans, and utensils she wanted. But the jackpot came when she uncovered a couple of boxes she'd never seen before. One contained a treasure trove of yellowed documents, photos, family histories, and other keepsakes passed down by her mother's family. The other was full of journals in assorted colors, filled with her mother's handwriting.

How could Mom have written in diaries all those years without my ever seeing her do it?

In the same box with the journals, she found a stack of handwritten letters from her father to her mother, held together with a red ribbon, that were written during a year her mother had spent studying international law at Oxford in London when Katrina and Franny were small.

I guess we were too young to remember that, but I don't recall Mom ever talking about studying abroad either. Maybe it was a sore spot between her and Daddy?

Katrina's stomach sank when she opened a large manila envelope containing assorted collections of cards and letters, each in its own envelope, and held together with a rubber band. One had postmarks from the months before her parents were shot. Another was dated the year Aphy was at Oxford. Yet another short stack of loose letters, without envelopes, was written before the twins were born, but after her mother had stopped dating Vincent. All of them, no matter the date, were signed either "Love you, Vincey," or "Yours always, Vincey."

The manila envelope also contained a couple of faded black-and-white photos. In one taken at Windansea, Vincent and Aphy were standing under the shack in their bathing suits, with Vincent behind Aphy, his arms around her waist and his chin resting on her shoulder. They looked like they were in their late twenties, which would have been about right for law school. A second photo, taken some years later, had Big Ben in the background. Vincent was kissing Aphy's neck as she turned her face away from the camera, laughing. She was wearing her wedding ring.

Well, that confirms my speculation about why she never talked about London. Did I even know this woman? Or Daddy, for that matter? Was she involved with Vincent during her entire marriage? Do I even want to read these journals and letters? It seems like our "loving family" was a giant lie.

"That's enough boxes, or I'm going to have to hire a moving van just to bring this stuff back to the house in a few months," she said, hastily stuffing the envelopes back into the box and tucking the cardboard flaps into each other before Goode could see inside. She wanted to go through them later, slowly and in private, before deciding whether to reveal the contents to him.

She felt embarrassed and confused. What if Vincent turned out to be the killer—and her mother was the motivating factor—in a plot that had gone horribly wrong? Could it have been a revenge response, because she still wouldn't leave Peter? I.e., if I can't have you, then no one can?

"Good enough," Goode said. "Now that you've marked them so efficiently, are you ready for me to move them back inside?"

"Yes, thanks. Go ahead."

He stacked the boxes carefully back into the lockers, with the markings facing forward for easy identification the next time she came back. Meanwhile, she tried to get her mind off her discovery before Goode sensed something was wrong and started questioning her. To head that off, she started telling him stories about her family, which seemed like a good way to get to know each other better anyway, when they weren't competing for who could get what witness to say more or keeping things from each other.

Are we doomed to repeat the same mistakes as my parents, hiding information from one another, but for different reasons?

"This stack of *Playbills* is from the Broadway productions that my mom sang and acted in before she went to law school," she said, holding up a random sample of the glossy booklets. "This is a photo of my parents' wedding reception. Look how big her pregnant stomach is. Dang. How did she even get off the couch and stand up straight, carrying that load?"

Goode glanced at the photo and laughed, but not for long. With one sideways peek at her face, he must have seen that she was churning inside, no matter how hard she tried to hide it.

"What's going on?" he asked. "What did you find?"

"Nothing," she said. "I was just looking at the wedding photo."

Goode shook his head and shrugged. "Okay, if you say so."

What is he, a frickin' detective?

"I'm just a little emotional going through all these boxes," she said. That much was true, and she hoped it would be enough for him to back off. It wasn't like she was *never* going to tell him; she just needed some time to process it all first.

"I get that," he said. "I guess you'll tell me when you're ready."

"Okay, Detective Surfer Man, enough with the questions. Let's finish up here and go to Bronx Pizza."

"No argument there," he said. "Let me load these last boxes, and we can head out."

Goode turned back toward the job at hand, then pivoted one more time. "I've been meaning to ask you, what genealogy services did you submit your DNA to?"

That's a weird question. What's he up to?

"Ancestry and 23andMe, why?"

"Oh, just wondering."

"I know you, and you are never 'just wondering' about any-thing," she said.

"I was curious, is all."

"I guess you'll tell me when you're ready," she said, echoing his earlier refrain.

"Oh, all right, Miss Smarty-Pants. Once you get your profile, if you also upload it to GEDmatch, that lets law enforcement use possible matches to help solve crimes. So, I was wondering if you'd thought about allowing them to do that once you get the results. It might help us figure out who has a hidden agenda in these murders."

Because Katrina didn't know that, she hadn't considered it. "I'll have to think about that, but if you think that would help, then yeah, I can do that. My profile should come back any day now. By the time we're done, my family's entire life will be an open book, though at this point, I'm a little scared to find out how it ends."

After inhaling pizza slices and Diet Coke on the outdoor patio in Hillcrest, Katrina felt fortified enough to get through the rest of the afternoon. But as much as she was enjoying Goode's company, she was quietly dying to shut herself in her apartment to read her mother's diaries and letters.

Back at her complex, Goode parked in the driveway below her balcony where Teddy Kincaid sat in his car all night, watching for intruders. As she helped Goode unload the truck and wheel the furniture and boxes upstairs on the dolly, she peppered him with questions to research in the CAIR system.

"If you can get me the names of the neighbors the cops interviewed, I can see if they still live on the street. Maybe I can get more information from them," she said, helping him maneuver her mother's antique wooden desk against the wall in her home office and a wooden bookcase from the old family room against the opposite wall.

Who knows what I'll find in these desk drawers after he leaves.

"Sure, no problem," Goode said, stopping to drink a glass of water in the kitchen between loads. "I meant to tell you about an interesting discovery I made last night. I found that list of Vitaleron investors, and Brandon Winchester is on it for ten million dollars. I specifically remember you quoting him trying to mealymouth deny being an investor without outright saying so. As you pointed out, it wasn't listed on his disclosure form, which constitutes a major campaign violation."

"Wow, that's big. Thanks for the tip," Katrina said. "He's an investment banker, so that could be his own earnings, but it also could be family money. His dad owns a bunch of racehorses, along with a major stake in the development company that recently bought the La Valencia hotel in La Jolla." Turning to look at him, she asked, "Do you think that means he and his dad are part of the cabal too? That would explain how Darla knows so much about it."

"Yes, it would. I'm starting to wonder if he wasn't using her to get a taste of the sex drug and that bribe from Darren. If he decides it's too expensive to divorce his wife while he's waiting for trial, then maybe Darla will walk away and stop protecting him."

Katrina smiled at that notion, which would help them both. "Let's hope. Can you leak the investor list to me, so I can write the ten-million-dollar

Winchester story? There might be some other surprises on that list, too, if we put our heads together."

Goode leaned against the wall and gave her that sexy half smile with his eyes. "I don't see why not," he replied. "Let me run it by Stone. He said he didn't want to know everything I'm doing while he's out, but this could work in our favor."

After bringing the last load inside, Goode came back into her apartment one more time and closed the door. He held out his arms, letting her decide if she wanted to hug him again. When she did, he held her close and kissed her neck, which made her jerk away as she recalled the image of Vincent kissing her mother's neck. Goode pulled back immediately, as if he thought he'd pushed too hard.

Gazing into her eyes, he said, "Goodbye, sweet Katrina." Then he gave her a long, soulful kiss, letting her go before he couldn't stop.

"Maybe next Saturday I'll invite you over to my house, and we can go through the Double-Judge file in the CAIR system together," he said.

"Will there be wine involved?"

"Is that wishful thinking or a serious question?" he replied, flashing his most mischievous smile.

"Just a question. Sounds dangerous, is all. You know what happened here last time we did that. Just remember, Teddy will be waiting for me to come home like a protective papa."

Goode raised his eyebrows questioningly. "Unless you give him the night off."

His remark hung in the air for a minute until Katrina shook her head and laughed. "Thanks again for your help today, Surfer Man," she said, leaning forward to open the front door. "I'll talk to you later."

"Unless I talk to you first."

CHAPTER 29
KATRINA

Saturday/Sunday

As Goode was giving Katrina that long, soulful kiss at the front door, her mind went back to the last time they locked lips in that very spot, after drinking wine at the end of an excruciatingly long workday. The kissing started on the balcony, then moved indoors, where Katrina was leading him toward the front door to leave.

Only, the urgent, all-encompassing sexy mouthful of a kiss wouldn't stop no matter how hard she tried. She got lost in it. So, they ended up against the wall, with her hands willingly pinned behind her, before dropping to the floor, their limbs tangled around each other, their clothes flying off, and rolling around like crazed rabbits. Until they were startled out of their skulls by the sound of Linebacker Dude's tires crunching on the driveway below.

Despite the risk of losing their jobs, Katrina could feel them getting closer to reliving that moment, knowing that soon, they wouldn't be able to hold off anymore. She was trying to delay that for as long as possible, at least until after she'd written the most important stories about the Fontaine–McMurphy case and the corruption scandal that she and Goode were uncovering. Or until the story became so big and deep that no one could object or take her off it.

I mean, look at Vincent, for God's sake. He's constantly trying to put the two of us into one conflict or another, forcing us to school him into behaving like an ethically responsible newspaper publisher. I can't imagine why Mom, a federal judge who I always thought was grounded and ethical, was so drawn to him. Maybe she thought he was devilishly impish and reminded her of her theater days. Or maybe he knows how to please a woman. Ewww. I don't even want to think about that.

Once Goode was gone, Katrina headed into her newly furnished home office and started opening the drawers of her mother's desk. Most of them were empty, but she did find more loose photos—of Katrina and Franny as kids, her parents, the family together, her mother's theater headshots, and her more recent judge portraits that still hung on the wall in the federal courthouse.

She had no clue where her mother had hidden the box of journals and letters, because Katrina and her aunt Athena had split up the house when they packed everything up. But it was possible that one of the lady-lunch friends Athena brought in to help might have found the hidden box and sent it to storage.

The house did have an attic of sorts, which was unusual for West Coast homes, though it was more like a crawl space. Aphy had always made sure to keep the twins out of there, so it could have been the perfect hiding place.

"It's such an old house, I don't want you getting hurt," she would say. "You could step in the wrong place between the beams and fall through the plaster ceiling."

Two years after the judges were murdered, Athena fell off a ladder at her house, hit her head, broke her spine, and died of a massive stroke a few days later. So, the box's origins would remain an unsolved mystery.

Pawing through the box of family artifacts, Katrina learned about the many faces of Aphrodite Chopin, aka Aphy the Greek. Dead for more than five years and Katrina was still learning new things about her.

Her maiden name was Onassis, and, as one might wonder, yes, she was a descendant of the wealthy shipping family. Aphy's father, who went by the nickname Zeppo because he was always doing Marx Brothers imitations, was a distant cousin of Aristotle Onassis, but distant enough that his family had none of that wealth.

Zeppo was a self-made man who made a modest living at the Greek restaurant he opened in Point Loma, enough to buy the house that Katrina's parents eventually took over. Zeppo worked hard, but he also played hard. He drank too much, raced cars and sailboats too fast, and died in a fiery crash while celebrating his fortieth birthday, leaving his wife Zelda alone to raise their teenage daughters Aphrodite and Athena.

Zelda was not one to live like a victim, torturing herself with worries about paying bills. She simply set her mind on finding a good provider and soon married into an old San Diego family that went back several generations. But she insisted on keeping the house in which she and her late husband had raised their daughters, claiming she didn't want to upset them. Her new husband, Cliff, didn't like it, but he gave in because he was in love. He often complained, however, that Zeppo's ghost wandered the halls at night, and he swore that Zeppo watched while he and Zelda had sex.

But that chapter of Zelda's life didn't last long either. She and Cliff died in a freak accident involving a runaway bus, a train, and the car they were driving home after a party. The crash generated a healthy insurance payout, which is how Aphy could afford to escape to New York City to fulfill her dream of singing and acting on Broadway. The same insurance settlement also allowed her to return home and pay for law school. Or so she told Katrina and Franny.

Opening the dusty box of journals, Katrina pulled out a short stack and curled up to read them in the corner of the familiar old dusty-rose couch that came from the old family room. By the time she came up for air, the sky was dark, and she saw Aphrodite Onassis Chopin in a whole new light.

For starters, Katrina learned that the real reason Aphy quit acting and came back to San Diego had more to do with the director who got her pregnant, then pushed her down a flight of stairs after she refused to get an abortion. The fall triggered a miscarriage and also broke her left ankle in three places, which ended her career as a professional actress who also danced on stage. If anyone asked about the slight limp she had for the rest of her years, she claimed someone accidentally tripped her during a performance of *The Club*, causing her to fall off the stage.

"I packed my bags, flew home, and never performed again. I don't miss it a whit," she always said, though her overly dramatic tone said otherwise.

Katrina found a *Playbill* for that musical, listing Aphrodite Onassis as having a named singing role, versus being a chorus member, which proved that her mother was telling the truth—about that, at least.

Mom, why did you feel the need to tell us all these made-up stories? Was it because you were ashamed? Or were you trying to make your life sound better than it really was?

Katrina's energy was sapped after she'd read several of the early journals and a stack of letters. She was having difficulty processing all the new information, her mother's written words echoing in her mind. Especially the last entry she read, which was so disturbing that she slapped the journal shut for the night.

He threw me down that flight of stairs like I was of no more value to him than a big sack of jasmine rice. As if I meant nothing to him. And our baby? He didn't give him or her a second thought.

Getting up to stretch, Katrina poured herself a glass of Chardonnay and took it out to the balcony, where she waved to Teddy, who was leaning against his car below. He waved back.

Hoping to replace the forced-abortion scene with something more benign, Katrina went back inside. She emptied a take-out container of Mongolian beef with broccoli onto a plate and heated it in the microwave, then watched a rom-com on Netflix while she ate. There was no sense buying a TV or setting up a cable account when she would be moving to Point Loma in a few months.

When Goode called on her cell, she let it go to voicemail. If it were any other time, she'd love to talk, drink wine, and laugh with him. But at that moment, she didn't know what to say. To him, or to anyone, actually.

The few remaining scraps of her family had been taken from her that day. It felt like she'd lost them all over again. It also made her question everything about her life.

She'd always thought of herself as Katrina Chopin, the daughter of two happily married federal judges. But now, only a few journals and photos later, her mother had become a total stranger. And she hadn't even gotten to her father's boxes of history yet.

The next morning, Katrina slept in until after Teddy was long gone. After slipping into her comfy loungewear, she walked up to her mailbox, which was past the carport near the street. She hadn't checked it in a couple of days, because having only just moved in, she rarely received anything important. Keying open the lock, she found her first phone and gas-electric bills and an unexpected envelope from 23andMe.

She was excited that her results had come back so quickly. She'd been itching to get going on this story.

Turning her face toward the sun, she meandered past the pool and up the stairs to her apartment, where she made herself a mug of green tea, mixed with peach-pineapple chamomile. Sitting down at her dining room table, she ripped open the envelope containing the DNA results.

The Greek ancestry on her mother's side was cited on the first page as predicted. But she was confused when she didn't see any listing for English, Irish, or Polish ancestry for her father's family. Instead, she saw origins from Australia, specifically New South Wales, and Hungary.

"Huh?"

When she turned to the second page, it listed only one possible close relative—a half sister, Meredith Battrelle. Katrina was so startled to see the Battrelle name that she knocked her tea over on the table before she could even glance at the few more distant relatives listed.

Paralyzed, she couldn't move as the pool of brown liquid began to spread. It took a few moments before she regained control of her legs. By the time she jumped up to grab a dish towel and mop up the mess, the puddle had reached the papers, which she gently swabbed.

She was able to read through the soggy, blurred type that Meredith had sent in her DNA recently as well. The paperwork suggested Katrina go to the website to access the family tree that Meredith had started constructing there. She opened her laptop, which was already on the table, and read over the names on Meredith's family tree: Meredith's mother, Ruth Winston Battrelle; her father, Vincent Battrelle; and her brothers, Michael and Alex.

"Oh, fucking hell!" she shouted. "You have got to be kidding me."

She sent the family tree listing to the printer she'd brought back from storage, so she could show it to other people.

Katrina's body felt like a human lightning storm. She was shaking from her belly outward, as stress cramps curdled her lower intestines. Even her fingers were quivering. But based on what she'd discovered the night before, she knew this had to be true.

It was a horrible yet scientific confirmation that her mother, Judge Aphrodite Chopin, had lied to her husband and her children their entire lives—and probably also to Vincent Battrelle, Katrina's birth father.

The only bright spot she could find was that if her other dad, Peter Chopin, wasn't a blood relation, then she'd been living all these years with a crippling fear of Huntington's disease—and of intimate committed relationships with men—*for nothing*.

She'd always felt a deep connection with Franny. How could she not after sharing their mother's womb for nine months? They knew things about each other without even having to say them out loud. At least that's how she felt. She assumed he felt the same, which is why she believed in her gut that he couldn't have killed himself. She would have seen it coming.

She thought that Franny took after their mom, which is why he'd always felt too close to her. According to Katrina's perceived sense of parallelism, she should have taken after her father, at least a little. But she'd actually felt like an orphan as soon as Franny died, because she'd never really felt a close connection to either of her parents. It was like something was just, well, missing.

She and Franny never had a mom who made them a bag lunch to take to school or who was waiting for them when they got home, like Peter's mother, Ida. Rather, Aphy was a working mom who gave her kids lunch money and keys to let themselves in to do their homework and help get dinner started.

At least now Katrina knew why she didn't feel a deep connection to her father either. He was caring and loving, but they really had nothing in common. Except for the compulsion to personally distance themselves from other people. She shared that trait with him, Franny, and her mom, too, come to think of it. They really were a disjointed family, all existing on their own independently rotating axes. Growing up with all that space was probably why she felt suffocated when anyone got close to her. Everyone except Franny and, more recently, Goode.

That's where being a newspaper reporter came in. She'd always tried to fill those empty places in her psyche with work. Work kept her busy on that treadmill that never stopped. It also helped to distract her from her emotions and, if she had too much time on her hands, loneliness. The adrenaline bursts kept her feeling alive. Seeing her byline on a story gave her a sense of accomplishment. She received immediate gratification when readers and sources called or emailed with their reactions. Good or bad, she didn't care. At least she was getting attention, admiration, respect, and sometimes fear for her investigative triumphs.

In analyzing all of this with her therapist, she realized that her long-standing habit of having sex with unavailable men was her subconscious mind's way of trying to find connection, even though her conscious mind would never allow her to actually make one.

That kept her on an endless path to self-sabotage, telling herself she needed that kind of connection to be "healthy," all the while creating conflicts, primarily the Huntington's, that pushed men, and even women, away. At least with women, she was just looking for a friendship, but with men, a promising start had to be thwarted before they ever got to the *having children* discussion. She had to bend her mind to consciously accept that that excuse was now moot.

Pacing across the living room floor, she clutched her hair in one hand and tugged. She felt like she was going to Crazy Town. It almost made her want to call Goode and propose an impulse rendezvous. If they had sex and got pregnant that night, while she was still young enough to have a baby, she could have a child right now if she wanted—without worrying that she would give it a degenerative nerve disease, come down with it herself, or both.

"Fucking Mom!" she sputtered. "I can't fucking believe this."

The sad part was that she had no one to tell except Goode, or maybe Joanne, because every other close relative she'd ever known was dead. That left only her new family, who would be so shocked by the news they would probably hang up on her.

As if I'd really call Meredith, Michael, or Alex Battrelle right now. Let alone Vincent.

Goode was the only one who would understand how much of an emotional and professional clusterfuck this was. She'd yet to tell Joanne the minute details of their theories about Vincent.

But I'm definitely going to have to tell her about this. Linda too. And, of course, Vincent. I cannot get my brain around the fact that he is my father, *especially after his weird pseudo-seduction act the night he invited me over to his house for a drink my first week at the paper.*

The funny thing was that she'd had a fleeting thought when she was at the storage facility: When she'd pulled out the photo of her mother and young Vincent, he'd reminded her of Franny, who was about that age when he died. But she'd pushed that thought away so fast it hardly registered. Because, how could that be? She wished Franny was around so they could discuss this bombshell now, especially in the context of all those fights he'd had with their "father" about Franny's drinking.

"How can you be so irresponsible?" Peter would ask rhetorically. "How can we even be related?"

She'd always thought that Peter was just frustrated, but now she wondered if he'd had some kind of sixth sense. Peter was always a moderate drinker, so that predilection of Franny's had obviously been passed down from Vincent, who drank a lot, but whose son Alex apparently took drinking and drugging to a whole new level. How ironic that they'd all been in family therapy together, not knowing this enormous hairy secret.

So, who am I, really, now that my life is an even bigger lie than it was last night? The daughter of an über-rich boozer and possible murderer? A guy who may, or may not, belong to a cabal of wealthy businessmen who bribe congressmen and count on the police chief and sheriff to further their agendas and hide the truth, knowing their pal Vincent's newspaper would cover it up? This can't be happening.

Was it possible that her mother didn't know who the father of her babies was? Was she having problems with Vincent and broke up with him before she knew she was pregnant? When she started dating Peter, did it all happen so fast that she just hoped the twins were his? Or did she already know she was pregnant, and leave Vincent because he wanted her to have an abortion, just like the director? Did she have some latex allergy or psychological delusion that made her unable or unwilling to use condoms?

However it happened, Peter had assumed he was the father of her children. He'd told Katrina several times that he was "damn proud" to marry Aphy.

Katrina went over to the box of her mother's journals and dumped the rest onto the floor. One at a time, she looked for the dates written inside the front cover until she found the one that covered the year right before and after her and Franny's births in 1980. It had a red cover and had no special identifying markings. Inside, Katrina found the entry she was looking for:

> It's happening again. I'm pregnant and Vincey isn't ready to be a father. I know because I brought up having children in casual conversation last night and he failed the test. "I've got things to do, Aphy," he said. "There's so much life to be lived. We're too young to be tied down with rug rats running around. I want to finish law school, start my own business, and enjoy spending time alone with you." "What if I get pregnant?" I asked. "I'd pay for you to take care of it, of course, you know that. I'd go with you, and hold your hand, knowing that we'd get another chance down the road after we get married." That was enough for me. He would never hurt me like that monster in New York, but I'm not giving up this beautiful baby. So, I'm going to cut him loose and find a good man who is willing to take on this responsibility. There's that nice, cute guy in my contracts class, Peter Chopin, who I always catch looking at me. I tried to smile at him the last time, but he looked away and blushed. I'll have to convince him to ask me out for coffee. I guess I should've learned from the first time that the rhythm/pullout method is not reliable, but if this is going to work, I'll have to be so "overtaken by passion" that I "forget" to use birth control altogether.

So, she purposely duped Daddy. She was more like Vincent than I realized.

Turning the pages was like living a lucid nightmare. Katrina learned how her mother manipulated this "nice, cute guy" into inviting her to coffee, then dinner. The next thing he knew, she was pregnant with twins, and they were getting married. The funny thing was that Aphy seemed to grow fond of Peter very quickly, probably out of necessity, but she seemed determined to make a go of it.

A few months later, she wrote:

> Peter is such a good man. He seemed overwhelmed at first by the prospect of raising twins with one more year of classes to finish. But he's grown up so fast and loves me so much that he's not even thinking about running away. If I grow to love him half as much as he loves me, it will be enough. It's a nice change to have someone take care of me who isn't trying to control me or my choices. We'll have a comfortable life, and everything will be fine. He'll make a solid father, and neither he nor the twins will ever learn that he isn't related to them by blood. Vincey was hurt and angry when I told him we couldn't be together anymore. He didn't understand what had changed. But I did it early enough that he never even suspected that I was pregnant. He'll never learn the truth either. So, he can have his own family with a docile wife who does what he tells her to. To be honest, he's been more of a playmate than a soulmate. He says he loves me, but he loves himself more. I feel more like a possession than a partner to him. I'm glad I found out now that he's not husband material for me.

That made Katrina feel a little better. At least her mother knew that Vincent wasn't the loving, caring man her father was, and in the end wouldn't make her happy. But it seemed that she could never let him go either. That she still enjoyed having him around as a playmate. So, she wasn't such a great person or wife material herself, which had become only too obvious since Katrina began this accidental journey of discovering who her mother really was.

She not only duped Daddy, she duped Franny and me too. How could she let us live our whole lives thinking we could come down with Huntington's any minute when she knew Daddy wasn't our real father? All she ever said was "Try not to worry. There's a good chance you'll never get it."

More than anything, though, it made Katrina feel sad and betrayed, not just for her father, but for all of them. She felt especially sad that her father had been used in this way, lied to and cheated on, that he was loved only a little in return for his full adoration.

But what most confused Katrina was that her parents had always seemed happy together. It seemed like her mother had grown to love her husband the way she'd hoped. So, maybe she wasn't cheating with Vincent at the Grant hotel. Maybe they were just having lunch. Katrina could only hope that whatever her mother did or said in those last months didn't get her and her husband murdered.

Then it struck her. If Vincent was the one who carried in the bottle of spiked lemon-infused vodka that apparently killed Patrick McMurphy, did that mean he also knew about, or may have even helped cause, the murder of his own son with the same narcotic cocktail?

Holy shit.

She had no choice. She grabbed her phone and called Goode. She couldn't keep these thoughts to herself any longer. Not now. Not when she had fully landed in Crazy Town.

CHAPTER 30
GOODE

Sunday

Katrina started talking before Goode even had a chance to say hello.

"Can you come over?" she asked. "I need to talk to you."

She sounded like she did the last Sunday morning, when she discovered that her car window had been smashed for the second time. Only worse, if that was possible.

"Are you okay?" he asked, worried that she might be injured or bleeding.

"No, not really."

"Are you hurt?"

"No, I'm just freaking out. I'll explain when you get here."

"I'll be there in fifteen minutes."

It was such a nice morning that Goode had been relaxing in the sun at his favorite café in Bird Rock, an older neighborhood in south La Jolla, with a latte; a prosciutto, Swiss, and spinach panini; and the Sunday *New York Times*. Hearing muted panic in her voice for the first time, he knew it had to be serious. So, he packed up his brunch to go and roared off in his van.

Knocking on Katrina's front door, Goode didn't know what to expect when she opened it. She was typically so pragmatic and rational, he was worried that the death threats and news of the connection between her brother's and Patrick McMurphy's deaths had taken their toll.

When she opened the door, her eyes were wet and a little swollen. He also saw the scattered mess of books on the orange shag carpet, some with their handwritten pages open. Were those her journals or a family member's from the storage unit?

As Goode came inside, closed the door, and put his arms around her, she folded into them, hugging him back like she didn't want to let go.

"What happened?" he asked softly.

"It feels like the world is spinning so fast that it's about to throw me into the stratosphere," she said. Pulling back, she reached down for some papers on the coffee table behind her and thrust them at him. "This came in the mail this morning. It's my DNA results."

Reading the first page, he saw nothing alarming. But as he turned the pages, he saw Meredith Battrelle's name and the half sister reference, along with the family tree listing with Vincent's name.

"What the hell?" he said, his mouth falling open and his head shaking back and forth involuntarily.

"That's what I said," she replied.

"Is this legit?" he asked in disbelief. "I mean, is this a reputable service?"

"It's in the top three in terms of customer reviews. I also sent a vial of my spit to Ancestry, which is rated even higher, but they take twice as long to produce results."

"So, this is true?"

"It looks like it. I've been reading my mom's journals, and I've learned some pretty disturbing information that supports this. Once I got these results this morning, I went back in and found the corresponding entries about her decision to lie to Vincent, and then my dad, after she got pregnant. It all matches up."

"So, Vincent doesn't know either?"

"As far as I can tell, she hid it from all of us. But she was still messing around with him during the marriage and possibly toward the end, when she was meeting him at the US Grant Hotel. I can't tell if it was for innocent lunches or for sex."

"Did you find all this out within the last twenty-four hours?"

"No, it started when I went to storage the first time. I just didn't get a chance to tell you. I also found out that my dad had a one-night stand with his clerk, then had her reassigned, three years before he died. He was seeing a therapist at the end, I think by himself. So, it sounds like the marriage was going through some rough times, but my parents never said anything to me, so I never suspected anything was wrong."

"Geez."

"Yeah. I found some letters from the clerk to my dad last weekend. Then yesterday when we were at the lockers, I found a photo of Vincent and my mom in London together after she was already married, but I didn't want to talk about it until I read these journals. I only made it through a few of her early ones last night before I got overwhelmed and had to stop. There are still all these others, plus some letters that I haven't gotten to, not to mention their laptops," she said, pointing toward the stack of computers on the dining table.

"Easy, there's no rush," Goode said, taking her hand. She was getting a little manic, and he wanted to calm her down so they could figure out the best path forward. If she wanted his help, that is. Maybe she just wanted his support or someone to talk to, but he was happy to do or be whatever she wanted.

"I'm not sure if you want my help, or if you just want a sounding board, but it seems like all of this could be relevant to the murders of your brother and your parents. Do you have a feel for that yet?"

"Yeah, I was thinking that too. The thing that made me call you was the question of whether Vincent helped kill my brother since he just admitted to delivering that bottle of vodka to Patrick McMurphy. If he did that with Franny, too, he couldn't have known Franny was his son."

"Right."

"So, I was wondering, what if Vincent wanted to be with my mom enough to put a hit out on my dad as an FOTC? Or when she refused to leave my dad, he got one of his cabal friends to put out a hit on both of them?"

"Or, what if your mom was in on a hit on your dad, and things just went horribly wrong?"

"Wow. That's dark. Killing a federal judge seems like a stretch even for Vincent, but there's no way my mom would ever go along with that. She might have found out about my dad's fling with his clerk, but it sounds like that was over and done with. I'd also bet that my mom had no idea about this cabal or that Vincent was hooked up with them somehow. But the more I hear about this group, the more likely the FOTC scenario sounds."

Katrina stopped talking for a moment and stared out the window. "This is all so surreal, I don't even know where to start."

This seemed like the right time for Goode to set some ground rules, or boundaries, as they may be.

"So, if you are asking for my help, I have to ask, do you want my help as a friend or as a police detective? Because it's going to be hard for me to unsee and unhear all of this," he said, gesturing toward the journals and laptops.

"Both," she replied. "Now you know how I feel when you keep telling me things off the record."

Goode nodded and smiled. "Duly noted," he said.

He didn't want to slow their momentum, but he thought he ought to point out one more key issue. "So, here's the thing. When we go through electronic devices, we always make copies of the hard drives first, so we don't accidentally delete or change anything. It can make a difference. Once we start opening files, it can modify the dates that the documents were last viewed, and if we accidentally hit 'save,' it can change the file itself. So, this makes me a little nervous, because we could shoot ourselves in the foot in terms of prosecuting the bad guys if we start messing with the evidence."

"But we're going through my parents' stuff unofficially, not as a police investigation, right?"

"Yes. I just thought I'd point that out in case we need to change it up partway through this exercise."

"Why don't we get started and make that decision if and when we find something? Even before this, you said that my life is in danger, so I think it would be better if we figure out who the bad guys are ASAP, gather the documentation, and get it into the right hands before they can hurt me or anyone else. If Vincent really is involved, then it's better we pin that down than keep theorizing. And if we do call in the RCFL, then it starts getting political because you were specifically told not to get involved in my parents' case and also to leave the Fontaine–McMurphy case alone. So, it seems like we're better off doing this totally off the grid."

"I can't argue with that logic."

"One last point. We have to agree that, since this is my family and these are my personal papers, I have every right to publish what we find."

"Okay. As long as I retain the right to try to talk you out of it if I think there's a better, smarter way or if we should stop to call in the RCFL. Agreed?"

"Agreed."

"Good," Goode said. "Let's start by going through emails on the laptops."

"One thing first. Something's been bothering me," she said. "We touched on this yesterday, but why do you think your bozo colleagues never seized the laptops or their office files?"

"I've been mulling that too. It could be an indication that the cabal was involved in this case from the start. That would explain why we never heard about any suspects—because they squashed the investigation."

"Or they purposely assigned low-performing detectives who they knew would do subpar police work," Katrina said. "Which wouldn't surprise me either."

"Now, now. Since I still haven't reviewed the investigative file, I don't even know who was assigned to the case yet. But after we go through your parents' stuff, we can switch over to my laptop, which is at my house, and search through the files in the CAIR system like we talked about. Speaking of which, would your brother's laptop be in the storage unit?"

"That's a good question. I went through some of his stuff after my parents died, but I can't remember because it wasn't important at the time. It was a blur then, and it's still a blur now. I don't know where else it would be, though."

"Because we'll want to cross-check names of the people involved in his resort deal with the Vitaleron investor list and the short list of cabal leaders that I wrangled out of Darla."

"Sounds like a plan."

Because this was Katrina's show, she got to direct it, which was strange for Goode given the professional line that had previously separated their respective, and sometimes opposing, investigations. But this new collaboration was an entirely different kind of deep dive. He rather enjoyed being able to learn from her while also gaining access to information he wouldn't otherwise have.

The dynamic duo spent the next couple of hours going through emails on the judges' personal laptops. Goode thought this would be safer, in terms of keeping the record intact, than going through the data files. If they didn't find any relevant or important emails, they agreed to review the data files next.

Mostly, he followed her lead. She was smarter than any detective he'd worked with at the SDPD, and she knew these players better than anyone else. It was hard not to watch her work. She was sexy as hell, so he couldn't help but sneak a peek at her every so often, taking notes as her brain gathered and analyzed information. It felt like foreplay—to him, anyway—heightened by the hint of a smile she gave him now and then.

When she asked him to come around the table and look over her shoulder at something, he happily obliged. With his face so close to her neck, he couldn't help but breathe her in. Not in a creepy way. At least she didn't seem to mind. He got the sense that she, too, knew it was only a matter of time before they gave in to those urges again.

CHAPTER 31
KATRINA

Sunday

It was a bit distracting to work with Goode across her dining room table. Although he wasn't gauchely staring, she could feel his eyes on her when he glanced away from the laptop. She could also feel the sexual tension in the room, knowing he was holding himself back out of respect for her wishes to maintain a professional distance. The ethical quandary seemed to loom larger in her mind than his. For him, the barrier seemed more of a bureaucratic nuisance, a protocol issue inflicted on him by management.

But as she saw him sitting there, with the strong but gentle hands that had already touched her private places, even she was starting to feel like this separation was getting to be too hard to maintain. They were both adults. Why shouldn't they be allowed to be together? What would it hurt? Who would even know? Teddy wasn't on duty until just before sunset.

Well, I would know. And because I'm honest to a fault, then Joanne might figure it out, which would force her and Linda to take me off this story, because them's the rules—you can't cover someone you're dating, or an issue in which your significant other is heavily involved—and that's not what I want. Just hold on a little bit longer.

Despite the sexual frustration, it was comforting to know they were attacking this project together. She hoped that would make the outcome more comprehensive and successful.

While Katrina focused on her mother's personal laptop, she gave Goode her father's work laptop, asking him to keep an eye out for emails that his colleagues should have looked for years ago. She and Goode discussed up front what those would be, and that he should flag and print out any from or about Peter's clerk, Vincent, or Vitaleron. Also, any messages from rando court observers, complaining citizens, and angry or aggressive defendants or attorneys.

Once they completed that round, she switched over to her mother's work laptop while Goode searched her father's personal laptop. Goode thought printing emails would cause less damage to the evidence than using the laptop to copy them or send copies to another email account.

Her phone had buzzed with an incoming call a couple of times since Goode arrived earlier. But seeing it was Teddy, she just ignored it. She'd see him soon enough.

Three and a half hours later, the only items of probative value they'd found were some old emails between Peter, Vincent, and Simon concerning Peter's investment in the original Vitaleron deal, which included a share in the building. There were no emails documenting Peter's withdrawal from that deal, however. Goode attributed that to Peter's desire to erase any trace of his involvement, which was also evidenced by the lack of mention on the company website that he was one of its original founders.

"It sounds like he pulled out in anger, but that could have taken place by phone," Goode suggested, posing it more as a question since Katrina knew the man better. "Either that, or being a judge, he knew that emails are a lasting written record that can expose questionable behavior."

Katrina cocked her head in confusion. "Questionable behavior? By my dad?"

"Well, by any of them. We don't know how it went down, but that might be a good avenue for us to explore."

"Yeah, you're probably right," she said. "I also haven't gone through the boxes from their court offices that I brought home, because I thought the laptops would be more fruitful. But maybe the answer is in the past, before people were so tied to their computers, and I should toggle back to searching for handwritten cards and letters. Since my stalker put those weird cutout notes on my car that mentioned my parents, he might have sent them something similar."

"I hadn't thought of that," Goode said.

He suggested that he scroll through the Word file directories on Peter's laptops next to see if any file names jumped out at him, but he wouldn't actually open any of them.

"If I see anything that looks like real evidence, I can make an unofficial call to a guy I know at the RCFL and ask if he'll make copies off the books, although that could still get us in trouble. I don't want to screw up and inadvertently change the record, but I also don't want this to implode, or to put us into the cabal's headlights by calling this in, even unofficially."

"No, I still don't want to take that chance," Katrina said. "Just open the damn files, and we can print them out if necessary. We just won't hit 'save' on anything. The paper isn't going to pay Teddy to watch over me indefinitely."

"Okay, here goes," Goode said.

Katrina stood behind him, looking over his shoulder as he opened File Explorer on the first of Peter's laptops. Neither of them saw any red flags in the files Peter had last viewed, even after scrolling down quite a ways.

"This is a dead end. Let's go to the Documents folder and scroll down that list," Katrina said.

Following her instructions, Goode slowly went down the file names until he came to a group that started with "Franny." The first was "Franny, autopsy."

Even though Peter had seemed dismissive of Katrina's suggestion that Franny had been murdered, he'd apparently explored that possibility himself.

"Oh, good," Katrina said. "Now I don't have to raise any red flags asking for it."

The file contained a description of the scene in Franny's two-bedroom condo on Crown Point, an upscale property on the water where he was found lying on the couch in his underwear. A smattering of colored pills lay on the glass coffee table next to the vodka bottle, some of which were smashed into powder as though he'd been snorting it.

"Did anyone actually test the bottle's contents, or did they just assume that he snorted the powder?" Katrina asked.

Goode scanned the report, and Katrina's instincts were correct, as usual. No one had tested the bottle of vodka. They simply identified the pills on the table as the source of the powder and cited his recurrent drug and alcohol treatment at the McDonald Center. When the toxicology screen came back with narcotics, they assumed he'd ingested the pills or inhaled the powder. It was easy enough to present what Katrina and Goode now knew was a flawed conclusion of suicide by acute intoxication from these meds, based on the results from the outside lab that tested the bottle on Patrick McMurphy's desk.

"Let's see who did the autopsy and signed off on the report," Goode said.

Sure enough, it was Dr. Clarence Thompson.

Going back to the "Franny" files, Goode hovered over the next one on the list, "Franny, Resort by the Bay."

"Click on that one," Katrina said. "That was his last project."

This file also proved to be important, because it contained Peter's notes, a roster of Franny's business partners, and links to news articles about the project, before and after it died, just months before Franny did. Vincent Battrelle, Darren and Patrick McMurphy, and Brandon Winchester were among the names that immediately popped out, along with several Katrina didn't know.

"I recognize a few of these others from the list of cabal members Darla recited to me at Jose's Friday night," Goode said. "They're on my phone."

Opening the Notes folder on his phone, Goode read the others aloud: "'Elmore Rayburn, Rick Rodriguez, and John Young.' So, it looks like these guys were pissed enough at your brother to have him killed. Just like Patrick. There isn't any information here about why they were pissed, so I have to assume it's about the millions of dollars they lost in this resort deal."

"That was the scuttlebutt, but do you think all these men, including Vincent, were party to that?"

"No way to know for sure, but as you and I have discussed, Vincent's name keeps popping up in business deals with people who end up dead."

"So, we need to research these three other guys: Rayburn, Rodriguez, and Young."

"I know a little about Elmore Rayburn," he said, repeating what Darla had told him about being a cabal leader. "I don't know anything about the other two."

A quick google fixed that. Although it was a common name, there was a Rick Rodriguez who was past president of the San Diego Downtown Partnership and owned a popular restaurant near City Hall named R&R. Goode explained that lobbyists, developers, and politicians frequently negotiated there over two-martini lunches. Their flunkies came back after work to sign paperwork over rib eye dinners and celebratory tequila shots, expensed with OPM, other people's money. Privacy was at a premium there, so deals were often done in private back rooms.

John Young was another common name, but the most likely candidate was a wealthy philanthropist who made his first pot of money from a biotech start-up in Silicon Valley, which he then parlayed into a portfolio of hotel and real estate properties in Rancho Santa Fe, a wealthy enclave northeast of La Jolla. He also owned a fleet of small planes and helicopters that he used to fly between his properties and car dealerships up and down Southern California.

By then, it was getting close to dusk. Katrina stood up from her chair, grabbed her lower back, and arched backward to stretch.

"It's almost the witching hour when Teddy shows up," she said, sending Goode a gentle hint that it was time to go.

Hearing it loud and clear, he jumped up, came around the table, and put his arms around her waist, prompting her to do the same to him.

It's okay, he's about to leave, so I'm not going to let him start something we can't finish. Besides, I could use one more comforting hug after the weekend I've had.

"Are you ready to go through your parents' investigative file together at my place tonight?" he asked hopefully. "I could pick up some wine and some takeout. Like I said, give Teddy the night off if you're really worried he'll wonder where you are."

But even as he said it, she could see in his eyes that he already knew she'd say no.

"Sorry, Surfer Man," she said, shaking her head. "You know how much I want to read those files, but I'll have to take a rain check. I've still got to go through those boxes from storage tonight, then try to get some rest. First thing tomorrow, I'm going to ask Vincent a bunch of confrontational questions before I hit him with the daughter-DNA news. I want to go to bed early, which may be silly since I probably won't even sleep tonight. If you find anything good, you can always call and interrupt me."

"I know some pretty good ways to get rid of stress, is all I'm saying," Goode said, smirking.

"I'm sure you do. I'll take a rain check on that too."

"All right, all right. I'm going," he said, giving her a quick kiss and tugging himself away.

He walked over to the door and opened it before she could beat him to it, and there was Teddy, standing on the doorstep.

"Hey, Teddy," Katrina said, startled and a little unsure how to handle this. She didn't know if he and Goode had met before or knew of each other from the SDPD. "This is my friend, Ken Goode. He was helping me move some furniture out of storage."

Teddy extended his hand and Goode shook it firmly. "Hi, Teddy, nice to meet you," Goode said. "Glad to hear you're taking care of our girl." Then came the awkward pause, as all of them realized that he'd just intimated that he knew Katrina intimately.

"See you later, Katrina," he said, making a quick exit down the stairs.

Teddy stood there, looking pleased with himself. "That your boyfriend pretending he isn't?"

Did he recognize Goode? Gawd, I don't need the drama.

"No, he's just a friend," she said. "Did you want to tell me something?" Normally, she came out on the balcony and waved to him after she heard him pull up. He'd never come to her door before.

Was he spying on me? He must have seen Goode's van in the visitor's spot.

"Yeah, actually, I did," he said, turning to point toward the driveway where he normally parked. "I tried calling you earlier today, but you didn't pick up, and I didn't want to leave this in a message, but a black Infiniti showed up here early this morning, around two o'clock. He started to drive down the hill with his lights off, but then he must have seen my vehicle, because he slammed on the brakes, backed up, and squealed off. You know anyone with a car like that?"

"Oh, my God! That's the car I was telling you about, the one that came by late at night and the driver tried to get into my apartment, remember?"

"Yeah, right. Sorry, of course. I guess I only remembered you telling me about a black Town Car."

"Different stalker. That was the Polish mafia in a black Town Car back in Massachusetts, because of another series of stories I did there."

"Got it, right. Well, it seemed like I spooked him, so hopefully he won't come back as long as I'm here, but we're getting to the end of my two-week stint. Maybe it was good he showed up, so your bosses know I'm still needed. You want to let them know, or should I?"

"I will let them know, or you can, whichever you think is best."

"I think it's best coming from me. So, if you can give me the details on his first visit, when he tried to get in your door, that would help," he said, pulling out a pen and a hand-sized spiral notebook from his breast pocket.

Given that she'd never told Joanne or Linda about that first visit, she thought this might seem odd coming from Teddy, but hopefully they wouldn't ask more questions. Because at this point, no one knew that Goode had been at her apartment at the time, including Teddy—at least as far as she knew.

"It was four or five weeks ago on a Friday night. Well, actually, early Saturday morning," she said. "It was before I had any furniture, so I was lying on my sleeping bag in the living room when I heard these tires crunch on the driveway. I looked out and there he was, with his lights off. I had the sliding glass door open to get some fresh air, and I smelled him smoking a cigarette. I made sure my deadbolt was set on my front door, and about five minutes later I heard the doorknob rattle, like he was trying to get in. Totally freaked me out. Thank God for that deadbolt."

"Must have been scary after you got that threatening note."

"Yeah, it was."

"Were you here alone?"

"Yep," she lied.

"Okaaaay," he said, pausing, possibly for dramatic effect. "Isn't your friend a cop?" Teddy asked, scratching his head.

Do all cops learn these Columbo techniques? Is he implying that he knows Goode was here with me and that he knows I'm lying about being alone? Vincent called me that night and seemed to know that Goode was here.

"Yes, he is, Teddy. But you already knew that. You just wanted me to know that you knew."

Teddy smiled and put his head back in a silent mock chuckle. "Yeah, pretty much."

"Well, let's just keep that to ourselves, shall we?"

"Sure. I didn't see anything untoward. You said he was here helping you move furniture, so I'm sure that's what he was doing."

"He really was, Teddy. Do you want to come inside and look?"

"No need. I'm just ribbin' you."

"Okay, good."

"But if you keep protesting, I'm going to have to mention that in my report."

Katrina knew that cops had a dark sense of humor and loved a good practical joke, so she just let it go. If she said anything else, he was right—she would look guilty.

"Ha, that's funny, Teddy. Well, I'm going to start making dinner. Thanks for letting me know about the black Infiniti. I'm glad you were here to scare him away."

As she was chopping vegetables for pasta primavera, Katrina tried to calm down. But after the conversation with Teddy, she felt more unsettled than she had for the past two weeks. So much for getting a good night's sleep.

I need to ask Joanne where they got Teddy's name. If it came from Vincent, then he's probably here to spy as much as he is to protect me, so maybe I'm no safer than if he wasn't here at all. But if that's the case, then who sent the guy in the Infiniti? If he came back at all. I almost feel like I'm in a hostage situation, but I don't know what the ransom is, who's in charge, or what deadline I'm up against. I hope it wasn't a mistake to send Goode home.

CHAPTER 32
GOODE

Sunday

After the surprise Teddy sighting, Goode had to sit in his van and take deep breaths for a few minutes before he could no longer hear his heartbeat pounding in his head.

Goode didn't know Teddy Kincaid from the SDPD, but he caught a weird vibe from him that he was not to be trusted. The kind of vibe that said Teddy not only knew who Goode was, he'd been waiting to catch him and Katrina together.

While he was still sitting in his van, Katrina texted him: Teddy says the black Infiniti came back at 2AM last night, but turned around and left after seeing Teddy's car. Should we believe him?

I'm not sure, he replied. Got a weird vibe off the dude. Want me to come back inside?

No, thanks. That's okay. But he put me a bit off-kilter too.

Part of him was concerned enough to consider staying the night in the visitor's spot, to keep an eye on things. What if Teddy tried to trick his way into Katrina's apartment? It felt like the wolf watching the henhouse to him, but she had told him to go, so he felt like he should abide by her wishes unless or until something else happened to up the stakes.

Because his date-night proposal had been rejected, Goode decided to stop off and treat himself to wine and takeout anyway.

Why the hell not. I deserve it after working all weekend, even if it was off-the-clock kind of work.

As he drove up his street, Goode felt like he was being watched, so he slowed down sooner than usual to check the cars parked on the street. A couple of houses before his, he passed a black Infiniti, but couldn't tell if someone was sitting inside because the windows were tinted, which was illegal in California. He couldn't recall if the Infiniti that had pulled under Katrina's balcony had tinted windows because it was too dark, but it wouldn't surprise him.

What concerned him now was that this same Infiniti seemed to be parked in front of his house on a Sunday night, watching and waiting for him to come home after allegedly stopping by Katrina's apartment the night before.

How does this dude know where I live? But more importantly, what if Katrina had been with me? He would have caught us going into my house together.

The only person he knew who apparently had been watching his place was Clover Ziegler's mother, and that was a good year ago now, even though he hadn't learned about it until recently. How would someone from the Fontaine–McMurphy case find out his home address? Probably from personnel files that a mole working for the cabal inside the PD, sheriff's department, ME's office, or City Hall would have access to.

This isn't good. If it's Walter Hall in this Infiniti, he needs to know that I'm onto him.

Pulling into his driveway, Goode tucked his gun into the rear waistband of his jeans, then got out and walked down the street to the Infiniti, where he rapped his knuckles on the driver's side window. He could tell that someone was, in fact, sitting in the driver's seat, he just couldn't see his face.

The window slowly rolled down to reveal Walter Hall, aka Linebacker Dude. The same dude posted outside Brandon Winchester's room at the Del, and the same jail deputy who had cut down the bedsheet with which Darren McMurphy allegedly hung himself.

"Can I help you?" Hall asked, chewing a bite of the half-eaten sandwich he was holding.

"Can I ask why you're parked in front of my house, Mr. Hall?"

Hall raised his eyebrows slightly. "Is it a crime to enjoy an Italian sub on a public street?" he asked nonchalantly, as if he wasn't surprised or concerned that Goode knew his name.

"No, it isn't, but you should tell whoever sent you that I know you've been watching me, and I don't like it."

"I don't know what you're talking about, Detective," he said. "I'm just minding my own business."

"I thought you were in the Bahamas anyway."

Hall started coughing, apparently choking after being called out. He took a loud pull on his soda and coughed a few more times before he caught his breath.

"You all right there, Mr. Hall, or do I need to call someone for you?"

"No, I'm fine," he said in a low, raspy voice.

"I think you should be on your way and finish that somewhere else," Goode said, "before I feel the need to pull out my weapon and protect myself."

With that, the engine started up, the tinted window rolled up, and Hall drove away.

Safely inside his cottage, Goode called Katrina to report what had just happened, only to learn that Teddy had recognized him and hassled her about it, which left them both questioning his motives and the real purpose of his "job" watching over her. She also elaborated on Teddy's report about chasing off the black Infiniti the night before.

"It sounds like they're getting nervous," Goode said. "I'm betting it's because of my conversation with Vincent at Torrey Pines. I think Hall has been following me and saw me meet with Vincent, with Darla, and possibly even with Artie Hayes in Hillcrest. If he followed us to the storage facility and knows that I was in your apartment both days, maybe he did come by last night, hoping to take incriminating photos of us."

"At two a.m.? I don't know. I don't like this."

"Yeah, me neither. They're turning up the heat, and my ass is getting hot, but it sounds like they're feeling it too. So, keep your eyes open at all times and be aware of everyone around you. Let's keep in close touch from here on out. I have a gun, but you don't. Now that I've picked up a weird vibe from Teddy, I'm not sure you're safe if I'm not there with you. I think you should tell your bosses that you don't feel comfortable with the way he showed up at your door to question you today, and it's time for him to go."

"I think that would raise too many red flags. Even if he's a spy, I think he was sent here to protect me, not hurt me, or he wouldn't have told me about the black Infiniti," she said. "Maybe he was just doing the cop black humor thing. He is older, and that generation has always gotten away with a lot of lame-ass misogyny."

"Yes, that's true. I will try to keep my testosterone to a manageable level, but I do want to make sure you're safe. And right now, I'm worried you're not."

"I know. Me too. After I confront Vincent, things will come to a head fast. Maybe then we can get all of this over with."

"Let's hope. In the meantime, call me if you want me to come over again, and I'll be there in a jiff."

"That's sweet of you. I will."

"Good night, Katrina. Stay safe and try to get some rest."

"I will. You too, Surfer Man."

With his stomach churning with worry and adrenaline, it took a couple of glasses of wine before Goode was able to get any pizza down his gullet. By that time, he was deep into the Double-Judge Murder file.

Reading the reports was as exciting as watching paint dry, because the detectives were so uninspired, unenterprising, and unambitious that Goode almost fell asleep. The only key point he found in the reports was the suggestion that the killer may have had a military background, because the seventeen long, pointed cartridges retrieved from the Chopins' bodies likely came from an AK-47 or an AR-15. But he knew that wasn't necessarily true, because AKs and their knockoffs were popular with white supremacy groups too. But seventeen was the maximum number of bullets the killer could fire from a single AR-15 magazine without having to reload.

The detectives documented in lengthy, but dry, detail how they'd reviewed both judges' dockets from recent years, trying to identify disgruntled defendants. Although they flagged a few with military backgrounds, they never interviewed a single one of them.

Other than the two neighbors who they talked to early on, the team talked to a few random witnesses here and there—with no mention of Peter's clerk, Julia—but developed no real leads. There was also no reference to Aphy's lunch meetings with Vincent Battrelle. Most disturbing was the discovery that not a single follow-up report had been filed in the past four years.

This is shockingly lazy police work. I'm embarrassed just reading it. I thought this would have been a huge investigation, given the highly public nature of this case. Was this woeful understaffing or purposeful negligence? Based on what I know now, I'd say the latter.

Goode jotted down the partial plate from the noisy blue Toyota Corolla that the one neighbor reported, in case it became important later on, and entered it in the Notes file on his phone.

He was about to sign out of the CAIR system when he had one last thought. Going through the emails reporting back to the homicide lieutenant on the periodic progress, or lack thereof, he scanned the list of people cc'd on them. Following the threads down, he was not surprised to see that one person kept inserting himself for no apparent reason: Lawrence "Bow Tie" Rayburn, the son of cabal leader Elmore Rayburn, the Franny-resort-project investor and spy technology developer.

CHAPTER 33
GOODE

Monday

The next morning, Goode was sitting at his desk after another beautiful dawn surf, ready to take on whatever came his way. But that zen feeling crashed to a halt as soon as he saw Maria's name pop up on his caller ID.

"Chief wants to see you," she said.

Apparently, Chief Baxter had had a change of heart about calling off the meeting. Goode hadn't been summoned to the chief's office since he'd received commendations on the Tania Marcus case and was welcomed to the Homicide unit as a full-time detective. But he could tell by Maria's voice that this was not going to be a warm and fuzzy visit.

Five minutes later, he was sitting in the same hard-backed seat that Stone described as the punishment chair. Goode didn't know the chief personally, but he sensed that Baxter was as uncomfortable as Goode was, which he hoped to use to his advantage.

He planned to feign respect but employ his usual techniques for determining whether the chief had been compromised. Based on Stone's description of their last meeting, Goode suspected that Baxter felt he had no choice but to tell the detectives to stand down.

"How's your buddy doing?" Baxter asked in a flat voice that lacked the compassion one would normally expect to prompt such a question. It sounded more like a disarming prelude to Baxter tearing a new hole in Goode's ass.

"As well as can be expected, I think," Goode said. "I was about to check on him when Maria called."

"I thought you'd be talking on a daily basis," Baxter said.

"We have been, but he does have a wife to take care of his daily needs at home."

"Yes, but you're his work wife," Baxter said, chuckling at his lame joke.

Goode smiled apprehensively, as he waited for the hammer to fall. *C'mon, get on with it.*

"You know why I called you down here, don't you, Detective?" the chief asked.

"Not exactly."

"I figured you did, because you've been up to all kinds of things that I specifically told your sergeant were off limits. I don't know if you're doing this because he's out on medical leave, and you think you can run wild without any supervision, or if you're just used to operating this way and I was never made aware of it because Stone covered for you."

Goode let that comment hang in the air, knowing that it would do him no good to engage if the chief was about to embark on another rant. It sounded like he was just getting warmed up.

"I told Sergeant Stone to stand down and leave the McMurphy deaths alone," the chief said, "so, what do you do? You harass Vincent Battrelle at the golf course. Why is he involved in this case at this point? He already told you what happened at the Fontaine mansion, and I don't know that those misdemeanor obstruction charges are even going to hold up. So, why are you still hounding him?"

"Because, based on the totality of the evidence we've gathered, some of which you don't know about, I believe that Mr. Battrelle is more involved in this case than we were previously aware of, and in more ways than I feel comfortable explaining at the moment, given that some of the information is coming from confidential informants," Goode said, citing a rationale he'd come up with in the elevator.

That retort did the trick, because the chief's body language markedly changed. He shifted uncomfortably in his chair, as if he couldn't find a position to allow his puckered butt cheeks to relax.

"Well, I don't know what that whole mouthful is about, but I think you need to stay in your lane, Detective, or you're going to find yourself in a situation that you didn't bargain for. The sheriff's department and the ME's office have already ruled Darren McMurphy's death a suicide and that Patrick McMurphy died a natural death. The tox results have only confirmed those findings. And since these two men were ostensibly going to provide witness testimony against each other in the murders of Simon and Victoria Fontaine, it seems that the case has reached its natural conclusion."

"I respectfully disagree, sir. We've been working other sources that fit into a bigger picture with the cabal working this whole scheme, including Darla Johansen. So even though Darren McMurphy is dead, she's been giving us intel that shows this is bigger than just the McMurphys."

"Darla, is that your confidential informant?"

"One of them, yes, sir."

"I don't think she's credible. Congressman Brandon Winchester says they were never officially engaged. She was just his side piece, and he's decided to stay with his wife. So, it sounds to me like she's got a big mouth full of sour grapes."

"Respectfully, Chief, I don't see it that way."

But if that's the case, then that takes away her sole reason for not testifying against him. She's probably champing at the bit right now.

"She wasn't willing to testify against him before, so now her reason to protect him is no longer standing in her way of fully cooperating with us," Goode said.

Baxter's eyes started to bulge as he wagged his finger at Goode. "Detective, tell me something. Do you want to get suspended for insubordination and not following orders? Because I'm telling you again to stand down. Darla Johansen is not a credible source, and I don't know who else you've got, but we're not hanging an entire case on her statements, I can tell you that right now."

"No, I don't want to get suspended, but, respectfully, sir, I haven't disobeyed any orders. I'm just doing my job. Are you aware that Vincent Battrelle admitted to me on Friday that he carried in a bottle of vodka to Patrick McMurphy as a favor to a mutual friend? I have documented proof from a private lab that the bottle contains a fatal cocktail of several narcotics, so his death was *not* natural. He was murdered, sir. I also have a source in the ME's office that can prove that the deputy chief has deliberately changed and falsified the toxicology report to make Patrick's death fit the preliminary findings of a natural cardiac arrest."

Baxter let out a long sigh and shook his head. "Detective, you have now put yourself, and me, I might add, into a very precarious position that could be dangerous for both of us. I can't go into details, but I'm—"

Goode could tell he was taking the chief to a breaking point, which was either going to be good or very, very bad for both of them. But he couldn't stop now. "Are you being pressured by the cabal, Chief? Have you been compromised?"

Baxter did his best to ignore him, his voice rising as he finished the thought that Goode had interrupted. "—telling you right now, I'm not going to let you take this charade any further."

"Do I need to go to the FBI to protect us both?" Goode asked. "Or do I need to report that you and Lawrence Rayburn are doing the cabal's work for them?"

With that, the chief's face turned bright red, and he started sputtering like a cornered animal. If Baxter were a skunk, Goode would be covered in foul-smelling funk by now.

Is he about to have a heart attack?

"That's it. As of right now, you're suspended for insubordination and making threats against a superior officer," Baxter barked, his spittle flying toward Goode at an alarming rate of speed. "Surrender your badge and your gun immediately, Detective."

Goode wasn't expecting that move. He knew he'd get a rise out of Baxter, because the chief's temper was legendary. But he didn't realize the chief was going to be this stupid. Shaking his head, he pulled out his badge and his gun, which he calmly and quietly laid on the desk.

"I think you're making a mistake, Chief—"

But Baxter wasn't finished. "If I find out you've talked to thc FBI, you're fired. You don't understand how politically sensitive this situation is. You may not see this now, but I'm trying to save your life, and your girlfriend's too. And don't even get me started on how many rules that relationship breaks."

"She's not my girlfriend," Goode said firmly. "She's a reporter, covering this case. That's it."

"So, you're saying you weren't hugging and canoodling in public on more than one occasion? That you haven't been cavorting around town, moving her furniture out of storage, and spending long hours in her apartment? This is the second time you've had inappropriate relations in a case you're working, Detective. You were warned."

"I'm not sure where you're getting your information, Chief, but I've done nothing wrong. Not in the Tania Marcus case and not in this one."

"Well, that's all in the eye of the beholder now, isn't it? If that's what you've been doing in public, I can't, and don't want to, imagine what you're doing in private. You're suspended until further notice. That should give you some time to think about how you've been conducting yourself on the job."

Feeling numb, Goode walked like a zombie back to the elevator. He stopped by his desk to pick up his things, including the stack of case files that he wanted to review again. He got into his van and drove on autopilot to Windansea.

CHAPTER 34
KATRINA

Knowing the conversation would get ugly and personal, Katrina called Vincent Battrelle on his cell to ask him to meet her somewhere off-site. The last thing they needed was his gossipy secretary listening with her ear glommed onto the other side of his office door. So, she suggested Presidio Park, a historic site in Mission Hills, where the first Spanish Franciscan mission and military fort were founded in 1769. The pocket community park was a public space but felt private, and it was only ten minutes from the paper.

"What's this about, Katrina?" Vincent said, sounding more than a little annoyed. "I've got a very busy morning."

"It's important, Vincent. And once you hear what I have to say, you'll understand why I didn't want to do this at work."

"All right. I'll see you there in fifteen minutes," he said.

This was her chance to find out once and for all whether Vincent was truly a bad dude or was simply associating with the wrong people because he needed their investments to keep Vitaleron afloat. She planned to start with the questions, which he would "deny, deny, deny," at which time she would whip out the DNA results. The goal was to deflate his warrior bravado and turn him into a pile of jelly.

Maybe then he'll tell me the truth.

Sitting on a cement bench under a eucalyptus tree, Katrina waited for Vincent with a mix of emotions. She didn't know how to feel: one, as a reporter, trying to break a huge story; two, as a daughter trying to figure out if her mother's lover had anything to do with her parents' and brother's murder; or three, as an orphan who was about to reclaim a birth parent she didn't know existed until the day before.

Her fingers were cold and shaking, so she tried to warm them against her cappuccino cup. Not only was it a chilly morning, but her high stress level had sent all the blood to her central organs, trying to keep them warm.

As Vincent approached, he stomped on the grass like an angry caveman, pounding the ground combatively to show how powerful and important he was.

If only he knew what I'm about to tell him.

Before she asked him anything about the McMurphys, the black Infiniti following her, or if he'd hired Teddy to spy on her, she wanted to confront him about his lunch dates with her mother. She hoped a roundabout approach would soften him up.

"Listen, I need to ask you some personal questions. I've been going through my parents' things, and I've come across some troubling pieces of history that I knew nothing about while they were alive."

Hearing that, she observed Vincent's testosterone-fueled energy diminish and watched him let his guard down a bit. "Okay, I'm listening."

"Were you and my mother having an affair before she died, I mean right before? I know you met up with her in London after she married my father, because I found a photo of the two of you in front of Big Ben. I also found her datebook, which listed a series of lunch dates with you at the Grant hotel right before they were killed. Were those lunches or intimate meetings?"

Obviously surprised by the question, Vincent raised his eyebrows and blew air out his lips in one long stream. "I guess a little of both," he said.

"So, you were having an affair?"

"If you want to call it that, I suppose so," he said. "But as I told you the night you came to my house a couple of months ago, I loved your mother very much. I never looked at it as some tawdry affair. She said she would never leave your father, but she did agree to see me now and again. She wanted a little excitement in her life, because Peter was kind and stable, but, sorry to say, boring. So, I took what I could get."

"Did you ask her to leave him?"

"Yes. Many times. And she always said no."

"Did you ever consider trying to win her back by doing anything that you might now regret?"

Vincent frowned, his shoulders tensing again. "What are you implying?" he asked.

Katrina tried to ask her next question in a nonconfrontational way to keep him from marching off before she could get to the others. "I'm trying to find out if, perhaps, you might have wanted to get my dad out of the picture somehow, and it backfired."

"Are you asking me if I put a hit out on your father and she got killed by accident? Really, Katrina?"

Katrina nodded, hoping that staying silent might help defuse some of the anger.

"Why would you ask me that? Even if that was true, I'd never tell you. Jesus. You're a reporter, for God's sake, and I've seen how little regard you have for my family and their privacy or well-being, let alone the well-being of your coworkers."

"I figured you'd say something like that, but you still haven't denied it."

"If I really need to deny it, I will. No, I had nothing to do with your parents' murder. That's a ridiculous accusation, and I think you know that. I would never do anything to harm your mother, and I had nothing against your father other than he got to sleep next to the woman I loved for more than thirty years."

"Okay, fair enough. Thank you for telling me that."

Vincent sighed before turning to look at her again. "Is that it?"

"No. As I reported in my stories, Darren McMurphy claimed there is a group of wealthy men who control this city behind the scenes through money and influence. Darla Johansen called it a cabal and described you as a Friend of the Cabal, meaning you're not an official member, but you're aware of what they're doing. Is that true?"

"Oh, not this nonsense again. I belong to many groups of wealthy businessmen, many of whom are investors in Vitaleron. So, in a broad sense, yes. But there is no group that calls itself a cabal or that has made me aware of any nefarious deeds."

"Well, I've got information that they were behind the deaths of Darren and Patrick McMurphy."

"What kind of information, Katrina? I hope you're not trying to print any of this in my newspaper, because it sounds like rumor, gossip, and innuendo. Without any proof, you'd be opening us up to a crippling defamation suit."

"Do you remember when I told you that I thought my brother, Franny, was murdered?"

"Yes, I do, very clearly."

"Did you know that the cocktail of narcotics that was found in his body after he drank lemon-infused vodka was the same one that was found in the bottle of lemon-infused vodka that you carried into Patrick McMurphy's house?"

Vincent's shoulders tightened again, and his face grew flushed within seconds as he turned to Katrina to reply, his voice growing louder with each word. "What are you saying? That I murdered them both too? Good God, Katrina, this is preposterous."

He stood up abruptly to leave, but Katrina quickly responded before he could storm off. "Wait, please sit down. I'm not finished.

You'll want to hear the rest of what I have to say. This is just between us for now, so you can calm down. I'm not going to promise I won't write about this, but if I do, it's a ways off. Certainly not for tomorrow's paper, okay?"

Shaking his head, Vincent sat back down but turned away from her, trying to control his breathing. "You're going to have to give me a minute. You really have a knack for making me angry."

"Almost like a son or daughter might?"

Vincent turned toward her again, his brows furrowed. "What kind of question is that?"

Opening her purse, she pulled out the paperwork from 23andMe and handed it to him. "Read this."

His eyes glued to the papers, he looked confused at first. Then he raised his eyes to meet hers, his expression now one of sheer disbelief as his face turned a ghostly gray. He clutched her arm, and within thirty seconds, his eyes welled up with tears.

"Is this really true?"

"Yes. I've got another website that's supposed to get back to me with results in another few weeks, so we'll get confirmation from a second source. You can send in your DNA for a straight confirmation, either to them or to a private lab that will turn around the results in a much shorter timeframe, but I'm pretty confident these are accurate."

"Why did your mother never tell me this? All that time, all that sneaking around. I don't know how many times she said she wouldn't leave her husband because they had a family. Is it possible she didn't know who your birth father really was?"

"I wondered that, too, but no. I've been going through her diaries, and she knew it was you. She knew it when she asked what you would do if she got pregnant and you said you would pay for her to 'take care of it.' That's when she made up her mind."

"Of course that's what I said. Because I thought it was a hypothetical question. We were so young. We had our whole lives ahead of us. But if I had to make that choice in real time—"

"You would have made a different decision?"

Vincent paused, shrugged, and with a sad half smile, said, "No, probably not. But now that I know this, I'll regret saying it for the rest of my life. She was my first love, my only real love. But I had plans. Big plans. I wasn't ready to be a father. I would never be where I am today if I'd gotten married and had two babies back then."

"Well, then. She made the right decision, I guess."

Vincent examined Katrina as if he were seeing her for the first time. "I knew there was something about you, and I always liked Franny. Saw a little of myself in him. You might be surprised to hear this, but now that I know you're my daughter, I can say you're the one child who is the success I always wanted."

Why am I not surprised that he turned this around to make it about him? Poor Michael, Meredith, and Alex, too, for that matter.

He stared off into the distance, his thoughts going who knows where, before she saw the apprehension creep into his eyes. "What do I tell Ruth? She won't be happy about this," he said, pausing. "But you know what? I don't care. You're mine, and she'll have to accept you."

Hearing this, Katrina still didn't know what to think or how to feel. Or what to say. But she wasn't surprised that he thought of her as a possession, because her mother had made the same observation. Before, she was *his* reporter, and now, she was *his* daughter. She hadn't known what to expect from him, so she couldn't prepare for how his reaction would affect her.

Well, now she knew. She felt paralyzed. Confused. Overwhelmed. It was all a bit much.

"So, what do we do now?" he asked. "What made you decide to send in for these results anyway?"

"It was supposed to be for a human interest story, a first-person column, actually, about my family's history. What with the murders and my brother's alleged suicide, the stalker who keeps breaking my car windows and threatening my life, and the whole fiasco with Darren McMurphy trying to kill me at the Del, Joanne, Linda, and I thought it would be a good vehicle to keep the narrative going, but in a completely benign way. Little did we know how it would turn out."

"I see. As a publisher, it sounds like a great idea, but as a private citizen, I don't know that I want my secrets and mistakes exposed to the entire city."

"It'll sell papers, though, right? I haven't even told Joanne or Linda yet, so there's still plenty of time for you to tell your family before we publish anything."

Shaking off the paralysis, she went back into work mode. Now that Vincent had calmed down, she figured he was primed to give her some real answers to her previous questions.

"So how about my questions about the cabal? Maybe you can elaborate a little more now that you know you can trust me."

"Can I, though?" he asked, raising his eyebrows.

This was her chance to confirm Darla's cabal leader names. If he didn't know who they were, that would be telling.

"Did you ever take a blood oath to be in a group with Elmore and Lawrence Rayburn, Rick Rodriguez, and John Young? I hear Patrick McMurphy and Brandon Winchester were both in it, too, but I don't know where that stands now."

"Listen, Katrina, my answers won't change. Yes, I know all those men, but I've certainly never taken a blood oath for anything or anyone, nor would I. It sounds like voodoo or witchcraft. Something a teenager would come up with."

Vincent shook his head in disbelief. "If I had known what was in that vodka, or that Franny was killed the same way, I promise you I would never have delivered that bottle to Patrick."

"Will you tell me who gave you that bottle now?"

"Yes, all right. It was Lawrence Rayburn. I've known his father for years. But, frankly, I'm shocked by what you're saying. If I'd known that to be true, I would've cut myself off from those men and disenfranchised them from Vitaleron. And if it is true, I promise you I will do that as soon as you can prove it, and I will support your publishing it in my newspaper. You have to believe me, Katrina. I may not be a perfect man, but I'm not a murderer. Not by any means."

"I'm glad to hear you say that, but, honestly, I don't know what to believe. I want to feel that you're telling the truth, but I need to find out what happened to my parents, whether they were killed by this same group just like my brother was. Because someone has been threatening me, and I need that to stop so I can get back to living my life. By the way," she said, looking him in the eye, "did you hire Teddy to spy on me?"

Vincent raised his eyebrows and smiled a little. "Well, since we're being honest here, I hired him because you insisted on writing that first-person piece that announced to the whole world that you were receiving death threats. But yes, I did ask him to report back to me what you were doing and who you were seeing. We go back a long way."

"I see. I know you were partners with my father in Vitaleron and on the building in Sorrento Valley, but then he disappeared from the paperwork. He's not mentioned on the website, and I couldn't even find any emails between you about it."

"It was done in a phone call. An angry phone call. He was not happy with me. He'd found out many years earlier that Aphy and I had gotten together in London, but he thought that was long over. So, it irked him when he saw us openly joking and laughing together in front of their friends at the University Club. He was jealous, plain and simple. So that was his choice. A bad financial decision in my opinion, but I understand why he made it."

"Do you have proof or anything in writing?"

"No, I don't, other than his absence from the next year's Vitaleron corporate paperwork, which is how I assume you figured this out. As I said, it was all verbal, but I followed his wishes to a T."

"What about my brother? Did you know the other investors were angry enough to have him killed? You all lost a lot of money."

"Yes, we did, but I had nothing to do with that either. You need to believe me, Katrina."

"If all that's true, then you should stop dodging the police and tell them what you know."

"I'll have to think about everything you've told me. You've dumped quite a load on me. Let me talk to Ruth and the kids. Maybe we can all have dinner together at the house."

"Why don't we give everyone a chance to digest this first. These DNA results just came in the mail yesterday, and I'm still reeling from them myself. I was an orphan on Saturday, and now I have a brand-new family who may not want me around."

"Well, they aren't going to have a choice, if I have anything to say about it, and as the head of this family and the primary breadwinner, I have everything to say about it."

Vincent stood up, gave her a quick sideways hug, and walked back to his Jaguar.

CHAPTER 35
GOODE

Monday

Goode was staring out at the ocean from his usual perch on the stairs at Windansea when Katrina called, jumping right in without saying hello again.

"So, I told him, he cried, then he gave me a sloppy, awkward hug," she said. "He denied being a member of the cabal, said he knew of no group that called itself that and he had nothing to do with any of the murders. He even promised to print whatever proof I can find that such a group exists and did this. Then he invited me to dinner with his family."

"Sounds like a well-rounded set of carefully worded denials," he replied. "Do you believe him? Did he seem sincere?"

"I want to, and yes, he actually did sound sincere, like it was really important that I think him incapable of such evil deeds. He told me that I was the successful child he'd always wanted. So that was kind of big. And weird. Oh, and he finally told me it was Lawrence Rayburn who gave him the bottle to carry inside to Patrick. So, now can I print that?"

"Really? That's a great get," Goode said. "It also fits with the other information we've been gathering. But no, not yet, please. We need to maintain the integrity of this investigation and the element of surprise."

A car drove past Goode with one truant teenager yelling out the passenger side window to a second truant teenager who was hanging out at the shack. Goode didn't say anything, waiting to see if Katrina had finished telling him her news. He didn't want to interrupt her train of thought, knowing what a big deal that conversation was and how anxious she'd been about having it.

"Wait, are you at the beach?" she asked, sounding surprised to have taken this long to figure that out. "It's ten thirty in the morning. Didn't you already go surfing this morning?"

"Yes, I'm at the beach, and yes, it's for the second time this morning. Everything was going great until the chief called me into his office, launched verbal grenades into my face, and accused me of having an improper relationship with you. When I asked if he was compromised and suggested going to the FBI to protect us both from the cabal, he suspended me and said he would fire me if I went to the feds."

Katrina paused. "I'm not really sure what to say. I'm so sorry. That totally sucks. What kind of verbal grenades?"

Goode explained how serious the situation was, and that it was only a matter of time before whoever had ratted him out—someone who knew Vincent, most likely—would do the same to her. This case was all about San Diego's microcosmic power structure.

"Get ready, because we're about to feel the full effect of being disruptors who are fighting to break open that power structure to expose the truth."

"My first impulse is to be scared," Katrina said. "But I like the way you described it, that we're 'disruptors.'"

As Goode filled in more details, including the meager investigative reports he'd seen in the CAIR system about her parents' murder, Katrina listened intently, like a good reporter should.

"Are you typing this up?" he asked, hearing her keyboard clacking.

"Yes, shouldn't I be?"

"Did I need to say this was off the record? I figured we were just talking."

"We are, but I still need to keep a record of what's going on. This suspension is huge. I think you should go public with it. It'll light a fire under the chief. Maybe then he'll do the right thing."

"I'm not sure that would get the intended result. I think he really would fire me, and then where would we be?"

"Why don't you go talk it over with Stone and tell him about your suspension? I asked Vincent straight out if he'd been a party to the hit on my parents, and he denied it, so now I'm going to track down my dad's clerk and do the same to her. But first, I'll see if she'll have lunch with me."

"Then what?"

"I'll feel her out and try to determine if she seems unstable, the kind of woman scorned who could do something rash. Then I'm going to ask her straight out if she shot my parents or knows who did. Exactly what your department should have done five years ago."

"Let me know if you need any help. I guess I'm a free agent for the foreseeable future."

After they hung up, Goode listened to the seagulls calling to each other and the waves crashing, the white wash crawling up the sand and withdrawing like a lace blanket teasing the shore. Thinking back over his time at the SDPD, he mentally listed the high points. Up until recently, there hadn't been many low points. Overall, his experience had been pretty good.

He'd worked his way from Patrol to Vice, always with his eye on getting to Homicide. With Stone's help, he filled in as a relief homicide detective for those who were out sick or on vacation, then finally won the big transfer after making a splash with the Tania Marcus case a little more than a year ago. Stone had cheered him on from the start, and now here they were, both sidelined. All due to the chief's temper and his corrupt involvement with these rich and power-hungry white men. Cabal, indeed.

This BS cannot stand. Maybe Stone's right, and it is time to call my new FBI buddy, Marty Watts. I want to see how their case against Winchester is going anyway. I'll tell him I've got more suspects for him to look at and fill him in on the new layers of the corruption scheme that we've uncovered. There's no way Baxter can fire me if I claim whistleblower status, but there's no way of knowing if I'll get a goddamned medal or if everyone will hate me for being a snitch because of the "thin blue line."

But before he could do anything, Darla called. She'd just learned that her so-called fiancé had reneged on their engagement after deciding to reconcile with his wife. It was too expensive not to.

"He didn't even have the balls to tell me himself, and when I called to confront him, he had the chutzpah to ask for my ring back. Says he needs to sell it to cover his legal costs. I told him I'd pawn it first. What an asshole. How could I have been so naïve?"

Goode didn't know how to answer that, but he'd been wondering that all along. He'd chalked it up to poor judgment, compounded by her love of spending the rich dude's money.

"So, you're ready to go on the record about him now?" he asked.

"You're damn right, I'm ready. What do you want to know? I'll tell you everything. No holds barred. Just show me that immunity deal and tell me where to sign."

Not knowing how long his suspension would last, he didn't want to screw this up by telling her that he now had no authority to make that deal, so he figured he'd let her talk, then ask Stone the best way to proceed. Because, regardless of what the chief claimed, Goode believed that Darla had these assholes dead to rights with inside information they didn't want to come out. Which was exactly why the chief had tried to discredit her.

"Okay, let's start by going over the names of the five cabal leaders," he said. "Last time, you recited a bunch of names without telling me who was who in the hierarchy."

"Last I heard, the Circle of Five was Elmore Rayburn, Rick Rodriguez, John Young, Patrick McMurphy, and my loser former fiancé. But since Patrick's Circle brothers decided to poison him, that leaves one open seat. And because Brandon is facing federal charges and will likely have to resign his seat, they'll probably ask him to step aside, if they haven't already, because he's no longer useful to them. Typically, there's a lot of jostling and behind-the-scenes lobbying to get one of these coveted seats. Even before Brandon got arrested, a major shake-up was in the works because Elmore is getting older and wants to step down. His son, Lawrence, has been vying for that spot, but he had to prove his worth first."

So that's why he's been inserting himself everywhere.

"What about Vincent Battrelle? Has he ever been one of the top five or in line to be?"

"No, like I said, he's more of an FOTC. I don't know if that was his choice or theirs, but he's not an inherently bad dude. He's more of a ruthless businessman who favors money over people."

"Semantics. But go on. Who's next in line?"

"Besides Lawrence Rayburn? There's been talk about Reggie Flanagan stepping up."

"Who is he, exactly?"

"He's the former mayor who was convicted of campaign laundering, but was able to get a presidential pardon from George W. Bush. Campaign contributions can buy anything these days. He went into real estate development like the rest of them and made a pile of dough. He's a long-standing member of the caucus, and he's a Vitaleron investor too."

"Right, now I remember. Where does this group do business? I mean, do they meet somewhere in a dark cave, light candles, and chant?"

"No, it's funny, the Circle of Five may be an über-secret group, but it holds business meetings out in the open—at the quiet little Empress Hotel bar in La Jolla. The meetings are on the third Monday of the month, when the bar is usually empty. They sit around the piano player, so no one can hear them, and act like a group of old friends, drinking and chatting."

"So, the next one would be a week from tonight?"

"Yes. They'll all be there. Sometimes they have contenders come in, you know, men who want in or have a proposal—and yes, it's always men, because it's a white male–only group. They usually have some dirty deed they want the group to do for them, but first they have to persuade the Circle that it's worth their while, financially or otherwise. That might be how Vincent got to know those guys. He probably offered the entire membership a chance to invest in Vitaleron, because a lot of them did. Some of them forked over pretty big sums, and a few even managed to get in on the human trials."

"So, my understanding is that when Darren told his dad that Victoria was causing problems and interfering with his plans to facilitate the FDA approval, the Circle had Patrick tell his son to 'take care of the mess,' correct?"

"I don't know that for sure, but that sounds plausible. Darren said the order came from his dad, but I know this group, and I'm sure Patrick either did it on behalf of the group or he felt pressured to do it, which is why both of them are dead now."

"Because they knew too much."

"Exactly."

"Throwing his son out of the family trust wasn't enough."

"I guess not."

"All right, thanks for the info. Let me talk to my sergeant, and I'll get back to you."

"Don't take too long. I can't really leave my place. Every time I look out my living room window, Brandon's bodyguard is parked outside in his black Infiniti. He's been following me too. I'm wondering if he saw us talking at Jose's the other night, because I didn't see him around much until after that."

So, I was right, and that explains why I got suspended this morning. They are worried. With good reason.

"Gotcha. Can you have a male friend stay with you? They're less likely to try to harm you if you've got a man around. But be careful. I'll try to get this thing hammered out, but we've got a few bureaucratic roadblocks to get past first."

"I doubt it. I lost most of my friends, male and female, when I rebuilt my life around Vitaleron and Brandon. And now they're gone too."

CHAPTER 36
KATRINA

Monday

Back in the newsroom, Katrina decided it was time to tell Joanne about the DNA results. She and Linda wouldn't want to run this story if Vincent Battrelle wasn't behind it, because this bombshell was about to turn his entire family upside down. Unless he wanted to go ahead with the story, of course. Even so, she would still have to consult the other family members, because, without their permission, the story would violate their privacy rights and reveal personal medical information, which would leave the newspaper open to a lawsuit. The question was, would their combined rights outweigh Vincent's?

She imagined that Vincent's wife, Ruth, would be dead set against it, whereas his sons, Michael and Alex, might not mind. And his daughter, Meredith? Who could say. Meredith was the reason this information had come to light in the first place. And because she seemed to hold little emotional significance for Vincent, she might even see this as a way to get her father's—and everyone else's—attention.

"Are you ready for this?" Katrina asked as she closed the door to Joanne's office.

"What now? Should I be worried?" Joanne asked sarcastically. It seemed almost impossible to worry this woman. Katrina wished she had her editor's temperament.

"No, but let's just say my DNA results are not what I expected," she said, handing over the paperwork.

Joanne's eyes almost rolled back into her head, and she wasn't even clowning around. "This is insane. Is this a joke?"

"No, it's not. It's from 23andMe," Katrina said.

"How the hell did *that* happen?"

"Remember I told you that Vincent mentioned he'd dated my mom back in law school and remembered her fondly?"

"Yes, but, wow. I didn't see this coming. Did you?"

"No, not at all. But I dug around in my storage units this weekend and found some old letters and diaries, so I was able to reconstruct the whole backstory. Vincent didn't know, and neither did my dad. It also turns out that my mom and Vincent were having an affair on and off for years all the way up until she was killed."

"Did your dad know about the affair?"

"I know he saw them together, flirting, and got jealous, which is why, after initially investing in Vitaleron, he pulled out after only three months. He knew they'd been together many years earlier, and then again when my mom studied abroad in London after Franny and I were born, but he thought it was long over. So, there was some history there."

"Wait, your dad was one of the original investors in Vitaleron? How long have you known that?"

"There's a lot I've been finding out lately that I haven't told you because it's more related to my parents' and my brother's deaths. I can't share all of it right now, either, because there's some sensitive goings-on down at the PD—"

"I'm sensing that Detective Goode is involved in this, too, then, am I correct?"

"Yes, and by the way, he was suspended and placed on administrative leave this morning, because he accused the chief of being corrupt, so—"

"Did he tell you that on the record?"

"Joanne, can I please finish telling you this first?"

"Sorry," she said, covering her mouth with her hand. "You've got me all aflutter with these bombs you're dropping."

"Right. It turns out that my brother was murdered with the same narcotic cocktail that Patrick McMurphy drank the night he died. Goode told the chief about that this morning, and Baxter basically said that he was putting them—including Goode's girlfriend, meaning me, who, by the way, is not his girlfriend—in a very dangerous situation. When Goode suggested going to the FBI, Baxter threatened to fire him. But we can't print any of this because it's all off the record, and since it involves my personal life, and Vincent's, too, it's one big cluster-you-know-what. Oh, yeah, we also finally have some names of the cabal leaders, and we're working on getting more. I didn't want to keep all of this from you, but at least now you know the highlights."

"My God, Katrina. Do you even sleep on the weekends?"

"Not this past weekend, especially after finding the DNA results in my mailbox. By the way, you know Teddy Kincaid, the retired cop who's been posted outside my apartment? Vincent admitted that he didn't just hire him to protect me, he also hired him to spy on me, which is *not* cool."

"He admitted that?"

"Yes, he did."

"So, what do we do now?"

"Well, Goode is going to discuss next steps with his sergeant, who is out on medical leave after having a meltdown in the chief's office over some of these same corruption issues. I need to talk to them to see what I can print. If we wait a few days, I think we can start chipping away at it. Some of the information came from my storage units—my parents' computer files, letters, datebooks, and journals—but I want to let the rest of it play out first so I can connect the dots. I promise that, eventually, we'll have a series of blockbuster stories. I've told Linda a little of this, but she seemed worried about keeping our jobs and protecting the paper's reputation, so let's not tell her anything more right now, okay? I don't want to take the chance that she lets this slip out to Vincent, because he could tell his cabal friends and the whole investigation would be compromised. We can tell her about the DNA results, just not the rest. Not yet."

At first, Linda was more giddy about the DNA news than Joanne, but the inevitable reality set in once she realized the Ruth-Meredith-Michael-Alex privacy-and-medical-rights conundrum could complicate a perfectly good story that readers would gobble up.

"And that's what I'm going to tell the Battrelles," she said, apparently disregarding any concern for Katrina's feelings about her newly discovered birth father. "I guess we'll give them a little time and see what shakes out. What a terrific story, Katrina. It's going to be a great read."

Katrina excused herself and left her editors to conspire, saying she had lunch plans with an old friend.

A database search for her father's former clerk, Julia Frangello, showed two women by that name in San Diego County, but only one who was the right age. Calling media relations for the federal courthouse, Katrina was told no such person worked in the building.

"Have you tried the Superior Court?" the spokeswoman asked.

That's right, she said she got a new job at the state courthouse down the street.

With one more phone call, Katrina found the answer she was looking for: Julia was clerking for a female civil judge in the Hall of Justice.

Because parking prices were outrageous downtown, Katrina used an app to find an affordable spot in the Horton Plaza garage. It made for a bit of a walk, but well worth the inconvenience.

The air was cool and breezy as she made her way down Broadway, but it was warm in the sun as long as she walked on the north side of the street.

After pulling open the heavy glass doors of the courthouse, she put her purse on the conveyor belt of the metal detector. The bailiffs gave her a once-over and deemed her safe to pass.

In the elevator up to the fourth floor, Katrina worked out what she would say to put Julia at ease. Even if the clerk had been friendly to her with the hopes of impressing her boss, Katrina saw no reason for a significant attitude change.

Finding the courtroom wasn't hard. But at 11:45 a.m., court was still in session. She knew the judge would call the noon recess any minute, so she took a seat near the door, where she could see Julia's blond head at a desk to the right of the judge.

Even while she was seated, it was obvious that Julia had gained some weight since Katrina had last seen her eight or nine years earlier, when she'd been relatively attractive in a tall, thin, and horse-faced kind of way.

The trial was a financial one, as boring and dry as it could get. But as soon as the judge broke for lunch, all the suits filed out the doors with their file folders, briefcases, and smug attitudes. Katrina approached Julia with caution, waiting to see if the clerk would recognize her.

"Is that Katrina?" Julia asked, breaking into a wide toothy grin.

"Yes," Katrina replied, relieved.

"What a nice surprise! Come up here and give me a hug!"

Approaching the wooden partition that prevented the lookie-loos from entering the sacred space where the judge sat with her clerk, Katrina stood at the precipice. Julia reached over and pulled Katrina toward her, causing Katrina's hips to slam into the barrier. Katrina immediately felt a sneeze coming on, her nose tweaked by the perfume with which Julia had doused herself that morning.

I'm not sensing any underlying anger or resentment here. If anything, Julia's almost too excited to see me. Unless that's underlying guilt she feels?

Julia looked her over, still smiling. "What brings you in today?" she asked. "Oh, where are my manners. I'm so sorry for your loss. Losses, actually. I didn't get a chance to come to either of the funerals."

"Thank you, Julia. No worries. Actually, I was wondering if I could take you to lunch."

Julia seemed pleasantly surprised. "Of course. That would be nice," she said. "Let me grab my jacket and purse."

The two of them rode down in the elevator in silence, surrounded by other clerks, lawyers, and jurors. Once they reached the lobby, Julia recommended a French bistro with outdoor tables on the next block.

The hostess offered to seat them outside, but Katrina said she'd prefer to eat indoors. Although she wanted privacy for this conversation, she also wanted people around in case Julia caused a scene.

After perusing the menus, they both ordered a salade Niçoise and a Diet Coke. A few minutes later, the busboy delivered ice waters and a hot baguette with a pot of whipped butter. Julia tried to break off a chewy piece that wouldn't come loose, fighting with it until she achieved success, and unexpectedly burst into tears.

Katrina had approached this lunch with no expectations, but she did anticipate that something like this could happen. She sat stoically, waiting to see where Julia's mood would go to next, hoping she might blurt out an unsolicited confession.

But that didn't happen. Unable to compose herself, Julia jumped up and ran to the restroom. The police had assumed that the killer was a man, but given that the driver was wearing a ski mask, it could just as easily have been a woman. Like Julia.

Katrina scanned the room for reactions, hoping to catch the eye of someone who knew Julia and might speak to Katrina later. But the few onlookers only glanced furtively her way, unwilling to meet her gaze.

When Julia returned to the table, half her makeup had been wiped off, presumably during the crying and nose blowing.

"I'm so sorry. I don't know where that came from," Julia said, plopping back down. "I didn't realize how much emotion I had pent up inside about your father."

"I get it. The same thing happened to me at the storage facility when I saw a little rocking horse that Franny and I used to play with," she said, pausing. "Are you sure it's sadness?"

Julia frowned, her brow furrowed with confusion. "What do you mean?"

"Well, I know about the affair, or fling, or whatever it was, between you, and how he had you transferred—"

"Wait, how did you—"

"—to another judge. How he asked you to stop calling and writing him, and how you left the federal courthouse so you didn't have to run into each other anymore."

Obviously embarrassed, Julia stared down at her lap, unable to look Katrina in the eye.

"I just found your cards and letters in storage when I was going through some of my parents' belongings."

"I'm sorry you had to find out that way," Julia said, glancing up now. "But if it makes any difference, I was in love with him until the day he died. He was such a good man. It was only one night. I'd been thinking about it for a long time, but then it just kind of happened."

"What just happened?"

"We were working in chambers. It got late, so we were eating takeout and talking, and one thing led to another."

"Uh-huh."

"He was feeling sad. He always seemed to be sad around that time."

"What time was that?"

"It was after he invested in Vitaleron. Initially, he was really excited about the new drug that Dr. Fontaine was developing. He thought it was going to make them all very rich. But then three months later, he decided to pull all of his and your mom's money out. That's when he started moping around. I didn't know or understand what was going on, so I gave him a hug to cheer him up, and we started kissing. You probably don't want to hear the rest."

"No, I get the picture. He was worried he'd lost the love of his life, because my mom was flirting around with someone else."

"Vincent Battrelle?"

"Yes," Katrina said, hoping this spontaneous admission might lead somewhere fruitful. "Do you know him?"

"Not really. He came to the courtroom a few times to take your dad to lunch around the time of the Vitaleron deal."

"Did you see him in the months before my parents were killed?"

Julia frowned. "Why would you ask me that?"

"Can you just answer the question?"

"Of course I didn't," Julia said defensively.

"Why does it sound like you're not telling me the truth?" Katrina countered.

"I am, but it sounds like you're trying to accuse me of something, like going behind Peter's back with his former business partner. I would never do that."

"Uh, no, not at all. I was only asking if you'd seen him. Are you sure you're not trying to hide something?"

Julia shook her head dramatically. "I'm not. It's just . . . Okay, I did see Mr. Battrelle, but he told me not to tell anyone. He took me out for a drink after Peter had me transferred and asked if Peter had ever cheated on his wife. I told him yes, but it was just the one time, and it wasn't going to happen again because we no longer worked together. I was so flustered about how he would even know about that night that I got up and left. I didn't even finish my second glass of wine."

"Is there anyone who could have seen you with my father that night in his chambers? A janitor, a bailiff, or a security guard whom Vincent could have paid to get the information? I'm sure he bought you drinks to lower your defenses so you would admit it, which you did."

"No, I don't think anyone saw us. We were in his chambers with the door closed," Julia said. "And yes, I think you're right. I said too much because I was tipsy, and Vincent said a bunch of stuff that made me feel manipulated and embarrassed. I felt so bad after I inadvertently blurted it out, because even though I was hurt and angry, I still didn't want Peter to get in trouble or to blame me. I was still so in love with him I couldn't even sleep. I missed him like crazy. We'd worked together for twenty years."

"Yes, I know."

"Why would Vincent Battrelle care so much?"

"He probably wanted to use the information to try to get my mother to leave my dad."

"Well, that's pretty conniving."

"That's a good word for it. Listen, Julia. I have to ask you. Do you know anything about my father's murder or who might have wanted to kill him?"

Julia pulled her jacket down and adjusted her skirt, then went back to staring at the table. "No, not really."

"Not really? What do you mean?"

"No, I mean no. I don't."

"But you hesitated. Like you *do* know something."

"No, I don't. I'm just nervous. This whole conversation is very upsetting. I feel like I did the night Vincent took me out for wine."

"I'm not Vincent Battrelle. I'm just trying to find out who killed my parents and why."

"What about Vincent? It sounds like he wanted your dad out of the way."

"Yeah, I already thought of that, but he denied it. Just like you."

"Only I'm not guilty. And I wouldn't have the money to pay someone even if I wanted to. He does."

"It still seems like you're holding something back."

"Well, I'm not. Like I said, I'm just nervous." Pushing her chair back to stand up, Julia grabbed the strap of her purse and slung it over her shoulder. "I'm really sorry, Katrina, I'm going back to the courthouse. My stomach is upside down, and I couldn't eat anything if I tried. I hope you find what you're looking for."

CHAPTER 37
GOODE

Monday

Kicking back in Stone's living room with a beer he'd brought over, Goode gave him the lowdown. Listening intently, Stone drank an entire bottle of a sugar-free sports drink that Dr. Costello recommended to keep his electrolytes in check.

"Damn, Goode, you've been busy chasing down these corrupt bastards," he said. "You don't even need me around, do you? Don't answer that."

Goode was proud that he didn't have to leave anything out about his investigative time with Katrina, given that she'd rejected his invitation to come to his house for wine and file searching.

"It's so aggravating that the chief is calling her my girlfriend when literally nothing is going on," Goode said. "By the way, we should open a murder case on her brother."

"We'll get there, eventually. But let's wade through this other stuff first," Stone said. "Like getting the ME to change the manner of death for Patrick McMurphy from natural death to homicide. That's going to take some maneuvering."

"True. So, now that I've been suspended, they can't do anything to me if I have sex with her, right?"

"Back to that, are we? The answer is no, but I would steer clear until we see our way through this case."

"You know I had to ask."

"I know, buddy. You never let a good opportunity go to waste."

Goode took a long pull off his IPA and let Stone process all the new developments while they watched a soccer match, Liverpool versus Manchester City, on cable. Stone needed more processing time than Goode, but he usually got there in the end.

"So, the vodka bottle tested positive for narcotics, but the toxicology report says Patrick didn't have those drugs in his body? How do we get around that?"

"Thompson altered the report in the computer, but I've got a copy of the original, before his changes. Artie's in-house toxicologist friend, who did the lab work, was smart enough to print one out."

"Is it someplace safe?"

"What do you mean?"

"I mean, I wouldn't put it past that thug, Walter Hall, to break into the ME's office, and into your house, too, to root around for whatever case files and paperwork you've got lying around."

Goode tapped the side of his head. "I like that you're always thinking, my friend. Don't you worry. It's in my van in a lockbox inside a cooler underneath a tarp and an old wetsuit. He would never find it even if he broke in."

"Don't think he won't try. That guy's nuts. I had a friend check him out. Had to do something to keep myself busy while I'm incapacitated. My toenails were starting to curl."

"What did you find out?"

"He's a former marine. Dishonorable discharge for excessive violence, if you can believe that. He beat up his sergeant in Afghanistan after taking too many steroids."

"Great. A roid rager."

"He quit the drugs, I guess, and went into rehab. Brandon Winchester's a former marine, too, so he took Hall in, gave him a job. That's where the brotherhood loyalty comes from."

"What I want to know is, how Hall had time to get a job as a jail deputy when he was working for Winchester and chasing us around?"

"That's the crazy part. He'd only just started working the jails the week Darren 'hanged' himself, so the cabal must have inserted their guy to get in and get out after the kill. Just like in Afghanistan. I'll bet he was gone immediately afterward, because didn't you say he was in the Bahamas with that newspaper editor who was forced to resign?"

"Yeah, he went there after Winchester's arrest, but he must have come back for the kill. Now he's following Darla Johansen around and hanging outside my house eating Italian subs. Glad to see the bonk on your head didn't kill your memory."

"Yeah, I've been drawing up flowcharts while I've been watching football."

"Isn't it time for you to come back soon?"

"Yes. In fact, now that you're out, I should get back in there. Someone's going to have to start preparing warrants. Although the chief will probably make that difficult."

"About that. That's why we can't do all of this on our own. I think you're right about meeting with Marty Watts."

"Even after the chief threatened to fire you?"

"He had to be bluffing. That would never fly. Besides, we need Watts's help with this meeting on Monday. If he can mic up the place like he did at the Del for Katrina's meeting with Winchester and Darla, then we can nail the Circle of Five, if we're lucky, while they're planning their next kill. Hall came by Katrina's place in the middle of the night again a couple of days ago, but Teddy's car, parked under her balcony, scared him off. Teddy Kincaid. You know him? He's retired now, but he was one of us. He knew me for whatever reason, but I didn't recognize him."

Stone shook his head. "Name doesn't sound familiar. But I think you're right about Watts."

"I wanted to keep this in-house, but it's gotten too unwieldy with the chief ranting at you and suspending me. It's also spilling over into the county's jurisdiction, at the sheriff's department and ME's office. If Winchester and his lackey are still chasing people around, it sounds like he's actively doing cabal work even after he's been charged and is out on bail. I didn't know he was part of the Circle of Five until today."

"So, if you're sure this cabal was involved in Katrina's brother's death, what about her parents' murders?"

"It's possible, but too soon to tell. Katrina and I were on the same page about Vincent Battrelle until Darla said he wasn't an official cabal member. Katrina confronted him after learning yesterday that he's her birth father, which is a whole other long story, but he denied everything pretty persuasively. So, she thinks he may not be as involved as we originally thought, but we may not know for sure until the meeting Monday night. Besides the Circle of Five, we don't know who all is going to show up."

"Right, but that means you probably shouldn't go, because some of these folks might recognize you. That's another reason to call Watts."

"Exactly. On to the next thing, which needs your immediate attention. After Darla found out that Winchester was staying with his wife this morning, she said she was ready to sign an immunity deal, which is partly what prompted my visit today. Can you handle that while you're on medical leave or ask someone else to draw something up? I didn't want to tell her I was suspended now that she's finally primed to nail her crooked ex."

"Why don't you call Watts right now and ask him to come over?"

"Done."

Within the hour, they were briefing Marty Watts in Stone's living room. If you'd told any of them two months earlier that they would be plotting their second sting operation together, they would have laughed you out of the room. But after the takedown at the Del had gone so smoothly, they were all mutual fans.

Watts nodded, taking it all in, as Goode brought him up to speed. "I'm impressed that you put all of this together so fast," he said. "We thought the case had gone to shit with the McMurphys out of the picture."

"I'm sure that's exactly what the cabal was hoping for," Goode said, "but Darla Johansen finally came through with the juice we needed."

"Good to hear. And don't worry, Goode, Baxter can't fire you under these circumstances, especially if we can prove that he's your mole. Based on the bizarre interactions you two have had with him recently, he's definitely acting suspicious and paranoid. If Goode's instincts are as on the money as they have been in the past, we may have to recruit him to join our team. Sorry, Sergeant," he said, laughing in Stone's direction.

"I won't let him go without a fight," Stone said, "but he's always been his own man, ever since we were kids."

"Well, thanks to you both," Goode said. "But I have to give credit where credit is due. Even though her life is being threatened on an ongoing basis, Katrina Chopin has been helping to move this investigation along with her reporting. I can't say that we're working together, per se, because obviously we're on different teams, and we haven't been able to share certain things with each other. But she's certainly pulled more from interviews with witnesses like Doreen McMurphy and Michael and Vincent Battrelle than I've been able to. She's also given me informal access to information she's recently gathered from her parents' computers and personal papers, which I'm embarrassed to say that our department never seized during the Double-Judge investigation. And that's why we are where we are today."

"Understood," Watts said, declaring this as the first unofficial meeting of the Cabal Task Force, or CTF for short, because the feds loved acronyms.

Watts agreed that they should launch another joint operation, in which he and his team should mic up the Empress Hotel bar before the cabal meeting, and if all went well, they could make arrests that same night. In the meantime, they would explore the backgrounds of the current Circle leaders as well as the proposed new members, Lawrence Rayburn and Reggie Flanagan.

"We welcome any and all information. Goode, you don't have anything better to do this week than surf anyway, right?" Watts asked, slapping the suspended detective on the shoulder.

"Now that you mention it, nonstop surfing sounds like a great idea. But yeah, I can fit in some backgrounding."

"Can I see that toxicology paperwork you mentioned?" Watts asked. "I'll need to make copies of it."

"Sure, I'll be right back. It's in my van," Goode said. "Can we get that immunity deal with Darla Johansen locked down today? She was pretty fired up about Winchester this morning, and I don't want to lose momentum in expanding the list of charges against that bribe-taking bastard."

"Absolutely," Watts said. "I'll call the US Attorney's Office right now."

As Goode walked along the brick pathway from Stone's house to the street, he stopped to read his latest texts from Katrina. About a minute later, he heard a car pulling away from the curb and looked up to see the black Infiniti speeding away.

"Are you effing kidding me?" Goode muttered, sprinting toward his van.

Was that asshole tapping into my calls somehow? Or did he put a tracker on my van?

Goode knew he'd made sure to lock the van's sliding side door, but when he got there, it was not pulled to completely. Tugging on the handle, he yanked the door all the way open.

Jumping up into the cargo area, he practically dove toward the cooler, the top of which was open. As he dug down, under the folded clothes, tarp, and wetsuit, he was relieved to see that his lockbox was still there. If he hadn't come outside when he did, that lockbox would probably be gone.

So much for the fail-safe storage locker.

Unlocking the box, he breathed a long, deep sigh to find all the paperwork intact. "Thank God. We are going to get you, Walter Hall, you little shit, and send you to the Big House."

Back on the street, he leaned down and ran his fingers along the underside of the van and around the wheel wells.

Boom.

After extricating a tracking device from the left wheel well, he promptly stomped it into tiny pieces, which he brought inside and presented to Watts as he described what had just happened. Watts immediately called FBI headquarters for authorization to move ahead with Operation Cabal, the name for the upcoming sting.

"I'd better take the original toxicology report and notebook into evidence before that thug tries to steal them again," Watts said. "*You* can take photos of them for *your* files."

CHAPTER 38
KATRINA

Monday

On the drive back to the newsroom, Katrina mulled Julia's strange behavior in the context of her claim that, "no, not really," she didn't know who might have killed Katrina's parents. By the time Katrina was sitting at her desk, she was convinced that Julia was lying.

Julia's body language and speech pattern had conveyed that she was indeed nervous, but her comments indicated she was also scared to tell the whole truth. If Julia wasn't the one in the ski mask, she might very well know who was.

Katrina typed Julia's name into the database to do a more thorough background search, including property, criminal, and civil records, and names of family members and associates. Julia's record was clear, other than a couple of parking tickets, which she'd paid on time. She'd never married, and she owned a house in Santee, a small city in East County where it was hotter and prices were lower. She had no roommates, but she did have a brother named Gino, who was five years older and had lived with her intermittently.

When Katrina typed in Gino Frangello's name and approximate date of birth, up came his rap sheet: breaking and entering, assault with a deadly weapon, drug possession (methamphetamine), and carrying unlicensed firearms while possessing narcotics. He'd been sent to the county psychiatric hospital several times on a 5150, meaning he was considered a danger to himself or others. He was also former military, discharged four years after enlisting in the army, which fit with him knowing how to use an AR-15 as the murder weapon. His current address was an RV park in El Cajon.

Wow.

She found nothing about him in the newspaper archives, but a search on Facebook turned up several of his posts on the page for the Proud Boys' local chapter. One of them featured recent photos of him and other men holding protest signs touting white supremacy and gun rights and threatening to "take out" anyone in government who stood in their way. His hair pulled back into a ponytail, Gino wore jeans, cowboy boots, a wifebeater tank top, and a red bandana tied around his forehead.

This is big. Could this be who Julia was talking about, if only by a slip of the tongue?

Katrina wanted Goode's take, but he wasn't answering his cell, so she texted him.

Can u call me? Had weird but promising lunch w dad's clerk. Ran check on her. May have found our killer: her brother—Proud Boys member, former army soldier, rap sheet w guns/drugs/assault.

This discovery called for a face-to-face interview with Gino, but Katrina knew better than to go alone. He sounded like a dangerous and potentially unstable guy. After such an emotional lunch with Katrina, Julia might call to warn him, especially if that was the person to whom she'd inadvertently referred. It might be safer to confront Julia again with this hunch first, remind her that the Unabomber's brother had turned him in to authorities, and see if she would do the same.

While Katrina waited for Goode to call her back, she called the DMV to ask what vehicle Gino Frangello was driving in June 2010, when her parents were murdered.

"I'll check, just one moment," the clerk said, typing the information into the DMV database.

Katrina tapped a pen on the desk impatiently as the clerk scrolled through Gino's file.

"Sorry, hon, this guy's got a long record. Let's see: In 2010, he owned a Toyota sedan, which was impounded for nonpayment in December of that year."

Oh, my God.

"He also lost his license due to receiving his third DUI in five years. He had two more DUIs after that, still without a license, but driving someone else's car."

"Can you tell me if that sedan was a Toyota Corolla? Or if it was blue?"

"No, sorry, hon. We don't store that information in the database."

"Can I get the license plate number, then?"

"Sure thing," the clerk said, reading it off to her.

Now all I need is for Goode to confirm that this plate number matches the neighbor's partial-plate report and we're home free.

The question was, did Gino act on behalf of his sister, or was he hired by Vincent or the cabal? If Vincent had tracked down Julia to ply her with drinks, he could have done the same thing with her wacko brother. Maybe Julia mentioned him during their cocktail conversation, and Vincent had his boy, Teddy Kincaid, run a background check for him.

Katrina's mind was churning with possible scenarios. It made sense that Julia would have complained to Gino that she'd been used and tossed aside by her longtime boss-crush, and with or without her knowledge, he'd decided to avenge her honor. Gino could have watched Julia gain weight, crying and miserably alone, and took it on himself to assassinate the judge and his wife. Maybe he never even told Julia that he'd done it. Maybe she only suspected, but never wanted to know for sure, which was why she'd said, "no, not really."

Based on what Goode had reported after going through her parents' file in the CAIR system, this new lead advanced the murder investigation more than anything his colleagues had ever found.

It was late afternoon when Vincent called her cell. "Katrina, my brilliant daughter," he said, chuckling nervously, as if he didn't know how the greeting would be received.

He sounds a little manic. That's new. I also don't know how to respond to this intimate salutation.

"Have you checked your bank account today?" he asked.

"No, why?"

"Because you'll find a gift in there. I wanted to explain why I gave it to you."

"Okaaaaay," she said cautiously, logging into her online banking account.

"I talked to Ruth after you and I met in the park, and, as I suspected, she did not take the news well. She not only doesn't want to have dinner with you, she wants a divorce. She started screaming, hitting me in the face and chest, and gave me a bloody nose. It was not pleasant."

"You didn't hit her back, did you?"

"No, of course not. She confronted me with the suspicions she's had all these years that I was 'carrying on with that whore,' as she called your mother. She said she'd done her best to ignore it, but now that I was shoving these DNA results in her face, and trying to bring you into *our* family, that was the last straw. She told me to pack a bag and leave the house. I told her that if anyone was going to leave, it should be her, because I pay the mortgage, along with everything else. She's never worked a day in her life."

Well, she took your shit, put up with you sleeping with the woman you loved more than her, and raised your kids. That's a lot.

"I'm sorry to hear that," Katrina said carefully.

"Yeah, well, in case she does anything funny with our bank accounts, like finding a lawyer to freeze them, I wanted to make sure you had a token of my affection to prove what I said this morning, that I really do want you to be part of our family. Just because Ruth doesn't want you around doesn't mean you can't be. She's gone now, so we can get together without her. I'm sure the boys will welcome you; they always liked Franny. As for Meredith, she's her mama's girl, so I'm not sure what to expect there. Anyway, I just wanted to tell you, so you knew where the money came from and why."

"It's not necessary to give me money or to prove anything to me, Vincent. I don't want anything from you. I hope you know that."

"Yes, which is precisely why I wanted you to have it. Besides, you're a Battrelle now. You should dress like one and live like one. I'm just sorry we didn't find out sooner."

They were still on the phone when Katrina clicked on the account where the newspaper directly deposited her paychecks.

"Okay, I'm opening my checking account now," she said. When she saw the deposit of $5 million, she almost dropped the phone.

Are you effing kidding me? If I take this, he's going to expect something in return. I can almost guarantee he'll try to coerce me into doing things I don't want to do. This is life-changing money, but I don't want the grief that I'm sure will come with it. He's going to have to take it back.

"Vincent, I can't accept this. Seriously, this is crazy."

The strings-attached theory aside, Katrina had always lived as a minimalist. She didn't buy much in the way of material goods, especially pieces of furniture, because she didn't want or need them. If the *New York Times* called, she wanted to be free to up and leave on a moment's notice. That's why she didn't spend much, and as long as she knew it was generally less than what was coming in, she didn't bother to budget. But money was clearly far more important to Vincent, because he saw it as a way to manipulate and control people, and he apparently had plenty to spare. How much of a fortune he'd amassed, however, she couldn't even begin to estimate.

"Don't worry. There's plenty more where that came from. I'm going to my lawyer's office in the morning to add you to my will, before anything else happens," he said, which she found oddly foreboding.

He doesn't mean another murder, does he? I don't like the sound of this. He's not hearing me, and now he's trying to give me even more money. As if his promise of more wealth would persuade me to let him control me for the rest of my life.

"What do you mean, 'before anything else happens'? Like what?"

"I don't know. Ruth's pretty angry. She has quite a temper."

"I hate to hear that the two of you are fighting over this. Sounds dangerous."

"Yes, it can be. That's one of the reasons I loved your mother even more. She didn't have a violent bone in her body."

Wait. I never thought of this, but did I have this ass-backward? Could Ruth have been the one to hire someone to kill my mom out of jealousy, and my dad was just collateral damage? Or is Vincent giving me all this money because he's the one who put out the hit, and now he feels guilty, knowing he also had a hand in poisoning his own son?

Katrina's phone beeped with call waiting. It was Goode. Finally.

"Vincent, that's my other line. I've got to go. Thank you for thinking of me, but I don't think I can keep this money. We'll talk about it later."

"That money is yours, Katrina. I'm not taking it back."

"Okay. Gotta go. Bye."

When she picked up the other line, she heard the waves crashing in the background again.

"Hey, it's me," Goode said. "Sorry I couldn't call you before, but it's been a hell of a day. Linebacker Dude broke into my van while Stone and I were meeting with Marty Watts from the FBI at Stone's house."

"You're kidding. Did he get anything?"

"I don't think so. I think he was in the van when he saw me come out of the house, but I didn't get there in time because I was in the garden, reading your texts. When I looked up, I saw the Infiniti tearing off. Luckily, he didn't get any of the case documents I had locked up for safekeeping in there."

"That's lucky. Listen, lots going on here too. Did you see my text about the clerk's brother?"

"Yes, that does sound promising. Even the PD's Keystone Kops team recognized that the killer was probably former military since your parents were likely shot with an AR-15."

"Right, that's what I said. I kind of remembered that from my initial briefing in 2010. But get this: The DMV says Julia's brother, Gino, had a Toyota sedan at the time of the shooting, so that fits too."

"Wow. What do you want to do?"

"That's what I wanted to ask you."

"Well, I'm out of commission, but Stone is going back to work tomorrow or Wednesday. We can let him know what you found out, and maybe he can run it up the chain. The original team isn't going to like us horning in, but this is pretty great information you've come up with."

"I had a different idea."

"What's that?"

"Why don't you and I go talk to Julia tonight and see if she'll admit to us that she either knew or suspected that her brother was involved, because it sure seemed like she was hiding something at lunch. She acted pretty erratic, breaking down and crying after we ordered, then she ran off before our food was served."

"But then what? I can't arrest anyone right now."

"I know. I was thinking maybe we could convince her to turn him in. You know, like the Unabomber's brother did."

"That's not a bad idea."

"I also thought that, after I showed up out of the blue today, she might have gotten in touch with him. If we don't do something now, I'm worried that he might feel like he needs to cover his bases and come after me. We still don't know who smashed my car window and left me those threatening notes. What if it was him?"

"Excellent point. But how would he know where you lived?"

"I don't know. If Vincent or the cabal hired him, he could have gotten it the same way Linebacker Dude found my address and yours. By the way, this is off topic, but Vincent deposited five million dollars in my bank account today. If that's not guilt talking, I'm not sure what is."

"Five million dollars? Are you effing kidding me?"

"No, I'm not."

"Damn. That's life-changing money."

"I know. That's what I said. I feel like I should give it back. I don't want him to feel I'm beholden to him, and if he had something to do with my parents' murders, then I shouldn't help him ease his guilt with a payoff. But what's even more life changing is that I don't have to worry about getting Huntington's disease anymore."

"Huntington's disease, why?"

"My father had it in his family, so Franny and I both had a fifty percent chance of getting it. We never wanted to get tested so we didn't have to live our lives in fear, but that didn't really work. But now that I know Peter isn't my real father, I don't have to worry or push away men who might want to have kids with me. It's an enormous relief."

"I can imagine. How come you didn't tell me about that before?"

"It didn't come up. But it would have eventually, I'm sure."

They both paused to let that sink in before Katrina got back to business. "So, you up for coming with me tonight to Julia's house in Santee? That way, she can't run like she did at lunch today. We'll tell her you're a detective, because I think your presence will make her take this more seriously. She doesn't need to know you're suspended."

"Okay, sure. I'm in."

"Meet me at the parking lot at the paper in fifteen? We can go in my car. Your van is too loud. We want to go in stealth mode."

"See you then."

CHAPTER 39
GOODE

Monday

Julia Frangello lived in a white ranch house with gray trim and patches of peeling paint across the front. The landscaping consisted of a couple of spindly rosebushes whose bug-bitten leaves were turning yellow next to the garage door. The whole place was badly in need of love and care, just like the owner, by the sounds of it.

Sitting in Katrina's Land Rover across the street, Goode and Katrina could see right into Julia's living room through a picture window, because, for whatever reason, she had no blinds closed or curtains drawn.

"Maybe she feels invisible, like no one can see her," Katrina said, as if she sensed what he was thinking. It seemed as if Julia didn't notice or care that everyone could see her boozing it up in the recliner, where she was watching TV with a mangy brown dog the size of a small horse at her feet.

I sure hope that isn't a German shepherd.

He only felt safe around that breed if he was working with a trained K-9 drug-sniffing dog, because they could chomp down on a suspect's limb pretty hard. He'd seen the blood and exposed tendons for himself.

"You want to wait a few minutes and see if she moves, or should we just go in?" Katrina asked.

"Let's wait. She might have dinner in the oven," he said. "Since we know she missed lunch, we don't want to get between a hungry woman and her food."

Katrina tapped his arm playfully. "My guess is it's microwaved leftovers, so it should be quick if that's the case."

"You're probably right."

In the end, it was lucky they waited, because a rough-looking dude pulled up on a motorcycle, removed his helmet, and marched purposefully toward the front door, his ponytail swinging with his swagger.

"That's him. I recognize him from Facebook," she said excitedly. "I bet she called him, just like I said."

"You're pretty good at reading people, so you're probably right."

They watched him fling open the screen door and enter without knocking, the outer door slapping closed loudly. The dog started barking but stopped after Gino wrestled with him briefly on the throw rug at Julia's feet.

Gino let go of the dog and stood up to face Julia, who was still in the recliner, sipping from a wineglass big enough to put out a fire. Then Gino started yelling, his arms flailing wildly. His voice was so loud they could hear it outside. Katrina rolled her window all the way down to see if they could make out what he was saying, but it was just a dull roar. They thought it best to stay in the vehicle so as not to draw his attention.

Gino's bellowing upset the dog, which started barking again, sensing that his owner was in danger. A couple of minutes later, Gino came flying out of the house like a wild man, shoved the helmet back on his head, and roared off down the street on his bike.

"Angry and unstable much?" Katrina said. "Did I mention that he's been taken to the county psych hospital as a 5150 a few times?"

"Sounds about right," Goode said. "I hope he doesn't come back while we're here, or we might have to call in another one."

"Hey, did you get the partial plate number for the killer's blue Toyota out of the CAIR search? I got Gino's full number from the DMV to compare."

"Yeah, it's right here in my phone," he said, showing her the number the neighbor reported.

"I knew it!" she said, beaming. "It's definitely him."

"We make a good team," he said, smiling back.

Once they saw Julia get up from her chair, looking rattled, they gave it a few more minutes, thinking that she'd gone to the kitchen for a bucket-of-wine refill. They were right. When she came back into view, her large glass was full again. She paced back and forth a few times, shaking her head and talking to herself, before settling back into the chair.

"Now?" Katrina asked.

"Yes, let's go."

They walked single file to the screen door, climbed the two steps, and were barely able to fit side by side on the tiny square of cement that was Julia's front stoop. Katrina rang the doorbell, hearing it sound off loudly inside.

Heaving herself out of the recliner with a grunt, Julia appeared at the door, her dog a few steps behind, barking again. Julia seemed spooked and flustered, as if they'd caught her dancing naked. The dog, which yapped at them through the screen, obviously didn't like, or wasn't used to, strangers, and the noise made it impossible to make a move or communicate further. Julia seemed frozen, unsure of what to do.

"If you put your dog in the bedroom, we can hear each other talk," Goode yelled over the din.

Julia nodded, shuttled the dog to a back bedroom, and closed the door, saying, "It's okay, Gino."

"She named the dog after her brother?" Katrina whispered. "That's love for you."

"How did you know where I lived?" Julia asked when she came back. "And how long have you been standing outside?"

"Public records. We just got here," Katrina said in a measured, calm voice to try to ease Julia's paranoia. Goode had heard her use that tone with him on a couple of occasions but never recognized it as a technique until now.

"I'm just surprised to see you, is all. Twice in one day," Julia said, attempting a fake smile to mask her obvious fear and discomfort. "I'm not sure why you're here."

"I know you said you couldn't help me, but I think you can," Katrina said. "I want you to meet Detective Goode with the San Diego PD. We're here to talk to you about your brother. We just saw him fly out of your house after yelling at you. Was that about our lunch today?"

At a loss for words, Julia shook her head again and muttered to herself.

"What's that, Miss Frangello?" Goode asked.

"Nothing," Julia said. "I just don't understand what you want from me."

"I think we can shed some light on that," Goode said. "May we come inside for a few minutes?"

Julia hesitated for a moment, then opened the screen door and waved them inside the living room toward a ratty couch with faded flowered upholstery. Katrina and Goode sat down as requested while Julia sat back down in the recliner. Adjusting it to a more upright position caused the chair to jolt forward and the wine to slosh out of her glass.

"I guess I should have put my glass down before I did that," Julia said, laughing nervously. After dabbing the wine droplets off her T-shirt, she took a gulp and set the glass on the table next to her.

"I'd offer you some, but you said this was only going to take a few minutes," she said.

"Not necessary, thank you, Miss Frangello," Goode said, taking the lead as they'd agreed outside.

"You can call me Julia," she said.

"We appreciate you letting us come in, Julia. Like we said, we heard your brother yelling. Did you call and tell him that Ms. Chopin surprised you today with her unexpected visit?"

"He called me, actually," Julia said. "But yeah, it was a weird day, so I told him about it."

"Do you know where your brother was Thursday, June 3, 2010, the day that Ms. Chopin's parents were shot in front of their house in Point Loma?"

Julia's mouth dropped open with shock at such a direct question. "What do you mean?"

"Just what I said. I'm asking if you know where he was. Have you been to the Chopin house for holiday parties and such?"

"Um, yeah. But why are you—"

"So, you knew where their house was. Katrina got the distinct impression today that you were hiding something from her. After reviewing our files, I saw that you never volunteered any information to the police during the investigation into these murders. We think you're trying to keep your brother's trip to the house that day a secret. Is that true?"

Her top lip quivering, Julia started to cry, which she tried to counter by shoving the wineglass into her mouth. But when she tried to take a sip, she choked, spraying out a burst of wine like a fountain.

"You all right, Julia?" Goode asked.

Julia plonked the wineglass down on the table and started coughing as she tried to breathe again.

"Take your time—we're in no rush," he said. "If you didn't do anything wrong, then you have nothing to worry about. Can we get you a napkin, maybe a glass of water?"

Julia nodded vigorously, her face bright red. Katrina got up to get a glass from a kitchen cupboard and opened the fridge to search for filtered water. She found a pitcher of it right next to the gallon jug of white wine.

Katrina handed Julia a napkin and set the water next to her wineglass, which, even after the skirmish, was still half full. But Julia seemed to be breathing easier now.

Switching tactics, Goode and Katrina stared at Julia in silence, an approach that often pressured people into filling the empty space with conversation. Or a confession.

"I don't know what to say. I had nothing to do with the murders, and I don't know where Gino was that day. He never told me. But he was doing meth and acting crazy around that time. I saw in the paper that the neighbor reported seeing a blue Toyota Corolla driving away and that it had a loud muffler. I didn't want to suspect my own brother, so I never asked him. He always protected me, growing up. But then he got into drugs and joined that Proud Boys gang. I didn't like the changes I saw in him, but he was still my brother. He's all the family I've got. So, when he called me today, asking if I could loan him some money, I told him that you'd stopped by."

"And?" Katrina asked.

"He hung up, rode over here, and started yelling questions at me. I told him I didn't tell you anything because I didn't know anything."

"What did he say exactly?"

"He didn't really say anything new. He just got mad again about what your dad did to me, and then he left."

"Your brother served in the army. And he has an AR-15, right?" Goode asked, pretending he already knew this.

"Yes, he was in the army, but I have no idea what guns my brother has or doesn't have. He works at a gun store in El Cajon. It has a shooting range in back, so he's around guns all the time."

Katrina looked at Goode, mouthing *what the hell?* Obviously, a man with his criminal and mental health record would never be allowed to work at such a place *legally*, but the people of El Cajon had their own views on law and order. Lots of disruptors out there, although not the same kind as Goode and Katrina.

"Let me ask you something. If you knew that your brother was guilty of shooting your former employer and his wife, wouldn't you want to do something about it? Wouldn't you feel a legal and moral imperative?" Goode asked.

"But I don't know—"

"You just said you read about the blue Toyota in the paper, and you suspected something at the time but didn't ask, right?"

"To tell you the truth, I tried not to think about it. I used to tell Gino how much I loved Peter, how hurt I was when he had me transferred. But that was before, when Gino was more stable. Before he joined that group and started hanging out with the men from the gun store."

"And then what?"

"Well, he just changed, is all. I don't know, I guess it's possible."

"Julia, do me a favor and think back to that day," Katrina interjected. "It was a Thursday evening in June 2010 when they were killed. Where was your brother working at that time?"

"Nowhere. He'd just gotten laid off. I had to call the police because he was saying crazy stuff, like he was going to 'hunt them down like dogs.' I didn't know what or who he was talking about. I figured he was hallucinating from the meth. Thank God he stopped doing that when he went to jail on those felony assault charges. Jail got him clean. But he still drinks too much. He lost his license years ago, but he still drives that motorcycle when he has somewhere to be."

"So, you never put two and two together and thought he meant my parents when he said he was going to 'hunt them down like dogs'?" Katrina asked.

"No, but when you say it that way, it sounds like maybe I should have."

"Do you remember his license plate at the time?"

"No."

Katrina read it off to her. "Does that sound familiar?"

"I don't know."

"Well, I got that from the DMV today, and it matches the Toyota's partial plate that the neighbor reported to the police, along with the noisy muffler. You remember his muffler dragging on the ground?"

Julia nodded and started crying again. "I tried to block it out. This is all my fault. I should never have told him what happened between me and Peter."

Katrina got up and put her hand on Julia's shoulder, hoping to make her feel safe enough to do what they hoped she would—turn her brother in.

"You're familiar with the Unabomber, right?" Goode asked, taking advantage of Katrina's instincts. "You know the only reason he went to prison was because his brother turned him in?"

Given that she'd worked her entire life as a court clerk, Julia was indeed aware of that. She nodded again.

"Are you ready to do the right thing, and give us a statement?" Goode asked.

As Julia stared straight ahead, her breathing grew more measured. She nodded, as if all the fight had gone out of her.

"Good for you. We're really glad to hear that. One last question, though. Do you think he did this on his own, or is it possible that someone might have hired him to do it?"

Julia briefly looked hopeful, as if maybe this hadn't been Gino's idea, but her mood turned again, as if it really didn't matter in the end. It was a horrendous, unthinkable deed either way.

"I don't know. I guess it's possible. But who would do that? Vincent Battrelle?" she asked, looking at Katrina.

"We're still investigating that," Goode said, gesturing to Katrina with a head nod toward the door, indicating that they should go outside to discuss next steps. Neither one of them had expected this to go so well, and Goode didn't want to wait and potentially lose Julia's rational state of mind to denial-and-retreat mode.

"Excuse us for a moment, would you?" Goode asked.

Julia seemed happy to have a moment to herself after what she'd just promised to do.

Outside, Goode suggested they call Stone and see if he would agree to send their most senior team member, Detective Ted Byron, to take Julia's statement. But Katrina was one step ahead of him.

"That's fine, but I want to stay for that and then go back to the paper and write a story about it, if not tonight, then tomorrow. As long as Julia agrees."

"Do you think that's safe? We still don't know if he was hired or if he acted on his own. That may not come out until we can get him into an interrogation room, and I can't do that until my suspension is lifted, possibly next week."

"That's true, but I still want to be here for it. These are my parents. She never would have admitted any of this if I hadn't gone to see her today and asked you to come here tonight to catch her brother yelling at her."

"All true. But I'm thinking of your safety and the shit show at the PD if we go outside the chain of command to snatch this arrest away from the assigned detective team."

"Which was purposely not investigating anything anyway, so who cares? They're all corrupt, right?"

Goode still hadn't told Katrina about the big sting planned for the coming Monday night.

Should I? I know her well enough by now that I can trust her not to expose our operation. Don't I?

After mulling it over quickly, he didn't want to give the chief a real reason to fire him or for her to slip and tell Vincent about the operation beforehand. A little voice in his head told him to tell her only what she needed to know so she would agree to hold off on printing anything.

"Listen, I can't tell you all the details, but—"

"Are you effing kidding me with this right now?" she hissed loudly at him. "Haven't I earned the right to know all the details? These are my parents, this is my story, and this is my find! You can't take that away from me. I told you that before."

"Whoa, you didn't let me say what I was about to say, which is this. You obviously can't tell anyone about this, but we have a big sting operation planned for next Monday night. So, if Gino was hired by Vincent or the Circle of Five—that's what the cabal leaders call themselves—that would be great to know in advance. But it also might tip them off. We didn't even tell our own chief about the sting after the way he reacted at the mention of bringing in the FBI. I'm simply asking you to hold off writing anything. I promise it will be well worth your while. That way you won't screw up the operation, which will be bigger and more important than our sting at the Del. I hope you know you can trust me by now. But you can't tell your editors, because if Vincent finds out, it will compromise our entire operation."

Katrina looked perturbed. "I can't agree to all that, but I can explain the urgency of keeping this between Joanne, Linda, and me until next week. They'll get that. So, you're going to call Stone to get Byron over here to take her statement while I stay to listen and write it up? Then I sit on this for a week until the big fireworks, which I get to cover exclusively, correct? I can sit outside in my car and watch you guys set up and go in. Then, when everyone comes out in handcuffs, I can be there with a photog to capture the scene?"

"We can work it out, but that all sounds fine. Just do me a favor. I know you have your doubts about Vincent's guilt now, but remember you were the one who said that five million dollars feels like a guilty payoff."

"Yeah, I know. Don't worry, I'll make sure Vincent doesn't find out."

"Okay. Let me get ahold of Stone."

Luckily, Stone was in a great mood after their meeting with Marty Watts, so he was amenable to sending Byron out to take Julia Frangello's statement. In fact, unlike the old Stone, who was all about following the rules, postseizure Stone was excited about showing up the other detective team, which had done nothing to advance the investigation due to the corruption scheme that he, Goode, and the FBI were about to expose.

"To hell with protocol. I'll be back to work Wednesday, and after the sting the following Monday, I'll ask again to have the Double-Judge investigation reassigned to you. But once we take out the Circle of Five, I don't think anyone will fight me, let alone question me when I make you the lead detective, especially with this statement in our back pocket," Stone said. "In fact, I think you should pick up this Frangello dude for questioning Monday morning. We can hold him while we're doing the sting, so if he was hired by these clowns, he'll be another point of leverage for us. If he wasn't, then no harm, no foul. We'll just look like bigger geniuses."

"What have you done to my buddy, the cautious, kiss-ass, rule-abiding Sergeant Stone?" Goode asked playfully. "I really like the new you."

"Passing out and having stress seizures gives you a whole new perspective on what's important. My therapist helped me see that it really gums up the works to be scared of things all the time."

Within the hour, Detective Byron was on Julia's doorstep with a video-recording kit. Julia said she had no problem with Katrina noting down what she said and taking video on her phone for the paper. And this time, she didn't hold back.

Julia told them everything, starting with the years of innocent flirting between her and Peter Chopin, which culminated in their after-hours coupling in his chambers. His immediate cold shoulder and her transfer to another judge. All the cards and letters she'd written, and Vincent's invitation for drinks. She couldn't recall clearly, but she thought she might have mentioned her brother to him, noting that Gino had been very supportive.

She also told Byron about Gino's descent into drugs and delusion, followed by his joining the neofascist group. How she cried for days after hearing that Peter Chopin had been gunned down in his driveway. Her brother never said another word about the judge until his verbal explosion that night, and still hadn't explicitly mentioned the shooting.

CHAPTER 40
KATRINA

Monday

On the drive back to San Diego, Katrina felt an adrenaline high, along with a tremendous sense of accomplishment and relief. She'd waited so long to find her parents' killer, after swallowing years of frustration with the police's inaction. It was like a huge weight had been removed from her shoulders.

She had uncovered enough evidence now against Gino—Julia's statement about his erratic behavior, his car, his license plate, his military background, and his familiarity with and illegal access to guns—for Goode to trap him into confessing, or at least incriminating himself. Julia said he'd been working at the gun store since he got out of jail, where he'd met the store owners, who were brothers and Proud Boys members, through mutual friends. This was enough to get his parole violated, but what if Goode couldn't get his suspension lifted by next Monday?

"How 'bout some wine at my place?" Goode asked. "Seems like a good night to celebrate. Since we can't go out in public without people spying or tattling on us, we can have a cocktail while we research the cabal leaders. We can park your Land Rover at the paper and take my van, so Hall or Teddy won't see your car outside my house."

Katrina knew this would be asking for trouble, but at that moment, she didn't really care. Goode was suspended, so technically neither one of them could get fired over it. But at the same time, they both knew the inherent problems the Circle could cause for them if they were exposed for going to bed together, which is where Katrina knew in her gut they'd end up if she accepted the invitation. All this waiting was getting really old. For both of them.

Still, it felt like everything was coming to a head, and she was at the center of the vortex. She hadn't trusted her bodyguard, Teddy Kincaid, since she learned that he'd been hired to spy on her. And as the list of people suspected of stalking her, including Teddy, was narrowing, she could feel her anxiety levels rising as the danger to her life escalated. She didn't want or need saving, but Goode was the only person she could trust right now.

"I'm not sure that I'm safe anywhere I go at the moment, but being with you feels like the safest," she said. She didn't want to say this out loud, because it felt a little sappy, but she wondered if it was because they'd been two orphans, a man and woman coming together like yin and yang to make one another feel whole.

Goode gave her thigh a gentle squeeze. "It's nice to hear you say that. I'm glad," he said.

They traveled the next ten miles or so in silence, both off in their own brains.

"You have better taste in wine than I do, so why don't we stop at the liquor store, and you can pick out what you want," Goode said. "I also don't have any food. Want to grab a pizza?"

Katrina looked over at him and smiled. He was being so nice. No sarcasm, no jokes. It felt like a date. A real date. No competition, no conflict. They'd reached a comfortable place where things were now on a course. There wasn't much they could do about it except ride along and run for cover if a projectile came their way.

"Pizza sounds good."

"Okay, great. I'll call in an order to Carino's right now, and we can stop at Dick's Liquor on the way. What do you think about the works, with artichokes?"

"Yes. Whatever that is, that sounds divine."

"Carino's is an old neighborhood favorite. The works means pepperoni, sausage, bell pepper, olives, and onion. That okay?"

"No onion, please," Katrina said, hoping he wouldn't be upset, but if they were going to be in each other's faces, onion was a no-go.

"Right, good point. It's been a long time since I had to worry about that," he said, chuckling.

After they'd switched out their cars at the *Sun-Dispatch*, Katrina texted Teddy to let him know that she had some business to take care of.

I don't know when or if I'll be coming back tonight, but don't worry. I'm safe. You're still going to watch my apartment, though, yes?

He texted back: If you're with your non-boyfriend, I'm sure you're safe. And yes, I'm paid to be here either way.

"He knows we're together," Katrina said. "I said I had some business to take care of, and he just assumed. He thinks he's so damn smart."

"Well, there's no coming back from him seeing us together on Sunday. So, I hope Vincent really isn't part of the cabal, or he could blow it for us."

"They probably think we're canoodling anyway, not researching and investigating," she said.

"Who knows what they're thinking. All I know is, there's no winning for losing. Since they think we're having sex anyway, and I'm suspended, what the hell? We're in a bubble. We're technically not breaking any rules, so I say 'fuck it.'"

"So, you're dead set on doing that?" she asked coyly.

"Not if you don't want to. It's totally up to you."

"Let's see how it goes," she said. "My nerves are kind of shot. It might not be the best time."

"Sounds like the perfect time to me. But I'm easy either way."

Armed with a nice Cabernet and a hot box of pizza, Goode led Katrina into his one-bedroom cottage. It wasn't messy, per se, just so crammed with flotsam and jetsam that they had to follow a path that had been carved between the piles. Not what she'd been expecting.

The path went from the front door into the kitchen / dining area, where a table doubled as a desk, with stacks of files and a laptop. To the right were the bedroom and bathroom, in between built-in shelves and a cubbyhole decorated with faded family photos. A wood-framed glass door at the end opened onto a cute brick patio lined with clay pots of geraniums and calla lilies.

"Is this your eating area or your office?" she asked playfully, pointing to the kitchen table as she set the pizza on the stovetop, the only space she could find. "I'll let you move your files. I don't want to lose your place."

"Thanks," he said. "It's both. As you can see, there isn't a lot of square footage to work with. When I got divorced, I ended up with a lot of junk that Miranda didn't want, and I've never gotten rid of it or had money to replace it with nicer versions. It's not that I'm holding on to it for psychological reasons, I just haven't had the time or motivation to go through it and throw stuff away."

"Maybe I could help you with that, like you helped me with repacking the storage units," Katrina said.

Because it's pretty damned cluttered in here.

"It's also that I want to live in La Jolla, where I can't afford a bigger place unless I give up being near the beach, which I'm not willing to do.

Believe it or not, I don't even use most of this stuff, so it's just taking up space. I guess I don't think about it because I never have people over."

"Don't worry, I get it. We're both busy. I'm not here to judge."

Even so, Goode looked embarrassed, which made Katrina feel bad. Like she'd said too much. She didn't mean to criticize his living space. It was just so jam-packed with unnecessary crap. Not like hoarder crammed, but definitely dusty and musty, too, since they were so near the ocean.

Goode retrieved a corkscrew from a kitchen drawer and popped the cork. "Since I don't drink wine as much as you do, all I have are these cheesy old wineglasses. See? You've made me self-conscious about my life and how I need to move on from the past. But that's a good thing. Now I'm feeling motivated. Out with the old and in with the new."

He gave them both big pours and handed one to her. "Cheers!" he said, clinking his glass against hers. "Let me attack the office / dining table so we can sit down. Or we can sit on the couch if you want. I just need to move a few things."

"The office/table is fine," she said.

"No, now I'm on a mission," he said. He picked up the books and stacks of magazines that were on the couch and moved them to a pile nearby. "My brain isn't organized like this, if that's what you're thinking."

Katrina laughed. "You're funny. I *was* wondering that, actually. Good to know."

"Here," he said, gesturing toward the newly uncovered beige couch. "Have a seat while I clear these folders from the table."

"Those aren't anything to do with my parents' case, right?"

"No, those are all online in the CAIR system. I told Stone that we should open a homicide case for your brother, by the way, and he said we need to sort out the Fontaine–McMurphy case first. I also figured your parents' case took precedence over your brother's, right?"

"Yes, that makes sense, especially after getting Julia's statement tonight. I hope Gino doesn't give you any problems. Or that she doesn't break down under pressure and tell him, and then he runs."

Goode stopped what he was doing and looked at her. "You know, you're right. I was so excited about getting her to talk and planning for the sting that I didn't think that through."

"Maybe it would be better to talk to him tomorrow, in case he goes back over to Julia's," she said. "She doesn't seem like she's good at keeping secrets even when she's trying to."

"So, it's decided," he said. "I'll take Byron over there tomorrow to get a better feel for Gino and make sure he's aware that we know he's in an illegal work situation. If we threaten to call his probation officer, that should keep him in line till I'm off suspension."

"Good idea."

After Goode made room for them to sit at the table, he asked, "You want to have this wine first, or are you too hungry to wait?"

"It would be good to eat something. Long day."

Katrina had been worried that Goode lived in a cool bachelor pad with many dark corners where he could seduce her up against the wall and into oblivion before she was ready to decide to get intimate again. She'd also been worried that he would judge her minimalist lifestyle and her lack of substantive relationships. So, she was actually relieved to discover that he had a cluttered divorcé's cottage. His outer appearance was so flawless, if his internal life weren't complicated, he wouldn't be more than a Ken doll.

"Madam," he said, pulling out a wooden chair with a cushion for her to sit at the table, which he'd set with paper towels as napkins and plain white plates.

They sat kitty-corner to each other, munching on pizza, drinking wine, and shyly smiling at each other. The pressure to act felt imminent in a way that it hadn't before.

Maybe I should just hang out for a while and then go home.

"You look like you're thinking about something," he said. "What is it?"

"I'm not sure I'm ready," she said. "It feels like everything is coming to a head, and I don't want to get lost. I want to feel grounded, like I know what I'm doing."

Since when did you ever feel like that when you had sex? Thinking and feeling grounded are the last things you worried about with men. You just gave in to the moment and went with it. But that's because none of them ever meant anything or had real potential before.

"Are you talking about sex?" he asked. "Because, like I said before, really, no pressure. It's totally up to you. We can wait, no problem. We can just do some research on Lawrence Rayburn, and I can drive you back to the paper to get your car. Just say the word."

"Okay," Katrina said. "Let me go wash the pizza grease off my hands, then. You can pour me another glass of wine, though."

"I'd be happy to," he said.

The bathroom was teeny and cramped but clean, although the towels were damp and smelled a bit musty. Her eyes looked red and tired in the mirror, but she felt like she was starting to relax.

When she came out, Goode had cleared the plates and set up the laptop between their two chairs. Nice and cozy.

As she sipped her wine, she relaxed a little more as he nuzzled her neck. He gave her control over the keyboard and mouse and let her lead him through the many pages of their Google searches, from Facebook to blogs to old news articles and Beach and Tennis Club newsletters—anywhere she could find a mention of Lawrence "Don't Call Me Larry" Rayburn.

In a surprising find, they discovered news articles and gossip blogs that discussed the "friendship" between Rayburn and "spree killer" Andrew Cunanan. Like Stone said, Rayburn had gone to school at Bishop's, a private school in La Jolla. Although he was ten years older than Cunanan, a fellow Bishop's alumnus, Rayburn got to know Cunanan through friends in the gay community in Hillcrest. Rayburn, who was gay but not out to his conservative, homophobic parents, said he admired the way Cunanan operated, because he was so out and so free, so charming and so good at befriending wealthy older men who spoiled him with gifts, cash, and dinners, often in exchange for sex.

Then the handsome young Cunanan abruptly left San Diego on a national killing spree, shooting five people, including clothing designer Gianni Versace in Miami Beach. Cunanan ultimately died of a fatal self-inflicted gunshot to the head in 1997 while being pursued as one of the FBI's ten most wanted fugitives.

"Wow, I didn't see that 'friendship' coming," Katrina said.

Although Rayburn later denied knowing Cunanan very well, his quotes rang hollow, especially in light of the earlier stories. "I wonder if Cunanan shared some of his tricks with Rayburn," she said. "This article says Cunanan's dad was an embezzler and that Andrew maxed out all his credit cards. He also abused painkillers and alcohol, so maybe that's where Rayburn learned which pills to use to make it look like my brother overdosed. It worked so well, he did it again with Patrick McMurphy."

"I can picture them sitting around, having seminal discussions about how to manipulate, steal, or even kill, probably staged as fantasy-type conversations, facilitated with expensive scotch," Goode said. "I'm sure Rayburn became more dangerous as a result of their friendship."

"Yeah, I think that would be a good topic for your interrogation," she said. "I know I'd ask him about all that."

"Would you now?" Goode said, coming in for a kiss, which Katrina allowed. It was nice, not aggressive. His mouth was warm and tasted like wine, and her neck, which he'd been rubbing, was pretty stiff and sore.

"I still can't decide if Vincent is a bad guy or not," Katrina said. "He sounded genuine when we talked in the park, even more than he did the first time he told me about Alex being MIA. But I still have no idea if he was aware that Alex did illegal transactions for cabal members in the Caymans."

"Katrina, this is your family now, so I'm not sure you can be objective. Why don't you wait and see what comes out when we question Gino. If he says he was hired by Vincent or someone from the Circle, I think you'll have an easier time making that assessment."

On that note, Katrina yawned. She felt more tired than frisky. She was happy to have a nice, quiet evening with this attractive, sexy man and feel no pressure to go any further. This felt real, and he wasn't going anywhere.

"So, I'm going to go home tonight," she said. "I don't want to give Teddy or Vincent any reason to come looking for me before the big sting. Everything will change after that."

"You're probably right. I'll take you back," he said, getting up to go.

"I'm not in a rush, though. You can sit down," she said, tapping the side of his thigh. "I'll finish this glass of wine, and then we can go."

Goode sat back down. "I just don't want you to feel uncomfortable. Anytime you're ready."

They chatted about Goode's sister and the last time he saw her, which had been a while, and by then Katrina's glass was empty.

Standing up, they were making their way along the path to the front door, single file, when she put her hand on Goode's shoulder. He turned around so they were face to face in the dark, cramped space, with the moonlight streaming through the glass window in the front door. It felt very déjà vu.

"Before I go, I want to tell you something, so you have a full understanding of what's going on in my head right now," she said. "It's not that I don't want to. But for the first time in my life, I don't feel like I *have* to be noncommittal because of the Huntington's. I didn't tell you about it before, because I was still living in the fear of that disease, which made me have all kinds of unhealthy, meaningless sex with unavailable men *for years*, because I told myself I couldn't have anything real. I went through lots of therapy before I could even admit I was doing that. So, now that this feels real, well, it's kind of terrifying. Does that make sense?"

"Yes, absolutely, and even though I don't have the Huntington's in my past, I do have a history of attracting damaged women. So, now that I've found a woman who is beautiful and smart and has her head on straight, it's equally terrifying to me. Although I'm willing to overcome my fear right now if you want to—"

"Ha. That's funny. Just kiss me."

Goode was obliging, taking her in his arms and giving her a sensuous, deep kiss. She felt all melty inside, just like the night in her apartment. The old urges lapped at her like a flame, testing her. But the voice of reason she'd learned to listen to in therapy kept them at bay.

You can wait for it. It's only a matter of days, maybe a week, tops.

"I'm sorry if this is too soon, but I think I'm falling in love with you," he said into her hair.

"Me too," she whispered.

"What?" he asked. "Say that again."

"No, you heard me. Just take me back to my car," she said, kissing his cheek. He turned and kissed her on the mouth one more time, then took her hand and led her out to his van.

CHAPTER 41
KATRINA

Monday/Tuesday

Back at home, she lay in her bed, all tingly and flushed. Hugging an extra pillow against the length of her body, she relived every nuzzle, kiss, and touch from that evening until she finally fell asleep.

The next morning, Katrina drove to work feeling giddy, proud that she hadn't followed her old patterns of jumping into bed without a second thought. She was finally acting like a rational, well-adjusted adult. Her therapist would be proud too.

Taking a deep breath, she headed into Joanne's office to tell her about her adventures with Julia and Gino Frangello, slapping her notebook for emphasis as she described her interview.

"So, you can write that up for today?" Joanne asked brightly.

"No, I can't, and here's why."

She explained that her hands were tied until she knew what Gino was going to say—if he was going to confess or deny killing her parents, and whether Vincent or the Circle of Five had hired him or somehow had influenced him into doing it.

"What's the Circle of Five?" Joanne asked, confused.

"Which brings me to the other big news," Katrina said, going into a longer explanation and a preview of Monday night's sting operation. "It should be like the Hotel Del, only bigger and more final, so we really need to wait for that, because once again, we can't tip off Vincent or the Circle, because some or all of these murders are related, including my brother's."

Joanne's eyes opened wide as she listened, making all the right noises. But she obviously felt she needed to drop the reality hammer. "You know this is going to take up a lot of space in the paper, and none of that happens without Linda's approval," she said.

"Yes, I know. But we have got to make her promise that she won't tell Vincent or anyone else at the paper, I mean no one, or it could screw up the whole operation. I promise I will have a prime seat, and we can bring a photog and maybe even another reporter—I was thinking Norman Klein—while we wait outside the Empress Hotel for them to be paraded out in handcuffs. I've been promised the exclusive story in exchange for waiting to publish."

"I see," Joanne said.

"So, I suggest that I spend the next few days researching and writing up short stories about everyone we know they're hoping to arrest so Linda can determine how much space we'll need in Tuesday's paper. You guys can edit the stories in advance, then I'll make the finishing touches when I get back Monday night, and we can post them all online. But we can't tell anyone else until the sting is over, or the whole operation could be blown."

"I understand, and I think Linda will too. Your plan is sound, and we'll have everything ready to go once you get back Monday night to add the action and color to the A-matter," she said. "And I love that we'll have the exclusive."

"Of course!"

Katrina said she still had to run this by Goode and Stone, but she also wanted to write up the story about Patrick McMurphy's toxicology results and how they matched the same vodka-narcotic cocktail found in her brother's blood at the time of his death. If they waited until Tuesday to run it, she hoped to say definitively that authorities believed the same person or people caused Franny's and Patrick's deaths.

"This is so exciting!" Joanne said. "Let's go tell Linda."

Linda practically had an orgasm while she was listening, taking frantic notes as Katrina described the overall plan in the context of everything that she and Goode had been up to over the past few weeks.

"No wonder they're trying to destroy your reputation by saying you two are 'canoodling.' They're scared shitless," Linda said. "Vincent asked me what I thought, and I said, 'If I know my girl, she's doing everything by the book. I haven't seen anything to suggest otherwise. And anyway, she's your daughter now, so if she colors outside the lines a little, what are you going to do, fire her? Or disown her? She's got your genes, for God's sake. She's good at what she does. Leave her the hell alone.'"

"What did he say to that?"

"Before, he would have been frustrated and angry, but this time he just gave me a big grin. He may not feel the same way once he finds out we've been hiding this giant scoop, though."

Feeling more hyped than ever, Katrina got to work researching. Because she already had what she needed on Lawrence Rayburn, she moved on to his father, Elmore, along with John Young, Rick Rodriguez, and the wannabe Circle member, Reggie Flanagan.

With Goode's off-the-record help, she also wrote up a story about how Brandon Winchester, who was still refusing to resign from his congressional seat, could be looking at additional conspiracy-to-commit-murder charges in connection with the McMurphys' deaths, because Walter Hall worked directly for him, and Hall was the last one in Darren's jail cell.

What I really want is an interview with Darla Johansen, to ask her why she helped Darren McMurphy try to murder me, only to turn around and snitch on all these guys. But that would probably get her killed. I'll hold off on that until next week.

CHAPTER 42
STONE

Wednesday

Eager to return to work, Stone woke up early Wednesday morning. He showered as usual, but he also shaved for the first time since leaving the hospital, nicking his chin in the process. Swabbing the bloody cut with a scrap of toilet paper, he left the house without remembering to remove it. Kelly was too busy getting the kids ready for school to catch it on her usual once-over.

His health scare, which had prompted four therapy sessions over the past two weeks, gave him a chance to seriously rethink his approach to his job. As he told Goode, the long days on his couch helped convince him that it was time to lose the fear, shrug off the criticism, and do the work the way he knew it should be done, but without internalizing all the grief.

This ongoing corruption was wrong and needed to be stopped. But that would require him to stand up to the chief for the first time and do what needed to be done to expose the cabal. But he had to be savvy about it. Until the sting on Monday night, he would have to pretend to acquiesce to the chief's wishes that he shove the investigation under the proverbial rug.

It was quiet in the Homicide unit when he arrived, primarily because Goode wasn't there to welcome him with a joke or witty quip. But Stone was prepared this time when Maria called him to come down several minutes after he'd settled in at his desk with a mug of bad office coffee. That was another thing he'd vowed to change. He was going to take Goode's advice and order a cappuccino machine for the unit, even if he had to pay for it out of his own pocket. As Goode liked to say, life is too short to drink bad coffee.

Coffee mug in hand, Stone took the elevator down to Baxter's office without any apprehension this time. He figured the chief simply wanted to ensure that his earlier message to stand down had gotten through, in spite of the cracking blow to Stone's head and everything that came after it. Stone was ready to nod and smile but firmly tell the chief that he needed his best detective back in the unit ASAP.

"Hey, Sergeant, how are you feeling?" Maria asked, tapping her chin to alert him to the bloody scrap of tissue. Her compassion was real. He wasn't sure what to expect from the chief. If Baxter still felt guilty and responsible for Stone's injuries, he would milk that for all it was worth.

"I feel like a new man," Stone said, amazed at his calm mental state even though he was about to enter the chief's office. The blood pressure and antianxiety meds were doing their job nicely.

"Great," she said. "I'm so happy for you. Go on in. He's waiting for you."

This time when Stone opened the chief's office door, Baxter was sitting at the head of the big conference table. He immediately stood up with a broad smile.

"Welcome back, Sergeant. It's good to see you. You're looking better than I've seen you in a long time. Sit down. Sit down."

Stone did as instructed, sitting kitty-corner to the chief, and casually sipped his coffee, Cheshire Catting inside, as if he wasn't secretly working with the FBI to take this man down.

If he tries anything, I'm going to shrug it off and not ruminate about it, like we talked about in therapy.

"So, Sergeant. I wanted to apologize for anything I said at our last meeting that may have contributed to your injuries. I feel horrible about what happened."

"Thank you, Chief," Stone said.

Baxter stared at him, apparently waiting for him to take some accountability as well. But Stone sat silent and blank faced. He was going to make Baxter work for this.

"Okay, then. Moving forward, I wanted to review what I said at our last meeting and make sure we're still on the same page. As you know, I had to suspend your detective because he wasn't taking this matter seriously. It's out of our hands, and that's just the way it is. With both of the McMurphys gone, there's no one to prosecute for murder, so we can close the Fontaine case as solved. It's purely a bureaucratic matter now."

Stone maintained his neutral expression as best he could, trying not to fall back on his previous habit of growing agitated and frustrated as he prepared to ask his next question.

"What about the lesser charges—obstruction and evidence tampering for Michael and Vincent Battrelle, the conspiracy-to-commit-murder charges for Brandon Winchester, and the theft of property and conspiracy charges for Darla Johansen?" he asked.

"I heard that the Battrelles' charges were pleaded down to misdemeanors, and if you want to waste your time with those pissant charges, I guess that's up to you. I thought you'd be happy to let the feds fold those into their case so as not to duplicate efforts. They've got plenty of resources that we don't, and I'm not going to pay overtime for you to keep working a dead case."

"With all due respect, Chief, my team spent a lot of man-hours putting this case together, and it's still very much alive. We're happy to work with the feds on their case, but these charges are not only legitimate, they are strongly documented, and they fall within the

Fontaine murder case, not within the feds' bribery and campaign corruption investigation."

The chief's expression reflected that he was perturbed, but Stone could see that Baxter had been advised to keep his cool as well, possibly so as not to expose the Circle any further.

"I see. If you feel that strongly about it, hurry up and finish it up, then. It's just that the work Vitaleron is doing is so important to our core business community. Many influential people who have invested in the company have told me they want to see it back on track as soon as possible, and that dragging the Battrelles through the court system isn't going to help further that agenda. The community would like to see those charges dropped or minimized significantly, because they feel that it's not just a black mark on the city, but it's hurting our image nationally and in the financial markets. And I have to agree."

Translation: He's talking about the cabal and the rich men who invested in that sex drug, many of whom may be one and the same.

"That may be so, but it's our job, Chief, and I think they'll have to understand that. No one escapes the rule of law."

"Yes, of course, but—" Baxter said, his cheeks turning red, a sign Stone recognized well.

"And in that vein, I respectfully ask you to reinstate Detective Goode immediately, Chief," Stone interrupted. "He's my best detective. Probably the best in the department, as you told me yourself when we brought him into Homicide full-time over a year ago. I need him back."

The chief was trying to hold his anger in check, but Stone could see it was building up. If the sergeant kept pushing, Baxter would explode, as he'd seen him do in the past. Stone had half a mind to offer him one of his pills.

He needs these meds as much or more than I do.

"Are you all right, Chief?" Stone asked. "Can I get you some water? You don't look well."

"I'm fine," Baxter said, breathing out a long and loud breath.

"Deep breathing. Good for you," Stone said. "I've been getting lessons myself."

The chief shook his head. "This job is harder than it looks. I like it, but I think it's getting time to retire here soon. Or I'll end up in the hospital like you did."

"Yes, Chief. So, about Goode."

"All right, all right. Fine. But not until Monday. He needs time to feel the full weight of his actions. He was questioning my integrity, and I can't have that. No one threatens Chief Baxter, and certainly not a smart-mouth like your boy, Goode. We don't need the feds sticking their noses into our business. He claimed that reporter isn't his girlfriend, but I have my doubts. Make sure you tell him to keep his distance from her. She's always up to something, and we shouldn't be feeding her any information. Even Vincent Battrelle is wary of her. His own hire. That can't be good."

"Thank you, Chief. I'll let Goode know he can come back Monday. I'll have to limp along without him until then."

"I'm sure you'll be fine. Thank you, Stone."

With that, Stone got up with his mug, which was now empty, smiling to himself that he'd made it through the meeting unscathed and had gotten exactly what he'd come for. He'd put the chief on notice that they weren't going to drop the case, he'd gotten his buddy reinstated, and he'd kept quiet about the rest. The chief would find out about the FBI raid in good time.

"Bye, Maria, have a good day," Stone called over his shoulder.

"You're right, you are a new man, Sergeant," she called back. "Good for you."

After the elevator doors closed, Stone felt like doing a little leprechaun jump and kick, but given the security camera in the corner, he simply imagined doing it.

As soon as he got back to his desk, he called Goode, who answered on the first ring.

"How'd it go?" Goode asked.

"Just like we planned, if not better. I asked for your immediate reinstatement, knowing the chief wouldn't agree to that. So, you're back Monday, after you've had the chance to 'feel the full weight of your actions.' And he's convinced that Katrina's your squeeze."

"God, the man's obsessed with that. Anyway, I'll be feeling the full weight of my actions even more when I talk to Gino today, suspension or not. Byron is meeting me at the gun store and shooting range in fifteen. After that, you and I meet with Watts to talk raid logistics at noon. I'll swing by the back lot at ten till to pick you up. If anyone asks, tell them I was taking you to a healthy lunch. Wife's orders."

"Got it. See you then."

CHAPTER 43
GOODE

Wednesday

The Pistola gun store and shooting range was housed in an old bowl-ing alley in El Cajon. Anyone who didn't know better would think the building, located at the end of a deserted and dilapidated strip mall, was closed and unoccupied. It was the perfect cover.

Goode only knew this because he'd asked Byron to run property, business, and social media checks so they weren't walking in cold. As Julia had indicated, the owners were two brothers and Proud Boys members, who probably trusted Gino even more to sell their guns and run their shooting range *because* he was a convicted felon.

"So, you flash your badge while I introduce the both of us, and Gino won't think twice," Goode told Byron. "Then let me do the talking. Just back me up if things go wonky. I've got the rest covered."

"No problem. I'm here to serve."

"That's what I like about you, Byron."

Inside, the place fit the definition of *shady*. It was so dimly lit that Goode could barely read the labels on the guns that lined every wall. All the windows were covered, as if the store also served as a secret meeting place and bunker, if need be.

Gino was working alone at the counter near the door to the range, which was in the nonworking bowling alley section. The shooters would stand at the heads of the lanes where the bowlers used to roll their balls, and fire at the paper targets where the pins used to be. It was shorter than regulation for police training but worked fine for the average Joe Cowboy or biker gang member.

Goode and Byron purposely dressed East County casual in jeans, T-shirts, and baseball caps, so as not to raise Gino's suspicions.

"What can I get you, gentlemen?" Gino asked. "Haven't seen you around these parts before."

"No, probably not," Goode said. "But we're actually not looking to buy a gun. We're here to talk to you, Gino."

"Oh, yeah? What about?"

Gino may not have been using meth anymore, but even former users have undeniable visual characteristics that give them away. Their hands may shake, their teeth are often bad or missing, and the purple shadows under their eyes don't ever fully fade away. In a word, they're jumpy, and that was Gino to a T.

"I'm Detective Goode, and this is Detective Byron," Goode said, cuing Byron to quickly flash his badge, put it away, then put his hand on his hip next to his gun, streetwise communication for "Don't mess with me, or I'll shoot."

"We were talking with your sister last night, and now we're here to talk to you."

"So that was you in the Land Rover across the street?"

"Yup."

"What about?"

"Her former employer, Judge Peter Chopin."

"What about him?"

His eyebrows raised, Gino seemed a little spooked, just like his sister. When he reached under the counter, Goode wondered if he had a call button under there, like they did in banks, to alert security that they had an intruder or robber situation. Or if he was reaching for a weapon.

Byron saw Gino reaching, too, so he stepped closer to the counter and moved his hand into a more active position to draw his gun.

"Easy, now. Let's stay calm and keep both hands on the counter where we can see them," Goode said. "Like I said, we're just here to talk. As you can see, I'm not even armed today, but my partner is."

"Okay, talk," Gino said, his hands on the counter now. He'd clearly had enough past dealings with the cops that he didn't trust them.

"Well, we wanted to start with a warning. We know you have a felony record and are working here illegally, which we could easily report to your probation officer."

"Yeah, so? My employers don't care. They're my brothers, and they're giving me a chance to work to keep a roof over my head. Nothing wrong with that."

"But it would send you back to jail."

"Whatever. I'll be right back here when I get out."

"With your Proud Boys brothers?"

"That's right."

"Where were you on Thursday, June 3, 2010?"

"How the hell do you expect me to remember that far back? That's five and a half years ago."

"Your blue Toyota Corolla was seen and heard driving away from the scene where Peter and Aphrodite Chopin were killed in cold blood with an AR-15 that evening," Goode said, going with his gut about the gun.

"I don't know anything about that."

"Really? It was all over the news. One of the neighbors reported hearing your noisy muffler and seeing your license plate."

"Wasn't me."

"You had and probably still have an AR-15, though, isn't that right?" Goode asked.

"Yeah, so what. A lot of us former military have 'em."

"As a convicted felon, you know it's illegal to own one, right?"

"We've already been over that."

This guy clearly thinks that laws don't apply to him.

Goode looked at Byron to signal that this wasn't going anywhere. They were going to have to do more than banter, but Goode was powerless as long as he was suspended.

Dammit. I want to arrest this guy, but I can't take him downtown and interrogate him until I get my badge back.

"Let me ask you, Gino, did someone hire you to kill those judges?"

"No, not at all. I wish they had. All I know is that that Peter Chopin dude screwed my sister, then fired her. She loved that job, and he just tossed her aside like a used tissue."

"How did you find that out?"

"I knew something was up. She was lying around in her housedress, crying into her jug wine every night, getting fatter, looking miserable, and sleeping with her dog. Then a big bald guy came down here and explained to me what was going on, and it all made sense. He was really getting me going, saying that the judge deserved some comeuppance. That he should pay for what he did. That we had to protect our women and our families, not let them get used and abused like that. And he was right."

"Did he give you any money to do that?"

"No, we were just talking."

"So, what did you do?"

"You here to arrest me? Because that's all I've got to say right now. Other than I never liked that judge's liberal politics either."

"No, Gino. But we'll see you around."

At that moment, two older dudes with long gray beards, one in a cowboy hat and one in a baseball cap, burst through the front door, guns raised, as if they were entering a saloon shoot-out.

"What's going on here?" one of them shouted. Just as Goode figured, Gino had hit a call button, and these were either the owners or two clowns they used as security.

"Easy, boys, we're all good here. We were just leaving," Goode said as he and Byron walked past them as coolly as they could. He really hated coming in to a situation like that unarmed, but he had no choice. It had to be done. "We'll catch you later, Gino."

Outside, Byron looked questioningly at Goode as if they should have done more, like haul Gino in for selling guns illegally.

"But then we'd waste our chance to interrogate him, because I can't do that until Monday," Goode reminded him.

Without a second gun or the power to arrest and question Gino, the visit had gone as far as it could have. "Besides, what if Gino reported me? I could be fired for doing what I just did. It was best to get out of there, pronto, especially with the clown brothers pointing guns at us."

Goode said they would come back Monday morning, both of them armed with guns and a warrant to search Gino's residence while they held him in a cell downtown until after the raid, when Goode could formally interrogate him without risking a tip-off to the cabal.

"You can get working on that warrant today, in fact," Goode said. "By the way, you heard him say it was a big bald guy who tried to provoke him into avenging his sister's honor, right? Sounds like Teddy Kincaid to me. You know him? He's a retired SDPD cop and a lackey for Vincent Battrelle."

"Really? I don't know him, but I can ask around."

"Yeah, do that, but only with a few trusted friends. We have at least one mole in the PD and who knows how many more in other departments, but I'm still searching for the nest. Anyone who knows him might be tainted, so be careful."

So, the dude Vincent Battrelle hired to be an armed guard at Katrina's apartment for a couple of weeks, allegedly to protect her, sounds like the dude who poked this guy's buttons to kill her parents. Unbelievable. If that's true, my gut says he did it on Vincent's behalf. If I'd known this last night, I would have insisted she stay at my place. She's not safe under that smug asshole's watch. So now I've got to call Katrina and tell her. Vincent is not *a good guy, but I don't see how he gets held legally responsible for their murders unless he paid Gino.*

CHAPTER 44
KATRINA

Wednesday

Katrina was sitting at her desk when Goode called her cell.

"Are you ready for this?" he asked.

She could hear the wind blowing and the waves pounding in the background, so she assumed he'd finished his meetings and was back to hanging at the beach as a free agent.

"Yes. What's up?" she asked.

"Five years ago, a big bald guy shows up at the gun store where Gino works to tell him what a scumbag your father was and how he needed to pay for having sex with Julia and then tossing her aside like a quote, used tissue, unquote. My money says it was Teddy Kincaid."

"Are you serious? And this guy's allegedly been watching my back?" she said. Concerned that her pod-mates were overhearing their conversation, she got up from her desk and headed for the stairs to the rooftop patio. "Did he pay Gino to do it?"

"Gino says no, they just talked. But I'm not sure I believe him. All I know is you might even be less safe with Teddy outside watching you and your place, because that's some fox-watching-the-henhouse bullshit. And I still don't think Vincent is a good guy, no matter how much you want him to be, because my gut says that even if no money was exchanged, Teddy riled up Gino on Vincent's behalf. If I know Vincent, he'll say, 'Oh, but I just wanted him to scare Peter, to expose him and to screw up Aphy's marriage so she would leave him. I didn't know he was going to shoot Peter, and I certainly didn't want him to shoot the woman I loved.'"

"Yeah, that is what he would say, almost verbatim," Katrina said as she stepped out on the patio, where it was windy but there were no unwanted ears listening. "It also sounds plausible."

"Well, then he shouldn't have approached a trigger-happy meth user to do his dirty work, should he? I'll press Gino for more details when I can do a real interrogation Monday, while my team searches for guns in the shithole I'm sure he's living in."

"You can't do that before Monday?"

"Unfortunately, no. Stone tried to get the chief to let me come back this week, but Baxter wants me in time-out until then. That means I'll have to do all of this the morning before the sting. Talk about a long day. But that's the only way we can prevent triggering suspicions or phone calls to Vincent. If Byron arrested him today, I couldn't question him, plus we couldn't chance that he might call a Circle-affiliated attorney. As it was, we narrowly escaped getting shot at by two gray-bearded chuckleheads who burst into the store with guns drawn. It felt like a slapstick comedy set in the Wild West of East County."

Katrina laughed at the image, but only because Goode came out of it safely. That was her Surfer Man, pushing the envelope and taking chances even when it was dangerous. Just like she would. "Just one question. Why would you show up unarmed to a gun store? Talk about looking for trouble."

"Uh, because I had no choice? I did what needed to be done to catch your parents' killer and to protect you."

"That's sweet. I'm just glad you didn't get hurt, is all. You're my knight in shining armor." Switching to a more serious tone, she asked, "So, what do I do about Teddy? It's scary and annoying that he's been watching my place this whole time under false pretenses. I was feeling safe up until he started making cracks about you, but this feels untenable now."

"I'd tell your editors what Gino said and see if you can get Teddy replaced with someone who doesn't have a questionable agenda. The clock is ticking, so you really only need someone through the weekend. I'd be happy to do it, but we both know that that isn't going to fly, suspension or not."

"But won't firing Teddy have the same effect as arresting Gino before Monday?"

"That's a good point. I could sit in my van and watch Teddy to make sure he doesn't try to break into your place or let Hall get past him next time. It's either that or you come stay at my place while Teddy watches your place. But you'd have to figure out a way to hide that you're with me, and I don't see that happening."

"I'll talk to Joanne and Linda and let you know what they say."

As they talked through the options, Linda was very pragmatic about the whole situation.

"We can't fire Teddy Kincaid without Vincent finding out, which pretty much leaves our hands tied until Monday night," she said. "But that also means you're unprotected, maybe in even more danger, in the interim. Give me a few minutes to think about this."

In the meantime, Joanne took Katrina to her office to wait. "Is Goode still suspended this week?" she asked.

"Yes," Katrina said, pausing. "Why?"

"It seems to me that your life is more important than the rest of this, so if you want to ask him to sleep on your couch until this is all over, I'd say that was okay. I'll defend you if need be. Technically, you're not covering him this week, so it's a gray area, but I think it's something we would overlook if anyone found out, given the circumstances. We want you alive, and this development that's come to light with Gino Frangello, Teddy Kincaid, Vincent, and your parents is, shall we say, a little out of bounds for our ordinary protocols."

I know I've been telling her that Goode and I aren't a thing, but does she really not know that we are very close to a thing, we just haven't slept together yet?

"I appreciate you saying that. That is very true. But I don't see how he gets in without Teddy knowing. Although Teddy thinks we're sleeping together anyway, which we aren't."

"I know. I can tell you might have feelings for Goode, but I have faith that you've stayed on your side of the line while you've been covering this story. Maybe Goode can come up with a witness protection plan or some other creative excuse."

Katrina couldn't tell if this was a wink-wink, nod-nod suggestion, but she didn't care.

"Thank you," she said, surprising Joanne with a hug. Her editor was the closest thing to a mother that she had. In fact, Joanne felt like more of a mother to her than her own mother ever had.

Fifteen minutes later, Linda called them back into her office.

"I've made an executive decision. We'll tell Mr. Kincaid that his services are no longer needed, because we've decided that Katrina needs a higher level of security, and leave it at that. For the next five nights, Katrina will be staying at the Embarcadero Hotel downtown, which is noted for its security measures. This location will be a secret to everyone but the three of us until further notice. Thank you, ladies."

After preparing to tell Goode that he could sleep on her couch until the sting, Katrina felt a bit shell shocked.

I'm kind of relieved, though. It would be awkward to kiss him on the couch or to even cuddle in bed without feeling like I was breaking Joanne's trust. But now no one will know what we're doing. If we do anything at all.

When she informed Goode, his first reaction was to deflect his personal feelings by saying he needed to check her car for a tracking device.

"If you really don't want to be found, we'd better make sure your car's clean," he said. "Why don't you go home and pack your things—then I'll meet you at the paper to give your car the once-over before you head downtown."

"Good idea. This will actually be fun, staying in a five-star harborside hotel for five nights. Room service, a premium movie channel, and a heated pool."

"Sounds great, like a mini vacation."

"At least now I have a chance to be safe without putting us into an awkward position," she said. "We can still talk on the phone and take moonlight walks along the promenade. Hopefully we'll have more freedom after the raid, when all the bad guys are in jail, and no one is watching us."

"I was liking the idea of staying at your place and throwing it in Teddy's face."

"I guess Linda didn't like the odds on that one."

"I suppose I can't blame her."

CHAPTER 45
GOODE

Friday–Monday

Over the weekend, Goode enjoyed a couple of tasty meals in Katrina's room, followed by strolls along the Embarcadero. They were careful to choose entrées and sides that were big enough to share to keep the editors in the dark that they were ordering for two.

Outside the room, he spent most of their time together scanning the lobby, lawns, and walkways for anyone suspicious who might pull out a gun and shoot them. They might have been safer spending that time apart, but they were getting pretty attached to each other.

Stone managed to retrieve Goode's badge and gun from the chief on Friday afternoon, though he had to do the Vague about why he needed them early. Stone brought them over to Goode's place Sunday night so he could hit the gun store first thing in the morning.

On Monday morning, Goode was up before his coffee brewer turned on automatically at five thirty. But because this was going to be a long-ass whopper of a day, Goode skipped the dawn surf. He couldn't afford to lose his edge by going into the day with zen brain.

The gun store opened at nine o'clock, so he and Byron were parked outside, locked and loaded, by 8:45 a.m., as were Stone and their other teammate, Detective Bill Foster, in front of Gino's RV at a rental park a few blocks away.

By then, Byron had obtained the warrant to search the RV by citing details they'd gathered from their impromptu conversation at the store and tidbits Goode had culled from the early Double-Judge investigative reports.

When Goode and Byron walked in at 9:02 a.m., Gino was alone at the counter again. This time, he immediately reached underneath to hit the call button, a move they'd anticipated.

"We're here to take you downtown for questioning, Gino," Goode said. "Let's go."

"I want a lawyer."

"That's fine. We still need to take you downtown."

Goode stood facing him while Byron walked behind the counter to put him in cuffs. Gino tried to resist as a stalling tactic, but they were already driving off in Goode's Explorer by the time the two bearded clowns pulled up in a beat-up Chevy truck.

"See you, boys," Byron called out to them.

"Watch it, they might shoot out your tires," Gino said from the back seat. "They're like big cats. They don't like to be teased."

Down at the station, they put Gino into a holding cell while they waited for Stone and Foster to come back with whatever goodies they'd found in the RV. It wasn't long, because Gino's meager belongings fit into a duffel bag.

Goode watched patiently as Stone dumped out the bag's contents: There were five guns, including one AR-15.

"The place was a smelly, dirty little hole, with wrinkled paperwork strewn all around. We overturned the seat cushions and searched inside a blue-and-white cooler, where he had his most important documents assembled. Just like you, Goode," Stone said, laughing.

Goode could take a joke, but this one made his face turn red. "I've already learned my lesson on that one. No need to rub it in."

"We didn't find any drugs, so he's probably clean."

Stone was in prime form, stating orders with more quiet authority than Goode had ever seen.

"Let's run the serial numbers on all these guns," Stone said. "See when they were purchased and by whom, and if any other law enforcement agencies have run searches on them."

"We're going to hold Gino until after the raid and interrogate him tomorrow as planned, though, right?" Goode asked.

"Right. If he hadn't asked for a lawyer, I'd say go question him now. But, after the sting, we should have enough information to arrest this dude for the Double-Judge murders."

Gino's guns were a surprising mix of mutts. Because none of them was registered to him, and he didn't hold a permit for any of them, Goode figured he'd collected or traded them as "burners" to sell illegally under the table, probably out of the store. When bad guys wanted to get rid of burners, guns that were hot or used in a crime, they often relied on middlemen like Gino to find them new homes and earn some cash or bartered goods on the side.

With the AR-15 in hand, Goode told Stone he was going to run over to the crime lab to see if he could get a tech to let him jump the line for a ballistics test to compare the bullet with those pulled from Peter and Aphrodite Chopin's bodies.

As he stood at the reception desk of the crime lab with the AR-15 in an oversize plastic evidence bag, Goode was disappointed to learn that Dwight Pepper was on vacation.

"Who's the supervisor today?"

"That would be Carrie Valdez," the receptionist said, buzzing him through. "I'll let her know you're on your way back."

"Thanks."

Carrie Valdez was a short, squat woman with a torso like a cannonball.

Fitting for the job.

"What can I help you with? Detective Goode, right?" she asked.

"That's right."

"I've heard about you," she said, grinning wickedly.

"Really? All good, I'm sure."

"Mostly. You're a bit of a pain in the ass, I hear. A stickler too."

"Yeah, that's me."

"Just kidding. Mostly," she said, smiling again. "What case is this for?"

Goode gave her just the case number, not the name, so as not to arouse undue attention, which was the last thing he wanted right now.

"Got it. Let me go pull those bullets, then we'll fire this baby into the chamber and take a look."

She came back with the evidence envelope, and off they went.

"Could I ask you to put on gloves before you handle it?" he asked.

"See? There you go," she said, rolling her eyes. "You know I do this every day, right?"

"Just being safe. Depending on what results we get, I was also going to ask you guys to do a fingerprint and DNA analysis on this weapon. Might be too much time has passed between events, but I'd like to give it a try."

Valdez fired the gun into an underwater chamber that sent the cartridge into a receptacle. After retrieving the fired round, she examined it under a microscope along with several others from the envelope.

It took all of fifteen minutes for her to give him another big grin. "Detective Goode, this is your lucky day. These bullets are a perfect match."

"Thank you, thank you, thank you," he said. Based on their quick camaraderie, he thought it would be okay to give her a friendly hug, which elicited a giggle. "Can you please hold on to all of this for now, including my fingerprint and DNA analysis request? And please don't catalog or enter it in the computer until I get back to you with instructions, which probably won't be until tomorrow, okay? This is very hush hush."

"Sounds intriguing. You got it."

The only way he could describe his reaction was ebullient. Damned ebullient. He couldn't wait to tell Katrina. Even though he still couldn't say for sure that Gino had pulled the trigger, once his suspect heard about this development, he might be willing to talk about Teddy Kincaid without waiting for a lawyer. But Goode was torn about whether he should even ask.

We don't want him calling a lawyer who might be tied to Teddy or Vincent in some way, or it could have a ripple effect on who shows up tonight. I'd like for Vincent to stroll into the bar as he normally would, or stay away if he isn't affiliated with the cabal as he claims.

Goode drove back to the station as fast as he could. His confidence boosted by the ballistics victory, he decided to risk asking Gino a couple of questions. But they still weren't going to let him near a phone to call an attorney until the morning.

Pulling Gino out of the holding cell, Goode set him up in their smallest interrogation room and turned up the heat. He had a hunch that, as a former meth user, Gino would quickly feel the effect of a small, hot space. After a few minutes of watching him sweat, Goode knew he'd made the right call.

"Is your AC broken or what?" Gino asked. "I've been in a lot of these rooms, and this one's the worst."

"Listen, Gino," Goode said, "this is only going to take a few minutes. I know you said you wanted a lawyer for the interrogation, but I just got some information I wanted to share with you before we go that route. So, all you have to do is listen. I think you might change your mind."

"I'm not going to do that. I've already said enough."

Despite all of Gino's bitching, Goode had a feeling he wouldn't be able to help himself, and he was right.

"I think you might actually *want* to talk to us. Just hear me out, okay?"

"Okay."

"You told us the other day that you owned an AR-15, remember?"

"Well, 'owned' is not the word I used. I didn't buy it, if that's what you mean."

"So where did you get it?"

"A friend gave it to me for loaning him my car."

"Was this around the time the Chopins were shot?"

"I told you I don't remember anything that far back. I'm only talking about the gun, because I do remember that."

"And who was that friend?"

"It was that big bald guy I mentioned to you earlier. Real nice guy. Said his car died and he just needed a loaner for a day while it was in the shop. So, I said okay. When he returned the car, the gun was in the trunk. Said it was a gift. What does this have to do with anything?"

"Teddy Kincaid, right?"

Gino looked startled. "Yeah. How did you know that?"

Goode nodded knowingly. "What would you say if I told you that gun was used to kill Peter and Aphrodite Chopin?"

"You're shittin' me."

"No, I'm not. Is Teddy Kincaid still a nice guy?"

"Fuck. He set me up," Gino said in a low growl, clenching his fists.

"So, when you said you didn't get paid to kill the Chopins, you were telling the truth."

That's his ticket to freedom. All he has to do is talk.

"Damn straight," Gino said looking up and right at Goode. "I was in the army, and they trained me how to kill and slit your throat with a bayonet, but once I got out, I had no reason to do any of that. Besides, I was already on probation, and I wasn't going back to jail, let alone prison. No way, no how. When Teddy got me going about my sister, I really wanted to give that Peter Chopin some payback, but I'm no fuckin' Rambo. I guess he played me, and he thought he could play you, too, because that's exactly what you thought I would do. Don't quote me, but I could kill that fucking asshole."

"It's okay. We've got some other stuff going on with this case today, so we need to hold you for a while until we can get it sorted out. But trust me, it's for your own protection. And if things go as planned, you probably won't need that lawyer."

"Well, I'm supposed to be working today, so I'll be losing a whole day's pay. I'm not too excited about that."

"Better than going to death row for two murders, though, right?"

Gino nodded. "Yeah, you got that right."

Feeling pumped up, Goode ran home to change into an all-black getup for the nighttime portion of the show.

Meanwhile, the FBI sent in their team to mic up the Empress bar and post hidden cameras to capture the cabal members' faces. To prevent leaks about the operation, hotel security cleared the bar of all staff and closed the doors while the bureau's team worked. The mics were concentrated mainly on the high-top tables around the grand piano, where the meetings typically started at 7:00 p.m.

The hotel was festively decorated with wreaths, mistletoe, and shiny Christmas tree balls, so the primary team of Stone, Watts, and Chris "CD" Dougherty, another supervisory FBI special agent, agreed to meet at the bar, dressed in red and green, at six o'clock. They also decided to wear disguises of fake facial hair and Santa hats, because they had no idea who, besides the Circle members, might show up and recognize them.

Each of them would be equipped with high-tech earbuds allowing them to listen to the suspects' conversation without the background noise, which would be filtered out. They would communicate with their respective teams outside the hotel by secure encrypted texts.

Before the Circle meeting started, a team of twenty-five agents would assemble on the La Jolla Recreation Center tennis courts a couple of blocks away, where they would pretend to play a tournament until they received direction to start the raid. The long unmarked white comms truck would be parked nearby, staged to look like the tournament hub, where a team of agents would process the sound and images picked up in the bar.

Watts explained that the primary team's earbuds would be activated inside the bar as soon as he texted the comms truck that the meeting was about to begin. At that point, the recorded conversation would be relayed through a voice-activated program to produce written transcripts in real time. There would be a slight delay in the output, but Stone, Watts, and CD would receive the transcripts on their phones.

To avoid being recognized by cabal members and an unknown number of lower-ranking members and associates who might show up, Goode and his fellow detective teammates were the designated "eyes" on the street, reporting to their supervisors who was entering the building. Once the *GO* signal for the raid went out, they would join the FBI agents in climbing several floors via the fire-emergency stairwell to the bar and assist with the mass arrest.

From there, the suspects would be led downstairs in handcuffs or zip ties to buses that would transport them to SDPD headquarters to be interrogated and threatened with exposure to ruin their public lives if they didn't turn on each other.

CHAPTER 46
KATRINA

Monday

At 5:30 p.m., Katrina met up with Norman Klein and photographer Chip Johnson in the newsroom. The plan was to take her car to La Jolla and park a block from the hotel, where they would camp out until Goode signaled that the raid was starting. At the last minute, however, she and the editors decided that the trio might draw too much attention if they were seen dressed in black and sitting in the same car, so Chip ended up driving separately and taking a long lens.

Katrina was so excited, she felt like her body was a centrifuge in a lab. She imagined that the blood in her veins was moving so quickly that she was almost levitating. She'd been in high gear all day, which she knew was not good, because she didn't want to burn out. But the editors were driving her crazy. Up until the very last moment, they kept asking for changes to her mini bios about the arrestees and the A-matter for her main story.

"Sorry, but we've really got to go," she finally said.

It was six fifteen by the time she and Norman were parked with their cappuccinos, which were supposed to keep them going for the rest of the night. Katrina realized too late that she hadn't factored in their inevitable restroom needs.

Goode stopped by to say hello and was opening the passenger side door when he realized that Norman was lying across the back seat, practicing to hide from passersby who might recognize him.

"Hey, Detective Goode, what's up?" Norman said, sitting up abruptly.

But Goode was clearly in no mood to be social. Katrina hadn't warned him that Norman was coming with her, and this was the first time she'd seen Goode give off such an annoyed vibe. He basically refused to engage with Norman, as if he didn't have a right to be there, then slammed the passenger side door.

"Gotta run," he told Katrina. "I'll text you when Stone sends us the *GO* signal."

CHAPTER 47
GOODE

Monday

Goode, Byron, and Foster had been sitting in silence in the Explorer near the hotel's front entrance for thirty minutes when Goode saw a man in the rearview mirror.

"Man approaching, wearing a Santa hat," he said. "I can't make out who it is yet."

Sitting in the back seat, Goode didn't want to turn around and be caught looking, so he scooted over until he was directly behind Byron on the driver's side to get a different angle in the rearview. "I don't recognize him," he said. "But don't turn around and look."

As the man got closer, Goode saw that it was Clarence Thompson from the ME's office. He immediately ducked down and lay flat until Thompson passed, then texted Stone to let him know:

Thompson coming in now.

Young, Rodriguez, Winchester, and both Rayburns all here, Stone texted back. Must be parking inside.

Goode was pissed. They'd been sitting outside in the dark, thinking that no one but Thompson had arrived, when in fact, the cabal members had apparently been parking in the interior garage, which he and Stone had dismissed as too small to monitor.

Might be nice if you'd let me know that before, Goode texted.

Sorry, lots going on, Stone replied. Will try to send updates, but need to focus on what's happening here.

Stone's next texts came in a series of short bursts:

Flanagan just walked in.
Mayor!!!
Walter Hall. Figures. Someone called out "Hey, Kincaid" when a big shaved-head dude walked in. Vincent's goon?

Goode texted back: Yes, so Kincaid and Hall are in this together??? Shoulda seen that coming.

Stone again: That a-hole Allegro from jail is here. Looks like meeting is about to start. No sign of V. Battrelle. Will try to send interim updates before I hit GO, but may be no time.

Goode: Good luck!

CHAPTER 48
STONE

Monday

Stone was a jumble of eagerness and nervous energy. Watts was more Goode's contact than his, so Stone was worried he would feel out of place running a sting operation with two supervisory FBI agents he didn't know that well, one of whom he'd never met before.

"They need us as part of this operation because we know the local players," Goode told him that afternoon. "Don't smaller-ize yourself. You're just as important as they are."

Stone reminded himself that he was the sergeant in charge of helping the FBI to direct the operation, but his medical episode had undermined his overall confidence. Although the meds and therapy were helping him find his way back, he still had work to do.

He usually shrugged it off, but that night, he was thinking about how much smarter Goode was than him. He admired the way Goode's mind worked, and he enjoyed helping his buddy succeed. Goode was the one who had seen this case for what it was from the start.

He should be the one directing the operation, not me.

Stone had never discussed these self-doubts with anyone, not even Kelly, but he confided in his therapist. She'd been trying to help him neutralize them because she thought they'd been contributing to his condition. After he told her about his long relationship with the Mini Tuber, she reminded him that he'd been the one who had taught Goode how to surf, who had helped Goode get the job at the SDPD, who'd greased Goode's way from Vice to Homicide, who was Goode's most vocal cheerleader, and who helped Goode work all his homicide cases.

She's right. He didn't do it alone. I was there too. So, quit it.

Stone's therapist had also given him self-affirmations to chant into the mirror every morning, which he'd been repeating all day: *You are worthy, you are smart, you are capable. You have nothing to fear but fear itself.*

After repeating them five more times in the car, he walked tall into the hotel in his black pants, green long-sleeved shirt, Santa hat, and fake mustache and goatee. He made sure to arrive early to scout out the table that would give them the best view of the action.

The bar was completely empty when he strolled in at 5:50 p.m., which put him a little more at ease. He ordered a tall glass of ginger ale with extra ice so it would last for a while and claimed a table with three chairs, kitty-corner, and at the opposite end of the room, to the piano.

His FBI counterparts, Marty Watts and CD Dougherty, sauntered in a few minutes later.

"This is the perfect table, Stone," Watts said. "Well done."

With that, Stone felt like he was back in the game, laying his hand protectively on his fanny pack, which held his gun. The agents said they'd hidden their weapons in the black backpacks they hung over their chairs, as if they were casual travelers.

Slowly, one by one, the Circle members and their associates filed into the bar and ordered drinks. Like Stone, some wore Santa hats, as if the meeting was a holiday party among friends. When Baxter strolled in, Stone felt his heart racing as he furiously texted Goode.

OMG, Baxter just arrived!!! So, he IS the mole!!! What if he recognizes me?

Don't worry, Goode texted back. Stay cool and you'll be fine. He is ours now.

Despite Goode's attempts to reassure him, a wave of nausea came over Stone, his lower abdomen gripped with cramps. He also felt a tightness and some sharp pains in his chest, but after he took a few deep breaths, the symptoms passed.

Stone couldn't stop watching Baxter, who eased his way through the group and clapped the other men on the back before he reached the bar, where he joked with the bartender. They clearly knew each other.

That effing bastard Judas. He must be a regular at these meetings. That whole rant in his office and his indignation toward Goode make perfect sense now. We were getting too close. Goode saw this coming, but I didn't want to believe that a man I'd worked with so closely and for so long could be one of these corrupt jackals.

Seeing Baxter glance over at the table where Stone sat with the two agents, Stone quickly averted his eyes and shifted around in his chair so his face was turned away from the chief.

I can't afford to let him recognize me and alert the others. It could jeopardize the whole raid.

At 6:30 p.m., the piano player came in and sat down, tinkling Christmas songs on the keys. Stone wondered when the transcripts would start showing up on his phone. He was no lip-reader, and he couldn't hear what anyone was saying.

Stone saw Walter Hall acting buddy-buddy with the group, too, laughing and drinking whiskey with a big mid-fiftyish man with a shaved head. When Stone described him to Goode by text, they agreed that it was likely Teddy Kincaid.

All the pieces are finally coming together, Stone texted.

All this time Kincaid acted like Hall was the enemy, Goode texted. What F'ing BS.

Does this mean Kincaid's the cabal's goon, not Vincent's? Or is that one and the same?

Excellent question, Goode replied.

It was 6:55 p.m. by the time all the players were settled in and Watts sent the alert to the comms truck. With Patrick McMurphy gone, that left only four voting Circle members, who were seated at a round table where they could hear each other over the piano, leaving one open chair for a fifth person to join them. A group of nonvoting members sat within listening distance of the Circle, but the only other men Stone recognized were Lieutenant Allegro and Lawrence Rayburn. As head of the Circle, Elmore Rayburn, who looked to be in his seventies, started the meeting. "First order of business is to thank Congressman Brandon Winchester for his service as he steps down to deal with these bogus federal charges," Rayburn said. "He will remain on the board for tonight's meeting, voting on new members as his last act of brotherhood."

"Amen, Brothers," the others chanted. "Thank you, Brother Winchester, for your service."

"First, we will vote on the replacement for Patrick McMurphy, whom we had to clean to protect the Circle," Rayburn said, gesturing for Reggie Flanagan to sit in the empty fifth seat. Flanagan sat down with his gin and tonic, nodding with deference to the others.

"How do you plead, Brother?"

"I plead that I will pledge my loyalty to the Circle and carry out the duties as laid out in the Text," Flanagan said.

"Thank you, Brother Flanagan. You may leave us while we vote."

Going around the table, each member tapped on his glass with a pen to register his vote, once for yes, and twice for no. Flanagan was voted into the Circle on a vote of three to one, after which he was brought back to the table to participate in the next vote.

"Next order of business is to vote on the proposed replacement for Brother Winchester," Rayburn said. "As you know, I will be stepping down within the next year to do some traveling with my dear wife, Judith. My son, Lawrence, has expressed great desire to join the Circle and has shown devoted efforts to carry on my twenty-year legacy. If he is voted in, I can help train him. He has worked hard to further our interests by following our instructions and has also acted proactively by following his own initiative."

So, Patrick McMurphy was never the *Circle leader, like Darren claimed. It was this guy, Elmore Rayburn.*

Elmore Rayburn gestured to his son, Lawrence, to pull up a sixth chair. "How do you plead, Brother?"

"I plead that I will pledge my continued loyalty and devotion to the Circle and will carry out the duties as laid out in the Text," Lawrence said.

"Thank you, Brother Rayburn. You may leave us while we vote."

Counting Flanagan, the board now had five voting members. This time the vote was unanimous, most likely out of deference to the elder Elmore.

"Now that we have the full five-member-voting Circle present, Brother Winchester may stay and cast the next vote as an emeritus. The next order of business is a report from Brother Clarence Thompson, one of our esteemed soldiers."

Called to the table, Thompson described how he'd followed orders to keep other agencies from investigating the deaths of Darren and Patrick McMurphy. He'd made sure that Detective Goode and his sergeant, Rusty Stone, did not attend either autopsy. He'd issued a news release characterizing their deaths as a suicide and a natural death, respectively. He had also gone into the computer system to change the outcome of toxicology tests on Patrick McMurphy's blood by deleting all traces of narcotics, leaving only the alcohol.

"We've been working in cooperation with Chief Baxter to end the Fontaine investigation and close these cases as soon as possible," Thompson said.

"Thank you for your service, Brother Thompson."

"You're welcome, Brother Rayburn."

"The next order of business is a report from Brother Allegro, another esteemed soldier."

Sheriff's Lieutenant Tony Allegro reported that he'd made sure Walter Hall had been "hired" as a deputy in time to get into Darren McMurphy's jail cell, strangle him with the bedsheet, hang his body from the light fixture, then cut him down with a box cutter. He'd held Stone and Goode at bay by refusing to cooperate with them at the jail and deleted Hall from the shift log on the computer so no one could trace that he'd been on duty that afternoon.

"Excellent work, Brother Allegro."

"Thank you, Brother Rayburn."

"The next order of business is a report from Brother Baxter, one of our most esteemed soldiers."

Dropping the smiles and banter face Baxter had displayed while talking with the mayor next to the piano, he approached the Circle table with an expression of respect. For the next ten minutes, he described how he'd told Stone to stand down with such force that he'd put the sergeant into the hospital. He'd also suspended Goode for insubordination and threatened to fire him after he suggested discussing the Fontaine–McMurphy case with outside authorities.

"I'd like to think they've both learned their lesson, but I can't guarantee they will fall in line. Stone and Goode seem determined to pursue the lesser charges, despite my best efforts to discourage them. But to go further at my level would only draw undue attention that would not be in the Brotherhood's best interests. We'll need to call on our brother in the DA's office to help with that."

"Thank you for that detailed report, Brother Baxter."

"You're welcome, Brother Rayburn."

"Our next order of business is a dual report from Brothers Teddy Kincaid and Walter Hall, two of our most esteemed soldiers."

Joining the Circle table, Kincaid and Hall reported on the comings and goings of Katrina Chopin, the investigative reporter and sister of Franny Chopin, the developer they had cleaned after he'd cost members of the Brotherhood, and the Circle in particular, a fortune in losses. They reminded the Circle that Katrina was also the daughter of the two judges they'd cleaned after her mother had threatened to expose the group's role in her son's death.

"The son of our late brother, Patrick McMurphy, tried and failed to kill Katrina Chopin at the Hotel Del. Since then, death threats and smashed car windows, even the knowledge that she is constantly being watched—nothing seems to deter this woman," Kincaid said.

"She's also been secretly working with Detective Goode to investigate her family's deaths, as well as the McMurphys'. We strongly advise that you take immediate action to stop those efforts," Hall chimed in.

"We believe she and Goode are having sexual relations, so it shouldn't be hard to clean them in a single takedown," Kincaid said. "Brother Hall and I can present options, or you may simply convey your wishes, and we'll see that it gets done."

After sending the two men away for what proved to be a 6–0 vote, Hall and Kincaid were given the go-ahead to "clean" Katrina and Goode however they saw fit and as soon as possible.

Holy shit!!! After a report from Hall-Kincaid, they just voted to "clean" you and Katrina. Clean = kill, Stone texted Goode. We also now have a recorded admission that they previously "cleaned" Katrina's entire family.

Once the Circle concluded the incriminating votes and discussion, Watts and Dougherty looked to Stone with a questioning thumbs-up gesture to confirm it was time for the *GO* signal. Stone gave an enthusiastic nod in response.

With that, Watts and Stone sent out the signal to their respective teams to start the raid. When they'd timed it earlier, it had taken the agents four minutes to march briskly from the Rec Center to the hotel, and a few more to climb the stairs and burst into the bar.

It's GO time! Stone texted his team.

As soon as he'd sent the text, Stone glanced up from his phone and over at the group of associates to find Baxter staring at him, frowning. The stare continued as Baxter's expression slowly changed from suspicion to panic. As his mouth fell open, he stood up, pushed his way through his colleagues with some urgency, and escaped into the hallway.

Either he got hit by a sudden need to empty his bowels, or he just figured out who I was. Or both.

"I think Baxter just made me," Stone whispered to Watts.

"Well, go after him," Watts hissed back. "Have Goode meet you downstairs and arrest that asshole for conspiracy to commit murder!"

CHAPTER 49
KATRINA

Monday

Around seven o'clock, when Katrina knew the Circle meeting was due to start inside, she and Norman walked over to the Rec Center to use the restroom and gather some color for her main story, as the FBI agents pretended to play tennis while waiting for the *GO* order.

"Goode seemed a little high strung tonight," Norman said.

"What do you expect? This is a huge deal for him and Stone, working a joint sting operation to take down a bunch of the city's high-profile officials and businessmen. I can't even imagine the stress he's under."

"Yeah, I guess so. But he didn't have to be such a dick."

"It's not personal, Norman."

"I know. I just thought we were buds."

"No, Norman. You aren't buds. He's a detective, and you're a reporter."

When they reached the tennis courts, they saw the white command center parked on the street and the agents either hitting balls to each other or huddled around the benches, talking.

"When we see them line up, we'll know the raid is starting. That'll be a good shot for Chip," she said, texting the photographer to come over. "We'll need to get out of their way, or we'll get trampled."

Most of the agents had short hair, even the women. Katrina had heard about the dress code, which went way back to the days of J. Edgar Hoover. If they weren't wearing tennis garb, they would be wearing suits.

While she and Norman stood at the railing above the tennis court, Katrina saw a familiar figure walking up the street. As he got closer, she felt increasingly anxious. It was Vincent, who cocked his head curiously as he approached.

It's too late to hide or run for cover, so I'm going to pretend I didn't see him and come up with some excuse to be here. Maybe he didn't actually see me.

"Katrina," he called out to her.

Shit.

Still, she didn't turn.

Let him think I'm someone else.

But it was no use. "Katrina!" he said more urgently, only a few feet away now.

Katrina grabbed Norman's arm and whispered, "Don't say a word. Let me handle this." Then turning toward Vincent, she spoke as casually as she could. "Oh, hey, Vincent. Fancy meeting you here. What brings you to La Jolla and the Rec Center of all places?"

But her attempt to deflect fell on deaf ears. "What are *you* doing here?" Vincent countered suspiciously.

He's clearly on edge, which must mean that he's on his way to this secret meeting. I've been giving him the benefit of the doubt this whole time, but now he's here, and I can't deny it. God, Vincent. I hope I didn't get the wrong information and you're actually one of the Circle members. Or trying to become one. I don't know if I could stand that.

"You know Norman Klein, the cops reporter?" she asked her father innocently.

Vincent nodded at Norman dismissively, then looked back at her for an answer to his question.

"Linda wanted me to mentor Norman, so I'm giving him the scenic tour of La Jolla while I drop some invaluable investigative journalism tips. We were just about to mosey down Prospect to George's for a drink. You want to join us?" she offered, figuring he would refuse the invitation.

She hoped this move would defray his suspicions, and that him being there was simply a weird coincidence. Anything so that her father wasn't associated with the cabal in any real way.

But I know in my gut why he's really here, and I can't afford for him to alert his cabal friends about his suspicions on why we're here.

Apparently Vincent was satisfied, because his expression and tone softened. "No, thanks, I'm meeting some business associates at the bar in the Empress Hotel. And since your drinks are work related as well, go ahead and put them on your expense account," he said, chuckling good-naturedly.

Katrina smiled awkwardly. "Thanks, Vincent, I will. Have a nice evening."

As Vincent crossed the street and headed toward the hotel, Norman gazed at her in disbelief, his eyes open so wide she thought his eyeballs might pop out.

"Don't say anything," she said. "Be quiet and let me think. He's going to be pissed once he learns that we knew exactly what he was walking into, but there's nothing we can do about that now."

CHAPTER 50
STONE

Monday

Stone practically tripped over his own feet trying to run down the fire stairwell as he heard Baxter's footsteps echoing throughout the cement structure a floor or two below him. In his haste, turning corners while grasping the banister so he didn't fall down, Stone lost his Santa hat but didn't stop to pick it up.

There's no time to go back. I don't need it anymore anyway because he's already figured out who I am.

Because Goode was the last person he'd called, Stone stopped long enough to hit the redial and speakerphone buttons on his cell phone before continuing his hustle down the stairs.

"What's up? Is something wrong?" Goode asked, concerned.

"It's Baxter," Stone said, trying not to talk too loudly as he panted for breath. "He made me, then ran out of the bar. Now I'm chasing him down the fire stairwell. So be on the lookout for him downstairs when he comes out. As soon as I get there, I'll let you know which way he goes after that."

"Then what?"

"Then we arrest Baxter."

"Copy that."

Stone had made some progress with his new exercise routine, but not enough for this. He was so out of breath, he was worried he might pass out, so he tried more affirmations.

You're close. Keep going. You can make it. You have to.

He heard the squeak of the door opening at the bottom of the stairwell, then the heavy door banging shut.

Baxter's not in great shape, either, so he won't get too much of a lead on you.

Finally reaching the bottom, Stone heaved the door open and looked right and then left, but didn't see Baxter. So, he made the most logical choice and veered toward the front entrance, on the opposite side of the building, where he knew the long line of agents would arrive any minute to start the raid.

"Okay, I'm at the front entrance," he told Goode, still holding the phone. "I don't see you. Where are you?"

"I was out front already, so I saw him come out and start running up the street toward Prospect. I'm chasing after him now. See me?"

"Yep."

"Good. See you in a minute."

Goode was about half a block away when Stone saw the detective take a flying leap onto the chief's back and land with his full weight, forcing Baxter face down onto the strip of grass next to the sidewalk.

Jogging the rest of the way toward them, Stone arrived just in time to watch Goode pull Baxter's wrists together and hear the satisfying click of the metal cuffs locking.

"Tom Baxter, you have the right to remain silent," Stone said, still out of breath, but enjoying every minute of it. "Anything you say can and will be used against you in a court of law. You have the right to an attorney. If you can't afford one, one will be provided for you."

"Wait, stop! What are you doing?" Baxter said, interrupting the obligatory Miranda warning. "Listen to me! I infiltrated this group to do exactly what you're doing!"

"Did you tell anyone?" Goode asked.

"No, I was doing it on my own. I was trying to protect you guys. But you wouldn't listen. Had to do it your way. They threatened me. Said they would hurt my wife if I didn't go along. They'll hurt you, too, Goode, and your girlfriend."

"Who's 'they'?"

"Lawrence Rayburn, his father, and the rest of them. They just voted to take you both out. Ask Stone."

Stone nodded to confirm. "You looked pretty friendly with all of them tonight, Chief," he interjected.

"That's funny, Santa," Baxter muttered. "How else was I going to act? Like the fat old fool you are?"

Goode looked at Stone, frowned, and shook his head. "Don't listen to him. He's just trying to get into your head," he said. "He's lying, trying to save his own ass. Chief, I'm sure no one forced you to donate money to Winchester's campaign, and I'll bet you're a Vitaleron investor as well."

Stone nodded. "Probably is. Listen, Chief, we'll have to sort this all out later. But right now, we're arresting you with the rest of your brothers, and then taking the lot of you downtown for questioning."

Stone saw a metal bench on the grass down the street a bit. "We're going to cuff you to that bench while we go finish this raid, which I'm sure is in full swing by now."

The two of them pulled the chief to his feet and dragged him down the sidewalk to the iron bench, which had a green patina from the salt air, and recuffed Baxter to one of its arms.

"Don't go anywhere," Stone joked before turning to Goode. "He should be safe there until we get back," he said.

CHAPTER 51
KATRINA

Monday

A few minutes after Vincent had walked out of Katrina's sight, the agents started streaming toward a box where they dropped their racquets and formed a single-file line. It was like watching an ant colony or a beehive, communicating in its own language. She could see the adrenaline pumping through the agents' bodies as they stood tall and alert, marching quickly toward the hotel.

"It's on. Let's go!" Katrina said, running across the street so they were parallel to the advancing formation of agents. "Wait a sec," she said, stopping to take a few shots with her phone. Chip, their photographer, ran past them to get ahead of the group and capture the agents' dogged faces.

"We need to be near the buses to watch the bad guys being loaded in," she said, referring to the two large white vans that had already passed them and were now parked in the back lot and on the side street.

"Count the number of agents, and I'll do the same. Then we can compare," she called out.

"Okay," Norman replied breathlessly, trying to keep up.

"Dude, you need to get some exercise."

Standing outside the back entrance to the hotel now, they watched the agents slow down just outside, bending down to pull guns from ankle holsters, under their athletic pants, or inside jacket pockets, before filing into the fire stairwell and disappearing inside.

"Goode said it wouldn't take long to get the suspects on the floor, handcuff and arrest them, read them their rights, and bring them out. They'll probably be out within fifteen minutes."

"Are you guys dating, or what?" Norman asked.

"Did you seriously just ask me that question in the middle of a raid?"

"Are you seriously trying to get out of answering my question because we're in the middle of a raid?"

"I would never do anything to jeopardize my job," she said. "That's my statement."

"Whatever," he said. "That was a nonanswer."

Katrina ignored her young coworker, who didn't seem to know when to shut up.

Boundaries, dude! No wonder he has no friends and can't get a date. He can be so annoying sometimes.

"Count the people in handcuffs when they come out, and I'll write down their names. There may be a few surprise faces I don't know, but hopefully you will."

Just then, Katrina saw in the distance an older man running up the street in front of the hotel, crossing to the other side, and Goode chasing after him. Goode caught up to him, leaped onto his back, and forced him to the ground, where he cuffed his hands behind his back. Stone sluggishly brought up the rear.

She watched as Goode and Stone pulled the man to his feet and cuffed him to a metal bench, where they left him before heading back into the hotel.

"What the hell?" Norman said. "I think that's the police chief!"

The reporter duo jogged over to the bench, where they tried to get Baxter to talk. "I have no comment," he said, turning away to avoid eye contact.

From there, they headed to the hotel's rear exit, where Goode had told Katrina to wait for the arrestees to be escorted to the waiting buses.

CHAPTER 52
MARTIN WATTS

Monday

Once the voting was over, the group of cabal leaders and associates went back to drinking and merrymaking, calling out song requests to the piano player and singing out of tune.

Moments after Watts had sent out the *GO* signal, Vincent Battrelle sauntered in, shuffling around to shake hands all around before sidling up to the bar, where he ordered a double shot of Macallan.

What the hell? He missed the whole meeting. He didn't vote, but he's here now, so he's clearly an associate. He was also involved with Aphrodite Chopin, so who else would have reported the threat to expose his or the cabal's part in her son's murder? Because that's what got both judges killed. Not Vincent's jealousy or Gino Frangello's urge for revenge.

Watts watched the faces of the group for any sign that Baxter had alerted them about recognizing Stone in the bar. But he saw no indication until he came to Walter Hall and Teddy Kincaid, who were intently reading a text on Kincaid's phone.

Watts immediately sensed the heightened tension in their bodies. Shifting into high alert, they started pulling other men into a huddle and showing Kincaid's phone around.

But before the men could instigate a group response, the throng of agents stormed the bar, shouting, "FBI! Everybody down on the floor! Everybody down! Hands behind your backs!"

Vincent didn't move, looking shell shocked with the rim of his glass in his mouth.

"You too, Mr. Battrelle," Watts said as he moved next to the newspaper publisher. "Put your drink down. Then lie face down on the floor, please."

Appearing confused, Vincent did as he was told. "But I haven't done anything wrong," he said.

"Down!" Watts barked, which sent Vincent to his knees, hands first and then face down on the floor as instructed.

CHAPTER 53
GOODE

Monday

Stone and Goode fell in line with the agents as they swarmed into the bar. Goode headed straight for Teddy Kincaid, who was already on the floor. "I'm sure this guy's got a gun on him," he said, going for Kincaid's ankle, where he had one holstered, and removing it from his person. "Clean me, my ass, Kincaid."

"Fuck you, pretty boy," Kincaid muttered into the carpet.

Goode didn't see Kincaid's hand go into his front pocket and retrieve a Taser, but he felt the jolt of pain as the powerful electric shock zapped his leg. Losing his balance as his knee buckled, he fell to the floor as one of the nearby agents turned and fired his gun into Kincaid's thigh, sending a stream of blood spurting.

"You hit my artery, you asshole!" Kincaid screamed.

But after Kincaid had tased Goode, none of the agents were eager to help him. They were too busy trying to pull all the suspects' hands behind them and attach zip ties to their wrists.

As soon as Goode recovered, he searched around to find Hall, eager to zip-tie and disarm him before Goode could be tased a second time by another foe with a grudge against him. But an agent had already done the job for him.

With Hall's wrists cuffed behind him, Goode pulled up Hall's pant legs as well. "I know this guy's got at least one gun," he said, finding weapons on both ankles. "Clean this, you fucking scumbag."

"Bite me, asshole," Hall growled.

With the two hit men safely apprehended, Goode pulled Kincaid's belt from his pants and used it to tie off his bleeding leg.

"We're going to need an ambulance for this one," he called over to Watts, who nodded with an unusual, but quite understandable, hint of a smile.

The room was one big roar of agents ordering cabal members and associates to lie still and be quiet while they were being apprehended. Cabal members, in turn, were saying, "You're making a big mistake," as each one was arrested, read their rights, and sandwiched between two agents, who walked them downstairs.

Goode watched the wealthy men's expressions—a mix of shock, dismay, and arrogance, as if they were thinking, "Who do these jerkoffs think they are? They'll never be able to make this stick. Not in this town. This town is ours."

Not anymore, you low-life losers.

CHAPTER 54
KATRINA

Monday

Minutes ticked by as Katrina and Norman waited impatiently on the street, until they heard the stairwell door open and an echoey buzz of voices approaching.

"Here they come," she said. "Take down any interesting details you notice about them, too, okay?"

"Got it," Norman said, his eyes lit up with excitement.

One by one, the bastions of corporate and governmental power were led out, cuffed with their heads either hung in shame or raised high in defiance. In addition to the Circle leaders, the group of twelve included the mayor, Walter Hall, Teddy Kincaid, and a couple of guys she didn't recognize.

So, Hall and Kincaid were both *in on this? What a traitor that Teddy is. I still can't believe he was outside my apartment, trying to scare me silent while pretending to protect me—for almost two weeks. And what about Vincent, my own father? Did he know this bald thug was a cabal hit man when he hired him to spy on me?*

After a pause, one more man was led out. It was Vincent, and he was furious.

Looking directly at Katrina and Norman, he vigorously shook his head and practically spat on them with disdain. "You knew about this, and you didn't even try to warn me?" he asked rhetorically. "I can't even look at you. You're disgusting. I'm going to fire both of you. But you'll see—this is all one big misunderstanding. I told you I was meeting some friends for a drink, and that's what I did. I walked into the bar, and they arrested me."

Vincent kept walking toward the bus, then turned around and said, "The least you can do is call Milton Biggs and tell him to get me out of this."

"I can't," Katrina replied. "I'm writing this up for tonight, but I'll tell Linda when we get back."

"Linda knows too? Of course she does," he muttered. "You're all a bunch of backstabbing ingrates."

"Be quiet, face front, and get on the bus, Mr. Battrelle," the agent holding his arms ordered.

At the end of the line were Stone and two men Katrina assumed were the supervisory FBI agents. Goode trailed behind with a couple of detectives she recognized from his team, then took off down the street, apparently to go collect the police chief from the bench where she and Norman had last seen him.

"Excuse me, can you stop for a minute and give us a statement?" she asked one of the supervisory agents. "I'm Katrina Chopin, and this is Norman Klein, from the *Sun-Dispatch*."

"Supervisory Special Agent Martin Watts," he said, extending his hand for a shake. "And this is Supervisory Special Agent Chris Dougherty. We put this operation together in cooperation with Sergeant Rusty Stone and Detective Ken Goode of the SDPD, but as you can see, it was done without the knowledge of their chief, Tom Baxter, and the mayor, Jack Norton, who were arrested tonight, along with eleven others. The group calls itself the Brotherhood. Their five leaders are known as the Circle of Five, all of whom were arrested."

"Can you confirm my list of arrestees?" she asked. "I think I'm missing a few."

"Sure," Watts said, listening as she read them off. "You're missing Clarence Thompson, the deputy chief medical examiner; Sheriff's Lieutenant Tony Allegro; and Vincent Battrelle, whom you already know. He came in late, but he's obviously an associate, so we're going to question him."

"Was he arrested too?" she asked.

"Yes, he was. He came in after the vote, but he made sure to shake hands with the entire group."

"What are the charges?"

"For now, these men were arrested for conspiracy to commit murder, but we're looking at charges under the RICO Act as well."

"Can you tell me what the gist of the meeting was? I was told there would be a few votes."

"Yes, that's true. There were."

"Can you say anything more?"

"Not on the record."

Oh, geez, not this again.

"I've got to write this up for tonight, so anything you can say on the record would be great."

"They voted in a couple of new members, took reports from several associates, then voted to put out a hit on two private citizens."

Who is it this time?

"A hit? Can you tell me who the two citizens were?"

"Not on the record."

"Okay. Can you describe them but not give me their names?"

"I'd rather not, but you'll probably find out anyway. I respect your work, and I'm very sorry about the loss of your parents and brother. To answer your question, it was a police detective and an investigative newspaper reporter, both of whom were working the Fontaine–McMurphy case. You can probably guess who they are."

Oh. My. God.

"Let's talk in the next few days," Watts said. "I hear you have some information that would be very helpful to our investigation, which I'm hoping you might share with us. I'll be reading your stories. Have a good night."

"Thanks," Katrina said, then called out to Stone, who was talking to his team. "Sergeant, can I ask you a couple of questions?"

"Hello, Katrina," Stone said, who seemed to be on high alert and yet more relaxed than she'd ever seen him. "Just a couple—then I have to go. We've got a long night ahead of us."

"They actually voted to put a hit out on me and Detective Goode?"

"Yes, they did. Right after admitting to 'cleaning' your brother and your parents, which is their code word for killing. Apparently, your mother threatened to expose the cabal for killing your brother," he said.

So, she did believe me. Why didn't she tell me?

"Sorry to say it so bluntly, but the 'cleaning' admissions are what made these arrests possible tonight," Stone went on. "I'm not sure the FBI wanted me to release that, but I feel that you, especially, deserve to know."

Katrina wasn't expecting this to happen, but her professional armor started falling away, leaving her standing there as an orphan, vulnerable and alone, who had finally confirmed that her reportedly suicidal addict brother had been murdered, just like her innocent parents.

By this group of evil sociopaths that apparently includes my birth father.

The impact hit her in the gut. She could barely stand upright. Her knees felt weak, but she resisted. She had a job to do, and her bosses expected the moon.

"Thank you, Sergeant," she said, her eyes brimming with tears that dripped on her notepad. "Sorry. I wasn't expecting to hear that. After so long."

"It's all right, Katrina. I know it's a lot. I'm so sorry for your loss, but at least now you know," he said. "I'd give you a hug, but in this crowd, someone might write me up for sexual harassment."

"Thanks anyway. I appreciate the thought."

"I've got to go. I'll let Goode talk to you on the record just this once. Special occasion," Stone said with a twinkle in his eye, glancing around for Goode, who was not behind him as expected.

A moment later, Goode came running up, an expression of embarrassment on his face. He whispered something to Stone and then to Watts, who both looked annoyed, but said nothing out loud so as not to alert the media.

When Goode saw Katrina crying, his expression immediately switched to concern as he turned toward her. "Let's go into the stairwell, so we can talk," he said, putting his arm out when Norman tried to follow. "Sorry, this is just for Katrina."

"I'll be back in a minute," she called to Norman over her shoulder. "I'll meet you at my car. Call and let Joanne know it's over and we're coming back."

Safely inside the stairwell, Goode pulled her to him and hugged her tightly. Katrina sobbed like she'd never sobbed before, with the sound of the buses pulling away in the background.

"Let it out, and breathe," Goode whispered. "It's okay. I'm here."

"What did my family do to deserve this from these bastards?"

"It's all about money. Lost money and hubris. That's all these greedy assholes care about."

After taking a few deep breaths, Katrina was able to pull herself together. "Thanks for the hug. I've got a story to write. What was all that about with the whispering? Was it about Baxter? I saw you guys cuffing him to the bench earlier, but I didn't see him in the group that was loaded onto the buses."

"You don't miss a trick, do you? I just went back to get him, and all that was left were these," he said, holding up a pair of metal cuffs.

"You're kidding!" she said.

"No, I'm not."

"Do you have any idea where he went?"

"No, no idea," he said. "But I'm going to make some calls and see if I can find out."

"Okay. In the meantime, you want to give me a quote about how it feels knowing this group put a hit out on you tonight?"

Goode thought for a minute, then said, "If they want to kill me for doing my job and standing up to greed and avarice, then I'll take the hit. But, thankfully, we stopped them before they could hurt you, me, or anyone else. As of this moment, the cabal, the Brotherhood, the Circle, whatever you want to call them, is dead with a capital *D*. Starting tonight, we are cleaning up government, we are cleaning up City Hall, and we are cleaning up this police department. And if the justice system works the way it's supposed to, these men will go to prison for a very long time."

"You sound like you're running for office," she said, smiling and wiping her wet face with her jacket sleeve. "Why was Vincent arrested if he's not part of the cabal?"

"Apparently, he came in after the voting was over, ordered a drink, and boom, we raided the place. So, he got caught up in the sting. He'll be questioned about his involvement with this group. We know they're his investors at Vitaleron, so he's obviously an associate, at the very least. We just don't know how much he knew or if he was complicit in the murders—and who knows what else this group has been up to. It sounds like they've been around for at least twenty years, so murdering your parents, the Fontaines, and the McMurphys, the Vitaleron bribes, and the campaign shenanigans are probably just the tip of the iceberg."

Feeling a little overwhelmed, Katrina had more than enough to write another blockbuster story. "I guess I'd better get back."

"I'll be up all night and crazed for a few days, but I'll see you soon," he said, giving her a quick kiss on the cheek before running off to join the others.

Norman was waiting by the Land Rover, antsy as hell. "What took you so long? Joanne had a bunch of questions I couldn't answer. I told her you'd call her on our way back," he said.

"Well, she'll just have to wait. I need you to be quiet on the drive back, okay? I've got to craft my lede and the top of my story, and this is pretty personal for me."

"Why does everyone keep telling me to—sorry, I'll be quiet."

CHAPTER 55
GOODE

Monday/Tuesday

At SDPD headquarters, the arrestees were detained separately to prevent them from strategizing, trying to revise history, or coming up with a common story. The smaller players would be interrogated first and given the chance to save their own asses in exchange for incriminating information about their "brothers."

As a task force member who knew the local players and had reviewed Katrina's personal materials in addition to the Double-Judge case file, Goode was tasked with interrogating Lawrence Rayburn. Although he was the Circle's newest member, he had long been working diligently from the inside to assist the Brotherhood in carrying out all of its crimes.

Before Goode went in, Watts gave him some intel on Lawrence, describing him as "the kind of guy you love to hate," which reflected research Goode had done on his own: He always wore a bow tie to show that he was a neoconservative like his role model, Tucker Carlson, a FOX political commentator whose journalist father, Dick, had run unsuccessfully for mayor in 1984 and ran in the same circles as the Rayburns. The two families were viewed by some observers as wealthy conservatives known for spewing inflammatory rhetoric to further their party's interests, and thus the Circle was born.

Once Goode faced Lawrence across the table, he confronted him about the hotel district tip that Darren McMurphy had given him as leverage. Rayburn's pride and his instinct for self-preservation quickly overtook any scintilla of loyalty.

"I helped the mayor set up that district, and if you give me immunity, I'll tell you whatever you want to know," Lawrence said. "I know how these FBI public corruption operations work. Trying to get the little fish to turn on the big fish. The mayor, the police chief, Congressman Winchester, and even my father are much bigger fish than I am. I keep files on everyone that could help you."

"I'm not authorized to give you any kind of deal, but I can tell you that you'll have to give us something pretty damn juicy for the US Attorney's Office to even consider giving you immunity," Goode said.

"If you aren't authorized, then let me speak to someone who is," Rayburn said.

"Let's see what you've got to offer first. We're all hands on deck here, and it's the middle of the night, so right now, I'm all you've got."

"Are we being recorded?"

"Yes, we are."

"Well, I'll just start, then."

Goode nodded for Bow Tie Rayburn to start spilling, which he did.

"Let's start with Chief Tom Baxter. Do you know where he is? We cuffed him to an iron bench on the street during the raid, but he was gone when I went back to get him," Goode said.

"No idea," Rayburn said.

"Okay, well, did he ever give you any indication that he didn't want to cooperate? He claimed that he only did so because you—and he mentioned you specifically—threatened to hurt his wife, just like your group voted to kill me and the *Sun-Dispatch* reporter, Katrina Chopin, tonight."

"We may have indicated that he should cooperate or there would be repercussions, but he was all in. He went above and beyond, in fact, as soon as he learned how much money he could make with just a small investment in Vitaleron. I saw the dollar signs in his greedy beady eyes, Detective," Rayburn said.

"I see. All right, continue."

Rayburn nodded. "Mayor Jack Norton and I both wanted to impress Patrick McMurphy, who was second to my father in terms of Circle seniority, because Jack knew I'd been working to show my dad that I was worthy of stepping into his shoes when he retired. So, I told Jack that if he helped me get into the Circle, I would help bring him up the ranks so he could join, too, someday. But first he'd need to get in the game and amass some wealth and property. I had to keep him motivated, so I didn't tell him that public employees aren't usually granted a Circle seat, because you're either born into that path or you're not.

"Franny Chopin's resort project failed because environmental activists lobbied it to death with the California Coastal Commission and the San Diego Planning Commission. So, I came up with a work-around. Knowing that Darren McMurphy was looking to earn points with his father, too, I told him to propose a deal to Patrick that would give him the authority to build on the same property as Franny's dead project. In return, Patrick would buy the mayor a nice fat new home that Jack and his wife could never afford on their own. I identified a mansion that was already owned by Patrick's development corporation, which Jack's wife loved.

"So, one of Patrick's shell corporations purchased the mansion, then transferred it to Jack, as a bribe, essentially, for the mayor to spearhead the creation of a new district where Patrick could build a beautiful resort on Mission Bay. The plan was advancing quietly until the McMurphys were publicly outed for causing the Fontaines' murders. Once we got them both out of the way, my dad and I put a team together to build the resort ourselves."

Lawrence smiled as he splayed his open palms to either side, indicating that he was not only finished, but also damn proud of his accomplishments. "That's it in a nutshell."

"Why did you want so badly to be part of the Circle?"

"As you can imagine, being gay in a homophobic far-right family has been an uphill battle my whole life," he said. "It took a long time for my father to see me as a worthy son. My other siblings had his support from day one, but he withheld it from me until recently, when he finally had to admit that I'm an asset. I became a lawyer to win his respect, but my alleged affiliation with Andrew Cunanan in the press set me back big-time. That's when I decided to go into public service. It's not like I needed the money, but I thought I could be more useful on the inside, and I was right."

"Uh-huh. Then what happened?"

"As time went on, I also wanted power and, to be honest, more influence. I had no interest in being a politician, but being the mayor's chief of staff could only take me so far. I figured the way to win my father's respect would be to further the Brotherhood's interests while also keeping its hands clean. So, I arranged for Walter Hall to 'take care' of Darren McMurphy in jail, and then I gave Vincent Battrelle that vodka to give to Patrick McMurphy as a gift, just like I did to Franny Chopin."

"My understanding is that Franny had been sober for a year at that time. Why did he drink the vodka?"

"Because he'd just lost everything. He initially turned up his nose at the lemon flavoring, but we were hanging out, and I told him to pour some cranberry juice into it. Down the hatch it went. I didn't tell him what else was in it."

"Didn't he wonder why you didn't drink it with him?"

"He knew I was sober, so he didn't think twice about my can of Diet Coke. After he was dead, I staged the table with the pills and the powder."

"I see. Where does Vincent Battrelle stand with all of this?"

"What do you mean?"

"Was he involved with the hit on Franny?"

"No, it was done on behalf of the resort investors, who included every Circle member and some of us in the lower tiers as well. We all lost a ton on that deal, including Vincent. He found out about the hit afterward and was a bit broken up, to be honest, because I guess he and Franny used to yuk it up together on the golf course. But he's not part of the Brotherhood. He's never felt the need or desire to be. Nonetheless, he understands what we are and how we operate. He must have explained that to Franny, so I'm sure he knew who he was dealing with and that he'd have to pay for his failure one way or another. For all I know, he may have known the vodka would be his last drink. I think Patrick understood that as well, because he was one of the Circle members who voted to clean Franny, and he had to know we'd used lemon-infused vodka, because it was in the newspaper."

"Did you learn that trick from your buddy Andrew Cunanan?"

Rayburn shook his head and frowned. "Where did that question come from?"

"You just admitted that you two were friends. I read about it after he killed all those people."

"I said 'alleged affiliation.' I hardly knew him at all," Rayburn said, steely eyed.

Goode could see that he wasn't going to get anywhere with that line of questioning, so he moved on. "What about the judges? Was Vincent involved in that murder?"

"Only tangentially. He uses Teddy Kincaid for his side jobs, so he confided in Kincaid that Aphrodite Chopin had threatened to expose that her son was murdered. She suspected that Vincent knew about it, because he kept trying to get her to leave Peter over some fling he had with his clerk, and I guess he got a little too aggressive about it. So, Kincaid did the job himself and framed the clerk's brother for it. He used the brother's car and gave him the gun afterward as a gift, which was brilliant, really. We were all impressed."

"So, Vincent ordered that hit?"

"No, what I'm saying is that he gave enough information to Kincaid for him to bring the matter to our attention, so the Circle voted to clean the Chopins to protect the Brotherhood. Vincent was devastated once he realized what had happened, but that was long after the fact. He stopped coming around for a long while, but eventually he must have seen how naïve he was for thinking we wouldn't rectify that situation."

"The Circle members and the Brotherhood at large, you're all investors in Vitaleron, correct? So, he must have come back for that money."

"No. You've got the timing backward. The investments were made before any of the Chopins were cleaned. So, he knew he could never really cut himself off from us. He'd basically sold his soul to us to get Vitaleron up and running, and he needed us to keep it going. So, whether he's an official member or not is really immaterial."

"I see."

"One more thing, and this is important. The Circle had nothing to do with the Fontaine murders. That was between Darren and his daddy, which is what started this mess and got them both killed. We wanted to protect our investment in Vitaleron, sure, but the Circle never voted, or even suggested, to have the Fontaines killed. Dr. Fontaine was going to make us all a lot of money, and many members were counting on that drug to enhance their long-term virility. We never would have put ourselves out there so publicly in such an inartful and, frankly, enormously stupid way. We have that idiot Darren to thank for that."

"You realize that this Brotherhood of yours is dead, though, now, don't you?"

"Maybe. Don't forget that we still have at least fifty lower-tier members out there, and they can easily vote in a new Circle of Five to lead them. If you want their names, you'll have to get me a deal first."

How soon he forgets that he was just in their position and managed to have Darren McMurphy killed. But he might be right, as distasteful and repugnant making a deal with this creep is to every fiber of my being, not to mention my feelings for Katrina.

"I'll have to discuss this with the people in charge. We're just gathering information at this point. This has been helpful, but I wouldn't count your chickens. You personally poisoned two people and just voted to put out hits on me and Katrina Chopin. Don't forget that."

Goode's gut churned as he watched Lawrence sit back in his chair looking smug. "I'm too useful for you guys to pass this up," Lawrence said. "So, I'll just wait here while you run my offer up the chain. And would you bring me a hot cup of coffee while you're at it? This one is cold."

The hell I will. I'm not your effing waiter. The utter entitlement is nauseating.

Goode got up to leave the room without responding, but still had one important question that he wanted to seem like a throwaway.

"Hey, did you loan Doreen McMurphy a Xanax when you were over at her house recently?"

Rayburn cocked his head, trying to remember. "Yes, as a matter of fact, I did. She was all out."

Bingo. Gotcha. There's one more attempted murder charge.

Goode couldn't get away from such pure evil spawn fast enough.

He told me all of that like he was reciting his résumé. Without a shred of remorse. But he could still end up like that "idiot" Darren, cut off from his family and their money for being a rat, and strung up in his jail cell.

CHAPTER 56
KATRINA

Monday/Tuesday

The newsroom was frenzied when Katrina walked in with Norman, but her colleagues stopped what they were doing to stand and clap as she made her way to her desk. It brought tears to her eyes.

Damn, they never did that for me in Northampton.

As she smiled and nodded to her coworkers, she noticed that most of them smiled back, but a few, including Jerry, were either stiff faced or scowling with jealousy that she'd landed the biggest exclusive scoop in the paper's history.

That's okay. The catty pettiness was even worse at the Record. *No one congratulated me after I won the award for my Polish mafia series, and I was gone two weeks later.*

When Linda pulled Katrina into her office, it was clear that the new executive editor had mixed feelings about the situation, specifically Vincent's arrest.

"Just what we need for some great PR," Linda said sarcastically, rolling her eyes. "I'm about to call the attorneys to see how to proceed on that."

But on the bright side, at least Vincent couldn't try to stop them from publishing anything this time. Linda said she was sure that her protégé was going to take them to Pulitzer heaven.

"It will be our first, and with you on staff now, I know it won't be our last," she said. "All of your other stories are ready to go as soon as you top that A-matter. I assume the biggies were all arrested tonight. Anyone we missed?"

"Besides Vincent? No. They nabbed the mayor; Clarence Thompson, the deputy chief ME; and Tony Allegro, a sheriff's lieutenant, but we can come back with their bios tomorrow. Oh, and Teddy Kincaid."

"Wow, okay. I wasn't expecting that name, but maybe I should've been. So, what's your lede?"

For once, Katrina didn't have to think any more about it: "A dozen city officials, wealthy businessmen, and their henchmen were arrested on suspicion of conspiracy to commit murder tonight in a joint raid by the FBI and San Diego Police Department. The arrests came after the group admitted in a recorded meeting at the Empress Hotel to arranging hits on two federal judges and their developer son, as well as two defendants in the Fontaine murder case. The group leaders, known as the Circle of Five, also voted tonight to 'clean'—their code word for 'kill'—this reporter and homicide detective Ken Goode for their respective investigations into these murders."

"Oh, my God, Katrina. I'm so glad we got you into that hotel this past weekend before they could hurt you. Anyway, excellent work. Write it up!" Linda said. "You've got forty-five minutes."

Joanne came over as soon as Katrina sat down at her computer. "I'll have Norman send you what he's got, but if I know you, it's all in your head or notebook," she said.

"Yeah, not to take anything away from him, but we were together the whole time until I sent him to the car."

"You never know. He might surprise you."

Linda was right. Norman sent over a quote from a longtime La Jolla couple he'd talked to on the street: "The mayor, a sheriff's lieutenant, and the owner of the newspaper? Wow, there goes the neighborhood," the woman said sarcastically.

At first, Linda didn't want to include Vincent in the man-on-the-street quote and told Katrina to use ellipses.

"But if he goes to prison, we're going to look silly in retrospect having left that out," Joanne said.

Linda had to agree.

By the time Katrina got home, it was close to midnight, and her nerves were a raw, frazzled mess. She emptied the last of the bottle of wine into her glass, cautioning herself that that was all she could have. The next few days were going to be long and arduous. She couldn't afford not to be at the top of her game.

Even though Teddy was gone—in fact *because* Teddy was gone—Katrina felt relieved from the nagging fears and impending doom that had been keeping her awake at night. She was confident now that it was either him or Walter Hall, or both, behind the threatening notes and smashed car windows.

The only thing that still concerned her was that the police chief had escaped from custody. It eased her mind a bit when Goode sent her a reassuring text:

Can't give you details yet, but I wouldn't worry about Baxter being a threat. We think he's long gone. At 1:00 a.m., she was crawling into bed after a long hot shower when Goode texted her again, this time about his interview with Lawrence Rayburn.

Call Watts and tell him you'll trade transcripts from Circle meeting and my interview w Bow Tie Rayburn tonight for yr personal papers re Vincent, yr brother, parents. He said Vincent made deal w devil re Vitaleron but wasn't complicit in murders. Thought u'd want to know.

That brought another round of tears, triggered by sheer exhaustion and a deep sense of relief. The last thing she wanted was for her new father to be a complete villain. She knew he wasn't a great guy and that the Vitaleron investments were the satanic deal to which Goode referred. Still, she was thankful he hadn't played an active role in killing his own son and the love of his life, for his sake as much as Katrina's. That would be a lot to handle.

I'm sure there's more to the story, but it was thoughtful of Goode to stop during a crazy night to tell me these things. He's a good man. I wish he was here now, so we could debrief together. But I guess we'll have plenty of time for that later.

The next morning, Katrina took Goode's advice and called Watts. He agreed to the exchange, which they did in the newspaper parking lot. His eyes were bloodshot and bleary, and he talked faster than she could think, probably hepped up on triple espressos like Goode.

"Thanks for this, and I'm sure we'll talk again in the coming days," he said. "Keep up the good work. We wouldn't have gotten this done without your stellar investigative work."

She thanked him for the materials he handed her, of which she read every word in the privacy of her car. Goode was right—these papers did provide many of the answers she was seeking. They would also make for another long, emotional day, writing another great story.

After almost six years of wondering what had happened to her family, it felt amazing to finally have closure. She wanted the perpetrators to be punished to the fullest extent possible.

Vincent called at noon, after being released based on Lawrence Rayburn's statement. When she took the call up to the roof patio for privacy, it seemed that he'd already overlooked her failure to give him a heads-up about the raid. He seemed more focused on repairing her damaged perception of him.

"I meant what I said, Katrina—I would never have done anything to hurt your mother, and now that I know that these people killed her *and* Franny, my son and your brother, I'm going to see if I can divest all of them from Vitaleron. I can't bring down the company over this, but I've got Michael looking into it. Maybe we can do it slowly and find a hedge fund or venture capital firm to fill the funding gap. But neither of us wants to do business with the La Jolla mafia, because that's who these people are. It devalues the company. Not to mention all the bad PR."

"Vincent, I appreciate you saying that, but you knew who these people were when you took their money."

"Not really. I may have been naïve, but I never thought they were so greedy that they'd kill people. I know that if I want to earn your respect, I have to tell the truth, so that's what I'm trying to do. I hope you'll forgive me for whatever I've done—" he said, his voice breaking, "that contributed to your family's deaths. Because it was my family too. I'm so sorry, Katrina. I really am."

I'm still not sure if those are real tears or more Machiavellian manipulation. Now that I know he's my father, I want to believe him, but after everything that's happened, it's still really hard for me to trust him. He always talks a good game, but we'll see if he does divest from this group and its money.

"Thanks for the call, Vincent. I've got to run. As you know, I've got a big follow-up story to write. I might call you for a quote, unless you want me to use what you just told me, which would be great, actually."

"Use whatever you want. This is all going to come out anyway. And it's better it comes from you. By the way, Meredith and Michael are fine with the DNA story. You can call and interview them if you like. Ruth is on her way out of town for a cruise on the Italian Riviera with Nancy Fontaine and Doreen McMurphy, so I didn't ask her. She probably won't even see it until she gets back. Alex is still on the fence. He's already feeling embarrassed because he and so many of his clients have been arrested recently, but I'll talk to him again."

"Oh," Katrina said, her brain switching gears. "That's great news. Thanks, I'll get on it as soon as I put the cabal story to bed."

Katrina was pleased to hear that at least two of her half siblings had accepted her. She was looking forward to writing up that first-person account, which would be far juicier after this raid. But she scratched her head about the cruise on the Riviera.

Are these women skedaddling out of town because they were involved or complicit somehow? Or is this just an innocent girls' trip?

Before going back down to the newsroom, Katrina tried to process what Vincent had just said. It occurred to her that she should dive back into her mother's journals to find the last entry before her death, to see if she could glean anything new. With any luck, Aphy would mention confronting Vincent about her suspicions that Franny had been killed. If there were any lingering questions or contradictions, Katrina would confront Vincent herself.

After turning in yet another blockbuster A-1 story, Katrina was in such a hurry to get home that she took the stairs two at a time to reach her front door. A week or so earlier, she'd picked her mother's journals off the floor and put them back into the box. But now, she dumped them out all over again, opening each cover until she found the most recent. She didn't even wait to pour herself her usual glass of wine before digging in.

The last few pages described Aphy's lunch meetings with Vincent: A couple of times, they had impromptu sex, but mostly, they just talked. Just like he said.

> Vincey keeps trying to convince me to leave Peter.
> I feel like a broken record because I've told him no
> 1,000x. He keeps bringing up Peter's alleged fling
> with Julia. I didn't believe it at first, but when I asked
> Peter about it he got kind of hinky and said she

hadn't worked for him in a few years. I asked why and he said she'd developed a crush on him, so he had her transferred. So, Vincey's probably right, but I let it go. Peter and I don't need to discuss it further. It would just cause more pain and heartache, because I'm no angel on that front either. Vincey brought it up again this week, so I changed gears and mentioned Katrina's theory that Franny was murdered by his investors, who include Vincey. He got this strange look on his face. "What?" I asked him. "What do you know? Tell me." He wouldn't answer. He jumped up, and said he had to run to a meeting. When I asked him again at our next lunch, he changed the subject. I finally told him that if he didn't tell me what he knew, I was going to the police and the newspaper, because clearly something was up, and as a judge and a mother, I needed to have this question investigated. And until he told me the truth, there would be no more lunches. That made him very angry, but I'm used to that. We'll see what happens.

That was her last entry. Aphy and Peter Chopin were murdered two weeks later.

CHAPTER 57
KATRINA

Later in December

Working obsessively seven consecutive days to finish the series, including a few hours on Christmas, Katrina tied up the Fontaine and McMurphy murders and the takedown of the Brotherhood. She also explained the hows and whys of the group's order to kill her brother and parents. Vincent registered his opposition to her quoting her mother's last journal entry, because he thought it made him look complicit, but he ultimately relented.

Katrina took a couple of days off to recover, then came back fresh and ready to tackle the next topic. It felt good to shift gears as she explored her newfound family and the unexpected wonders of genetic genealogy. How, after being orphaned by tragedy and murder, she learned her true birth father was the owner of the newspaper that had only recently hired her.

She already knew her half brother Michael from interviewing him about the Fontaine murders and was pleased to talk with him again at his office at Vitaleron for a more positive and personal story.

"I knew I liked you," Michael said, coming around his desk to give her a warm, welcoming hug. "You're one of the only women

I've ever seen stand up to my dad. The other one was Victoria, and that personality trait got her killed. I wanted to thank you, though. After watching you and taking notes, I feel more able to stand my ground with him."

"My mom stood up to him for many years, and I'm sorry to say, in the end, that got her killed as well," Katrina said. "Even though Vincent wasn't legally responsible for her murder."

Alex, who was out on bail awaiting trial, finally agreed to an interview, so Katrina talked to him and Meredith, both at a family dinner and individually over coffee.

When she was done writing the story, she realized she'd left so much material on the table that she had enough to write a book.

Her first-person account ran a couple of Sundays later, taking up the entire top half of the front page and continuing on two full inside pages with photos and pull quotes. Her instincts about the salability of her story were confirmed when she got calls, emails, and flowers from the TV network morning shows, as well as stations across the country, that wanted to interview her on camera. She also got several voicemails from a well-known literary agent in New York who wanted to fly in ASAP and meet for drinks to talk about her soon-to-be *New York Times* bestselling tell-all memoir.

Vincent called to compliment her, describing the story as "a masterpiece that caused a stir" everywhere he went, from the beach club to the golf course.

"So, I was true to my word, wasn't I? I let all of that about the Circle be printed in my newspaper even though those men were my friends, or I thought they were, anyway. I know you may still not believe me, but I swear I didn't know what they were up to. But, listen. Turns out we can't give their money back from Vitaleron. Michael says we've been scraping by since the Fontaines were murdered, and we still have one last phase of human trials to get through. So, I'm sorry, Katrina, but that's not going to happen, at least not right now."

Why am I not surprised? Sometimes there are things that are more important than money, but I guess he and I will never see eye to eye on that.

"That's disappointing. I think that if you don't divest them from your company, you're going to have a harder time raising capital moving forward. But you're going to do what you're going to do."

"I know where you stand, and I'll keep that in mind. But on to more enjoyable topics. Can we have dinner this week? Michael and Meredith both called this morning to say you did a great job on the article."

"Thanks, yeah, they called me too. I'll think about it. A lot of people want to talk to me, and I need to think about what all of this means. What I want to do next."

"You're not thinking of leaving the paper, are you? You're the best goddamned reporter we've got."

"Thanks, but I've decided to write a book about this whole saga, so I need some time off to put a proposal together."

Vincent was supportive of the idea, and they left it at that. "Why don't you take a day off and get some rest. In fact, take two!" he said jovially.

Katrina had already cleared taking a month off with Joanne and Linda, but now that she also had Vincent's blessing, what she really wanted was a longer leave of absence. Writing a book proposal would allow her to fully process everything that had happened, but it would also require more research. She still had to go through the rest of her mother's journals and her parents' computers, where she was sure she would discover untapped resources that would help flesh out the story even more.

Most importantly, she needed to figure out how to deal with her new identity. With Vincent's $5 million gift, she wasn't even sure if she should stay at the paper, working for her hardheaded father, or if she should try to find another job elsewhere.

After some time away, I might say 'screw the whole reporter thing' to become a full-time author. I could even open up shop as a private investigator.

Bottom line, she wanted to spend some time with Goode, both in private and in public, without having to hide from their bosses or spies they didn't even know were watching.

For the immediate future, she set her sights on a trip to the wine country in Sonoma and the Napa Valley, where she rented a house while she worked on her book proposal. She'd already asked Goode to join her for a couple of weeks at least.

"We can sleep as late as we want. You can go play while I work a few hours. Then we can go wine tasting during the afternoon, and hit a different gourmet restaurant every night."

"When do we leave?"

CHAPTER 58
GOODE

Sunday

After reading Katrina's massive story about her DNA journey to a new identity, Goode sat on the steps at Windansea and sipped his second latte of the morning.

It was hard for him to picture how he could be any happier. He was in love with a brilliant, beautiful woman who loved him back, and they were planning a romantic getaway to wine country.

She's not even the least bit difficult. Who would have thought.

While he looked forward to spending time locked away in their own little bubble, naked and free to do what they wanted, whenever and wherever they wanted, his work life had vastly improved overnight as well.

After obtaining a rush warrant for Chief Baxter's cell phone records, Goode was able to access the texts from the night of the raid. Although Baxter had warned Terry Kincaid after he'd recognized Stone, despite his Santa hat and fake-beard disguise—Abort! We've been infiltrated!—it was too late to carry out any contingency plan they might have had.

But then, after somehow getting free from the handcuffs, perhaps by asking a kindly senior citizen to dig into his pocket, where he probably kept a handcuff key on his key chain, Baxter immediately texted his wife:

I'm sorry. I was trying to protect you. I'm heading south to our special villa to hide out for a while. I'll be in touch when it's safe.

Figuring that "south" meant Mexico, Goode contacted Baxter's wife to try to get more information, leveraging her cooperation by threatening to charge her with being an accessory after the fact and abetting a fugitive. Although she gave him the address of their villa on the shores of the Sea of Cortez, the place was empty when Mexican authorities arrived. As the manhunt continued for the disgraced chief, Goode, Stone, and Watts figured it was only a matter of time before Baxter was captured, extradited back to the US, and arrested on charges that didn't allow for bail.

Just as Goode had telegraphed, Katrina's investigative series touched off a maelstrom of public pressure to clean house from top to bottom—at the SDPD, City Hall, and the sheriff's department, with an eye on any other departments that had a law enforcement role. Although they had no immediate proof that Sheriff Helmsley was tied to the cabal, only his lieutenant, they kept looking. Same with the ME's office. And, based on Baxter's comment at the meeting about their "brother" in the DA's office, the search was on for that mole as well.

Lawrence Rayburn did end up making a deal with the feds, but because he was an admitted killer, his immunity fantasy went unfulfilled. Still, it sickened Goode to hear that Bow Tie got a lighter sentence for his cooperation than he deserved.

Back at the PD, Stone was encouraged to take the lieutenant's test and was told he would get the next open slot if he passed. Although Goode was also encouraged to take the sergeant's test, he said he wasn't sure he wanted to move into management, because he enjoyed basic detective work so much.

I'm also damned good at it.

But after solving the biggest cases the department had ever seen, he was also getting the hard sell by Watts to join the FBI. Watts gave up once he learned that Goode was aging out, however, which was fine with Goode. He honestly couldn't be more fulfilled in his job unless he got paid to surf full-time.

On that note, he got up, downed the rest of his latte, and sauntered over to his van to grab his board. So what if the ocean was a little cold. It was winter. Fifty-eight degrees. That's what wetsuits are for. The tubes were a beautifully clean green. They were glassy and hollow. And they were calling his name.

ACKNOWLEDGMENTS

I want to thank the people who offered me emotional support and helped me get my facts right, as well as my beta readers, who made sure those facts made it onto the page accurately and in a compelling fashion: Géza Keller, Bob Petrachek, David Byington, Lisa Churchville, Scott Dreher, Bunny Amendola, Jacob Bruce, and Larry Welborn. Also, thanks to my agent team, Joe Veltre, Hayley Nusbaum, and Joslyn Jenkins, and to my editing team at Thomas & Mercer, Alexandra Torrealba and Clete Smith.

ABOUT THE AUTHOR

Photo © 2023 Géza Keller

New York Times bestselling author Caitlin Rother has written seventeen books—ranging from crime novels to narrative nonfiction and memoir—including *Down to the Bone*, *Death on Ocean Boulevard*, and *Body Parts*. An award-winning investigative reporter for nineteen years, Rother has had her work featured in *Cosmopolitan*, the *Los Angeles Times*, *The Washington Post*, *The Boston Globe*, *The San Diego Union-Tribune*, and *The Daily Beast*. Her more than 250 media appearances include *20/20*, *People Magazine Investigates*, *Crime Watch Daily*, Australia's *World News*, and numerous shows on Netflix, Investigation Discovery, Lifetime, HLN, and REELZ.

A popular speaker, Rother also works as a writing-research coach. For fun, she binges on limited series, sings and plays keyboards in a jazzy bluesy trio with her partner, and swims in the ocean. She holds a BS in psychology from UC Berkeley and an MS in journalism from Northwestern University. To learn more, please visit https://caitlinrother.com.